Creed of the Guardian

Heart of the Warrior
Book Three

By

C.R. Richards

Book design by ebooklaunch.com

For Dad
Master Sergeant - United States Army
(WWII and Korea)

Chapter One

SETH D'ANTOINÉ PUNCHED his fist into a helpless bundle of hay secured in the airship's hold. Trapped like mindless livestock, he and his best friend—his squire, Riley Logan—had been herded inside a reinforced section of the hull. The suffocating enclosure was typically used to house mounts for the Jalora Legion's traveling rangers. Fortunately for all concerned, the battalion wasn't taking horses with them to North Marsh.

"Great gulls! Would you stop? I'm near death, and you want to punch things." Riley gripped the porthole with one hand and covered his mouth with the other.

"You're already airsick? We haven't set sail yet. Our journey to North Marsh Outpost spans three days. The trip will be a rough one if you don't settle your stomach. Can't you make some concoction?"

Ignoring Riley's glare, Seth leaned against the hold wall. The Lion Ring on his finger pulsed to the beat of his angry heart. It, too, resented being caged by their uneasy allies. The Jalora was the force for good on Erthe. Its Legion consisted of men, each of whom had been bonded in service by a Heart of the Warrior ring. Every such talisman clung to its bearer's left middle finger, feeding off the host's blood. Seth lifted his Lion

Ring and regarded it. His blood surged and ebbed with the tide inside the yellow crystal.

"They've no right to cage me like a beast! I have things I must do."

His thoughts returned to the hidden passageways boring through the granite body of the Obsidian Citadel, his former duty post. A few hours before the Legion caged him, Seth had chased his murderous half-brother, Julian, to the battlements. Mercenaries had been waiting for him there, ready to fight. His new Lion Friend, Lord Fausto De Quintaro, and the men of Valdeon had stood with Seth to drive the villains from the stronghold. Fausto had vowed to return to Valdeon with rebellion in mind. Seth desperately wanted to go with him, but the Jalora Legion had other plans in mind for the new bearer of the Lion Ring.

"Aye. But you've been grousing for the last half-hour. Please give me a little peace so I can calm my aching head." Riley swayed forward with a groan. "Tell me what happened when you met with that foul-tempered uncle of yours. As quietly as possible, if you please."

Seth's uncle, Esteban D'Antoiné, was a prince of Valdeon and bearer of the Hawk Ring. His very name sent Seth's temper surging. Esteban's intrigues had ripped their family apart.

"Hawk was the ranger who bargained with the assassin Pavel Sandor on Marianna," Seth reminded his friend. "My uncle found Mother when I was a baby and promised her he would protect us by keeping my existence secret. Hawk assumed he had Pavel under his control. We both know his madness was uncontainable."

Seth ran a hand across his face. "My uncle claims he sends us with the Phoenix for my protection."

Riley sighed. "Who knows what waits for us at the end of this journey. I'm not sure I trust that uncle of yours. It seems to me he should have waited for Cardinal Dragon to return."

He made a sound point. Cardinal Dragon, as head of the Legion, should've been consulted before Hawk sent Seth off to the farthest reaches of Andara. Seth folded his arms and fell silent. Hawk was flying on a hidden path and taking Seth with him. Seth and Riley needed to escape this airship and find Seth's Right-Hand, Wolf.

Thoughts of his missing mentor sent Seth's anxious fingers picking at a stray splinter clinging to the wall. He'd searched the hull for a way out, but the corral had been built to keep beasts inside. A few small windows covered in steel mesh had been placed around the enclosure to give the horses fresh air. Through one of these small openings, a pair of wide green eyes now appeared and stared at Seth. He reached out gently with his power. Curiosity ran both ways.

Then a voice added a comment. "You see, son. Remember this day. The Lion has returned to Andara." A man's face joined the young boy's in the crisscross of steel mesh. "He's coming with us to learn how to be a ranger."

"Are you going to teach him, Dad?"

"No." The man laughed. "A gentleman like the Lion couldn't learn anything from the likes of me."

The little boy's smile turned into an unhappy frown. "You're plenty smart, Dad."

Seth let out a frustrated sigh. A chance of birth had made him heir to Edmund the Leo, King of Valdeon. But birthrights and riches didn't matter in the heat of battle. True honor was in a man's actions. Courage was located in the heart willing to risk everything to protect those who couldn't defend themselves. Seth's bloodline didn't make him any better than this loving father, who also fought for his family.

Pushing away from the wall, Seth used his powers to move unseen among the ribbons of sunlight. A cold blast of winter chill struck his face as he stood before the open vent. This goodbye from the Obsidian Citadel felt harsh.

Hovering midway up the mountain fortress above the Legion docks, the airship floated hundreds of feet over the city of Lea. Seth had no idea how the boy and his father had managed to perch outside his window. Putting a finger through the mesh, he lifted the little boy's chin.

"The Lion!" The boy gasped with wide eyes. "You've come to speak with us."

"So, he has."

Short-cropped blond hair rested well above the collar of the father's olive UR Army uniform. Three tan stripes on the lapel marked him as a master sergeant within Seth's new battalion. Sharp eyes, accustomed to spotting unenthusiastic cadets, held Seth's gaze as if he may be waiting to see this new Lion's reaction.

Seth held his left hand against the mesh and let the child's small fingers smooth at the Lion ring. Floating in the center of the Heart Crystal, the great beast's head swayed back and forth as it followed the boy's movement.

"Your dad is a modest man." Seth nodded at the sergeant. "This is my first time traveling with the army. I'm certain I can learn a great deal from him if he's willing to teach me."

"The name's Sergeant Duncan, my lord." The grateful father smiled down at his son's proud face. "I'm honored to help you in any way I can."

"Why have they locked you in the hold?" the boy asked.

Seth and the boy's father well knew the answer. The rangers wanted to use their new Lion and his gifts to restore power to the Legion. His uncle, Esteban the Hawk, was ever evasive and harbored secret ambitions for Seth. The Legion's collective fear, however, was keeping Seth in a cage. Throughout the continent of Andara's history, a man of pure Valdeonian blood had been named Lion Protector by the Jalora. Born of two ancient rivals, Seth was the first Lion with mixed blood. He'd sensed his battalion's uncertainty and heard the hushed whispers as soon as he'd boarded the ship. But how to explain such blind fear and hatred to a child?

"Sometimes people fear what they don't understand..."

"But the Jalora gave you its ring," the boy said, touching the beast's head with a final stroke. "Shouldn't that be enough?"

"You are a wise soul, my little friend."

The great ship began to rumble, then eased as the crystal engines fell into their usual rhythm. The shuddering wall shook bits of hay from the bales onto the floor—small compensation for horses confined to such suffocating circumstances.

"I'd better see you back to your mum."

The little boy waved to Seth and then sank out of sight. Sergeant Duncan lingered a moment, however, and dug into his pouch. He took out a long, black string of some kind of dried plant or herb and handed it to Seth with a nod. Seth sniffed the gift while attempting a smile. Sickening sweet with overtones of leather from the sergeant's pouch, this present wasn't something Seth would willingly put into his mouth.

"Tell your squire to chew on it until his stomach settles. It shouldn't take more than a bite. I've seen some air sickness in my day, but not as bad as he seems to have it."

"Thank you, Sergeant." Seth, sorry to watch them go, stepped a few paces back. They were sure to be the only friendly faces he'd see in a great while.

Making his way across the hay-littered floor, he stopped by Riley and handed him the black string. "It's from a friend. He says you should only take a bite. It's sure to settle your stomach."

"You've made a new friend in an empty cargo hold? Aye, that's you all over."

Riley, too, sniffed at the stringy object, but he had the courage to take a tentative bite. He wrinkled his nose and swallowed with a big gulp. Closing his eyes, Riley leaned his head on his arm. The soft hum of relief told Seth the sergeant's remedy was working.

Then the engines roared to life again. The hay prison shook and swayed as the ship suddenly lifted into the air.

"Great gulls!" Riley cried. "I don't think I can stand three days of this."

"I'm more concerned about what happens when we land." Seth gripped the nearest post and hung on tightly as they ascended into the unknown.

Chapter Two

THE DOOR BURST open with a boom. White Tiger stood before Seth and Riley. Thinning hair, faded with age, clung close to his scalp. Small scars covered his face and hands. These relics of wounds spoke of many battles and a lifetime of experience. Seth had surprised the old ranger on the battlements of the citadel once. Luck had been with Seth as he knocked the warrior off his feet. He wouldn't get the chance again. Power radiated from White Tiger, who looked ready to strike. Gray eyes now ruthlessly examined Seth. Clearly, he'd not entertain any mischief.

A squire stood next to the ranger. Matching White Tiger's age, he held the same sour frown. A growling predator feline, forever captured in bronze, clung to the collar of his uniform. The squire's indignation focused on Riley. Neither man seemed impressed by the Lion and his own faithful squire.

"Stand at attention, Ice Lion. I'm not the stable hand."

Seth pulled Riley to his feet. They hurriedly assumed respectful stances. White Tiger was second in command of their new battalion. He'd also been a friend of Seth's father. The old ranger was someone Seth hoped to win over. Disrespecting his authority wasn't a good idea.

"We've set sail and are well away from the docks. I doubt you can cause much mischief now." White Tiger stood aside and motioned them into the hall. "Phoenix will be meeting with his new apprentices in a few moments. You're to join them."

More apprentices? Seth hadn't seen any other young men waiting to test in the arena of the Obsidian Citadel. Of course, his attention had been focused elsewhere at the time. His uncle had taken Riley and the Lion Friends hostage, forcing Seth to test for his naming into the Legion.

Now, they followed White Tiger down a long corridor. Several doors—each expertly labeled with the contents of the room—lined the walls. Armory. Storage. Oats. Someone had gone to a great deal of trouble to keep the hold orderly.

A sign marked "Upper Deck" was shaped like an arrow and hung at the bottom of a flight of stairs. According to the sign, Seth and Riley had experienced their first Legion takeoff from one of the "Lower Decks." A few more flights up finally brought them to the "Main Deck." Here, the transport ship began to look less like a massive warehouse and more like a military building. The walls were painted a green-gray color from floor to ceiling. Sanitized and tidy, the deck could have passed for an infirmary. The ship's captain was a champion of order.

White Tiger slid open a set of double doors, crystal lanterns giving off a surprisingly cheery glow in the interior, windowless room. Rangers sat solemnly on benches lining the walls of the chamber. Their ash-colored uniforms contrasted starkly with the green-gray walls.

White Tiger pointed to a group of nervous young men sitting in a cluster at the far corner. Dressed in the olive drab uniform of Legion apprentices, they stood apart from the rest of the battalion in every way.

"Ho! Lion!"

A massive young man with dark-brown hair and pointed sideburns waved to him. This was Anders the Bear, Seth's opponent during testing at the Obsidian Citadel. Seth had won the battle, earning his ranger name, 'Ice Lion.' Judging by the huge grin on Bear's face, the other man had forgiven the defeat.

"Well, don't just stand there like a couple of wallflowers." White Tiger jutted an impatient finger again. "Go join the other apprentices."

Seth and Riley walked past the rows of higher-ranking rangers. The Jalora's transmitted power, garnered by these men in years if not decades of training, pulsed as low hums while tendrils of white light drifted in gentle waves across their skin. They were justice incarnate and servants of the Light, whose blades never hesitated. Today, they seemed uneasy, though, as Seth walked by. Quick probes and curious stares followed Seth's and Riley's steps. Hushed whispers reached Seth's sharp ears. He ignored such interest, keeping the ice walls about him.

"I was glad to hear you've joined our battalion, Ice Lion." Bear patted the seat beside him. "Sit quickly. Our commander doesn't look kindly on those out of place."

"Phoenix is an impatient man then?" Riley grumbled with dislike and added a quick "sir."

"Something happened in the Legion HQ. He has been in an ill temper since." Bear shook his head at Riley. "Phoenix is the commander of this battalion and a powerful deacon. If I were you, squire, I would clear my mind when he comes among us. A ranger's skill isn't required to sense your dislike of him."

"You'll find others more fitting of your disdain before our apprenticeship is over, Lion's squire." The young man sitting on Bear's other side glared over at the rows of rangers. "You'll have plenty of choices."

"This is the Stallion. He's a new apprentice as well."

Coal black wisps of fine straight hair flapped atop the Stallion's head as he nodded to Seth. The uneven tresses had the appearance of once-long hair having been cut short by a dull blade. Seth had seen enough of such cuts at sheep-shearing time on Marianna. The young man slumped back against the wall. Pulling on his hood, Stallion folded his arms with a pout. Anger. Resentment. Frustration. They raced about the apprentice in a wild fury. He seemed determined to broadcast rather than hide his emotions.

Fear. Its intensity pulled Seth's attention toward the young man sitting apart from their group. Curly blond hair dangled in swirls about his face. Thin, boyish shoulders hunched forward as the youth's body shuddered. An older man, his squire, sat beside him. Resting a gentle hand on the young man's back, the squire whispered soft words of comfort. Both ranger and squire stared down at the young man's ring as if they were looking at a death sentence. Shame. Disappointment. Terror. These emotions made erratic patterns about their bodies.

"That's the Badger. He's an Ephemeral," Bear whispered to Seth.

"A what?"

Lifting his yellow stone to show Seth, Bear tilted his finger to catch the light. A black bear floated within the dark yellow crystal. The beast watched its Bearer circling the surface with his finger.

"On rare occasions, a black circle forms around the outside of the crystal, the Jalora's curse on a bearer. The lucky ones die quickly. Others—the truly cursed—are deformed. They're bad luck for themselves and their battalion."

"How must it feel to know without question, you will be dead or mutilated at any moment?" Riley murmured with a wave of pity.

"Come to attention," White Tiger boomed from his place at the double doors. "Commander is present."

The rangers rose to their feet in an effortless and uniformed movement. Seth and Stallion followed Bear's lead as he joined his fellows. Gregory Baldemar flew into the room, his pale squire following. True to his animal spirit, Phoenix burned with fiery impatience. A head taller than most of his men, the deacon displayed golden curls that shined under the crystal lanterns in the windowless chamber.

All eyes were on Gregory—Phoenix—as he made his way to a single chair at the head of the room. He paused for a moment as if to take stock of his subordinates, and then sat with a grace befitting the crown prince of Heidelbrecht.

"At ease," White Tiger barked, and the rangers shifted positions.

"Get the men settled, Tiger."

"Yes, sir." The commander's second lifted his chin and eyed the group. "As you were."

Confidence. Trust. Acceptance. The feelings evoked by the mere presence of their commander hovered about the chamber. These men had complete trust in Phoenix and his strength as a leader. Seth heard no mutterings of complaint or curiosity as to their new mission. The battalion sat down quietly. Life resumed.

"To your duties, squires," White Tiger's own squire barked. "This isn't a pleasure cruise. We have our chores."

"I suppose that's me, Seth." Riley stood, rubbing at his stomach.

He fell in line with the other newcomers, who then attached themselves to the long line of black uniforms. Riley and the other apprentices sported tan vests, further designating them as from the Squire Corps. Leaving at a fast pace, he disappeared with the rest before Seth had the frame of mind to bid him farewell.

"They're in capable hands," Phoenix said at Seth's shoulder.

Startled, the apprentices jumped to their feet and snapped a quick salute. Phoenix returned it. He raised a slight golden eyebrow at Seth. Questions flashed from his blue eyes, yet he didn't linger long. Their commander came to stand before the middle of the bench. He regarded his new apprentices with an unnerving intensity.

"Henry the Badger," he said at last. "Come stand before me."

The doomed apprentice took a hesitant step and winced at the effort but tightened his jaw against the pain. Stumbling forward, as if an invisible force had propelled him, Badger moved across the chasm to stand near Phoenix. Though he shook uncontrollably, he struggled to remain upright before their superior.

Phoenix reached down to the apprentice's ring and lifted it to show the rest of the troop. "The black ring around your crystal proclaims you are an Ephemeral."

"Yes, sir. Much to the shame of my family."

Harsh vowels and his abrupt accent grated on Seth's ear. Tslavia and Valdeon were bitter enemies. Seth was a child born of both royal houses. Most Tslavians vehemently objected to his existence. One notable exception had become very dear to him. His Aunt Charlotte, queen of the Isle of Carlotta, had accepted him out of affection for his mother. Would this unlucky young man, Badger, share her tolerance or hate him for his father's blood?

"I must tell you, apprentice, I do not believe in the Ephemeral myth." Phoenix released the ring and clasped his hands behind his back. "I knew a ranger who started as an apprentice with this on his ring, just like you. He rose above the legend to distinguish himself as a servant of the Jalora. Now he's a high-ranking deacon."

Young Badger's terror seemed to lift, and a reluctant grin formed on his lips. Hope. It was a much-needed gift for Badger and the entire battalion. Morale immediately appeared to boost among the rangers. The atmosphere in the room felt lighter to Seth. Phoenix had shown wisdom. Leadership, it would seem, was a valuable skill.

"Western Beta has thirty rangers in our troop now. You have twenty-nine resources from which to learn. Choose for yourself, apprentice. Don't let something else choose for you."

White energy from Phoenix's body suddenly stretched out to encircle the Stallion in the Jalora's power. Their new commander withdrew his touch with a fleeting grin.

"Calhoun the Stallion."

The commander's words were cut off by bellows of laughter from the rangers. Stallion gave them a murderous glare. The apprentice was ready to fight the entire ship in his current temper. He looked at Phoenix and seemed to reconsider the idea.

"It's just Cal, sir. Calhoun is a family name."

"Regardless, it is good to see the Stallion Ring aglow with the Jalora's power. Many a decade has passed since the ring shone with life. It brings hope."

The Stallion Ring glowed brightly on Cal's finger, clearly pleased by the Phoenix's words. Seth examined the young man's somber face a bit more closely. Straight black hair framed square features. His pale complexion was in sharp contrast to the dark hue cut short against his head. He didn't seem any more pleased to be aboard this vessel than Seth himself felt. The Stallion Ring at least brought hope, unlike the Lion Ring, which inspired uncertainty.

Phoenix stepped toward Seth's new bench-mate. Bear's grin threatened to expose his full set of teeth. Their commander offered the Bear a pleased smile.

"You did well in the battle today, Bear. Next time take a more careful assessment of your opponent."

Their commander's blue eyes then turned to Seth. A light touch drifted along the outskirts of the newest recruit's mind. In less time than thought, Seth raised his defenses to block Phoenix's probing. The touch increased in pressure, and so did Seth's defenses.

Phoenix gave Seth a mischievous grin. "You are full of surprises, Ice Lion. I don't care what the Hawk says. Soon, we must have a long talk."

Their commander turned back toward the group. "Welcome to Western Beta Battalion, apprentices." He lifted his voice. "We've been deployed to North Marsh Outpost to relieve Western Delta Battalion. Reports have shown one or two small battles in the past six months involving aggressive wildlife. I don't expect much trouble from any two-legged assailants. We can pass the time training our apprentices."

Rounds of laughter boomed from the old hands here. Seth didn't like the sound of it.

"This is going to be a long apprenticeship," Stallion murmured.

Chapter Three

RILEY FOLLOWED UNSTEADILY behind the long line of men as they plodded down the corridors of the main deck. The ship lurched, and so did his stomach. He took another bite of the bitter root Seth had given him. Ignoring the sour taste, he let its juice run down his throat and into a grateful digestive system. Someone tapped him on the shoulder. Thick, mud-colored hair rested in short strands against the young man's head. An oval face, containing signs of a life lived in the outdoors, blanched under the crystal lamps.

"The name's Lucas. I'm the Stallion's squire." Brown eyes pleaded with Riley as he motioned toward the root. "Give us a bite, will you? Men were not meant to ride the skies."

Riley pulled off a piece and offered it to the other man. Lucas then chewed on the root with an intensity Riley well understood. Obviously, Riley wasn't the only one wishing they were already on the ground. The other squires marching before them walked on steady legs, however, even as the ship swayed in waspish air currents.

A wave of heat and the smell of boiling vegetables struck Riley as they entered the galley. He swallowed hard against a nausea squeezing his empty stomach.

Taking a deep breath through his mouth, he followed the others to stand around a large wooden counter at the center of the kitchens.

Roland, Phoenix's squire, waited for them. Serene porcelain features remained placid as his keen eyes followed them about the room. If ever a perfectly formed creature had been put upon the Erthe, it was Roland. He nodded his head at his second when the squires had settled down. Somehow, Arthur understood the intent of the wordless order.

"We head to North Marsh. It's a wet, cold, and miserable place. Don't expect a wide variety of elegant meals from those kitchens. Learn to love boiled vegetables." Arthur waved off the groans. "Let's be thankful for the extra barrels of ale from Heidelbrecht."

Squires of all ranks cheered. No punishment for the lack of discipline came from either of their seniors. Instead, Arthur and Roland seemed to enjoy the pleasure of their men. Signs of comradery were evident in Riley's new battalion. Their assignment here might not be as bad as he'd thought.

"And for the benefit of our new apprentices, if you've never peeled a potato, don't worry. You'll be an expert by the time we land at the outpost." Arthur gave them a good-natured chuckle.

Riley had the sudden sensation eyes were upon him. Roland stood at the far door, watching the apprentice squires with keen interest. How had he managed to move so quickly and without being noticed? The pale squire gave Riley a nod and then left the kitchens, an amused grin stretched across the perpetually silent lips. By the green, green fields. What was so funny?

Asking the man outright would do no good. No doubt Roland couldn't or wouldn't speak.

The squires suddenly broke into groups, merrily chatting with each other and going about their duties of preparing the meal. Arthur took Riley by the arm and pulled him aside. A troubled mask of disapproval altered the features of his worn face.

"It would appear you've caught the interest of the Phoenix's squire," Arthur said with a frown. "I'm not sure if that's a good thing or a bad thing. Roland is a dangerous swordsman and a strict leader. He doesn't tolerate any mischief among his men."

"Aye, sir." Riley rubbed at the back of his neck. "I've seen him fight. He held his own against the Lion before my ranger used his fancier moves."

A massive man dressed in an apprentice squire's uniform thundered across the kitchen. Dark hair clung tightly to a large head. Broad shoulders pushed two of his comrades off balance as he passed between them. Bright green eyes, wide in excitement, found them. His sizable muscular bulk hurried over to stand before Arthur.

"You'll never guess what's to happen!" he cried, clutching his side.

"Take a breath and tell us, Gudal." Arthur folded his arms with an amused grunt.

"My ranger was picked over the Lion as head apprentice." He grinned broadly.

"Here now," Riley said. "What are you on about?"

"This is Gudal, squire to the Bear," Arthur said. "May I present the Lion's squire."

"The name's Riley Logan." Riley shook the offered hand and winced as it completely engulfed his own. "It was your ranger Seth tested against in Lea."

"Yes, indeed. Esteban the Hawk asked him personally."

"Well, you tell your ranger not to get too comfortable as head apprentice. Ice Lion is bound to advance quickly," Riley assured the Bear's squire.

"Come now, little friend." Gudal gave out a booming laugh. "Ice Lion is new to the legion. I'll admit his swordplay is impressive, but he knows very little else. Your ranger will be an apprentice for years."

"Care to make it interesting? Perhaps we can say fifty credits?"

Gudal grinned and shook Riley's hand again. "Done, though I feel a bit guilty taking another man's money so easily."

"I was wrong about you, Logan." Arthur slapped Riley's back. "Dante, the Leo's Squire, wasn't making a joke by choosing a Marianna boy. He was teaching a kindred spirit. Swear an oath you won't let those Valdeonian squires turn you into a fancy-pants idiot. Stay just as you are right now."

"How do you mean?"

"An apprentice is assigned to his new troop right after he is named. Cardinal Dragon will most certainly put Ice Lion with the Lords of Valdeon. Wolf leads them. Wolf's hellhound, Basilio, commands the squires serving those Valdeonian rangers. I don't envy you, Logan. He won't be easy on you just because you're the Lion's Squire."

"It isn't all doom and gloom." Gudal tugged at Riley's arm, nearly pulling him off his feet. "You're with us for now. Come meet your new comrades."

Dark looks and whispers followed them as they passed their fellow squires. Riley stared right back at them, lifting his chin with a defiant glare. They were gentry from stuffy palaces. Let them be standoffish. He had no time for such people.

"Let's join the apprentice squires," Gudal said.

"Stuffy bunches of nobs aren't they?" Riley grumbled. "Well, my queen named me an earl. That's good enough for my ranger. It should be good enough for them."

"I'm no gentleman from castle walls either." Gudal frowned with a shrug. "Your pedigree isn't what has them nervous. They share their lords' concern about your ranger."

"Worried about Seth? Why?"

"Never in the history of Andara has there been—if you will excuse the expression—a mix-blood son of the D'Antoiné house bearing the Lion Ring. They are uncertain what this means for the Legion and Andara. Give them time. They'll come around."

"Aye," Riley said. "I don't mind their slights against me. It wouldn't be the first time. But Seth is a different subject altogether. They need to give him the respect he deserves as the Lion, or the Jalora might remind them that *It* chose Seth in the first place."

Great gulls. They had enough on their hands without being castaways from their new battalion. Well, Riley supposed he couldn't do much about it now. These rangers and their squires would have to discover Seth's importance on their own.

Chapter Four

JULIAN D'ANTOINÉ CLUTCHED at the blood-soaked tunic sticking to his side, fingers twisting the stained fabric. The wound had been a gift from his young half-breed brother, Seth, in honor of their murdered sire, Edmund the Leo. Grinding his teeth as another stabbing pain dug into his torso, Julian squeezed shut his eyes. Memories of Seth's blazing amber orbs haunted the darkness beneath his lids. This young Lion wasn't the weakling he'd supposed. His brother had grown powerful.

He let out a stream of undignified curses and slammed a fist against his stained cot. Julian had suffered another unpleasant surprise watching the testing from his hiding place in the arena of the citadel. A long-forgotten face haunted the stands. Esteban the Hawk had unexpectedly reappeared after decades in hiding. Watching the young Lion's battle in the sand below him, their uncle seemed eager to grip the boy's flesh in his controlling talons. Curse him! Esteban was better off dead and forgotten. He was one more challenge on Julian's growing list of problems.

Creaks and groans echoed about him. Their small airship—the last vestige of a Valdeon lost—shuddered in the moaning winds off the foothills of the

Border Mountains. His faithful, if not mad, ally had taken a launch to seek out a healer for Julian. Hovering over the border towns of Tslavia, Julian couldn't trust any medicine such vipers would give to a Valdeonian.

"I was a fool to have returned to San Leonora." He glared at his half-sister Zoya's stiff back and the unspoken disappointment she held for him.

Julian's first instinct had been to track the young Lion down on those cursed isles and cut their father's ring from his finger. Talisman and symbol of power, the Lion Ring gave its bearer the undeniable authority to rule Valdeon. Jackal thugs had used coercive persuasion to drag Julian back to San Leonora before he could seek out his half-brother. The doomed city was relying on Xavier the Wolf to bring them their boy deliverer—the Lion. They'd been disappointed when the streets were covered in Valdeonian blood.

Cursed by the Jalora and locked away in his palace, Julian had failed in his attempts to take the throne. His unrealized schemes might have saved the city from destruction. He would never know. Perhaps it was better to start with a clean slate and an empty city.

"What did you say, brother mine?" Zoya ran a fingertip along Julian's arm. "My ears must be mistaken. Julian D'Antoiné, prince of Valdeon, calls himself a fool?"

A twisted grin ruined the pleasing features of his sister. Long, dark hair fell in straight strands across the armor she wore. Always the worst kind of survivor, Zoya, Julian knew, had already calculated her brother's chances of escaping the ill-favor of Lord Gorman, the Jackal general who'd conquered Valdeon. She'd gone from a lady's silks and ribbons back to Jackal warrior armaments.

"Be still, Zoya! Despite the budding friendships you've made among our enemies, I doubt any of them would save you should I decide to throw your body overboard."

The door to his chambers swung open. Marcellus, Julian's ally, filled the space, his broad body tense as he pulled another figure behind him. Mad eyes twitched in uncontrollable fits until they finally rested on Julian.

Shoving the old man inside, Marcellus said, "Here is your patient, healer. If he dies, so do you."

"You see, Zoya," Julian said, hiding the sneer struggling to escape. "One of my followers is still loyal to his lord. Hurry, Tslavian pig, before I change my mind about keeping you alive."

He moved his hands away as the frightened healer knelt beside him. Gaunt and well past his good years, the old man gasped a wheezing breath. Had Marcellus snatched the man from a pig farm? His shaking, wizened hands didn't inspire much confidence. Julian turned his head as the ruined tunic lifted away. He had no desire to see his own innards exposed to the open air.

"Careful!" Julian growled when the fabric tugged at his tender flesh.

Warm liquid poured across his side, washing away the blood. Fingers gently mopped at the clinging residue. Then the old healer screamed. He pushed from Julian's body, rambling incoherently and gesturing for protection from his gods.

Letting his eyes drop to the gruesome hole, Julian stared at the ruined flesh. Gray scales surrounded the rim of the wound and spanned the abdomen to his sternum. They matched the roughness of his arm. His human side appeared to be losing its battle with his Changeling blood.

"Get out," Julian said, letting the fabric fall back down to cover the scales. "All of you!"

Zoya took Marcellus's arm while he pulled the old healer out of the room with the other. Hunger for blood and torture were in their eyes. The old healer would never see his people again. Julian spat as he watched them go. Theirs was a murderous match made in the bowels of hell.

He lifted the Sarcion Ring to eye level. Its green glow had diminished since the loss to the Lion. Had the Sarcion lost faith in him as well?

I only reward those who win, it said in his mind. *Disobey me again, and I will abandon you altogether. Suffer in your rebellion until I summon you.*

Julian let the ring drop. Another ally had left him. This one, unfortunately, he couldn't afford to lose. The essence of avarice and unbridled desire, the Sarcion, many claimed, was evil incarnate. Julian, however, found it to be the inspiration behind his ambitions. Somehow, he'd have to convince the Sarcion to give him another chance.

Then a Changeling stepped away from the shadows. Its face contained gruesome punctures from what appeared to be splinters of wood. Random clumps of black feathers jutted from its head. Julian had last seen his nanny Changeling watching from a lamppost in the thieves' district of Lea. It had disguised itself as a blackbird. Something had since gotten the better of the wretched creature.

"Well, what happened to you?"

"I met the one you call Xavier the Wolf." The Changeling pressed a finger gently against the punctures on his face. "He won't be easy to kill."

"We have a common enemy then." Julian pointed to the liquor on the sideboard. "Pour us a drink. We both need one."

"I have no desire for such things. The Wolf's flesh in my fangs is the only prize I will entertain to sate my hunger for revenge."

The Changeling dropped to its knee and removed the fabric covering Julian's wound and scales. A satisfied grin crossed its thin lips. The creature's gaze lifted to Julian's face. A brilliant glow of mischief swam within the black depths of its eyes.

"The young Lion didn't use the Jalora's magic when he struck you," the Changeling said, its fingers wiggling over Julian's ruined torso. "Lucky for you. Focus now on the scales that surround the torn flesh. Do not question, cousin. Focus now."

Staring down at the gray scales, Julian concentrated on their shape and texture. Then they began to move. The scales crawled across the open wound. Stacking and locking in place, they didn't stop until his torn flesh was completely sealed. Even the dried blood had vanished, covered by his new gray skin. This impressive trick would be helpful in future dealings with Lord Gorman.

"Why don't you use this magic to heal your face?"

"This Wolf is not an ignorant fool. He used the magic of the Jalora. We can't heal such wounds. You would do well to remember that, cousin. The Lion is still young, but soon he will learn his true power. Then you cannot stand against him."

The Changeling rose and stood away. It stepped back into the shadows, pressing its back against the wall. A strange material streamed out of the Changeling's neck, oozing along its skin. Iridescent slime formed a thick second skin. Then that layer puffed outward, similar to the way a ship's sail filled with air. Gray and shiny, the inflated casing looked like the chrysalis of a caterpillar. Julian leaned back and watched the light reflect in swirls of color within its surface. The sensation was oddly comforting.

Betrayed by his Jackal allies, he'd lost the Sarcion Ring's favor. The time had arrived to take his chosen road to the throne. The Lion Ring was out of his hands for now. Only one thing would challenge the young half-breed's claim to the throne—the Regent Medallion. Unfortunately, it had chosen the barbarian, Jorge Pacarro, as its bearer. Julian smiled at the pulsing colors in the casing. He and his new family would soon relieve the Pacarro of his golden burden. His fingers flexed with anticipation. Holding the barbarian's beating heart in his hand would be deliciously satisfying.

Chapter Five

JORGE PACARRO, the reluctant regent of Valdeon, stood at the mouth of the canyon. His sharp Pacarro eyes remained fixed on the rising sun. Its rays touched the prairie grass as it slowly rose in a blue morning sky. Jorge longed for the peace of a crisp vineyard morning he would never again know. A sigh of regret escaped his lips. He'd lost many things—among them, the gentle touch of a wife who had joined the Erthe Mother too soon and the laughter of a grandchild robbed from him before it had drawn life's first breath.

His new life marched past him, breaking the quiet of the moment with moans of fear and utter defeat. Children—those not orphaned by the invasion—clung tightly to their mothers. The old leaned on each other while the strong carried such supplies as they maintained. Eaten weeks before, no beasts of burden remained for the chore. Those of the population who lived on would bear the weight of survival upon their own backs from now on.

An older man dressed in a cavalry uniform took great gulps of air as he climbed on the rock to join Jorge. Alberto Mendoza was steward of San Marimosa, ruling the massive fortress while his son, Berto the Jaguar, served in the Sacred Guard. Alberto's loyalty to the Throne of Valdeon was absolute. A fierce soldier, he was an even better friend.

"This is madness, Jorge," Alberto grumbled beside him. "You are the regent of Valdeon. We need to see you to the safety of San Marimosa's walls."

"I won't leave these people." Jorge turned at last from the prairie, the beads woven into his rust-colored warrior braids clinking softly. "I see dust clouds on the horizon. An army comes toward San Lucida."

"Looking for the regent." Alberto tossed a small stone at the boulder behind him. "Being out in the open is dangerous."

"Yes, it is. You and your men must return as quickly as you can to San Marimosa. We must maintain our foothold in the West until the Lion returns."

"How long might that be?" Alberto threw another rock, this time with a bit more anger. "Let us escort you to the forest rim at least."

Jorge shook his head. "I have many tracks to hide as it is. Safe travels, my friend."

"And to you, My Lord Regent." Alberto slid off the rock formation and called to Captain Stephano, his most trusted officer in the cavalry. "We ride for home."

Massive horses, each towering five hands above their riders' heads at the withers, stomped impatiently in the dried grass. Bronze and crimson battle armor covered their heads and bodies. Known as battling horses, the San Marimosa stallions fought with hooves and teeth to protect their riders. Jorge had witnessed the famous San Marimosa Cavalry in action. They were a deadly force, but even these men couldn't defeat the Jackal on their own.

Captain Stephano barked orders, and the cavalry began mounting in their disciplined fashion. Made up of the most athletic men in western Valdeon, they refused to use stirrups. Their jump mounts were a favorite at parades. A few of the breathing line behind the captain hurried a bit faster as the massive horses pounded eagerly at the ground. Today, their acrobatics lost the interest of the miserable crowd of refugees.

"Remember, My Lord Regent." Using the stirrups to mount his massive horse, Alberto waved away Captain Stephano's proffered hand. "If we don't see you at the meeting spot in one month, I'll come looking for you."

Then the magnificent San Marimosa Cavalry, the pride of the West, rode off. They were the last tradition of a once great nation. Jorge said a prayer to the Erthe Mother for their uneventful journey homeward.

Jorge's son, Duarto, hurried up the rocks to join his father. With sharp features and rusty strands of shoulder-length hair, the Pacarro tribesman within him was emerging more and more each passing day. He'd been a changed man since the Regent Medallion appeared around Jorge's neck. It was as if the medallion had given Jorge's son purpose again. He had a new air of discipline and hardness about him. The people listened to his word, not as a son of the regent, but as a man on his own accord. Still, the absence of light and love was missing from his eyes. It would take time to return. If it ever returned.

"The last of the people have evacuated the city, Father." Duarto turned back toward the empty canyon. "Those who stay behind have hidden as best they could from the approaching army." His jaw tightened, and the hardness intensified in his eyes. "Madness. Why stay in a dead city?"

"Some remain because they can't bear leaving the only home they've known. Others, like Mario, stay to act as our spies." Jorge grinned at his son. "Still others fear I've gone mad trotting off to the mountains."

Perhaps to trust Esteban the Hawk Prince was a bit mad. Jorge had many questions he wanted to ask the long-absent ranger, chief of which was why he'd returned now. Esteban had never been the type to put the concerns of the people before his own. The ranger seemed to hold sway over the young Lion with obvious self-interest. Still, what choice did Jorge have? Their options for escape were limited. He couldn't very well protect a city ready to crumble at the slightest wind storm. No. Their future rested in the tenuous clawed grip of the Hawk.

"Come, my son," Jorge said, jumping down off the rocks. "It is time we disappear."

Chapter Six

XAVIER DE VINCENTE, Bearer of the Wolf Ring, gripped the wooden railing of the aging airship someone had named the *Sailor's Pride*. Gifted to him by Seth's aunt, the old tub definitely wasn't the fastest ship in the skies over Andara. Each mile they successfully sailed was a happy blessing. Gasping and groaning, it struggled to keep up with the agile *Wind Chaser* darting in the air before them.

Rafael the Fox captained his sleek "competing" vessel as it danced effortlessly in the wind currents. Lord of San Angelica, fabled harbor city of western Valdeon, the Fox had lived the sailor's life with enthusiastic gusto. His admirable acrobatics on this trip was designed to elicit envy from their young guardsman piloting the old tub.

Yuli the Otter, now at the helm of *Sailor's Pride*, had served under Rafael since his apprenticeship. He was a good pilot, but the impatience of youth caused Yuli to press their old engines a bit too much at times. One look from Wolf, and their impatient pilot eased off again.

"He'll have the engines rattling out of their chambers in a moment," Wolf told his silent companion, Tulio.

Tulio the Rabbit stood quietly beside Wolf. Dark cropped ringlets swept unchecked across his gaunt face. Their youngest crew member wasn't much for talking anymore. The fall of Valdeon had transformed him into a troubled old soul. Staring down at the treetops racing by beneath them, he'd been overly contemplative since Muellerton Outpost in Heidelbrecht.

"You would ask me a question?" Wolf clutched harder at the railing. He knew what Tulio wished to ask. The suspicion and sense of betrayal hung about the young man in panels of remorse. Wolf's jaw tightened against the sudden rush of anger. Tulio cast a poignant glance at the Wolf Ring.

"I saw you," he said at last. "You burned a letter in the fire. What was in it?"

The letter. Wolf wanted to forget its contents. Left for him by the last Jalora Master, Gustavo the Lion Claw, over a hundred years before, it warned of troubling things.

Wolf, third-in-command of the Sacred Guard, had been called by the Jalora as the young Lion's Right-Hand. He'd assumed the selection was made out of necessity by Esteban the Hawk's disappearance. Gustavo the Lion Claw's letter had foretold the Hawk's fall from honor. But his warning came too late. Wolf had learned firsthand how far the Hawk had strayed when Esteban tried to murder Wolf in cold blood.

Now Wolf dropped a hand from the railing and smoothed at the tarnished silver on his belt. "It was a warning. Esteban the Hawk has fallen and forgotten his duty. The Lords of Valdeon must remain vigilant against further treachery."

"Trust is no longer something I'll give away easily," Tulio said with a nod.

Stiff-shouldered and swimming in disappointment, Tulio descended into the bowels of the old ship. Such pain was only known to men who'd faced torture. Tulio had narrowly escaped death. If not for the Jalora and its Lion, their youngest would have perished the night their homeland fell.

Burning orchards. Dead eyes. Dangling feet. Wolf cast aside memories of that night. Grief was a luxury he could no longer indulge. The Lion had been sent away from his guard by an ambitious charlatan. They must find Seth and join him. Wolf, with the aid of the Right-Hand's power, was in constant awareness of their Lion's heartbeat. It pulled him toward the northwest.

"Dead ahead!" Yuli called from the bridge. "We've got company."

Hurrying to the front of the ship, Wolf searched the horizon just past the *Wind Chaser's* sails. Two ships waited for them in the diminishing glow of sunset. Wooden hulls. Wolf's breath eased a bit. They weren't the metal ships of their deadly enemy, the Jackal. One such Jackal vessel had hunted him across the plains of Valdeon as he tried to escape. The power of the Right-Hand had been needed to bring it down.

Joining Yuli on the bridge, Wolf grabbed two red flags and began to signal the *Wind Chaser*. Rafael eased his speed. The old tub slowly closed the distance between the two airships. The pair of them being near wouldn't make much difference in a fight, but if one of them had to abandon ship, proximity would make their escape route shorter.

"Those ships aren't moving," Yuli said. "This isn't exactly a good place to make repairs."

Indeed, it wasn't. The mercenaries were nearing the foothills of the Bloodtooth Mountains. Very few ships sailed along this route except those bringing supplies to North Marsh Outpost and other isolated stations among the Buells. This place was, however, the ideal spot for an ambush.

Sails swelling full of wind and speed, the strangers' ships suddenly burst forward. Cannon fire boomed in echoes of explosive noise. Their fire arced over the *Wind Chaser* with an eerie whistle. Wolf hung onto the railings as the empty air on either side of their hull exploded.

Cannonballs peppered the sky about them, causing Wolf to choke on the acidic drift of gunpowder. Smoke, though quickly swept away by the wind, blinded him as one of the cannonballs grazed their hull. The old tub rocked and shuddered while it groaned a dying breath. Wolf reached out blindly as the signal flags—their only means of communication with Rafael—fluttered over the side.

Movement registered in Wolf's peripheral vision. Tulio scrambled onto the bridge, which tilted with the pitch of the ship. His wide eyes took in their precarious position. Wolf grabbed Rabbit's arm just as he began to roll over the side.

"We've no weapons onboard. How are we to fight back?"

"Yuli, take us closer to the foothills," Wolf ordered. "We'll lead them away from the *Wind Chaser*. I have a plan."

"I hope it involves our coming out of this alive."

Wolf gave him a withering look prompting Yuli to lean hard on the wheel, using his weight to turn the ship. Effort and panic made a wrinkled mask of the young face. He gritted his teeth as the old tub creaked and groaned in alarm.

"Come and help me, Tulio," Wolf ordered. "We need to light a fire."

"What?" Yuli cried. "You're going to burn the ship? It's a long way to the ground."

"I'm aware. Hurry now."

Wolf kept a firm grip on Tulio as they raced a few steps down. His power and agility kept them on their feet, but they weren't prepared for the unpleasant surprise waiting for them below deck. Air whipped through the tight confines of the corridor. Wolf staggered back with a growl. Then pushing against the pressure of the makeshift wind tunnel, he moved forward. Speeding bits of wood and dried food slammed against their bodies with biting strikes.

"Wait here," Wolf said. "I've got to block the crack in the hull, or we'll be swept back on deck."

Gripping the small metal handholds meant for inclement weather, he pulled his body through the vortex. The galley walls were still mercifully intact. As he pushed around the corner and out of the wind, Wolf began to rummage through the room. He spotted a large board with several hooks of varying sizes embedded in its surface. The remains of old fish and herbs dangled from the board's surface. It would have to do. He grabbed the edge of the board and turned his nose away when the stench hit him. Ripping the wood from the wall, he hurried to the entrance of the galley.

While he summoned the Jalora's power about him, Wolf pushed against the rim of the galley's door and thrust forward toward the gaping hole in the hull's wall. Snow-covered evergreens zipped by in a wild rush.

"Eyes open, Tulio!" Wolf shoved the board against the wall and slammed the hooks into the hull's surface with a burst of power. "It should hold for a bit. Hurry now."

Throwing barrels and old crates in a pile, Wolf and Tulio stacked the fuel as high as they could. Wolf threw oil on the stack while Tulio struck his flint. Flames gripped the old wood in seconds. Swift-moving fire engulfed the ancient vessel, barely permitting them time to escape above decks.

"Let's move!" Wolf called to the bridge and continued his rush toward the nearest launch.

Wolf held the launch in place as Yuli tied the wheel, keeping the ship in a direct line for one of the mountain rock faces. His young guardsman jumped into the hovering launch as the old tub raced toward its death. He wasn't Wolf's ideal of dexterity as he tumbled over the benches toward the rudder. Tulio gave an angry rebuke and slapped Yuli's anxious hands away as the pair struggled with the mooring line. Wolf pulled his sword and severed the rope with one quick slash. The two young guardsmen fell backward with a startled cry.

"We have to time this perfectly," Wolf told Yuli, who'd taken the rudder. "I don't want them to see us, but let's not get crushed either."

The rock face drew closer until it was all Wolf could see before them. He leaned to the side as Yuli ruthlessly yanked the rudder and raised them at a breakneck speed off the deck. Their frantic pilot dove toward the tree line once they were clear. The old tub exploded in a massive ball of fire. Shards of wood and metal emptied in the air over the tufts of green and white.

Casting anxious glances over his shoulder, Yuli swallowed hard. "Next time, I get to captain the *Wind Chaser*, and Rafael can pilot the old death trap."

Chapter Seven

HOVERING BENEATH THE evergreen ceiling, Wolf and his guardsmen remained silent as they hid under the circling enemy ships directly above their heads. The sun's arms had retreated behind the mountain peaks, further casting them in shadow. Thick branches and a little luck hid their launch. Wolf slowed his breath beneath the green needles. Considering the last meeting between him and these tenacious hounds, revenge rather than money seemed the motive for the mercenaries' thorough searching.

"Why are they ignoring the *Wind Chaser*?" Yuli asked, keeping a firm grip on the launch's rudder.

"They search for the Right-Hand." Tulio let a dull gaze fall upon Wolf for a moment then turned his eyes back to the sky. "The *Wind Chaser* is preparing to attack."

Ignoring the silent rebuke, Wolf turned his attention to their comrade. Rafael was coming into an attack position. The small vessel's sails caught the wind as its crystal engines fired at full throttle. Its mad captain was taking on both mercenary ships.

"What's he doing?" Yuli's wide eyes stared at the fast-moving ship.

"Giving us the escape we were supposed to be giving him."

The *Wind Chaser*, a recreational vessel with no weapons, faced impossible odds against those fully armed warships. Wolf released an anxious breath. He must do something or everyone aboard the *Wind Chaser* would be lost. Their only option for survival, however, came at a high price. Possessing a terrible weapon of last resort, Wolf wasn't pleased to drain his strength before they reached Seth.

Massive sails cast deep shadows as the two mercenary ships turned to take the bait. Engines thundered in the orange and purple sky. Wolf muttered a quick prayer to the Jalora as the enemy vessels came about. Several cannon barrels protruded from the sides of their hulls—curse the villains. These mercenaries weren't interested in capturing their prey. They intended to destroy them. Rafael and the others had moments before being shot out of the sky.

"Take us behind the ships, Yuli."

"We don't have any weapons."

"I'm the weapon. Get into position," Wolf snapped. "Do it."

Yuli lifted the little launch through the evergreens. Brilliant fiery spheres of power shook them as he brought their tiny vessel into the wake of the enormous engines. A strange mix of cold air and heat struck their faces. Wolf ignored the sensation and moved into position at the front of the launch. Grim-faced, Tulio gripped the side of their vessel tightly. Wolf guessed young Tulio knew what was coming, but Yuli hadn't seen the power of the Right-Hand.

"Hold tight, Yuli. Stay in position, no matter what happens."

Turning toward the glowing orange and white, Yuli stared into the consuming fire of their engines. Wolf pressed his boots hard against the launch's hull. Gathering to him all his hate, fear, and frustration, Wolf struggled to contain the building pressure. Their tiny boat groaned as the overwhelming power pushed at its hull.

Then Wolf released that inner surge in one mighty growl. "For Valdeon!"

Designed as a weapon to protect and soothe the Lion, the Right-Hand's power was second in strength only to that of the Jalora Master. The Voice, as known in legends, thundered out of Wolf's being in a mighty wave of energy. It struck the nearest mercenary vessel in its engine. Twisted metal and splintering wood exploded in a brilliant cloud of dust and fire.

Yuli cursed and took the little vessel in a sharp angle downward to avoid the larger projectiles. Wolf fell onto the hull, his legs giving way.

"What did I say, Yuli? Stay in position!"

Wide-mouthed, their young pilot immediately righted the launch. He took a spiraling route back up behind the ships. Too late. The second vessel, seeing its partner crippled, had already started its turn toward the object of their hunt. They knew the Right-Hand lived.

The enemy hull grew closer, towering over their tiny launch like a hungry, predatory beast. Wolf lifted to his feet as death's shadow shrouded them. Shaking with the exertion of releasing the Voice, Wolf struggled to summon the power once again. Endurance was the maxim of the De Vincente family. He needed its strength now. Only this terrible destructive power within his being could save them.

"Wolf!" Yuli slammed the rudder to the right, narrowly missing the first cannonball. "Do something!"

Stabilizers sputtered with the strain as their vessel rocked precariously on its side. Yuli slammed his body against the rudder, righting the launch and sending them beneath the belly of the passing ship. Wolf's legs flew out from underneath him, and he began to fall. Arms grabbed him, righting him to a standing position. Tulio nodded and kept a supporting grip on Wolf's arm.

A looming silhouette washed over their launch. The mercenary ship was coming in for the kill. Wolf, body shaking with exhaustion, pulled the destructive power of the Right-Hand to him. It began again to build. Sweat-soaked hair clung to his forehead, sending stinging drops into his eyes. Cannons' mouths opened widely, eager to deliver his death. They were out of time and Wolf was unprepared to strike.

Then an explosion in the mercenary ship's mid-section slammed the vessel onto its side. The ship's body groaning, momentum rolled the wreckage over completely. Screams filled the skies as the doomed crew fell to the ground.

A ship soared toward them like a mighty predator bird. Its massive shadow zoomed over its kill with a roar of engines. By the Jalora! A black raven flew in the fabric of gold and green. Fausto De Quintaro, former Bearer of the Raven ring and faithful Lord of Valdeon, had found them. Miracles still existed in Andara.

Wolf let the gathering power of the Right-Hand dissipate with a loud cheer. "We'd better give Fausto some room, Yuli. Take us back to the tree line."

"You don't have to tell me twice, Right-Hand."

Yuli zipped the launch around with a quick spin. Wolf, falling hard on his backside, swallowed a stinging rebuke. They'd escaped death this day with the help of a dear friend. He could tolerate his young guardsman's enthusiasm this once.

Fausto's *Golden Claw* fed on the carcasses of its prey with savage revenge. It was a rare ship able to best Valdeonian vessels, though the Jackal had torn through their fleet like parchment the night Valdeon fell. Wolf savored this taste of vengeance with grim relish.

Finally, the *Golden Claw* eased into a gentle hover, waiting for Wolf and his guardsmen. Yuli landed their launch onto the deck. Cheers greeted them as the three Lords of Valdeon stepped in the ship.

Fausto stood at the head of the crew. Straight hair, bearing signs of his advancing age, fell in short strands against his head. He possessed a few more wrinkles now than when last Wolf had seen him. A new life lived in the rough had changed Fausto, but he still wore a light of hope about him. His best friend embraced Wolf with a desperate relief. Affection. Pride. They swirled about Fausto's body as he stood away.

"My eyes are glad to see you, my dear comrade. Phoenix told me of your daring escape." Fausto rustled a hand in Yuli's and Tulio's windswept hair. "And you too, my young lords!"

His attention left them a moment to linger on the *Wind Chaser* mooring alongside their ship. A father's eyes searched for the son he'd parted with the night Valdeon fell. Not waiting for the crew to tether them properly, Ernesto the Raven raced across the gangplank. He grabbed his father in a tight embrace. The typically solemn and controlled Raven buried his tears in Fausto's shoulder.

"Mother? Our family?" Ernesto wiped the wet from his face.

"They're safe and eager to hear news of you, my son."

Wolf prodded Yuli and Tulio toward the gangplank to give the reunited men a private moment. They would not have many more happy exchanges in the coming months, Wolf feared. Tulio dropped his head with a sad smile. Neither he nor Wolf had anyone waiting for them in Valdeon. They were alone, Tulio more than Wolf himself. Young Tulio was the last of Cristobal bloodline.

"Here comes the rest of our kin." Wolf pointed to Fox, Jaguar, and Ferret hurrying down the gangplank. "We are indeed fortunate our new family stays together, yes?"

"Indeed, we are." Tulio offered him another rare smile.

Rafael the Fox, leaving their squires aboard to tend to the ship, led the guardsmen across the swaying strip of wood. Dressed in the waistcoat of a Legion naval officer, he absently smoothed the piece of San Angelica lace waving frantically in the blustery wind. His sharp eyes stared keenly at Wolf.

"Charging straight at the enemy ships," Wolf said. "A bold move, my Lord the Fox."

"Some would say it was madness." Yuli grinned.

"I'd be one of those unlucky individuals," Berto the Jaguar grumbled as he and Lucio joined them.

Berto was Wolf's second in the Sacred Guard. A horse master from the fabled San Marimosa Cavalry in western Valdeon, he preferred hoof and saddle to airships. His lifelong friend, Lucio the Ferret, nodded with a ready smile stretched across his round face.

"I believe our friend the Fox had grown bored in your absence, Yuli."

"Ha! I didn't realize how foolhardy my actions were until I saw the first ship ripped apart." Rafael let a smile emerge. "Remind me never to be in the Right-Hand's line of fire."

"Indeed not!" Fausto joined them, shaking Rafael's hand. "I often compared Xavier the Wolf to a hurricane. How right I was."

Wolf laughed, feeding on the joy so long absent. His body began to sway. Familiar hands took his arms and led him to a barrel beside the mast. Loyalty. Concern. Relief. It emanated from Basilio, his squire. Wolf had thought him dead the night their world ended.

"Basilio! I thought you'd perished aboard our burning ship." Wolf declared.

"You there!" Wolf's squire barked at an unlucky sailor. "My Lord the Right-Hand has need of water."

Basilio knelt before Wolf as the sailor hurried below deck. A leather patch covered his right eye, altering the face once loved by Wolf's children. Wolf's squire had endured many hardships since their parting.

Fading scratches crisscrossed his hands. Basilio's fierce loyalty, however, hadn't waned.

"I tried to find you in the embers of San Rudalfo, My Lord, but the smoke was too thick. Failing to locate you or your body, I did my next duty."

Wolf took a cup of water from the nervous sailor's hand and drank deeply. The water tasted sweet and fresh. Fausto must've stocked his barrels in the springs of the Commonwealth. Handing the cup back with a nod, Wolf wiped at his mouth with a still-trembling hand. He quickly lowered it, but his squire hadn't missed the sign of fatigue.

"You found the heir to the Wolf Ring," Wolf guessed.

"Yes, My Lord. Stephano is in hiding outside San Rudalfo. After the Jackal left, we…we buried your family." Basilio looked away, swallowing hard. "My duty to you done, I fought my way up the border of Southbay to warn the Legion. My Lord De Quintaro found me just outside of Lea. I was eager to join you the moment I learned you were alive."

"Indeed, he was! Too bad you both missed all the excitement." Fausto grinned when Basilio gave him a sour face. "Seeing our young Lion do battle at the head of his men. Ah, it is a sight I shall never forget."

"His men?" Rafael frowned.

"For the Lion!" the men on the ship began to chant.

"You see, Rafael the Fox. We are the Lion's men."

Fausto pulled up his left sleeve. Running across his arm was the young Lion's mark. Here was Seth's newest Lion Friend. Wolf was pleased with Seth's wisdom.

Fausto was a former member of the Sacred Guard and a wise leader. They would need more men like him as they took back Valdeon.

"Out with it, Fausto." Wolf chuckled. "My guardsmen are impatient to hear."

"You should have seen him, Wolf. Our Lion stood defiant, his fierce amber eyes burned into Julian, the bastard prince! Seth drew the first blood. And then his mighty roar shook the citadel," Fausto said, eyes glowing with pride. "His faithful charged the battlements and forced back the mercenary scum who helped take our home!"

"He will be a mighty king!" one of the sailors cried. "It was my greatest honor to see him named." The naming. Wolf's anger and resentment rose again for a moment. He was the Lion's Right-Hand. Cardinal Dragon, motivated by foolish curiosity, had robbed him of seeing Seth tested and officially named into the Legion. Wolf had the power to see, of course, though doing so was ill-advised while he was weak. Curiosity rather than wisdom won out. Wolf gently probed the sailor's memory with his power.

Images of the Lion came into sharp focus. Seth stood over his defeated opponent, fierce and triumphant like the mighty Lion Spirit inhabiting his ring. Thundering applause and chanting filled the arena around him. His countrymen worshipped while the Legion feared him. The rangers, it would seem, still possessed common sense.

"We've come on a mission from the Lion's squire to find you," Fausto said, wagging his finger at Basilio when the man grunted. "Say what you will, squire.

Riley Logan has an abundance of common sense and courage. He stood up to the Hawk after all. Riley wants me to warn you about Esteban. The Hawk prince has plans to challenge you."

"Yes, I am aware. Esteban tried unsuccessfully to kill me in the forests of the Commonwealth. I sent a trusted ally to warn Dragon of his betrayal. What happened, Jason Coyote?" Wolf asked, directing his gaze into the crowd. "Come out into the open and answer me."

The stowaway sunk further into the recesses of the stairs descending below decks. Wolf motioned an impatient finger toward Coyote. The ranger, accepting the promise of Wolf's punishment, threw off his protective cloak and stepped out of his hiding place. The young man was pleased with himself. Wolf snorted. By the Jalora. He was a good spy, crafty and silent. Coyote had fooled Fausto and his men. They had no idea he'd been hiding on their vessel since Lea.

"Good day to you, Wolf." His uncertain grin greeted them. "As per your orders, I went to warn Phoenix about the danger to Seth. Imagine my confusion when I found the Partisan and his men surrounding the Lion. They were preparing to cage our lord. The fools approached him at a time when his rage had overtaken Seth. While I was trying to help my lord Lion, Phoenix attacked me." Rage flared in his eyes. "I woke in a jail cell at Hawk's command. A comrade of mine let me out, but I was too late. Phoenix took Seth. Esteban the Hawk had disappeared before Dragon returned."

Jason Coyote's account was undeniably accurate. He was a ranger incapable of lying. Coyote was also the Lion's First Marked. Nothing would make him betray or dishonor his lord. Gregory the Phoenix had much to explain when next he and Wolf met.

"I fear for Seth," Wolf said. "We're going to him now. I'll take Ice Lion into hiding to keep him safe from Hawk and our hunters."

"I'm your man, Right-Hand." Coyote bowed low. "Let me use my skills to help you."

"I suppose I have no choice. You'd follow us anyway."

Coyote grinned. "You know me already, sir."

Fausto shook his head as Coyote headed toward the *Wind Chaser* with Boyd, his squire hurrying to join him. "We must part again, my old friend. I have a rebellion to organize," Fausto announced.

"I wish we had more time before our parting," Wolf said, standing with Basilio's help. "Take care of yourself, Fausto. I thought you dead once."

"I'm too stubborn to die. Find the Lion. Tell him his people believe in him."

Wolf's heart was troubled as he boarded the *Wind Chaser*. He desperately wanted to join Fausto in Valdeon for the rebellion, but such wasn't possible. His first duty as Right-Hand was to find Seth before Hawk could reach him again. Curse Dragon to the devil. Hawk's ambition had separated the Sacred Guard from the Lion they were sworn to protect. Such bangtail mischief was impacting more than Legion politics.

Chapter Eight

SETH LEANED HIS head back with a sigh and counted the nails in the ceiling for the tenth time. A slow two days had passed as they sat in the belly of their ship. Boredom was the greatest danger to him and his fellow apprentices. The other rangers busied themselves with parchments and enjoyable hobbies. Such things seemed to be contraband for the bored young men in Seth's group.

"Bear?" Seth tapped the big man's shoulder. "Why are the crystals within the Heart of the Warrior ring different shades? I know each color denotes rank within the Legion, but why are ours a darker yellow than that of the other apprentices?"

"How is it the heir of the Leo knows nothing about the Legion?" Bear asked, anxiously regarding the rangers sitting in the center of the chamber. "You must have a care. The acolytes delight in testing apprentices. They'll look for any lapse in knowledge or stamina as a means of persecuting you."

"I know it too well," Stallion grumbled. "You aren't the only one aboard this ship against his will, Ice Lion."

Stallion—offering them no further explanation—closed his eyes tightly against the soft rays of the overhead light. Seth resisted his impulse to probe the young man. They all had their secrets. Stallion, however, seemed headed down a path toward trouble.

"We're in this together now. I might as well teach you both something since we have more than a full day left in our journey." Bear answered with impatience when Stallion grunted. "You already know the Heart of the Warrior ring turns clear when first put on the finger. This stage is called 'Selected.' The Jalora turns the Heart Crystal white when it feels a man is ready to start his training with the Legion. This time is also an opportunity to strip out the weak ones. Thus, the term 'Hopeful.' No guarantee is given, understand?"

Seth nodded. He appreciated the warnings of Dragonfly, Coyote, and Phoenix now. Though the Jalora and its Lion Spirit accepted Seth when his father had placed the Lion Ring on Seth's finger, his designation was merely an opening. Seth had still to prove his worth as Bearer. If he was found inadequate, the Jalora still could have rejected him. He caressed his Heart Crystal. The price of their parting was death.

"Apprentices rank in three levels," Bear continued. "Our new friends with the light-yellow rings are at stage one. They have just begun their journey. You and I are senior apprentices. Soon, we will join the Legion as acolytes."

"You mean we aren't in the Legion yet?" Stallion opened incredulous eyes.

"Oh yes, but we're not full rangers until we reach acolyte level one," Bear told him, motioning toward a small group of rangers with light green rings. "They are 'A-1s.' The darker meadow grass color marks a bearer as an 'A-2,' like Mantis or Gecko."

"I don't want to be under Mantis for a moment longer than I have to be." Stallion grunted with disgust and pulled his hood over his eyes.

"Holding onto your anger isn't wise," Bear said. "The acolytes train us. You'll be spending most of your time with them."

Entering the chamber with purposeful strides, White Tiger saluted Phoenix. They began speaking together in quiet tones. Second in command of the battalion, White Tiger had the enviable freedom to wander the ship. How many times in the past two days had he been able to smell fresh air?

"What about White Tiger?"

"He's an 'A-3,' the highest level of acolyte. Most rangers don't advance past an A-2. In the UR Army, White Tiger is a captain." Bear bumped Seth's leg. "Careful, Ice Lion, Phoenix is a 'D-2,' a deacon level two. He can sense your interest from across the ship. Our commander is very gifted."

"Are all the ranks the same? The darker the crystal, the higher the rank?"

Bear nodded. "Less than twenty percent of rangers make deacon level one. The percent decreases as the rank moves higher. Rarely does the Jalora promote its rangers greater than deacon."

"The purple Heart Crystals?"

"Things are a bit different in their level of the Legion. Bishops, like your uncle, wear the pale purple rings. They command the entire Legion and the UR Army," Bear said in tones of awe. "A cardinal—he has a dark-purple crystal—commands the bishops. Dragon has been the only cardinal chosen by the Jalora in a great many years." Bear stopped to watch the squires approach their higher-ranking rangers. "Suppertime. A blessed relief after this dull day."

Seth held up the Lion Ring to his eye, pondering the many generations and many colors it had held. Of course, the Lion Ring adopted a crimson hue on rare occasions. Six times in the past, as it had happened. Many referred to these Jalora Masters as 'Red Hearts.' Seth was listed among them in the Book of Ancients.

"And what does the Legion say when my Heart Crystal turns red?"

Bear gave him an uneasy hiss and turned to look about the chamber. "Take care, Ice Lion. We do not speak of the Red Hearts. They are sacred. I have no wish to anger the Jalora."

Seth had listened to his father, his disgruntled relatives, and the Jalora about his duty as Protector. No one had used the word sacred before. Seth regarded the Lionhead swimming in the belly of his stone on the gentle waves of his life's blood. He had no desire to be seen as a sacred relic.

Stretching his cramping legs outward, Seth accidentally kicked his mother's treasured guitar. He straightened in his seat with a sharp cry. It was the only thing he had left of her. Grasping the neck, he pulled the instrument into his lap and plucked gently at the strings. Seth didn't see anything broken, but it was seriously out of tune. He hadn't touched the guitar since his time on the Isle of Carlotta when he'd tried to teach himself how to play.

Plucking at the strings, he brought the notes into clear tones. Then he began to play. Struggling fingers suddenly were confident and skilled. How was this possible?

Music gives joy and comfort. It is a gift to be shared.

Bear smiled as he watched Seth pick at the strings. Seth's fellow apprentice appeared to be relieved by the sudden shift of the Lion's attention. Letting his smile come, Seth chose a peaceful tune he had learned on Carlotta. It spoke of soft breezes and azure waves. He'd not thought about his home for a long time and found he missed it. Thoughts of Aunt Charlotte and their sunsets sitting on the patio garden brought a sentimental air to his voice.

"Stop! You'll have us all jumping over the side of the ship in a moment!" White Tiger put a hand over the guitar neck. "Play something cheerful, Ice Lion."

Indeed, the mood of Western Beta had changed. Bored only moments before, the rangers were now melancholy and contemplative as if they all share a common sorrow. How could this be? Did the Jalora connect the Legion members in some way?

"I'll have a Kirkland tune while you wait for your woolie-headed squire to bring the dinner." White Tiger put his fists upon his hips. "Do you know 'The Rose and the Sword'? You should. It was playing in the Rollicking Rover the night you overturned our wagon."

"I'll try, sir."

Seth played the song he'd heard in Lea. White Tiger, tapping a foot to the tune, seemed pleased. The mood among the other men had cheered immensely as well. Seth followed "The Rose and the Sword" with a few Marianna pub tunes, much to the delight of his squire.

Riley came toward him at a merry gait. Seth's dinner teetered precariously before him.

"I'm glad to see you," Seth told Riley. Seth put his guitar down when Riley stretched out the plate. "Being the evening's entertainment was a bit unsettling."

"Aye," Riley said, stepping in to block White Tiger's line of sight. "I can imagine."

Legion meals were an improvement over UR Army food. Tasting Riley's touch in the spices, Seth savored his supper and was rewarded with a second helping. Riley had trained under Dante, the Leo's squire, who had earned the reputation of being the best cook the Legion had seen in a great many decades. The new Lion's squire had, in turn, earned the praise of his corps. Seth handed his second empty plate back to Riley with a genuine compliment. The gesture started their apprentice squires buzzing. Apparently, a friendly competition was about to ensue among the young men.

Full stomachs and eternal boredom cast a sleep spell over the chamber. Soon the rangers and their squires were snoring under the dimmed lights of the ship. Riley's head flopped on Seth's shoulder. Seth envied the other man's ability to block out all troubles for a good night's rest. Sliding carefully off the bench, Seth lowered Riley across its surface. Sleep wasn't coming for Seth.

Sitting crossed legged on the floor, he began to take deep, slow breaths. That he keep the Lion Spirit calm was essential. Losing control aboard such a tight space would prove deadly for those who traveled with him.

His attention drifted to a knothole in one of the floorboards. The cracks and circles within the wood held his gaze. They began to swirl, catching the browns and grays of the floor. Then the wild patterns disappeared, taking the ship and its passengers with it.

Suddenly he was standing back on the ground. Smoke and ruin surrounded him. The smell of battle was thick in the air as Seth walked through their army, which stretched across the grassy plains. Ahead of them, a town was in flames. Fear drifted on the breeze, coming from the UR soldiers and several fighters from the northern countries. They pushed forward into the waiting Jalora Legion. So few rangers left. Sorrow threatened to consume him. One more hard strike by the Jackal would mean the end of the Legion.

"You must save them, Lion. This responsibility I entrust to you," the Jalora said.

His duty had somehow brought Seth to this place. Where were they? Or better yet, when were they?

"What am I to do?"

The Jalora came about him with its power, holding him firmly. "You must find what was lost. Look in hidden places buried by the marsh."

Then a white stone, like a tile, floated before Seth in the hazy gray of the battlefield. Strange letters written in gold burned into the surface as he watched. It began to spin faster and faster until Seth couldn't see its original shape anymore. A brilliant white fell from the heavens and struck the stone, knocking Seth back through time and space.

Seth's head slammed painfully against the rim of the bench. Riley grunted but didn't wake. Clearly, this burden Seth was meant to carry alone. Wrapping his power about him, he stood up and silently made his way through the sleeping men. He winced as the double doors gave a small squeak when pushed open. Seth stepped into the deserted corridor and carefully closed the doors behind.

The Protector's engines hummed as he made his way above decks. Outside air, heavy with moisture and chill, tugged at the short, dark strands sticking out from beneath his hood. Drizzle kissed his cheeks but didn't linger on the skin. Pulling his cloak tighter, he moved toward the railing. They were flying on top of the rain clouds, and thick plumes of gray fluff blocked any view of the ground beneath. Oddly, the scene suited his mood. He too was lost in a fog of uncertainty. How was he to save the Legion? When must he start? Should he warn anyone? So many questions with no one to answer them.

Suddenly, the deck door closed behind him. Seth turned, ready to bumble out words of explanation. But his fellow here was only another escapee from White Tiger's unlucky group of apprentices. Slight shoulders leaned against the nearest mass. The ash of his cloak drained any sign of color from his face. Clutching at his side, the young Ephemeral held up his ring under the dim glow of the ship's exterior lighting.

"I'm afraid the apprentice testing has put a strain on your body. The pain will leave you in a few days," Seth said, awkwardly pulling the hood from his own head.

"Forgive me, Ice Lion," the doomed man said in a voice laced with pain. "I have disturbed you."

"Badger, isn't it? Please stay. I could use some company."

"You would speak in friendship to a Tslavian?"

"If you show me friendship as well. My mother, Anne Von Wolkhurst, was Tslavian, and my father was Edmund D'Antoiné, king of Valdeon. Are we friends or enemies?"

"We are cousins then. I'm Henry." Badger held his hand out for Seth to shake. "My father is, or rather was, your mother's older brother."

"I'm called Seth. You are a welcome surprise. I thought my only family was our Aunt Charlotte on Carlotta. You must come with me to visit her when we're set free from our apprenticeship."

Badger smiled a little and joined Seth beside the railing. Blond strands whipped atop his head as he rested his arms on the wood. Gray fluff floated placidly beneath the two of them. Flying above a land you couldn't see created an eerie sensation.

"You don't fear to be with me then?" Badger asked at last.

Seth tapped on the Badger Ring with the fingertip bearing his own. The two animals floating within their stones swam around to greet each other. Lion and Badger playfully bumped against the exterior of their crystal homes.

"Your animal spirit isn't worried. I think you should take its example to heart." Seth patted the silver holding his crystal in place. "The Jalora guides our paths, but we are the ones who choose whether to follow its wisdom or give in to despair." Seth shook his head. "I suppose I should heed my own words."

"I've heard rumors of your fight with the Bear and how you saved the life of the Phoenix. You follow the Jalora Code."

"You see! I've no notion of this code. I'm here by a stroke of fate. You're here because you earned your apprenticeship."

Badger stared at him in a mixture of pride and disbelief. "You must know the Code before we reach North Marsh, or the acolytes will torment you. It consists of four rules. Always trust in the Jalora, for it gives its light to the world. Do not disgrace the Jalora or yourself—you've joined as one. Dishonesty and injustice have no place in service. And the last is our maxim. Protect the innocent. Punish the guilty."

"Very good, apprentice."

Seth and Badger spun around. A sailor stood a few inches away from them. Adorned in silver from tunic to trouser, the sailor, Seth fancied, must enjoy living among the clouds. His long, white hair fell in light strands upon his heavy waistcoat. On his face shined annoyance and disapproval. Seth felt as if they'd broken a rule in school and were standing before the headmaster.

Sea-green eyes scanned them with displeasure. Seth shifted slightly under the man's gaze. The ranger's arms crossed the silver tunic just below his golden Jalora Legion insignia. It differed from their ground troop emblem. A golden anchor lay across the star where the sword should have been. Another badge identified him as belonging to the Western Atlanta Naval Battalion. Seth's eyes reluctantly flicked down to the man's left hand. A dark blue crystal burned brightly upon his finger. This ranger was a deacon level three, like Wolf.

"I am called Firefly," the sailor said at last, staring down at Seth's ring. "And what has the Jalora called you, apprentice?"

"Ice Lion, sir."

Firefly narrowed his eyes as power pulsed from his body in aggressive waves. "I hope you prove to be more of a man of honor than your predecessor, Ice Lion."

"Leo was a great man. It is unfortunate your measurement of honor differs from mine."

Firefly gave Seth a quiet laugh. "I don't care if you're under the Hawk's protection, boy. I'm the master of this vessel. I will flog you for insubordination."

His intense gaze shifted over Seth's shoulder. Straightening with a sudden curt nod, Firefly spun on his heels and disappeared into the darkness. Seth watched him go, angry and shaken.

"Ice Lion." Badger slapped him urgently on the arm.

Seth turned to follow Badger's gaze and found Phoenix standing directly behind him. Phoenix was staring into the darkness where Firefly had disappeared. The familiar flames of anger burned in their commander's eyes.

"Go below, young apprentices. You'll need your strength when we reach North Marsh."

They saluted Phoenix and hurried down the stairs to the main deck. White Tiger, fingers tapping in irritation against the double doors of their chamber, gave them a sour frown. They threw him a careful salute and scampered past him to join their sleeping battalion.

Badger delivered a relieved smile as they sat down on the benches side by side. "Firefly certainly seems to hold you in contempt."

"I can't imagine why. We've never met. It sounds as if the captain knew my father." Seth leaned his head back against the wall. "This trip just keeps getting better and better."

Chapter Nine

JULIAN UNFASTENED THE clasp holding his cloak in place. The air was stifling. Eastern Valdeon was an arid land. To his memory, though, it had never been this hot. Even the waters of Lake Leonora and the Leonora River were depleting under the glare of a burning sun. The temperature, much to his annoyance, didn't cool in the shade of the Great Inland Wall. Its thousands of Lion Heads roared down on him in impotent rage. These magical protectors hadn't fallen in hundreds of years. Now San Leonora was lost, the city's impassable gates penetrated by a betrayer from the inside.

Turning his face away, Julian avoided their empty stares. These guardians of San Leonora were lavishing their contempt on the wrong man. He'd wanted to save the city. Why couldn't anyone believe his intentions had been good? Someone else was responsible for their defeat. San Leonora's betrayer wore a mask and cowl. His plans were as mysterious as his identity.

This dark stranger was delighted to offer Julian the location of his father and the heir to the Lion Ring. He'd been on hand the night San Leonora fell to warn Julian about the impending invasion. The villain had admitted to aiding the Jackal by letting them inside the city by way of a hidden gate within the wall.

Whoever this masked coward was, he hadn't given Julian enough time to convince the city's defenders to make Julian regent. Now Julian spat on the dirt before him. Perhaps he'd allow Marcellus to exercise some of his more creative tortures on their mysterious friend when next he showed his masked face.

Julian stepped through the gaping maw of a dying city. While the fabled wall and its gates remained intact by the magic that had created them, San Leonora itself hadn't been as fortunate. Julian wrinkled his nose at the stench of death and human waste, the city's beauty trampled beneath the boots of these Jackal invaders. It was a filthy sewer now.

"You could sail anywhere in Andara and its surrounding isles, cousin." His Changeling nanny sneered at the miserable urchins running half-naked in the streets around them. "Why come back to this dead place?"

"My brother has a childish obsession for this city," Zoya said, giving him her most petulant frown.

"I should think you'd be grateful for my propensity for sentimentality, sister. Otherwise, you'd be selling yourself on the streets of Southbay." Julian turned his back to her. "Come, I must reach my chambers in the palace."

A poof of air and sickly sweet perfume announced Whisper, his tenuous ally. The little imp had introduced itself to Julian as Uther's ambassador to Andara when they'd first met. Rejected by Lord Gorman, the creature had willingly allied itself with Julian's cause. Whisper was unshakably loyal, but was it he the imp followed?

"Welcome home, My Lord Prince," Whisper said with a bow of its bulbous body. "Your unexpected departure was troubling. I'm glad to see you've returned to us safely."

"Yes, I can imagine." Julian exchanged a grin with his Changeling cousin. "We have much to discuss, Whisper. Join us in my chambers. They are still intact I trust?"

"Of course, Highness. I kept the pillagers out for you. Nothing was touched."

"Good. We need a base of operation. My chambers will be all the more convenient when I take back the throne."

Warning hisses followed them as Julian led his entourage down the crumbling path once known as King's Row. Absent were the golden tiles meant for the touch of a Jalora Master's regal feet. Bits of dulled gold clung to the ground where ragged children with bloodied fingers snarled as they passed. Then the urchins resumed their digging and scraping at any gold left behind the Jackal's initial plunder. The famous thoroughfare was in no better state than a farm road. Muck and debris littered the ground, forcing them to the sidewalk or at times off the central row altogether.

Hard men with hungry eyes stared out of the recesses of rundown buildings along their path. Momentary greed and lust were begrudgingly replaced by fear when the Changelings pulled their swords. Hungry men, no matter how desperate, still valued their skins.

"We take the launch next time, cousin." His Changeling nanny sheathed its sword. "I enjoy killing well enough, but why take such risk against these numbers? Though they appear to be nothing more than animals now, one day these men may understand how greatly they outnumber us. I've seen it before."

"Your point is well taken, cousin. Forget the rabble. We're here."

This part of King's Row, closest to the palace gates, remained intact as did the towering statue of Mikel D'Antoiné riding his stallion. The ornate iron rod gates, now repaired, were guarded by two ridiculous-looking Jackal soldiers sporting the blue feathered hats of the old palace guard. Encased in metal, they must be boiling in their filth under the heat of a Valdeonian afternoon.

A flash of dazzling light struck Julian's face as their path curved around Mikel's statue. The golden domes atop the Palace of Kings blazed in the insufferable sunshine. Julian held a hand up to block the reflection. Some fool had polished the precious metal rather than covering it with canvas to reduce the heat. Lord Gorman was making himself at home. He'd not be sleeping well in his brick oven palace. Julian stroked the fabric hiding his gray scales with a thoughtful grin. Let Gorman protect the treasures of San Leonora. All the better when Julian snatched the throne out from under his metal clutches.

Now Julian walked up the perfectly preserved mosaic steps and through the wide opening into the Grand Atrium. Once a marvel of architectural achievement, the dirtied glass panels hanging above them were covered in filth. White tiles—though cleared of the bodies of the city's defenders—still held the bloodstains of murder. Julian lifted his chin and took a faster pace. The palace cleaning staff—those not butchered by the Jackal—were neglectful of their duties.

"You crawl home after being soundly trounced by the Lion, Abomination? Better if you had jumped from the battlements of the Obsidian Citadel."

Laughter boomed from behind the sealed golden doors of the throne room. The sound filled the Grand Atrium, thundering against Julian's ears. Malevolent power lifted to the glass ceiling and rattled dirt from the panels. His Changeling cousins hissed at the Jalora's voice, waving their hands before them in protective spells.

"Come. I have no time to mince words with a defeated foe."

Julian lifted his chin and strolled a stately pace down the corridor leading to the royal family's quarters. Pride kept him from running. The Jalora knew. How could it not? The Sarcion had all but left Julian. He was exposed and vulnerable to the Jalora's vindictive power.

Forcing his eyes from the tatters of ancient tapestries and priceless portraits, he maintained his steady pace to the royal family's wing. The corridor remained empty in this section of the palace. Thick layers of dust covered the marble floors and any bones of ruined furniture.

"This is new," Julian said as they came to the entrance of the D'Antoiné family wing. "I should think Lord Gorman the type to sleep in a conquered king's bed."

Massive doors, thrown together from a hodgepodge of materials, blocked the entrance. They were tightly boarded and fastened shut with a heavy chain. Julian reached for the lock. Ancient power slapped at his fingers with a sharp burst of energy. Curse it! He yanked his hand away with a suppressed yelp.

"Nobody will go inside, My Lord Prince," Whisper told him. "An unknown magic haunts those halls. Even Lord Gorman will not enter."

Julian nodded with a momentary glimmer of satisfaction. The ghostly presence haunting his father's hall was an excellent judge of character. Julian had experienced the living magic's disdain the last time he'd tried to speak with his father inside the wing's parlor. Pain, disorientation, and sickness prevented him from crossing the threshold. No one knew where the magic had come from or its nature. Not even his father. Leo simply accepted its decision about his wayward son. He refused Julian entry, and they were forced to meet in the gardens. The conversation hadn't gone well. Soon after, Leo left San Leonora and never returned.

The group continued along the corridor, each step exploding into a cloud of dust. Cobwebs clung to the ceiling and spilled down the pillars in thin strings of white. Dilapidated crystal lanterns sputtered as they passed. They'd neglected Julian's wing of the palace. Typical.

He stopped before his bedchamber door. A subtle touch of the unfamiliar made him pause to regard the chains binding the chapel housing the D'Antoiné family crypt. The chapel doors, waiting for him at the end of the corridor, radiated with a new mystery. He'd never minded their presence in the past. Something was different, though. Had the Jackal hidden some magical weapon behind those doors? Perhaps Gorman feared the dead? Interesting. Shaking his head, Julian turned back to the business at hand.

At once, he pulled open the doors to his bedchamber. Stagnant darkness greeted him. Lanterns sputtered on as Whisper buzzed about the room. Dusty furniture. Filthy bedspread and pillows. The little imp had indeed kept everyone out, including the cleaning staff. Julian took a steadying breath then coughed out the foul air again. His possessions were intact at least. More importantly, the liquor cabinet hadn't been disturbed.

He made a lavish show of preparing drinks for his guests, handing the first to his Changeling cousin. His nanny took a great gulp and emptied the glass. Julian poured more of the expensive liquor. Then hurried to fill the cups of the remaining Changelings. Keeping them happy had become key to his future.

"You're up to something, brother." Zoya folded her arms and leaned against the wall.

"I mean to find the regent of Valdeon." Julian sipped the liquor, which was spicy and robust. Perfect for discussing treachery.

"And when you do?" she asked.

"I'll kill him and take the medallion from around his neck." Julian lifted a glass to his Changeling family and shared their laughter.

"Gorman will find out and stop you, brother." She shook her head. "Give up this mad obsession with a throne out of your reach."

"My family is with me now, Zoya," he told her. "You are free to join your Jackal friends. Plan to leave with them when we chase those stray dogs from our shores."

Zoya stormed toward the door, eyes glaring with hot anger. In such a mood, she was at her most dangerous. Julian had witnessed her stabbing many an enemy with those unforgiving eyes. None of them had survived her temper. His sister gave Julian one last look of contempt and slammed the door behind her. The Changelings burst into laughter.

"This sister of yours is a friend to the Jackal and loyal to their cause, cousin." The speaker let a hungry grin come across thin lips. "Shall I slit her throat?"

Marcellus, who'd remained blessedly quiet, pushed away from the corner. "You gave Zoya to me, My Prince. I will take responsibility for controlling her behavior."

Well, well. Marcellus still had a bit of a man in him. He'd been sullen since Julian's defeat at the half-breed Lion's hand. Disappointment and confusion were etched on his face when he saw his lord's bleeding body. Such judgment was the last thing Julian wanted from a madman. Marcellus's very presence was an irritant. Let him focus on his new obsession. To see him struggling to control the vicious killer that was Zoya would be amusing.

"You'd better go see to your woman then," Julian told him.

Several black orbs watched with cruel amusement as Marcellus hurried out the door after his new burden. Julian shared the magical beings' keenness for a bit of naughty fun. He was no longer obligated to keep the Sarcion's house. Let it deal with the two wayward pawns on its own.

"Someone must keep an eye on them, My Prince," Whisper said, licking absent lips.

"A task suited to your skills, imp."

One of the Changelings held the door open for their bulbous ally. The imp disappeared with a cry of glee. Julian frowned, staring at the closing door. Something had changed in Whisper. Rather than being just a floating blob of gold, the imp's head glowed with a strange pinkish light Julian hadn't noticed during their previous exchanges.

"You see it now?" his Changeling nanny asked. "Whisper was made by Uther. It possesses certain useful skills. Best to be on your guard against it, cousin."

His skin crawled. Julian thought about the times Whisper had come into his presence. He'd barely noticed the strange pressure against his mind. Now the imp's intruding touch was apparent as the little blob left the room. It had retracted its mental claws in favor of other prey. The treacherous devil had been controlling him! But who was controlling Whisper? Uther? Gorman? Julian would indeed have to guard against any more of Whisper's touches.

"Enough of Whisper, cousin. Tell us more of this Jorge Pacarro."

"He's a barbarian who follows the Lords of Valdeon like a stray pup." Julian slammed back another drink. "He won't be too difficult to handle."

"The Jackal are barbarians. You see what they accomplished in a night."

"Yes, but they defeated Valdeon by sheer numbers." Julian lifted his glass to them. "And with your help, of course."

"They say the regent hides in the West. His stronghold is a place called San Lucida. Gorman's mercenary forces are closing in. How are we to find this regent first?"

"They'll never locate a Pacarro tribesmen in his forest. Don't worry, cousin. You'd be surprised what a few credits can do," Julian said, walking to the wall across from his bed. "We put a bounty on his head. Pay for information. The West has been flattened and burned. Those who follow him will be desperate for the money. Loyalty doesn't fill an empty belly."

Running his fingertips along the bricks, Julian found a small indentation in the mortar. He pressed at the spot. One of the stones popped out with a slight whoosh. Julian pulled the hollow brick from the wall and dumped its contents into his hand. He let the thumb-length silver cylinder dangle off its long chain. His Changeling cousins backed away in disgust.

"It reeks of the Jalora's magic!" His nanny wrinkled its nose. "What is it?"

"This is a Heart's Blood Talisman. The Sarcion gifted it to me before I bore its ring." Julian grinned, hanging the chain about his neck. "It blocks the mind powers of the Jalora's rangers. I dare say even the Lion could not penetrate its defenses. This talisman thwarted my father, though he was a Jalora bishop."

"I sense its wrongness."

Julian shrugged and stuffed the cylinder under his tunic. "I shouldn't wonder. The cylinder contains liquid heart crystal from the Temple Cave. It was gained by a bit of murder many centuries ago. Willing or no, the Sarcion will help our cause. Now, let us travel to the West in search of Valdeon's wayward regent."

Chapter Ten

WET AND CHILLY flurries of snow typically frequented the foothills of the Border Mountains this time of year. Winter, much like its allies, had abandoned Valdeon. The drought was their new eternal tormentor. Dried branches, covered in fragile needles, sagged overhead to block parts of the trail. Jorge carefully avoided them. Small bends or breaks in a single brittle twig were a road marker to those who knew how to read such signs. Their enemies would most certainly have trackers watching for any mistakes.

Snaps and stomps echoed behind him in the dead forest. By the Erthe Mother! His tagalongs were louder than a military band. He turned with an impatient glare toward the oblivious refugees. They tugged the brittle branches off their dying trunks, kicked the rocks off the path, and chattered about the hardships they must endure. Their dust clouds floated in swirling waves up the tree trunks and into the hot afternoon sky.

"Erthe Mother, grant me patience."

His followers were sending clear signals to the Jackal. To disguise the passing of more than two-hundred bumbling pairs of feet before reaching the caves safely was impossible. Something must be done to conceal their tracks, or the Jackal would follow them to their promised sanctuary. They'd be trapped inside and exterminated like rats. It would mean the end of Western Valdeon.

If these people were part of the nomadic Pacarro tribe, hiding tracks wouldn't be a concern. Pacarro children were taught at an early age how to conceal their passing in nature. Parents took great care in showing their offspring how to be soft in their steps and leave no signs of their existence. The lessons took years and were critical to the tribe's survival. The Pacarro people were able to be invisible as they carried their tents, animals, and all their possessions across the plains of Valdeon. Jorge must train his new people in the ways of the Pacarro. They didn't have much time. Having them wander in the open for long was a risk, but he had no choice.

"Duarto," Jorge called to his son.

Startled at being summoned by his father's voice rather than their usual silent signals, Duarto missed one of the branches. Jorge chuckled as it struck his son in the face with a resounding whack. Duarto's lips moved in disgruntled curses as he came to join Jorge.

"Do you remember the small meadow where I first taught you how to throw a hatchet? Good. It's half a mile up the trail. Gather the people when we arrive. I must speak with them about our direction."

"Yes, Father. Are you planning to tell them where we're going?"

"No. I teach our people the way of the Pacarro. We won't reach the safety of the caves for many weeks."

"Weeks?" Duarto grumbled low. "You know very well the caves are a three-day march from San Lucida."

"Our sanctuary is for those who remain loyal to the Lion. They must be able to survive until he returns." Jorge gave his son a frown. "It will also give me time to weed out the spies among us."

Duarto and his hunters wrangled the people into the sad little meadow of dried grass. Stomping their feet on the parched ground, Jorge's followers shuffled about like anxious cattle. Men who had lost all courage stared down at the brown grass. Women, gaunt and frail, followed without question. Exhausted children clutched at the adults. These little ones had forgotten what playing or laughing was like. Jorge steeled his heart against his compassion for their grief and despair.

He stood on the rocky knoll at the edge of the meadow. Wisps of yellowed leaves grabbed at his trouser legs as they withered against the hot breeze. His gaze swept over the anxious faces. Many eager eyes met his glance while others shifted their faces away out of mistrust. Perhaps they were hiding secrets. Time would tell.

"Look at the path on which you've come," Jorge said, waiting until their heads turned back toward San Lucida. "You move like a cattle stampede. How are we to avoid Jackal soldiers if you trample everything in sight? No, my people, you must do better. I will teach you the way of the Pacarro. By the time we reach our place of safety, you will pass through any terrain like phantoms."

"And how long will that be?"

A red-faced blowhard stood, arms folded, in the center of the crowd. In his middle years, the man was unimpressed by the regent of Valdeon. Touches of gray drew thick lines in his thinning hair. A bushy silver mustache completed the work started atop his head. Dark, mistrusting eyes questioned Jorge with little or no sign of respect. All in all, Jorge didn't care for the features or the man behind them.

"Concern yourself with learning what I teach you. I'll worry about where we go." Jorge took an offered pack from one of the hunters. "Watch me. You will do the same with your belongings."

Emptying the pack, Jorge methodically showed them again and again how to position each item. He emphasized their possessions must be balanced and quiet. No clanging pans or jingling jewelry could give them away. Comfort and mobility were of importance as well. He directed the people to their belongings and told them to do the same. Hours passed while he and the hunters checked their packs. Satisfied his unenthusiastic pupils had made progress, he ordered them to move out.

"Duarto," he said. "Find us two camps for the night."

"Two?" Duarto gave him a sour frown. "You're going to play your entertaining game. I hated it when I was a child."

"You learned how to pack and unpack quickly, didn't you?"

"The people aren't going to like it any more than I did." Duarto shrugged and darted off toward the northeast.

Jorge allowed himself a little chuckle. Yes, he remembered the groans and dragging of feet as his tired son begrudgingly unpacked and repacked his things under a midnight sky. Duarto had been a boy then.

Now he was a man with discipline earned in a military career. This discipline was foreign to the refugees Jorge must train now. Indeed, they shuffled along the trail in exhaustion, flooded with self-pity.

Sunset crossed the sky over Duarto's first campsite. The sun had mercifully disappeared behind the mountains, adding a bit of respite from the day's march. Jorge gave the order to stop for the night. A collective sigh of relief rose from the tired souls before him. His followers began the business of setting up their sparse camp. Bedrolls blanketed the ground, forming tight circles. Dried fruit and bean paste exchanged hands. It was Valdeon's closest picture of a peaceful scene. Pity.

Signaling with an extended hand, Jorge stepped out of the way. Descending into the camp from several directions, the hunters banged daggers against swords as if some great battle had fallen upon their numbers. Screaming and panicked, the people huddled together in a circle like sheep. Jorge gritted his teeth as he observed the chaos. No. This behavior would never do. Valdeon was not a country of cowards. It was made up of the strong who forged their homes and livelihoods from the land.

"Are you sheep then, content to cower before your enemies? I will not lead cowards to the feet of our king!" Jorge slapped a silver platter out of one man's grip. "You will run when I say you run. And you will stand and fight when I tell you. Now pack up. You have five minutes. Everything left out of the pack stays here."

"Cruel barbarian! These women and children have endured enough," his staunchest critic growled. "Who are you to treat us this way?"

"I am the man who will keep you alive."

"And how do you propose to do that? How can you expect us to follow if you do not tell us where we go!"

"We will move on the strength of our courage and endure with the steadfastness of our hope," Jorge said calmly. "I take my people to a place where friends have hidden food and supplies. It will keep us safe until our true king returns. You can stay behind if you choose. Four minutes."

Jorge turned his back and walked at the head of the people who waited to follow him. Most of the packs, stuffed carelessly, were half full. He sighed and ignored their clumsy attempts. It would do for now. Judging by the signs his son had left to guide them, their new camp was a quick march up the road. Tomorrow was another day and a fresh opportunity to improve.

Neto stepped from the trees after they'd shuffled about in the dark for a few minutes. He handed Jorge a piece of torn cloth. It contained natural strands of undyed threads. Lighter than gauze bandages, the loosely woven fabric was in every kitchen in Andara. Cheesecloth. It offered no help in narrowing down the suspects.

"You were right, My Lord. Someone is leaving signs. They also made an arrow to point in the direction you walked." Neto grinned. "I changed it a bit. Whoever is hunting us will find themselves in the plains to our south."

"I'm glad you're with me, my old friend," Jorge said. "Any clues left behind as to who our spy may be?"

"My money is on the troublemaker."

Neto pointed a thumb toward the surly man who'd complained so vehemently earlier. He pulled a small handcart covered tightly with a metal lid. A large padlock warned off the curious. Jorge raised an appreciative, but reluctant eyebrow at the dried branches dragging the ground behind the cart. The man was keen to cover his tracks at least.

"They call him Santos." Neto rubbed at the white beard forming on a normally clean-shaven chin. "He moved to San Lucida a few months back."

"Keep an eye on our new friend," Jorge said. "And, Neto, tell the hunters to show caution. I don't like the looks of his cart."

Santos was a newcomer to their little part of the world. Virtually unknown, he had no one to vouch for him. His timing was unfortunate. Judging from the locked cart, this Santos had secrets. He'd been one of the last to join the rest of the camp. Had he insisted on keeping the cart? What was the reason? Jorge hoped he had answers before they journeyed too close to the caves.

Chapter Eleven

THE LIVING CARPET of evergreen boughs abruptly ended. Towering peaks of inhospitable rock rose into the sky, determined to block any life from encroaching into North Marsh. The Bloodtooth Mountain Range was a formidable barrier between the fertile ground of Andara's mainland and the decaying lands festering along its northwest coast. A collective groan circled the deck. The faint stench of damp, decay, and stale air wafted aboard the *Wind Chaser* as soon as it crossed the peaks. Wolf hurriedly pulled the hood of his cloak over his nose and mouth. What was the travelers' saying? If the vast mountains didn't keep you out of North Marsh, then the stench would.

A wall of wet struck him with an unfriendly welcome. Their ship lifted sharply in response as if to jump over the foul weather. Fox brought them above the rain-heavy clouds. Wolf suspected Fox was more concerned with the aesthetics of his ship than his comrades' wellbeing.

Small windows of open sky exposed the twisted and tangled skeletons of rotting trees. Frozen in time, they reached toward the heavens. Their pleading death cries remained ignored by a disinterested universe. This landscape was full of such gruesome sights.

Keeping a hand on the hem of his cowl, Wolf held the fabric out to block the chilling rain. Boredom was a real threat to dulled senses. Nothing appeared on the horizon but wet and rot for miles under a dim late-morning sun.

Then he caught sight of an eerie landmark jutting out of the marsh. The dwindling remains of an ancient stone building held back the bogs beneath them. It tilted in a forty-five-degree angle over dead trees. Impressive. The building was a testament to the cleverness of their ancient ancestors. Its ruins, covered in moss and other slimy things, crumbled a bit more each year. Someone had planted brightly colored pointers along the top to keep the landmark relevant. The once-impressive temple, however, was slowly losing its battle to survive.

Strange lettering of a long-forgotten language still made deep lines precisely engraved into the last remaining spots of clean stone. A "U" hung by itself, separated by a large crevice in the building. Then a "rsity" ran within the surface. Many suggested it was an ancient temple of knowledge, while others believed it was a military installation. Who could be certain? Wolf suspected even the Jalora had forgotten the building's purpose. Corpse Point, a rather gruesome, but accurate name, was now used as a signpost for ships to calculate their location in a vast bog.

North Marsh hid many such relics of bygone days. Most were covered under centuries of muck and water while others lay just below the marsh's slimy surface. The Legion had mapped safe routes across North Marsh centuries before. They'd lost interest in keeping the maps current when airships filled the skies and the Legion's coastal outpost was abandoned. Copies of the drawings remained, but were rare.

"Wolf," Rafael the Fox called over the rush of putrid wind. "Starboard. Two o'clock."

Favoring the port side this trip, Wolf rushed across the deck and leaned over the starboard rail. Fox and the other guardsmen crossed the distance to join him. Flapping wildly against the backdrop of marsh, a mercenary ship's red flag was an obscenity against the dull green and brown. The vessel was at full sail.

"Where is it going in such a hurry?" Berto asked beside him.

"I don't know, but it would appear they haven't seen us flying overhead."

"Her captain must be experienced to be keeping the ship at such a fast pace in this heavy rain." Fox signaled Yuli's squire in the sails to stand by. "What are your orders, Wolf?"

"Follow them. Our mercenary friends are coming suspiciously close to the supply line for the outpost. I don't like the idea of their being so near the Lion." A sudden stab of anxiety squeezed at his chest. "They're up to some bangtail mischief. We must find out for Seth's sake. Tulio. Wake Jason Coyote. He may know more about their route."

An infuriating eternity later, Coyote climbed onto the deck. Rubbing the sleep from his eyes, he gave a great yawn. Fox tapped his fingers impatiently against the railing as he waited for the Lion's first-marked to join them.

"We're headed north." A crooked grin squirmed its way onto Coyote's face. "Why didn't you turn west at Corpse Point? Has our captain gotten us lost?"

"Hardly," Fox said. "If you're sufficiently awake, look down. We have an unexpected traveler coming a bit too close to the Lion."

"He's already gone too far north for the outpost. Unless he plans to backtrack and sail in from the west." Coyote shook his head. "He seems to be headed on a northerly course. *Why?* I was stationed in North Marsh and then the Buells as an apprentice. No ports, cities, or outposts can be found in this direction. The weather is too foul. No, sir. The only thing resembling a building on this path lies to the northwest. Sea Point Outpost sprawls on the coastline, but it was abandoned by the Legion centuries ago. I think it was Samuel the Thunder Lion who named it uninhabitable. Only the mad or the foolish would try to reach it now."

"Or the ambitious," Berto said, pointing to the north. "Look! What are they doing in such a lonely part of Andara?"

Out of the thick rain clouds emerged the massive metal hull of a Jackal ship. Dwarfing the much smaller vessel, it coasted toward the mercenaries and slowed to a stop beside them. Wolf's gaze scanned the deck, but at this distance, he couldn't see much without his powers. He dared not use them for fear of attracting attention.

"Such places are perfect for talks of killing and betrayal." Wolf leaned against the railing with an impotent growl. "We see how far Julian's treason goes. Not only has the bastard prince sold out his people, but now he has given away all of Andara."

A heavy silence hung over the rangers. They had only this tiny vessel with no weapons. Then again, the *Wind Chaser* offered them concealment. Perhaps fate was casting them into a different role now. Wolf regarded their Lion's favorite spy. Coyote had come to them for a reason. Yes, it was time they took a different approach in dealing with these Jackal invaders. The element of surprise was their greatest weapon right now.

"What is to be done, Wolf?" Yuli asked.

"We won't let those vessels out of our sight. We must find out what treachery they weave for Andara."

Chapter Twelve

AFTER THREE-PLUS days locked below decks aboard a windowless vessel, the apprentices hoped for welcoming scenery and fresh air when at last the gangplank opened. Instead, *The Protector* deposited them in the middle of a boggy wasteland. Built from imported stone blocks, North Marsh Outpost seemed to be the only thing of substance for miles.

Seth shook off the mud clinging to his boots. He and his fellow apprentices had been ordered to unload the ship. They worked side by side with the UR soldiers while the rest of the ranger battalion sauntered off to the comfortable dryness of their barracks.

"The stench will kill us before any enemies do," Stallion grumbled.

"Rotting debris and the carcasses of dead animals," Bear said with a sigh. "It reminds me of home. I grew up on the border of North Marsh in Framburg."

"You need some better-smelling memories, Bear."

Stallion shifted the crate on his shoulder. Suddenly thrown off balance, the apprentice staggered backward and stepped shin-deep in the bog beside the path. A hand grabbed him before he could fall into the wet mudhole. The tight-jawed UR sergeant pulled Stallion back onto the trail. He shifted the crate forward onto the young man's shoulder with a grunt. Seth set aside his powers for himself. He didn't want to know what the impatient sergeants thought of their less-than-capable helpers.

"Careful there, sir," Seth said. "North Marsh is a deadly place. It isn't wise to step off the trail."

Their path from the slippery wooden docks was a quarter mile of moss-covered stone. Its color may have been gray once. Now brown and green crawled on the surface. Determining where the stone road ended, and the hungry marsh began was difficult. The constant pummeling of heavy rain wasn't helpful either.

"You've been here before, sergeant?" Seth asked.

Pleased by the tone of respect in Seth's question, the sergeant let go of Stallion and gave him a good shove toward Bear. Recognition came into the army man's eyes as he regarded Seth more closely. Then the colors surrounding his body changed. Approval. Respect. Regret. He'd been one of the UR sergeants responsible for training Seth's group of cadets when Seth had first joined the army in Lea. Well, at least someone was glad to have him along.

"I've been sent to this cursed outpost on three tours. The last time I was here, a soldier stepped off the trail on guard duty at the dock and sank into the mud before anyone could get him a rope."

A familiar face pushed through the line of soldiers carrying crates. It was Sergeant Duncan. He nodded his greetings to Seth and his fellow sergeant. The three other apprentices he ignored. Seth's friends seemed too tired and uncomfortable in their lot to notice the slight.

"Been showing our new helpers the sights, Ralston?" Sergeant Duncan asked, pushing a hand through his wet blond hair.

"This young lad almost went for a swim," the sergeant said with a snort. "The stench in your boots will be a good reminder to avoid the edge."

Stallion murmured something Seth hoped Ralston didn't hear. Ranger or no, exercising polite behavior around sergeants was best. They had a unique sense of humor and uncanny timing for the worse possible moment to exact revenge.

"You mustn't go outside the walls of the outpost after dark either, Lion," Sergeant Duncan told him. "Men have been known to vanish."

"From the looks of those walls and that gate, I'd say they plan to lock us in." Stallion grunted under the weight of his load. "Fine by me."

Stone walls rose up out of the marsh. Towering thirty feet above their heads, the determined moss seemed to be the only thing able to reach the top. Seeing from his vantage point was difficult but Seth fancied the outpost took on an almost half-moon shape.

"A supply ship comes once a week loaded with cargo." Sergeant Duncan kicked at a glob of mud. "Trust me, ranger. After a few weeks of this rain and muck, you'll be happy to unload supplies to break the monotony." He came closer to Seth. "Ho, Lion. Carry the crate high on your shoulder and lift with your knees. It'll ease an aching back in the morning."

"That's better." Seth nodded to him. "Thank you, Sergeant."

Then Ralston gave a loud whoop and pointed his stern finger at the line of unlucky UR soldiers. He stormed down the path and through the gates of the outpost like a charging bull.

"Not that way, pea brains! Why stomp through the mud puddles when you can walk on the boarded paths? Track one spot of mud on my barracks floor and I'll have you scrubbing down the whole building with your linens."

"I'd better see to the other line before they trample inside like a bunch of cattle." Sergeant Duncan chuckled. "I'm sure I'll see you again. Lion."

"I didn't think anyone could be worse than White Tiger." Stallion frowned as the sergeants headed toward their dry barracks. "They're trying to scare us."

"It is best to heed their warnings. I have seen the beasts that walk this marsh. They are to be feared, not dismissed." Bear moved forward again, following the sergeants through the gates.

Seth had better warn Riley of the dangers. If indeed he was able to see his friend. Their squires were assigned the unpacking of belongings and helping in the kitchens. Seth was beginning to envy Riley's position as a squire.

A new odor assaulted his nose. Harsh and acidic, it seemed to seep from every direction. Seth passed closer to the wooden surface of the door. He wrinkled his nose at the foul-smelling liquid the boards were soaked in—some treatment to prevent rot, he supposed.

"I wonder if my sense of smell will ever be the same after being here," he said, taking gulps of air through his mouth. "What have they soaked the wood in?"

Bear shook his head with a cough. "I've never smelled such a foul stench. Perhaps if we're lucky, the marsh will cover the odor."

"Badger will be disappointed to have missed all this fun," Stallion grumbled. "Not that I begrudge him the recovery time after…well."

"Yes, poor lad."

"Henry needs our friendship, not our pity." Seth pushed past them. "You'll see his strength soon enough. The Jalora doesn't choose its rangers idly."

Taking their direction from the chastised soldiers, Seth and his friends marched along boards lining the buildings. They didn't want to incur the wrath of White Tiger by stomping through the mud puddles filling the center of the courtyard. Seth staggered under the weight of his load and the boards bounced as he walked. Mud oozed over the sides, coming dangerously close to the soles of his boots. This path wasn't a much better route than stomping in the mire. He sighed. Pointing the fact out to the sergeants or White Tiger would do no good.

"Looks like we're not the only ones playing in the mud," Stallion said.

An acolyte stood on the far wooden path. Waving his arms at a handful of Legion squires, he barked orders as they carried crates through a maze of buildings at his back. Sneering when he saw Seth and the others approach, the ranger stomped a boot on the wood. Splashes of mud spurted in oozing clumps from either side of the path.

"The rest of the supplies have come at long last. Did we take the scenic tour?" Mantis pointed with an impatient gesture. "Put them in the storage shed over there."

Seth bumped Stallion's crate, propelling him forward. The young man's temper could win them extra duties if he stayed too long in Mantis's presence. Keeping them separated as much as possible might be best. Wet, tired and hungry, the last thing Seth and his fellow prisoners needed was a jog around the outpost.

"I can finish stacking these boxes," Seth told his fellow inmates. "Go ahead and find our barracks. I'll meet you in the yard."

"Very well. It has to be close to mealtime," Stallion said. "I'm starving."

Seth lifted the last crate and shoved it on top of the pile. He stood back, making sure the arrangement was neat and orderly. Unlike the other apprentices, he knew what being under the scrutiny of a sharp-eyed sergeant was like.

A sudden rush of power rippled up and down his spine. Eyes were on him. He turned around slowly. Two rangers stood on the dirt floor close to the back wall of the storeroom. The tallest, a white-haired man with thin features, smiled at Seth. His friend, much shorter with thick sideburns shaped to frame his jaw, gave Seth a nod.

They suddenly turned as one toward the door. Seth tugged his focus away from the two older rangers and turned to look over his shoulder. An acolyte stood in the doorway with his fists on his hips. Known as the Gecko, he was a friend to the Mantis. Tension held his dark features in a mask of impatience. His eyes contained such rage, Seth took a step back toward the crates.

Turning in a plea for intervention, he searched for the two older rangers. They were gone.

"Do you think, because you're the Lion you can dawdle while others work?"

Gecko stormed toward him. Though they'd never exchanged words, the ranger had taken an immediate dislike to Seth. His mere presence seemed to infuriate Gecko. This resentment was more than a hazing of his underling apprentice.

"I don't expect any preferential treatment, sir. Neither would I accept it."

"Be still! What to do the words of a coward mean?" Gecko spat upon the floor. "Oh, how your men cheered for you in the arena. What did they think when you ran to the safety of the Legion rather than fighting for their freedom in your homeland? Your family has brought about Andara's destruction. Even now the Jackal cross Valdeon's borders and attack my people in Southbay."

"You call me a coward, Gecko, but here we are in North Marsh serving the Jalora together."

Gecko flew at him, grabbing the front of Seth's tunic. He lifted Seth and slammed his body against the crates. Gecko's fist shook as he struggled to keep it from flying. Gecko suddenly dropped Seth and marched toward the door.

"The squires have prepared our meal. Get to the mess hall."

Then he too was gone, leaving a wave of anger behind him. Another enemy to guard against. What of the two older rangers who'd left when the altercation started? How had they exited the storage shed? Gecko had entered and gone again through the only entrance.

Seth pushed away from the crates and made for the courtyard—too many mysteries on an empty stomach.

Chapter Thirteen

SETH, DESPITE HIS anger, took light steps on the boarded path toward the mess hall. The familiar aroma of corned beef hash set his stomach rumbling. Wiping his boots off the best he could, he stepped in line behind a group of wet soldiers. Water dripped off their sleeves and onto the tin tray meant to carry their meals. Seth shook his drippings off the empty plate.

"They've got berry crumble for dessert," he said to the man in front of him. "The little bit of sweetness will brighten my day at any rate."

"Doesn't hold a candle to the crumble my missus makes," the man replied. "The army uses Commonwealth fruit. My missus insists on good Kirkland apples and berries from southern Heidelbrecht."

"Who knew there were so many different types of apples? My poor mother could only get the bitter apples we grow on Marianna. They aren't fit for baking, but the woolies like them."

"You're from the Grey Cliff Isles? Rumor has it, the Lion's squire is from there as well." Turning to Seth for the first time, the soldier's eyes widened, and he almost dropped his tray. "Forgive me, My Lord. I didn't realize."

An uncomfortable hush suddenly fell over the crowd of unsettled UR soldiers. Not until he received a dozen salutes did Seth realize he had the wrong mess. He was grateful for the emotionless mask he wore as a ranger. The uncomfortable heat from his embarrassed blush blossomed to the top of his head. He'd made a great fool of himself on the first day they'd arrived in North Marsh.

A young lieutenant was the first to retrieve his presence of mind. "May I assist you, My Lord?"

"Thank you, sir. I'm a bit lost." Resisting the impulse to smack a palm against his forehead, he muddled on. "Have the rangers and squires already eaten then? I don't see them."

"Oh, they don't eat with us, Lion." The lieutenant pointed toward the far end of the outpost. "The Legion has its own…everything that way."

"They're missing a good meal and even better company." Seth gave him a salute. "Good evening."

Stepping out into the rain-soaked courtyard, he could feel them now. Western Beta's power filled the space beyond the end of the UR courtyard. It must be the Legion's area. The buildings, positioned at the opposite end of the outpost, were well removed from those of the other inhabitants.

Excited whispers erupted from the UR mess. Wrapping the wind about him, Seth ran in a diagonal path on the droplets of rain across the courtyard. Anything to escape their adulation. Not many days had passed since he'd shared food with these men at the Obsidian Citadel. He'd done nothing to earn their respect.

The Legion's side of the outpost stood in complete contrast to the UR buildings. Stone structures made a mock village with a small courtyard. Scrubbed clean and freshly mortared, the buildings were watertight. Seth ran a hand along a massive wooden pillar supporting an awning circling the mess hall. Thick windows glowed with cheerful light and the warmth of comfort.

He pulled open the door and was immediately set upon by an attendant dressed like a concierge at one of the fancier restaurants in Lea. The immaculately dressed man helped Seth off with his cloak and almost pushed him onto one of the benches lining the walls.

"Your squire has left you clean boots, My Lord." He put Seth's cloak on a hook formed into the shape of a Lion's head. "The other apprentices await you in the hall."

Disappearing through the door, the fussy attendant left Seth to his own devices. He pulled off his muddied boots and picked up the clean pair waiting beneath his hanging cloak. Putting his dirty set where the clean ones had been, he sat back down with a sigh. All this fussing about was already grating on his nerves.

Inside the hall, fancy crystal lanterns sparkled on the ceiling. Rich linens of white and gold covered several long wooden tables placed uniformly in line along the mess. Beautiful glassware and silver clinked lightly on plates as the rangers ate. He'd experienced such luxuries at his Aunt Charlotte's house on Carlotta but had never guessed to find it in the middle of a mudhole. Perhaps that was the point. Food and comfort certainly brightened a man's mood.

Bear and Stallion sat at a table toward the back of the mess hall. Henry occupied the bench across from them. Seth sank into the seat beside the unhappy man. Immediately, a golden bowl appeared at Seth's side. Another attendant offered Seth hot linens to wash his face and hands. He took the cloth with a hesitant nod. Where had the Legion hidden these fussy patrolmen of etiquette? He hadn't seen them walking about on *The Protector*.

"I was beginning to wonder if you'd gone back aboard ship," Riley said, setting a plate of rich meat and steamed vegetables before him. "Better eat up, Seth. You're the last one to mess. We've already started cleaning the pots."

"Sorry," Seth said between bites. "I got lost. Did you know they have two mess halls?"

"Aye. Of course, they do." Riley took Seth's plate with a shake of his head. "You know very well why."

Seth and a group of friends had slipped into Legion headquarters in the Obsidian Citadel to look for the Book of Ancients. He hadn't understood the dangerous power he and the other rangers possessed until it was too late. His friends, ordinary cadets from his troop, had almost succumbed to the force. He learned well that day why the Legion separated its rangers from others.

Resting his head on the table, he closed his eyes. Hauling crates and trudging through mud hadn't been as burdensome as Gecko's blistering rebuke. He must find a way to help Valdeon before succumbing to his horrible guilt.

"Sleepy, Ice Lion?" White Tiger barked.

Seth jumped to his feet with a jolt. He must have fallen asleep at the table. Bear, Stallion, and Badger stood at attention, apologetic grimaces on their faces. The other rangers of Western Beta didn't share their trepidation. Their laughter filled the mess. Humor. Glee. Retribution. The emotions danced over the tables in merry ribbons.

"Your day is not yet over. Fall in," White Tiger told the exhausted apprentices. "The Jalora gives its rangers boundless energy, but you must earn it first. Report to the sergeant of the guard for your assignments."

The apprentices, now successfully chased out of the mess hall, were prodded toward a stone staircase. Seth hadn't noticed it in his exhausted haze. They took the steps at double time. Lines of other unlucky guards watched them as they passed. Sympathy was absent in the colors about their bodies, but at least he didn't see their humor here.

They took up posts in a dark section of the wall. An absent moon made judging whether they faced east or west impossible. The gates, he'd been told, opened in a due north direction. Tired and disoriented, Seth could only hazard a guess that they guarded the western section of the wall.

"I thought it was dull in the light of day," Stallion said. "Night doesn't do anything for the scenery."

Henry the Badger leaned against the wall beside him and looked down. "The smell hasn't improved either."

Seth wrapped his cloak around his shoulders against the bone-chilling mist. He'd just managed to grab it as they passed the hooks. Bear hadn't been as lucky.

He stomped his feet in an attempt to drive the cold away. The mist clung to his hair and face. He wiped it off without complaint.

Then a loud screech pierced the mist just below them on the other side of the wall. Henry and Stallion jumped back. Steel rang out as they pulled their swords. Bear shook his head and stepped between them to look over the side.

"Some unlucky animal has met its end."

Terror. Disgust and perhaps a bit of regret swirled about Stallion and Badger. North Marsh had claimed another life. How many two-legged victims would it devour before they left its rotting clutches?

Seth joined Bear at the wall. He stared down into the soggy shadows of the midnight marsh. How was he to search for this lost relic supposedly swallowed by the murky waters? Bogs surrounded the entire outpost. Unless someone had hidden the item inside these walls?

"I don't think I'll be nodding off on duty," Stallion said, sheathing his sword. "Are we sure those things can't climb the walls?"

"It would be your job to keep them from getting inside, ranger."

The cold brazier suddenly burst into brilliant flames. A UR soldier lifted his torch from the burning fuel. Hard lines around his mouth and eyes spoke of many nights standing guard. He nodded to Seth and walked back into the mist, settling on the battlements. His torch put off an eerie glow as he slowly made his way down the line of braziers.

"I think I hate guard duty." Stallion frowned, watching him go.

"By the time our watch is over, you'll know you hate it." Seth held up his hands to warm them by the fire. "I've seen my fair share when I was a cadet in the UR Army. The trick to staying alert is to keep moving. We should take turns walking along the wall."

Badger nodded and pulled his sword. "I'll take the first stroll."

"Are you mad? I'm not going anywhere near the edge of the battlements again," Stallion said.

Henry gave him a sad smile, lifting the Badger Ring. "Perhaps if I try hard, the Jalora will change its mind."

"Well, you can't go walking in the dark alone." Stallion pulled his sword and joined Henry. "Come on. Let's go look for a little trouble."

It was their good fortune not to find any over the rest of the watch. North Marsh had taken enough bones that night to sate its hunger. His watch blessedly over, Seth fell into the small cot reserved and prepared by Riley. Their squires had picked four cots in a room full of empty frames. Seth didn't care why or how Riley chose his bed; he felt purely grateful. Exhausted and chilled to the bone, he just wanted sleep. The last time his head had touched a real pillow, he'd been in the Lion Protector's lavish chambers at the top of the Obsidian Citadel in Lea.

Snores soon sounded around the chambers he shared with the other apprentices. They were fast asleep. He envied them. Slapping a hand over his face, Seth tried to block out the thoughts of Valdeon and his quest. He had to look for the item, but apprentices didn't have a great deal of free time. He only had now. Forcing his tired body up, Seth dressed.

The Legion courtyard was empty as he stepped out into a dark drizzle. Lifting the hood of the cloak over his head, Seth was invisible to all but ranger eyes. The magical fabric wouldn't help him avoid leaving tracks in the mud, however. He must use the special skills the Jalora had shown him on Carlotta. Summoning his power, he wrapped the rain and wind about him and raced across the courtyard until he was at the edge of the Legion buildings.

If I were an ancient relic, where would I hide?

Free of moss and other signs of aging stone, the Legion buildings seemed relatively new. He glanced across the outpost courtyard to the UR barracks and mess hall. All the buildings on the army's side of the outpost were wooden—an impractical hiding place in such a climate. No. This mysterious item waited in a permanent structure. It had to be something that wouldn't rot or sink.

His attention turned to a small patrol stopping to check the gates. They pushed on the surface, but it didn't budge. Satisfied the entry was secure, the patrol moved on toward the line of UR buildings. Seth couldn't imagine anything opening those weighty gates without the guarded mechanism atop the battlements. The hinges were planted deep within the ancient and unmovable stone walls.

Of course! What better place to hide an ancient relic than within indestructible stone walls? He darted lightly across the muddy courtyard and stopped along the west side of the gate. Seth rested a hand on the nearest stone. Each stone spanned the height and width of a man and was expertly cut and placed within the wall. Seth regarded the mortar around the stone blocks more closely. The white substance was a material he'd never seen. Running a fingertip along the lines it drew, he noticed that the grout cast a kind of glow. Its light wrapped around Seth's finger, tingling with soft pulses of power.

He closed his eyes for a moment, connecting with the power encircling each stone. Then he began to run beside the wall with his hand brushing along the surface. The relic might be hiding just below the stony exterior. Searching the base of the wall would take time, but this strange substance in the mortar could help. It would tell him if any other sources of power were contained within the wall.

Head down and mind fixed on his task, Seth was bitterly disappointed when he came to the east side of the gate. Right back where he'd started. He took his hand off the wall. The power withdrew into its stony home.

It has to be here. Think!

Casting his eyes to the heavens, Seth took a frustrated breath. He was missing something. Who would put magic in a stone wall without reason? Bouncing a fist lightly against his leg, he scanned the length of the wall again. His eyes moved from bottom to top and then along the rim of the battlements. Had he missed a clue at the top of the wall perhaps?

Then, as if in answer to a prayer, he saw a flash in one of the supporting columns midway up the wall. Suppressing a triumphant shout, he raced to the column.

The average man couldn't reach the flash without being lowered by rope. He grinned. His not being the average man was a good thing. Wrapping the wind about him, Seth stepped onto the droplets of moisture. He danced on the current as it lifted him to the flash.

Lodged at the center of a perfectly circular stone, the image of a lion's head stared out of the metal plate holding it in place. Seth braced himself on a toehold and touched the lion's mane. The iron plate popped open. Holding his breath, Seth reached inside and pulled out a roll of parchment. It was a letter.

"Dear Seth—Patience is the greatest virtue. Deepest regards. Gustavo the Lion Claw, Jalora Master."

Gustavo had died over a hundred years before. How had he known about Seth or his search for the relic? Dropping his hand, Seth let the parchment fall. Patience? This grand Jalora Master had single-handedly carved the Obsidian Citadel out of a mountain in a single night. Honestly, he didn't have any better advice?

Then another signal flashed from a column on the other side of the courtyard. Seth pulled the wind about him again and flew across the distance with growing urgency. The iron plate was identical to its brother. He yanked it open and found a second parchment.

"Dear Seth—The Jalora's wisdom comes from a place of ancient knowledge and goodness. Trust it always. Never forget. The Jalora chose you as its Lion. Deepest regards. Gustavo the Lion Claw, Jalora Master."

A third column flashed beside the UR buildings. Growling an insult to his ancestor, Seth chased the wind this time. His focus was beginning to fail, along with his energy. Slamming painfully against the wall, he was forced to cling to the rock to keep from slipping. Behind the iron plate was another letter.

"Grandson—Have I not said to be patient? Gustavo the Lion Claw, Jalora Master."

Seth slipped, plopping in the mud on his backside. He hit a fist against the stone wall with a growl. Getting angry at the Lion Claw was pointless. The man was dead and buried. Seth rested his head in his palm. What now? Was he just supposed to sit tight while the people of Valdeon suffered?

"Fancy a cup of tea? Or maybe something stronger?"

Sergeant Duncan stood a few feet from him. A patient smile rested on his face as he reached out his hand. Seth took it with a miserable nod. The sergeants, he realized, had been watching him from their window. What must they think of the Lion Protector's mad dash about the outpost walls?

"Ho, Lion," Ralston greeted him as he and Sergeant Duncan entered their chambers.

Seth took the offered cup of tea with a nod of thanks. "You must think me insane, running along the walls as I have been."

"I've been here three times," Ralston said. "I've never seen the walls glow the way they did tonight."

The magic in the walls had been meant exclusively for him, it would seem. Seth sipped at the amber liquid. Its warmth chased the chills from his body. Emma, their housekeeper from his childhood home, had often claimed a hot cup of tea could cure any ailment. Perhaps she'd been right. Even his frustration was leaving him as he sipped from his cup.

"Sometimes the Legion gives orders we don't quite understand. They seem crazy at times. Do you know why we follow those orders without question?" Sergeant Duncan asked. "The rangers speak to the Jalora somehow. I don't understand it, but they do. If we can't trust the Jalora to do the right thing, then what can we trust?"

Seth nodded and smiled. "I was trained as a cadet. It quickly became clear to me who runs the army. Sergeants have unfaltering common sense."

"Well, this is what my common sense tells me, Lion." Sergeant Duncan poured him another cup. "You're a good man used to being around regular people. When you get to be what you're meant to be, I know you won't forget that we're men. You won't treat us like pieces on a game board."

"You have my word on it."

Ralston shook his head with a grin. "Sergeant Dancer and I had high hopes for you, McCloud, or should I say, Lion. Thought you'd rise in the ranks to be sergeant one day. Too bad." He stood up and motioned toward the Legion courtyard. "The First Call is in less than an hour. You'd better get back to your barracks. White Tiger doesn't miss much."

Indeed, he didn't. Seth had some serious explaining to do. If the sergeants had seen the wall aglow, then every ranger in the battalion must have witnessed the same event. Keeping his quest secret would be much more difficult now.

Chapter Fourteen

SCREECHES FILLED THE chamber with the dread of a thousand banshees. The Horde's Cry invaded their barracks in the complete darkness of early morning. Jumping out of bed like a jackrabbit escaping the hot water of a stew pot, Cal the Stallion ran blindly through the room. He struck the wall with a painful thump.

The other apprentices didn't fare much better. Trousers half on, they tumbled out of bed. Henry the Badger smacked his toe against the cot frame, an uncharacteristic Tslavic curse spilling from his lips. Bear rolled out of the blankets and onto his knees. He knew better than to move.

Mercifully, Seth's power came to him. The Sight, a ranger's ability to see in the darkness, identified White Tiger leaning against the far wall. Silent laughter shook the old ranger's body. Then he noticed Seth's gaze locked in on his location. The delighted smile vanished. Curiosity replaced it.

"The morning sun doesn't seem to shine here, sir."

Seth picked up the crystal lantern on the nightstand by his cot. A warm glow filled the room. Curiosity. Respect. They continued to swirl about White Tiger. Fear, however, wasn't present in the feelings coming from his body. The emotion was justified. Such powers were uncommon in an apprentice. Seth was grateful for it. White Tiger would be someone to trust, but Seth must earn this ranger's confidence before he'd receive it in return.

"The sun doesn't make an appearance at all, Ice Lion." White Tiger turned to the other apprentices still fumbling around. "Get dressed. It's time you all learned how to be soldiers. I want you waiting for me in the yard in ten minutes!"

White Tiger marched toward the closed door. He stopped beside Stallion, who was holding his bleeding nose. Pulling the young man up by the arm, he slapped the apprentice's hands away from his face.

"I think the wall broke my nose!"

"It will make your features more interesting." White Tiger grabbed the nose and yanked it with a pop. "Looks straight to me. Now get dressed and wash up."

The men began pulling on their uniforms to the disgruntled sounds of Stallion's cursing. Seth tugged on the wet clothes and muddied boots he'd worn for his romp around the outpost walls. Even Riley's lightening skills couldn't anticipate his nighttime exploits. Stretching aching muscles, he tried to wake up before they reached the chilly morning air.

White Tiger stood in the middle of the Legion courtyard. Drizzle clung to his face and hair. Mantis and Gecko, flanking him on either side, each took a stoic stance. The two acolytes seemed resigned to stand in the rain with the apprentices while their comrades stayed inside. They'd dressed for the occasion at any rate. Large-billed hats kept their faces dry and the drizzle out of their collars. Seth seriously doubted the apprentices would receive the functional head covers.

"Gecko is going to show you how to march like proper soldiers. Then Mantis will teach you the sword this afternoon. I go to my breakfast," White Tiger said, stomping past them.

Marching and running around the outpost were activities Seth had become quite familiar with as a cadet in the UR Army. Gecko, reluctantly satisfied with Seth's performance, turned his full attention on the other apprentices. Seth was able to scan the wall for iron plates or hiding places he might have missed the night before. His searching continued to prove fruitless.

Luncheon wasn't the grand affair dinner had been. The apprentices, covered head to toe in mud, were exiled to the sheltered patio while Mantis and Gecko took their meals inside the mess hall. Seth plopped down on the wooden floor and leaned his wet head against the exterior wall. Bear and Henry joined him on either side while Stallion sat in the middle of the patio in a stupor.

Bursting through the doors, Riley and the apprentice squires came at them in a rush. Each of them balanced huge bowls of stew and hot bread. Seth gave Riley a grateful smile, though his friend could no longer see the expression hiding behind a ranger's unemotional mask. Devouring every bite of the stew, Seth turned his ravenous appetite onto the fresh bread. Riley took the empty bowl with a pleased nod.

"You need to make acolyte soon," he said. "I'm worried you might drown out here."

"I'll do my best."

Stallion hissed as his squire finished putting a bandage on his healing nose. He touched it tentatively and nodded his thanks. Lucas patted his ranger on the shoulder and headed back inside the mess with the empty bowl.

"Well, I'm off." Riley gave Seth a frown and followed the Stallion's squire back inside.

"You can just bet our acolyte torturers are having a warm dram of something," Stallion grumbled. "I hope they choke."

"Oh dear. My ears are burning," Mantis said, pushing through the doors. "On your feet!"

Seth lifted his aching body off the floor and followed the others as they trudged out into the courtyard. Mantis moved to their head. His steady pace took them past the barracks and away from the staircase leading up to the battlements. They walked through a narrow opening between the last Legion storage sheds closest to the stone walls. A pen area Seth hadn't noticed during his searching in the dark, opened before them. Surrounded by log fencing, it looked like a rundown paddock for horses and smelled even worse.

Mantis pushed open a wide swinging gate and motioned them inside. "Today, you start your journey to becoming full members of the Jalora Legion. How many of you have witnessed a ranger in battle?" Everyone except Stallion raised their hands. "The incredible moves he makes defy reality. His weapons fly at impossible speeds. He is undefeatable. This magic is called the 'Dance of Death.' It is perhaps the most well-known power afforded the Jalora's servants. I'll teach you this dance. Form a line."

The others listened as Mantis demonstrated the Dance of Death's stances. Seth recognized them as stances one through five. His father had instructed him in these beginning movements back on Marianna. Other, more motivated instructors had continued his lessons. He rubbed absently at his side where his ancient ancestor had delivered a particularly harsh example in the Realm of Dreams and Mist.

"Are we boring you, Ice Lion?" Mantis growled.

"Yes, sir," Seth said, groaning at his forced honesty. "I mean I always have something new to learn."

"The rest of you stand over there," Mantis ordered. "We are about to have an exhibition in swordsmanship."

"You caught me off guard, sir. I meant no disrespect."

The ranger had stopped listening and held his sword before him. "Stand ready, Ice Lion. I'm about to teach you a lesson in humility."

Seth blew out an exasperated breath and joined their instructor in the center of the small arena. Henry gave Seth a worried frown from the sidelines. The apprentices had no power to stop the impending madness.

Mantis was already in the First Stance. Seth regarded the ranger with an appraising eye. Mantis's skill was proficient enough for Phoenix to entrust him with the training of their apprentices. Mantis's pride, however, seemed to be the ranger's greatest weakness. This match would do nothing to build anyone's confidence, other than his own.

It is Mantis who will learn humility, the Jalora said.

Fighting among themselves was foolish. Mantis would certainly resent him afterward. Seth lifted his eyes, searching for help from the courtyard. No one walked about today except for their headstrong instructor and the nervous apprentices.

Then Mantis struck when he supposed Seth was distracted. Their teacher was, in fact, fast and precise in his aim. He swept his blade upward trying to leave a nasty mark on Seth's cheek. But Valdeonian steel sang as it instantly rose to block the Mantis's attack. The ranger gritted his teeth and came at Seth again. Anger. Hatred. Resentment. They flashed about Seth's opponent in wild swirls. The lesson was no longer a punishment. It had become personal. Mantis intended to draw blood.

Raw power pushed at Seth's control as the Lion's Roar rumbled low in his throat. Experience seen through immortal eyes stayed his hand. He allowed Mantis to attack without striking back, pushing the mortal to its highest level of skill. Then a vicious stranger's smile stretched across Seth's face. His exhaustion and chill faded. Fury and bloodlust replaced them. This mortal would soon understand his mistake, because the Lion Spirit had come to join the fight.

"You dare attack me, acolyte?" The wild roughness of the eternal voice sent Mantis scrambling back a few paces. "We shall see who draws first blood."

Then the Lion Spirit flew at the mortal. It slapped away his sword as if it were a blade of grass. Mantis fell on his back, propelling himself in the mud to escape the fury of his opponent. Fear. The Lion Spirit savored it like a juicy piece of meat.

Fire and a piercing screech came between them. Phoenix's blade slammed against Seth's sword, blocking it as Seth brought the weapon down toward Mantis. The Lion Spirit receded suddenly, taking its fury back into its stony home. Seth came to himself and lowered his sword. He bowed in respect to the deacon.

Phoenix glared at him for a moment longer, then turned his angry eyes on Mantis. "Get up! I'll have you scrubbing dirty pots for a month!" He thrust an angry finger toward the mess hall. "Report to the kitchens immediately."

Springing to his feet, Mantis bowed low with respect. He ran at top speed toward the Legion courtyard without looking back. Phoenix didn't watch him go. His full attention focused upon Seth.

"My office. Now."

Stomach churning, Seth followed silently behind the deacon. He'd lost control again and had almost killed a member of his own battalion. The rangers had a new reason to fear him. News of the altercation in the paddock had already spread. Everyone, including Riley, had stopped what they were doing to watch Phoenix with his apprentice. Frantic whispers rumbled under the awning as they passed the mess hall patio full of curious spectators.

Finally, they reached the Phoenix's office. White Tiger jogged up to join them inside, but Phoenix stopped him with a look. Fantastic. He'd not simply gotten Mantis and himself in trouble. White Tiger too would share in the Phoenix's anger.

Seth stood at attention, waiting for his deacon to stop pacing. His ill-digested lunch gurgled painfully in his stomach. Phoenix sat down hard on the corner of his desk. He was powerful and not someone to irritate.

Even the Spirit of the Lion Ring had deferred to his command.

Tapping the band of his ring atop the desk, Phoenix finally asked, "Who taught you the sword, apprentice?"

"My father, sir."

"We both know you're not giving me a complete answer. Give me the truth! You were performing the advanced moves of a bishop. Moves I myself cannot do. Now, who taught you those?"

How could he explain about his two instructors in the Realm of Dreams and Mist? Ghostly Lions from the past teaching their hated descendent? It was too fantastical. He remained silent.

"You're hiding things from me, Lion."

Phoenix came to his feet and moved behind the desk. He reached into the top drawer and pulled out three pieces of parchment. Old and water stained, the letters from Seth's ancestor remained neatly folded. Phoenix held them out to Seth.

"Gustavo the Lion Claw had quite the sense of humor."

"Yes." Seth sighed. "He's hysterical."

"Many would be interested in seeing these letters. Gustavo was a Jalora Master, after all."

"I will entrust them to you then, sir. I'm sure the Lion Claw would delight in being known as a jokester."

Phoenix gave Seth a small grin. "Very well. I'll have them safely transported to Legion headquarters. Do you have any other such parchments or relics for me then?"

Seth raised his blocks, straining to keep the unwelcome burden of his secrets. Phoenix placed the letters back in the drawer and sat down. His blue eyes regarded Seth with a strange sort of gentleness. Then the moment was gone.

"Beginning tomorrow morning, you will teach the apprentices stances one through five. Dismissed."

Seth saluted. Confused and stunned, he hurried out of the office and back into the courtyard. Why hadn't Phoenix punished him? He could have killed the Mantis. Others had expected the same thing. Rangers and squires alike lingered on the patio, waiting for some sign of Seth's impending doom. A collective disappointment rose from the crowd as the apprentices hurried across the courtyard to greet him.

"You're alive!" Bear slapped a heavy hand on Seth's back. "I thought Phoenix would kill you. I've never seen him that angry."

"And I've never seen anyone better with a sword than you!" said Henry.

Henry splashed around Seth with a new sense of awe. Perhaps the rebukes and whispers were worth the price of giving his downhearted cousin some cheer. Indeed, Henry swelled with excitement and energy.

"Well?" The Stallion put fists on his hips. "What happened?"

"I'm to teach you the sword starting tomorrow."

Henry yelped excitedly. "Come along, Ice Lion. I'm eager to learn."

"Peace, Henry," Seth said with a laugh. "Now I intend to catch up on my sleep. Tomorrow is soon enough."

"Sleep?" Stallion grinned. "I'm after a dram of the good stuff they reserve for rangers. Come on, you lot. Join me?"

The apprentices weren't frightened by Seth at least. Teaching them the sword might prove to be enjoyable. Besides, time in their presence doing something positive and productive would be a welcome relief. Seth yawned and headed to the barracks, leaving the others to their pleasure. For the first time in a long while, he wasn't dreading the following day.

Chapter Fifteen

THE PUTRID STENCH of decay seeped through pockets of heavy clouds beneath their hull. Rafael the Fox kept the *Wind Chaser* within their gray mass as they continued to follow, unseen by the enemy vessels. Wolf pulled his cloak more tightly about him. Cold and wet, the wind chilled his body as he kept unwavering eyes on the enemy sails.

Was he making the right decision? Leaving the Lion to wander about on his own was dangerous. What if the boy lost control? Wolf's gaze momentarily shifted to the animal's image floating peacefully within its crystal. He was a member of the Sacred Guard, duty bound to protect the Lion. Was this excursion folly? Or was their detour practical vigilance? The Jalora had remained disturbingly silent on the matter. A billowing burst of air escaped his lips and caught the wind. He had no choice. They must discover what infamy the Jackal had planned next.

A silent shadow kept the watch with him. Body still as the grave, Coyote allowed a slight furrow to struggle across his brow. This small display of somber sentiment was foreign to his features.

"What is it?" Wolf asked.

"We are very near the Great Divide within the Bloodtooth Mountains. This formation of two split peaks separates North Marsh from the Buells. It would be a strategic place to pass unseen into Andarian territories."

"Come to the bridge," Wolf said. "This news must be shared."

They crossed the deck at an urgent gait. The sudden movement drew attention from many around the vessel. Wolf waved his hand, beckoning the other Lords of Valdeon from their stations about the deck and riggings. Rafael the Fox watched them assemble at the base of the steps. He murmured a quick order to his squire. Stepping aside, Fox begrudgingly allowed the man to take the wheel.

"Watch out below, Berto!" Yuli swung down from the sails with an exuberant yelp. Jaguar gave him a half-hearted shove.

"Coyote has an idea of the Jackal's purpose in North Marsh." Wolf nodded to the Lion's First Marked. Coyote snatched an extra bit of rope tucked neatly between two crates. Kneeling amid their circle, he began to make a crude outline of the Bloodtooth Mountains.

"This is the Great Divide." Coyote tapped his finger in a large dip he'd formed with the rope. "Jackal ships with their tough metal hulls could pass over the mountains safely without being seen."

"I too am familiar with the Buells." Lucio knelt beside Coyote. "Most Buellanders won't go near the Bloodtooth Mountains. They consider them evil." He pointed along the representation of the eastern foothills.

"I've heard rumors of small smuggler communities among the trees. They don't like competition and have been known to sell information to the Legion about rival thieves. The Jackal would have to know the trade lines to avoid being seen by these blaggards."

Coyote gave Wolf a troubled frown. "Someone who knows Andara must have aided the Jackal in their planning. The routes Ferret spoke of are not well known to outsiders."

"That's impossible," Raven said. "Dragon would have sensed such treachery."

"The way he or any of us knew about the invasion of Valdeon? Andara and the Legion are about to be taken completely off guard." Wolf stared hard at his young guardsmen. "We must discover their plans or risk losing Andara."

An urgent whistle pierced the wind and rain. Yuli the Otter's squire waved frantically down to his young lord. Sprinting with all the endless energy of youth, Yuli flew toward the railing. He leaned dangerously over the side. Curiosity won over prudence, and Wolf and the other rangers hurried to join him.

"Are they mad?" Yuli pointed at the ships slowly lowering toward the ragged edge of the bogs. "If they stay on their current course, their ships will smash into the mountainside."

Then the two ships headed straight for the rock facc. Never slowing, the vessels appeared to be purposely trying to crash into the rock. Was it a strange suicide mission then? Wolf didn't think so.

The vessels, against all reason, suddenly disappeared. No fire. No crash. What bangtail mischief was this?

Ships didn't just vanish, and they didn't pass through rock either. Something wasn't right.

"Curious." Coyote traced a fingertip anxiously over the hilt of his sword. "Do we follow them?"

"Are you insane? I'm not ramming my vessel into solid rock," Fox said.

"We follow, but on foot." Wolf pushed away from the railing. "We're too far from the rock face for me to See anything with my powers. Keep us out of sight, Fox. Our only advantage is the element of surprise."

The *Wind Chaser* lifted higher into the gray ceiling. Then it came to a stop, hovering within the gray belly of wet fog. The cloud's body floated through the railings to spread across the deck before them. Wolf moved to the safety of a solid mast, as the thick mist covered his legs to the waist.

"Well, this isn't eerie at all," Raven muttered.

"Afraid of ghosts in the mists?" Yuli grinned at his solemn companion.

"Many bodies rot in this endless bog, My Lord the Otter. They have waited in an uneasy rest over the centuries," Coyote said. "Don't give them a reason to surface now."

Otter's grin vanished as another bank of gray rolled through the railings in a wave of nothingness. Scanning the foggy backdrop, he took quick steps toward Berto and Raven. Tulio the Rabbit joined his comrades like a phantom, not stopping until he was at their center. His arm pressed against Yuli's back as the two youths did their best to appear fearless.

"We'll take the launch and land at the base of the mountain," Wolf said when Rafael the Fox joined them.

"The climb is going to be difficult. Our squires will remain aboard ship."

Concern. Frustration. Loyalty. Careful restraint kept their squires from charging across the foggy deck. Wolf regarded Boyd, the Coyote's squire. Images of the young Lion and his woolie farmer companion formed in the man's mind while Wolf probed him. Coyote's squire stood with his lord as they protected the young Lion when Seth was helpless. Boyd healed the Marianna squire after they'd escaped the deadly clutches of the Dirge. Affection for Seth and Riley was evident in his memories.

"You have earned my trust, squire." Wolf gave Boyd a nod. "Fetch your pack. You come with us to guard the launch."

Basilio ordered the remaining men to free the small vessel from its secured perch on deck. Trust. Loyalty. Acceptance. The emotions pulsed from the squire's body as he held the hovering launch for Wolf. Basilio never questioned his lord's decisions. He was a good squire and a worthy man. Though the weeks of grief and uncertainty had taken their toll, Basilio still had faith in his lord.

Fox slapped Yuli's hands off the launch's rudder and took the pilot's seat. He lifted them up and over the railing, descending quickly through the rain-soaked clouds. Wolf held on. Fox's steady hand took them at a sharp descent toward the bogs. Skimming inches above the dead trees, their launch remained undetected by anyone save the ruffled wetland birds.

Panoramic snowcapped peaks towered above the marsh. White upon the jagged peaks turned the mountain tops into the growling maw of a wild beast. Stained a dull red by nature and the elements, rock protruded from its soggy base to form the mountain range. Wet and frozen stone turned a deep red where it met the white snow. Bloodtooth. Yes, that was the right name for these mountains.

"I think the crevice to our right will hide our launch," Wolf suggested.

Fox made for an opening in the red stone. Easing the engines to a slow glide, he maneuvered the tiny vessel forward. Steep walls rose above them on either side. Completely consuming the vessel's body, the crevice left just enough room for a skilled captain to turn about in the small space. Fox handed the rudder to Boyd and took the mooring line. He jumped onto a small ledge along the rock face and secured it to a rotting tree root long dead.

Wolf stepped off the side of the launch and joined Fox on the narrow ledge. "If something happens and you must leave, I don't suggest trying to retrieve the mooring line."

Boyd looked down at the jagged rocks below. "Sage advice, my lord."

"Keep your eyes open," Coyote called to his squire from the ledge. "I'll be back with presents."

Wolf lifted the hood of his cloak over his head. Gifted by the Luminawni, the fabric used to make Legion cloaks was infused with magic. It tricked the eye with patterns and light until rangers seemingly became invisible. Wolf's companions followed suit, effectively vanishing against the rock's surface. Now they were only visible to each other.

"Stay close. We follow the sheep trails heading west."

Placing the toe of his boot on the thin rock shelf, Wolf wrapped the Jalora's power about him and sprinted up the steep incline. He paused as the trail began to run parallel to the marsh below. His companions followed, with Jaguar taking up the rear. Satisfied they could keep up, Wolf continued to run along the perilous mountain sheep trails toward the last place they'd seen the enemy vessels.

The remains of tiny daisies swayed in a relentless wind along the rock. These reminders of green and color defied the land of eternal death below in North Marsh. Though winter was upon them, these flowers were heralds of the life growing in abundance on the other side of the mountain range. North Point—in comparison—was a green land with ferns and towering trees in a sprawling forest.

Stopping when the sheep trail ended, Wolf looked around to find an alternate path. He saw another trail a few feet above him. Using his power, Wolf sprang up the slick rock and secured a toehold on the trail. But then his boot slipped from under him, and he began to fall. Coyote grabbed his arm before he could tumble over the side.

"Careful, Right-Hand. I don't want to face Seth if harm comes to you." Coyote pointed to a wider trail several feet below them. "We may have better luck taking the low road."

Coyote stayed close to Wolf like a hovering nursemaid. The Lion's First Marked ignored any fits of annoyance from Wolf. His young guardsmen, for their part, tried unsuccessfully to keep their grins to themselves. Wolf, despite his initial reluctance, had to admit he was beginning to like the ranger.

Suddenly, their boots struck a broad rock shelf. Patterns in the stone swirled and folded, hiding the shelf's existence until they were upon it. The wind shifted suddenly from the south and came at them in a strong gust from the west. Pungent odors of dried blood and unwashed bodies found them on their perch. Raven gagged and turned his face away. A wise move as moments later a Jackal patrol appeared out of the rock face without warning.

Pressing their backs against the mountain, Wolf and his companions stood perfectly still. Wolf held a deep breath and hoped the others had thought to do the same. Braids soaked in old blood bounced on dirty armored chests. Repugnant and vicious, these cunning warriors had taken time to analyze the strengths and weaknesses of their enemies. The magic within the rangers' cloaks may have kept them hidden from normal beings, but these invading killers were anything but typical.

Wolf squeezed his eyes shut in relief when the patrol took a sharp turn into the mountain. He gave the signal for his companions to stay put while he carefully followed the patrol. Their boots pounded hollow within the narrow tunnel cut into the rock. Wolf ran a hand along the walls. Whatever device had created this hole was far more advanced than anything conceived on Andara.

Suddenly, a flash of ash zipped by him and attached itself to the last Jackal soldier in the line. Tulio's dagger sliced across the man's throat with disturbing violence. Wolf could find no signs of compassion swirling in the hatred that came with the attack. Flying forward with all the speed and stealth he could muster, Wolf threw Tulio over his shoulder and raced out of the tunnel.

Jaguar followed behind, dragging the dead Jackal with him. Wordlessly, he threw the body over the cliff and then covered the drag tracks along the fine ground rubble on the floor of the tunnel.

Wolf slammed Tulio against the rock face and put a hand over his mouth. Two Jackal soldiers had come to see what became of their friend. Their keen eyes searched along the stone shelf. Satisfied he hadn't fallen behind, they looked over the cliffside. Tulio shifted his body forward, but Wolf held him firm.

The two Jackal soldiers burst into laughter. Their raucous guffaws bounced off the mountainside in wrenching tones. Shaking their heads, the soldiers turned from the cliff and entered the tunnel once more.

"Not very sentimental, are they. Lucky for us." Rabbit backed away from Wolf's anger.

"I will not tolerate any more lack of discipline. You could've gotten us all captured or killed. Does your vengeance mean more to you than us?"

"How can you stand there and let them pass, Wolf?" Tulio pushed away from him. "I see these rabid dogs, and all I want is their blood. I want to make them hurt!"

"Do you imagine you're the only one who wants revenge? They hung Dulcina and the children in my orchards." The ugliness of his words reverberated against the blood-colored rock face. "I serve the Jalora.

Vengeance will come only at its word." Wolf picked up Rabbit by the front of his tunic. "Do not disobey my orders again."

He dropped Tulio and turned away from the disappointment in those young eyes. Such childishness displayed no concept of responsibility over personal interests. Wolf would love nothing more than to cut down every last Jackal on this mountain, but what of Andara? They must discover the threat to their world even if it meant giving up any chance for retribution.

Chapter Sixteen

HENRY THE BADGER, determination fixed on his face, positioned the tip of his sword over the toe of his front leg. Frustration. Anxiety. Resolve. They made bold colors about Seth's cousin's body. The First Stance in the Dance of Death reminded Seth of the beginning pose of a merry waltz. This association had helped him master the move. Of course, he'd had his share of falls as well.

"Go," Seth said.

Spinning the sword in an upward arc, Henry twisted his body around. Boots, filthy from hours in the mud, dragged behind. Tripped by his own movements, Henry dropped facedown in the sludge. Laughter thundered from the railings of the paddock. Bear and Stallion, each covered in mud, hurried to help Henry out of the oozy mess.

"The First Stance is impossible to do without falling!" Stallion wiped a hand over Henry's eyes and nose.

Bear handed the sputtering Henry a cup of water with a grin. "You must have patience. I needed many months to stay on my feet."

"Does it get easier?" Stallion asked.

"Stances two and three are harder than the first, if you ask me," Bear said with a sigh. "I've been an apprentice for three years, and I'm still no closer to acolyte level."

"I shouldn't wonder," Seth said, coming to stand before them. "Listen to yourselves. *I can't do it. I haven't mastered it.* Your powers don't work that way. No mortal can do this Dance of Death without the Jalora."

Power, ancient and wise, rose out of Seth's being. Its presence expanded in warm tendrils of energy until the entire paddock vibrated with exhilaration. The Jalora had come among them. It looked on the young mortals with eternal eyes. They were unsure of themselves but eager to learn. Even the one called Stallion held the desire to improve, though he tried to hide it.

They must be taught to serve me, my Lion.

"Set your weapons aside and form a line." Seth's and the Jalora's joined voices projected reassurance across the paddock. "You must learn to listen, my servants."

Then the Jalora reached its power out to each of them. Seth grinned as gasps of surprise and awe lifted over the mud of North Marsh. Golden bands of sun descended from the heavens in a rare cascade of warmth. They stared at the sparkling fingers of light touching their arms. Seth was delighted. He'd been blessed with the Jalora's touch many times. It kept him centered.

"Dance for me! Delight in my power!"

The apprentices came into the First Stance—grasping at the offered power. Their bodies spun and fell.

Jumping up, they tried again without pause. Seth sensed the Jalora's hesitation. It was holding back for some reason. Tingles of humor ran along his spine as they watched the filthy young men spin about in the mud.

"I am still absent in your dance. Call me, and I will come." Then the Jalora released more of its power, aiding the students to feel its touch.

The Jalora's mortal servant called Badger completed the stance, coming to a stop on his feet. "I did it! I mean, we did it."

The servant called Stallion echoed his excitement. He and the one called Bear stood on their feet. Excitement. Gratitude. Devotion. These glowed in bright ribbons about the muddied mortals.

"*I am most pleased,*" the Jalora told them. "*Each of you has been placed in this spot at this moment by my will. Cast away your doubts. Know that I have a plan for you.*"

When will you teach them how to wrap the wind about them? Seth asked the Jalora in his mind.

You're special, Lion. Every advantage my power can offer I will gift to you. We have a hard road ahead, but men like these will see us through.

Then the Jalora left them, taking its light and reassurance with it. Seth stumbled back a step, feeling the loss. Its presence during their lesson had been the longest the Jalora had stayed within his body. Henry stepped tentatively toward him, hands outstretched.

"It's all right, Badger. I'm fine. Try adding your sword as you do the First Stance."

"I'd do as he advises, apprentice."

Hands gripped his arms and turned him around. A familiar and welcome face unexpectedly appeared in the mud of North Marsh, a neatly trim mustache curved under dark auburn hair. Pleasant features reflected the ranger's naturally calm disposition. Ronald the Dragonfly offered Seth a warm smile as he leaned the young Lion against the paddock railing.

"How have you come to be here, my friend?" Seth asked at once. "Where's Donny?"

"The Legion has reassigned us to Western Beta," Dragonfly said. "My brother was eager to find Riley."

"He'll be pleased! Come and meet my friends. May I present Anders the Bear, Cal the Stallion, and my cousin Henry the Badger." Seth put a hand on his friend's shoulder. "This, apprentices, is Ronald the Dragonfly."

Wiping their filthy hands on dirtied trousers, the apprentices shook Dragonfly's hand. Though an acolyte, Seth's friend didn't share the standoffish attitude toward apprentices adopted by the rest of Western Beta. Rather, he seemed genuinely pleased to greet Seth's friends.

"You're about to meet our commander, sir." Bear pointed at Phoenix and White Tiger walking rapidly across the muddy yard.

Dragonfly gave the two rangers a respectful salute. "Ronald the Dragonfly, reporting for duty, sir."

"Are you now?" White Tiger snapped. "It's customary to report directly to your new commanding officer rather than going sightseeing."

"My apologies, sir. I was curious." Dragonfly cast a glance toward Seth. "North Marsh Outpost is...unique.

And I was most interested to see how Ice Lion was settling in."

Dragonfly pulled a parchment from his tunic and handed it to Phoenix. Their commander took it without comment. He read the orders, eyes suddenly shifting from Dragonfly to Seth.

"Western Beta is indeed fortunate. The Dragon himself has sent you."

"I requested the transfer, sir. Ice Lion saved my life."

Phoenix and Dragonfly exchanged meaningful looks. "Ice Lion has developed a habit of saving ranger lives. I also owe him a life debt." Phoenix nodded to White Tiger. "Come to my office, Dragonfly. We have matters to discuss."

The matters dealt directly with Seth, no doubt. He began to follow as the two rangers headed toward the courtyard. If they were going to discuss him, he had the right to hear what was said. But a sudden restraint stopped him.

"What a lovely rain shower we have coming." White Tiger pointed up to the dark skies. "A nice run around the outpost will do wonders. Get to it, apprentices. Double time!"

True to White Tiger's prophetic forecast, the clouds opened up a short time later. The sky released buckets of water on the only two-legged creatures foolish enough to be out in the weather. Seth's clothes were soggy and cold as they ran in formation toward the entrance of the Legion courtyard. White Tiger finally jutted a thumb to the barracks. They got the point.

Tumbling inside and basking in the warmth, the apprentices shared a collective sigh of relief.

"I hope White Tiger gets a blister on his backside," Stallion grumbled as he pounded the bottom of his boot. Mud and other unidentifiable muck oozed out. "What sense does it make for us to march around the inside walls of the outpost in a thunder storm?"

"I've stopped wondering." Bear dropped down on one of the stools. "I'm simply happy to be out of the storm."

Henry joined him on a nearby stool. He leaned his wet head against the wall and closed his eyes. A long sigh filled the little mudroom. Seth resisted the temptation to join his cousin in gloom. They all could use something hot and cheering.

"I'll ask our squires to bring hot tea."

"Make it something stronger, Ice Lion." Stallion gave him a tired grin. "I've got the taste of muck in my mouth."

Seth pulled open the door to the barracks corridor and stepped through. The patterns along the wood flooring dissolved. Gone too were the solid circles of light from the crystal lanterns usually hanging overhead. Mists, touched with magic, gently blanketed a sea of forest ferns. He was no longer in the outpost. Someone had brought him to the Realm of Mist and Dreams. No one knew where this mystical realm existed, but it wasn't North Marsh.

Two Valdeonian men stood among the ferns. Seth groaned as he recognized their features. Ignacio and Hugo D'Antoiné—former Lions and his "not dead long enough" ancestors—regarded him with disapproving grimaces upon their faces. His rather harsh and exuberant teachers hadn't appeared to him since he'd been hiding from the Dirge on the Isle of Carlotta. How had they known where to find him?

"What are you about, boy? Am I to believe you're a stable hand rather than the Lion Protector?" Ignacio waved an arm, sending the old-fashioned tassels on his tunic swaying. His thick beard moved in waves as he muttered a long stream of Valdeonian profanities.

"Indeed." Hugo's sour frown stretched the skin on his clean-shaven face. "Allowing a common ranger like the Mantis to belittle you. Does he dare assume his skills are adequate to train the next Jalora Master? The man is a buffoon, just like his grandfather before him. I don't know which one of you is worse, that fool or you for allowing such presumption."

"What can you expect from this errant generation? They have no sense of duty," Ignacio said. "First Edmund marries a Tslavian, and then Esteban disgraces the family with his lustful ambitions." He huffed and rolled his eyes. "Imagine! A De Vincente being named Right-Hand to the Lion. May the mighty Hawks turn in their graves from the disgrace."

"Hold your tongue!" Seth growled. "Wolf saved my life. I won't have you insulting him for it."

"And where is your Right-Hand? He allows common acolytes to impugn your honor."

"All rangers serve the Jalora and Andara equally. I'm no better or no worse than they."

"You understand nothing, boy." Hugo shook his head as if he were talking to a dullard. "The Jalora is jealous of its chosen master. It has charged the Sacred

Guard with the protection of your body and the upholding of your honor. They will punish any who insult you." He opened his arms wide. "What do you think happens when your guard isn't there to punish those offenders?"

Ignacio thrust his hands toward the heavens when he saw Seth still didn't understand. "The Jalora's punishment is far worse than any Xavier the Wolf could think up. Mark my words. This Mantis will be punished by fate's hand for his blasphemy."

"The Phoenix has already reprimanded him."

"And the will of the Partisan be done then? Fool! Phoenix bows to the Right-Hand," Hugo said, joining Ignacio in irreverent chortles. "Must you behave like a dim-witted woolie farmer your entire life? You are the Lion, King of Valdeon and the next Jalora Master. All others are lesser than you."

"Now I understand why Valdeon fell by Julian's hand," Seth told them. "Our family line has fostered nothing but arrogance and entitlement. I will not use my role as Lion to elevate the family D'Antoiné. I've done with you and your hate. Leave me alone."

"You'll be back, grandson, because the Jalora has willed it." Hugo sliced at Seth's back with the tip of his sword. "Here is something to remind you to watch your tone in the presence of your elders."

Seth tumbled through the mist as the sharp bite of Hugo's sword stung his back. Their laughter faded in the stillness of the rolling puffs of gray. Staggering forward into the unknown, Seth prayed they were wrong. Mantis and the other rangers in Western Beta feared him. They must be put at ease somehow. Andara needed every soul working together against the Jackal.

Two figures stepped from the ferns to block his path. He recognized them as the rangers he'd seen inside the storage shed on his first day at the outpost. How had they managed to enter the Realm of Mist and Dreams? Neither the Jalora or his ancestors mentioned other rangers with the ability to walk within its forests.

"Greetings, Lion." The tallest one's measured nod sent white hair swaying in an absent breeze. "I am called Elk. My comrade's name is Cougar. We've been waiting for you."

"How have you come into the Realm of Mist and Dreams? Did the Jalora send you?"

"We were comrades of your father." Elk gave him a warm smile. "Cougar and I have come to fulfill a promise we made to Leo. You are on a quest. We're here to help you."

Seth examined them both a bit more closely. Though not quite the age his father had been when he'd first come to his son on Marianna, they showed features that betrayed signs of middle-age. Somehow the two men had remained hidden from Phoenix and White Tiger. Or they camped outside the outpost someplace. No. The rangers' clean appearance discredited the idea. Their uniforms were neatly pressed and completely dry, a miracle in North Marsh.

"You know of my quest?"

"Find what was lost." Cougar's baritone rumbled among the gray clouds. "We were there the day the relic vanished. It waits for you, Lion."

"What is it?" Seth stepped closer to them, his excitement growing. "Where is it? I've been looking but haven't had any luck finding my mysterious prize."

"A wasted effort. It's not at this outpost." Cougar folded his arms with a grunt.

"Cougar," Elk warned. "You'll know when you're close, Lion. It will call to you."

"This relic is somewhere beyond the walls of the outpost then? Can you show me?"

"The way is not clear yet," Elk said. "The Jalora will guide us when it is ready."

"Maybe Phoenix can help?"

"You mustn't mention us." Cougar wagged a finger at him. "We are here to aid you, no one else."

"Very well. I suppose you have your reasons," Seth said. "I'll keep your presence secret."

"We will see each other again soon, Lion."

Elk's voice faded like an eerie echo as the men stepped back into the mists. Seth stared into the vapors until the realm engulfed the two rangers. Strange they hadn't returned to North Marsh with him. Back aching, he was too tired for any more intrigue today.

A tug inside his chest forced Seth to turn to his left. Someone was searching for him. The mists parted. A steady rhythm of rain slapping against stone thundered in his ears. He followed the drum-like beat out of the fog. Back stinging as the hot blood rolled down his skin, he pounded his boots on the battlements of North Marsh Outpost. Rain drenched his hair and clothes. Disoriented, he fell to the stone.

Two hands grabbed his arm and pulled him to his feet. Seth nodded. Stallion's frightened eyes examined his friend's exhausted features. Questions lay in their depths. Stallion ran trembling fingers through the stubble of straight hair atop his head. The strands defied gravity and the heavy wet of North Marsh.

"How long?" Seth leaned heavily against him.

"I saw you vanish, so I went looking. Hours have gone by. It's just past midnight." He pulled Seth's arm over his neck, holding him upright as they descended the battlement's steps. "We've got to get you inside before the watch changes."

A low, plaintive whistle drew their attention to one of the Legion storage sheds. Roland, Phoenix's squire, beckoned them with a stern finger. They had no choice, but to do as ordered. What would Seth say? How could he ever explain?

"You aren't going to tell Phoenix, are you?" Stallion asked the pale squire.

Roland shook his head and held open the door. Why was he willing to keep quiet about tonight? That was the question. Seth let it go when he noticed the fire burning in a portable brazier. Lanterns glowed about the room. He saw bits of cloth blocking light from escaping to the outside. In the center of the tiny space were a mattress and blanket. Roland pointed to it. Stallion got the idea and lowered Seth down.

"You were expecting me."

The squire gave him no reply. Expert fingers removed Seth's tunic and began to clean the wound with a strange smelling liquid. Wincing, Seth rested his head on his outstretched arms. Stallion sat down across from him, leaning his back against the wall. He ran a hand across his wet hair.

"Who did this to you?" he asked.

"You wouldn't believe me if I told you." Seth sighed. "No one would."

Stallion tilted his head. "Try me."

Perhaps the urge to disclose his secrets came from carrying their burden or the strange tingling of Roland's medicine. Regardless, Seth was tired of carrying the weight alone. His voice sounded tired and thin.

"I went to a place called the Realm of Mist and Dreams," Seth began. "You won't find it on Andara. I'm not sure where it is. I train in its fern-covered forest. You can see my instructors aren't the patient kind."

"They cut you."

"Yes, and worse." Seth gave him a bitter smile. "Two Lions from the past have volunteered to train me. Neither of them approves of my mixed blood."

"Ancestors cast long shadows." Stallion held out his Heart of the Warrior Ring. "I believe you, Ice Lion. My family has come back to haunt me as well. You heard Phoenix mention that the Stallion Ring has been inactive for a hundred years. It was last on a ranger's finger when the Jalora Master, Gustavo the Lion Claw, ruled Andara. My ancestor, Calhoun the Stallion, was the Lion Claw's First Marked. He had endured so much anguish and experienced such torturous pain in his service to his master, the Jalora granted the Stallion Ring a rest to rejuvenate. It was to stay inert until a Jalora Master walked the Erthe once more."

Stallion grinned down at his ring. "His legend is pounded into every little boy's head from the day he is born until he reaches sixteen. Each time a new Lion was named, Edanstein threw a festival in honor of the Jalora and Calhoun the Stallion. They gathered all the boys of age in my family into the throne room. The Stallion Ring had been bricked into the wall by the Jalora, you see. A hundred years passed as time and again young men tried to pull the ring from the stone. Then came my turn. I didn't think the ring would pick me. I almost vomited my dinner when it came away from the wall. Of course, the Jalora Legion had to pick that day of days to send a ranger to watch."

"Mantis."

"Yes, he called me a coward for not wanting to bear the Stallion Ring." Stallion leaned away from the wall. "I had dreams. I wanted to build things. You know, buildings and bridges." His quiet laugh touched softly against the walls. "I thought it was one grand mistake. Then I met you and saw what you could do. It made me a believer."

"Are we friends then, Cal?" Seth asked.

"You bet we are, Seth." Stallion again rubbed at the stubble on his head. "Besides, we have a shared tormentor. Mantis cut off all my hair. I won't forget it. In Edanstein, short hair on a man is considered feminine. We'll see how he likes it when I shave him one night."

Despite Stallion's sorry state, Seth burst into a laugh. "Come now. You don't mean it."

"His head and his eyebrows too." Cal chuckled. "You wait and see. He'll look like a bald duck."

Their laughter slowly faded. Blessed silence filled the shed. Roland's fingers began to work their way up to Seth's shoulders and neck. Seth closed his eyes and simply breathed as the sound of rain on stone faded.

Chapter Seventeen

RILEY HELD SETH'S muddy boots at arm's length with one hand and gripped the polish with the other. Great gulls. What a blessing and a curse that the rangers were issued two pairs of boots. Riley pushed through the laundry door with his back. Hot, humid air from the boiling washtubs struck his skin. In the damp confines of the room, he lost any progress he'd made drying out his hair and clothes.

Puddles of condensation continued to form on thirsty rock tiles. The Legion, Riley had been told, chose the material for its ability to absorb moisture quickly. They'd installed it in the bathhouse and the laundry. If it were up to Riley, all the buildings in the outpost would have these absorbent rock floors.

A practiced spin brought him around to face the other legion squires sitting about the tiled room. Wooden benches, well away from the washtubs and similar to the ones aboard *The Protector*, lined the room. They shared the same bottom-blistering rigidity. Riley could keep his trouser bottom dry aboard the ship at least, but nothing escaped the wet of North Marsh.

"Ho, Riley!" Gudal waved him over. "Come to join us in our favorite pastime? I don't think I've ever cleaned and polished as many boots in my life. Don't care to again once we leave North Marsh."

Big burly arms rubbed back and forth along the leather of his ranger's boots. Bear, at least, had some experience in keeping out of the deeper pools of mud. Lucas, the Stallion's squire, wasn't as fortunate with his own ranger's expertise. He poured brown muck out of one of the boots, shaking his head as it made an oozing pile beside the drain.

"I think my good ranger finds every puddle in North Marsh! The filth has gotten inside this time." Lucas shook the boot with a chuckle. "I'm certain it gave him an extra sunny disposition."

The levels of filth the rangers attracted had been their favorite topic of conversation over the weeks. Each had his grumbles, but if anyone else said a word against their ranger, a fight was sure to follow.

"I think our apprentices are the filthiest rangers in North Marsh. Perhaps in the entire Legion." Gudal threw his buffing brush into the wooden storage box beside his bench. "They haven't stopped stomping in the mud since they arrived."

"Aye. White Tiger would keep them marching in their sleep!"

Riley uneasily joined their laughter. The statement had been one of fact, not a joke. He knew Seth better than anyone and saw him staring out into the darkness when he thought no one was watching. Seth suffered quiet fits of funk after spending time under Gecko's tutelage. Something was bothering the Lion. Riley wished he could corner his friend and wrestle it out of him.

Arthur, White Tiger's squire, was laughing the loudest. "My ranger will teach them to stay alive, boy. He has a purpose behind what he does."

"I just hope Seth survives the lessons," Riley muttered unhappily.

"No given names or titles. It is against Legion rules," Arthur said. "The rangers leave their lives behind while they serve the Jalora."

"I should think you would know better, Earl Logan of Carlotta." The Mantis's squire leaned against the wall beside several freshly washed tunics. "Earl, ha! I can smell the woolie dung on your boots from here."

He was a thin, fussy-looking man a few years younger than the Phoenix. Thinning chestnut hair, wet with the damp, clung to his head. Grizzled brows accentuated a high forehead racing toward developing bald spots.

"Keep your tongue in your mouth, or I'll mop the floor with it, Harold." Gudal turned to Riley. "Don't mind him. He's still upset the Jalora picked his cousin as Heir to the Mantis Ring rather than him. Poor Harold had such high aspirations, and where did he end up? Here with us, polishing boots."

Storming toward Riley, the Mantis's squire ignored Gudal's insult and the spattering of laughter around the chamber. "I, at least, know who my father was, unlike the questionable lineage of the apprentice from Valdeon."

Harold put fists on his hips and leaned over Riley. "I've heard the rangers speak of your half-breed Lion's nighttime exploits. He runs around the wall, searching for ghosts. A few of the UR soldiers claim to have seen

Ice Lion make the bricks glow. Ha! I suspect drink was involved." Harold stood up straight again. "Do you know what I think?"

"Be still, Harold," Arthur snapped. "The Lords of Valdeon won't like this idle talk."

"Don't be a fool. The Sacred Guard has abandoned Andara and their Lion." Harold spat upon the tile. "Phoenix doesn't trust the half-breed any more than the rest of us do. I've seen him following Ice Lion at night." Harold thrust a finger in Riley's face. "Your ranger is mad. He's losing control of his powers, and everyone knows it."

The squires stopped their scrubbing, jaws hanging with uneasy shock. Boots and brushes stilled as an uncomfortable silence filled the laundry room. Aghast, they shifted all eyes to Harold. Riley had heard gossip concerning the Lords of Valdeon. They acted as guard for Seth. Wolf had proven his loyalty while on Marianna by saving their lives. Well, the Lords of Valdeon weren't here to look after Seth at the moment. It was up to Riley.

"You've gone too far, Harold. I won't have anyone saying a word against my ranger."

Riley put Seth's boots down beside the bench. He carefully rested the polish and cloth on the surface next to them. Then he stood up slowly until his curly head stopped at the other man's shoulders. Nothing new. He was short, even for a Grey Cliff Islander.

"And what will you do about it, woolie farmer?"

Riley's fist swung up to the man's jaw and connected with a bone-jarring whack. Harold flew back against the wet tunics, pulling one down on top of his chest. He stopped with his head against the wall, unconscious and soaked through with soapy water.

Another man, the Gecko's squire, fell upon the tiled floor. The Badger's squire stood over him, fists at the ready. He was an older man with gray rolling about his dark hair. Fierce eyes spoke of the many battles he'd survived.

"I am no one to fool with, boy. Begone!" The harsh Tslavian accent made the elder's words all the more threatening. Gecko's squire pushed away from him, sliding along the tiles on his backside. He slithered out the door with a final glare at Riley.

Roars of laughter and cheers thundered about the room. Several hands smacked Riley's back. Tumbling forward, he was carried away by their enthusiasm. Gudal caught Riley in a smothering embrace and rubbed his large hand on Riley's head.

"One punch! Best thing I've seen in many months."

"I'm the youngest of seven brothers. I had to learn to fight if I wanted to make it through childhood." Riley pointed down at the wet cloth. "Sorry about the tunic."

"No worries," Arthur said. "It belongs to the Mantis." His eyes suddenly went wide, and he stood up straight. "Attention!"

Riley twisted around with the crowd. Fine white hair strands framed the porcelain features towering over them. Roland moved through their numbers like a silent ghost until he stood beside the unconscious squire. Everyone backed away in a hurry. Their commander used the tip of his sword to pull aside the wet cloth. Frowning lips expressed his opinion of the deep bruise beginning to form on Harold's face.

Soundlessly sheathing his sword, Roland walked casually toward the buckets of soapy water. He lifted one and threw the contents on the squire's head. Harold sputtered and sat up. He stayed still as he found Roland standing over him with arms crossed. Every man in the room held his breath, waiting to see what their commander would do next. Twisting his hand with incredible speed, Roland produced a scrub brush. He threw it at Harold along with the empty bucket. Pointing toward the kitchens, he glared as Harold scrambled to obey.

"Thank the Mantis for scrubbing those pots so well," Riley called as he passed. "I don't think the food has ever tasted better since ranger hands laid upon it."

The room filled with their suppressed chuckles, but their humor faded as Roland came to stand before Riley. Saluting the Phoenix's squire quickly, Riley waited for the inevitable punishment. Whatever Roland tasked him to do was worth his moment of revenge.

Then their commander allowed a slow grin to stretch across his silent lips. He gave Riley a nod and walked silently back to the kitchens.

"Well, by my father's beard!" Gudal said. "I thought Roland would have you scrubbing the battlements with a hairbrush, Riley. He must like you."

"Or he doesn't care for Harold either."

"Either way, Lion's squire." Arthur took up White Tiger's boots again. "It's best not to anger Roland."

Riley moved back to his bench and sat beside the Badger's squire. "Thanks for watching my back. I'm confused as to why you would, though. Most of the Tslavians we've met haven't been too keen on Seth."

"I owe your ranger a debt, Lion's squire. He's the first to treat Henry the Badger as a comrade and equal, not like a weakling child. Your lord is clever. He gives Badger respect, but he watches out for him as well." The Tslavian squire gave Riley a faint smile. "Have you not noticed the fondness they have for each other? They are cousins. Didn't you know?"

Great gulls. Seth had more relatives in the Legion? Each day held a new surprise where his ranger's family was concerned. Young Henry the Badger seemed a decent fellow though. He and Seth were friendly toward each other, and Riley was glad of it. The Lion needed all the support he could muster.

"The name's Riley."

"I'm Selby. It is good to have you as a friend. My hope is Henry's next squire will feel the same."

"New squire? Do you mean to say you're leaving us already?"

"Who can say?" Selby shrugged. "The Von Wolkhursts thought it best to have an older man as the Badger's squire. They believe Henry needs looking after." Selby tugged at a strand of gray hair. "Squires can't keep up with their rangers after a certain age. It's a rare man who can."

Selby and Arthur were the oldest among them, come to think of it. Riley ran his brush absently along the toe of Seth's boot. He hadn't considered having to leave Seth on his own. Well, life handed out no guarantees, especially to squires.

Chapter Eighteen

WOLF STARED AT the walls by the entrance of the tunnel, willing his eyes to see through rock. The exercise was pointless of course. He must stifle his impatience as an example to the others—no easy task. Wolf sighed. Disciplined stillness had abandoned his young guardsmen hours before. Yuli had taken to pacing along the tunnel leading toward the belly of the mountain.

"Jaguar's been searching a long time," Yuli said.

"We don't know how long this tunnel is or where it leads. Berto could be a while." Fox leaned against the wall, his blade expertly plucking invisible dirt from beneath obsessively clean nails. "Why don't you help Tulio watch the entrance? Ferret and Raven will need a signal to find the tunnel again after they've finished scouting the ledge."

"I could've gone with Berto," Yuli said, rolling his eyes at a sullen Tulio. "I don't see why Coyote got to go."

"His jibes are slightly more annoying than your grumbles," Wolf snapped. "Now be still. I'm trying to concentrate."

Closing his eyes this time, Wolf reached out with the power of the Right-Hand. His energy raced through rock and over the moss-covered marsh to grab hold of

Seth's heartbeat. Time and space fell away. Wolf's consciousness hovered close to the Lion. Soon they would be able to speak with each other, no matter the distance.

Curiosity. Anger. Protectiveness. They burned in dazzling flames about the Lion. Something had happened or was going to happen soon. Wolf couldn't quite grasp it. Then the power released him. Cool air within the tunnel brushed against his face. Voices touched his ears. Distant at first, they soon became recognizable.

"Has Wolf done this before?" Coyote asked.

"I've never seen him this way," Jaguar said. "The power of the Right-Hand is typically known only to the Bearer of the Hawk Ring."

Wolf's eyes snapped open, and he found Coyote's face inches away. "What bangtail mischief is this?"

"You were…away a long time, Wolf." Jaguar rubbed at the stubble along his square jaw. He was trying hard not to ask what the other curious rangers wanted to know.

"Raven and Ferret haven't returned?"

"Not yet." Coyote, ignoring the sacred nature of the Right-Hand's power, asked. "You were with Seth, weren't you?"

"In a manner of speaking. We must complete our scouting quickly. The Lion is agitated."

Coyote blew out a loud breath. "That can't be good."

Indeed, Seth's raw mood was dangerous not only for the Lion but for everyone around him. Wolf's thoughts drifted to the deadly marsh at the foot of the mountain. It surrounded the outpost. Seth would have nowhere to release his fury other than inside the massive walls. No one was safe should the Lion Spirit be on the prowl.

Ferret and Raven raced into the tunnel. Their frantic eyes searched the space of faces to finally land on Wolf. The two rangers pushed through their comrades to stand before him. Excitement and anxiety swirled about their bodies.

"You've got to see what we've found," Ferret said. "You were right, Wolf. Andara is in trouble."

"Show me." The entire crew followed.

Ferret and Raven took point as they moved out of the tunnel and onto the rock shelf. Heading due west, they clung close to the cliffside. This section of the mountain had been cut flat by the same powerful tool used to form the tunnel. Its surface made a glassy sheen devoid of imperfections.

"What do we have here?" Coyote's voice was a hollow whisper.

His hand gripped a section of rock. Moving his fingers carefully, he pressed the surface and sent a cascading ripple across a large segment of the cliff. The facade was camouflage, painstakingly dyed to imitate stone. Clutching the fabric, Coyote lifted it carefully. Several launches hovered underneath. Small and sleek, they'd be perfect for skimming along the ground in an invasion.

Ferret leaned in for a better look. "These will hold numerous soldiers. I have more to show you."

Ripples of apprehension raced up Wolf's spine. He gave the signal to move forward. All followed Ferret for several hundred feet. Then he stopped suddenly and pressed his back against the stone. The thundering hum of crystal engines echoed out of the mountain. Wolf eased around Ferret until he came to the edge of the rock. Pulling all his power about him, he turned the corner into a nightmare.

A cathedral of stone opened before him. Hidden by an optical illusion, the cavern's entrance would appear to any airships or other travelers as a solid rock, just as it had always been. Closer inspection showed a horrifying truth. The Jackal had gutted one of the peaks and made themselves a hidden fortress from which to launch the destruction of Andara. All their planning and building had happened right under the Legion's nose.

The mountain's belly was alive with activity. Dumbfounded, Wolf could merely watch as men and wagons moved large pieces of metal equipment. Cannonballs, powder, and raw steel filled the space. Ships, too, were moored inside, safe from detection by the Jalora Legion. Their enemy was well on the way toward an invasion. Andara was wide open for the taking.

Then a group of men walked out of an antechamber toward one of the ships. An Andarian man was among them, deep in conversation with the Jackal. Wolf well recognized the hard features and the brutal baritone of his laughter. Esteban, the Hawk Prince, had been the one to aid their enemies. Julian. Esteban. They were both traitors to their country and Andara.

"Now we know how Esteban was able to get in and out of Valdeon so easily," Ferret said, hatred filling his words. "I say we kill him now."

"As much as I would love to see his life's blood stain my sword, we have higher priorities," Wolf replied.

His anger barely contained, he led them back out of the cave. He didn't stop his furious march until they reached the camouflaged launches once more. Choking on his churning hatred, Wolf focused instead on a duty that fate had imposed upon the Lords of Valdeon.

"The legion must be warned of Hawk's treachery. Then we have Seth's safety to consider. Esteban won't be content to share the throne of Valdeon." His gaze drifted out across the desolate swamp before them. "We must find a way to stop their progress. Or at least slow them down until our Andarian forces prepare."

Wolf slammed a fist against the rock. He was the Right-Hand, leader of the Sacred Guard. The Lords of Valdeon looked to him for leadership. He well knew their first duty was the protection of the Lion. But he couldn't stand by as innocent Andarians were slaughtered. It would be Valdeon all over again.

"I'm curious as to how fast these can move," Coyote said, pulling back the fabric to expose one of the enemy launches. "I should be able to reach Lea within a week after I stop by to have a little chat with Phoenix at North Marsh Outpost. We have some unfinished business." Coyote untied the mooring lines from one of the launches. "Any messages for Seth?"

"Yes," Wolf said, helping him pull out one of the launches. "Tell him I'm close by."

"Hop aboard, rangers," Coyote told them. "I need to collect my squire. Might as well give you a lift."

Wolf climbed on board. His gratitude to Coyote remained unspoken. They must find out how far this Jackal treachery had reached into the Buells and northern Andara. Such an investigation might mean abandoning North Marsh for a few days. Wolf didn't like leaving Seth on his own, but he must rely upon others to protect Seth for now. The Lords of Valdeon had sabotage to plan.

Chapter Nineteen

SNORES RUMBLED AGAINST the walls of the barracks. Seth, unable to slumber in the echoing cacophony, stared up at the ceiling while the other apprentices slept. He envied the temporary peace they'd found. His mind, racing with questions, wouldn't rest. Elk and Cougar had assured him the mysterious relic wasn't in the outpost. How was he supposed to find it while he was trapped inside these walls? Turning over onto his side with an impatient sigh, he smacked at his unlucky pillow. The entire quest seemed impossible.

Evil walks the battlements this night, Lion.

A shiver of warning raced along his spine, breaking through his frustrated thoughts. Seth sat up. The Jalora was unsettled. Its shivers of disquieting energy flowed into his arms and legs. He well recognized the sensation. Evil's gnarled fingers had last dug at his flesh when he'd been within the Obsidian Citadel in Lea. How had it found him out here in this dead swamp?

He dressed quickly and strapped on his sword. Waking his comrades without knowing the dangers first wasn't wise. If his suspicions were correct, they wouldn't be able to stand against the powerful darkness haunting the outpost walls. Seth moved through their sleeping bodies then quietly passed out the barracks door and into the mudroom. There, he pulled on freshly polished boots. Honestly, how did Riley seem to stay ahead of him?

His head covered with the hood of his cloak, Seth left the barracks. He stood in the center of the Legion courtyard, waiting for some sign of trouble. The outpost, he realized, was strangely quiet. Absent were the typical noises of an edifice rarely settling into sleep. Complete silence seemed to be the only thing out of place this night.

Then Seth noticed the section of battlement wall closest to the Legion buildings. All the fire braziers had been extinguished. Odd. White Tiger insisted the braziers burn all night, every night without fail. Either someone was mad enough to risk the ranger's temper, or mischief was afoot.

Seth crept up the stairs to the battlements. He crouched on the top step, scanning the platform before him. All seemed quite usual to the casual eye. A handful of guards stood at the wall, looking out over the marsh. Having spent many a night on guard duty as cadet and apprentice, Seth noted that something about their posture didn't seem right.

Sprinting forward, Seth went to the closest guard. He touched the man's shoulder. A small zap of power flared in the night. Suddenly, the soldier and his comrades fell to the stone floor, two lives extinguished some time before. Evil had brought murder among the men this watch and used its abhorrent magic to hide the crime. Seth had to warn the outpost.

Whoever had planned this midnight murder spree was well informed. The alarm bell was on the other side of the battlements where UR soldiers could easily access it. Legion buildings were thought to be safe enough. Phoenix and the other rangers should have been able to sense the presence of any evil seeking out mischief against them. Seth shivered under the ramifications of the murders. The Jalora's power was fading. Seth must restore it for Andara's sake.

Scanning the battlements with the Sight uncovered nothing. Perhaps the killers were gone? Of course, any evil strong enough to hide from Phoenix and White Tiger could still be lingering within the walls. Seth clenched his fists tightly. The alarm bell was at least a ten-minute run from his current position—ten minutes at top speed in the dark. No matter. He must warn the outpost. Pushing away from his hiding place, he ran toward the distant lights of the remaining braziers lining the battlement walls.

A figure, shrouded in shards of midnight cloth, stepped out of the shadows to block his path. Peeling, gray skin covered bone-thin fingers as they kneaded at the air between them. Multiple rows of jagged teeth glistened with oozing saliva. The ultimate personification of Death, this undead and undefeated champion of evil was a favorite soldier of the Sarcion.

"Well, here we have the half-breed Lion," the Dirge said, strangling on the words. "I'd hoped to meet you. Flesh such as yours is best when savored slowly."

"You can speak?"

Prisoners to their gruesome hunger for human flesh, the Dirge were typically limited to grunts and moans. The anticipation of battle changed them. Their fevered yearning grew to its peak when they smelled the fear of their enemies. Then they began to sing their terrible dirge. Agony and the promise of a brutal death spewed from their gaping maws. Armies, frozen with fear, fell to the ravenous appetites of the Sarcion's grisly soldiers. A mere handful of mortals had heard the Dirges' song and lived to tell the tale. Seth was one of the unlucky who'd been serenaded by their haunting tune.

"He hasn't quite lost his humanity yet, Lion," answered a disembodied voice.

Feathers fluttered in wild shadows against the backdrop of distant glowing braziers. In the center of a whirlwind, the quills clung together as they grew. A creature made from nightmares formed quickly from the chaos. Long strands of dark hair framed its sharp facial features. Black orbs stared at Seth while this Changeling's unnaturally thin lips stretched into an amused grin.

Another of its kind came to stand by the first Changeling's shoulder. "We have what we were seeking. Let us leave before more Jalora playthings awaken."

"No! I want his flesh!" The Dirge licked its multiple rows of jagged teeth. It seemed not to notice the oozing gray blood foaming along what remained of its tongue. Wild hunger burned in eyes half hidden under its cowl. The being took a few tentative steps forward.

"Stop, slave!" The second Changeling held a hand out toward the Dirge.

"Let it have its fun, cousin." His comrade grinned, tilting its head as it regarded Seth with curiosity. "The Dirge ask so little and give so much pleasure."

"Lord Gorman will be displeased if we lose another of these creatures."

"Gorman? Is this the villain who has struck an unholy allegiance with Julian D'Antoiné?" Seth growled out.

"Oh, little ice kitten." The Changeling wagged a long black nail at Seth. "Many a champion of the Jalora has met his end by Lord Gorman's hand. Do not seek him out. Best if you die before he finds you."

The Dirge, unable to control its impulses any longer, pulled a massive blade from beneath its shrouds. Tainted magic exuded from the crude weapon's serrated edge. The Dirge broke away from its handlers and flew at Seth across the distance with the swiftness of a foul breeze. Its feet, if the demon still possessed them under its shrouds, never touched the stone of the battlements.

Seth pulled his sword and took the First Stance. His blade swept upward to meet the Dirge's weapon with bone-jarring impact. He thrust their swords to the side, throwing the creature off balance. Arcing his blade again, Seth brought it down on the Dirge's shoulder. It screamed and staggered away. Then lifting its face, the Dirge exposed clear eyes and flesh-covered features that appeared to be almost human. Yes. Human, and thus still vulnerable.

It charged again, yowling in an uncontrolled rage. Summoning his ice walls in defense against its nerve-shattering song, Seth discarded his fear. He knocked the blade aside and thrust his sword deep into what remained of the creature's foul heart. Yanking backward, he freed his weapon from the Dirge's chest with a sickening slurp. His final strike took the monster's head from its shoulders.

"I told you it wasn't ready yet!" the Changeling snapped at its kin. "Lord Gorman won't be pleased." Then it turned tempestuous orbs on Seth. "We will meet again, Lion. I will kill you that day. We go now, cousin."

It turned and headed toward the battlement. The Changelings could use their powers to fly over the walls, but how had the Dirge managed? Had it climbed the thirty-foot-high stone covered in moss? Seth hadn't heard the humming of a crystal engine. He didn't see any sign of rope.

Leaning a hand against the stone, the Changeling turned those cold black orbs on its remaining companion. "Hurry! They wait for us. We must be swift."

"Come now, cousin. It won't take but a moment to kill this mortal plaything of the Jalora. Perhaps we will take the Lion Ring back with us?"

Drawing a curved blade from beneath its cloak, the Changeling stood ready. This villain wasn't a clumsy animal driven by its hunger. The Changeling was deadly with a sword. A malicious grin on its thin face signaled the creature planned to play with Seth for a while. Seth didn't know what these spies of evil had come for, but he couldn't allow them to leave.

"For Andara!"

Seth wrapped his powers about himself and flew at the Changeling with all the speed he possessed. A fist struck his torso, knocking the breath out of him. Such speed! The Lion rolled to the edge of the battlement, smacking painfully against the barrier overlooking the Legion courtyard. Stunned, he didn't have time to block the sharp stab to his right shoulder.

"How disappointed your Jalora must be right now." The Changeling swung its blade playfully in the space between them. "Your career as bearer will be a short one."

Primal fear and hatred rose within Seth's heart as he stared into the mystical being's black orbs. The Lion's Roar rumbled low in his throat. Gasping in short, panicked breaths, Seth desperately tried to concentrate. The Lion Spirit laughed at his struggles. Its vast power chipped away at the thin layer of control Seth still held.

Let me out, Bearer. The Lion Spirit growled. *I grow hungry for its flesh.*

"No! You'll destroy more than the Changeling."

You will soon learn, boy, I cannot be contained.

Then the beast was loose. Bursting onto the battlements in a massive wave of destruction, it struck the Changeling with a bone-crushing surge of energy. Laughter boomed in Seth's ears as the Lion Spirit fed. Slashing and chomping, the invisible beast delighted in the frenzy. Its destructive force, now free upon the outpost, didn't stop at the enemy's ruined body. Thundering along the battlements, the Lion's Roar shook the foundations.

Seth, a stranger in his own body, sat helpless on the battlements while the Lion Spirit devoured everything in its path. Flesh. Stone. Metal. It ate indiscriminately. Seth scratched his fingertips along the rock, trying to regain control. The Lion Spirit, however, wasn't ready quite yet to return to the confines of the ring. Seth prayed an outpost would still be standing when at last its hunger had been sated.

Chapter Twenty

SHARDS OF ROCK and mortar showered down from the cloud of debris. He lifted his arms in a vain attempt to protect his eyes and face. Suddenly, a twisted piece of metal landed inches from his leg with a loud bang—one of the fire braziers. The Lion's Roar had flattened and then twisted the container into a shapeless hunk of useless metal.

Seth leaned against the inner battlement wall, shaken by fatigue and horror. Such raw hunger! The Lion's Roar would devour all in its path. How would he ever control such a willful and powerful entity? His gaze fell upon the motionless Dirge. He recalled its unbridled frenzy. The Lion Spirit seemed as obsessed with its hunger for the flesh of its enemies as the Dirge had been. Would he, too, be a slave to the savage beast within him?

"You're too dangerous, Lion Bearer." The remaining Changeling shifted through the raining debris like a specter of death. "Lord Gorman warned us about the power you possess. I didn't believe until the beast came for me. Fate aided me in escaping its jaws tonight. The Jalora's beast will not get the same chance again."

It pulled a sword from under its cloak and held the blade steady before its body. This Changeling didn't share its comrade's propensity for play. It brandished the sword as a being intent upon killing quickly. Seth rolled away from the wall and tried to gain his feet—to no avail. The Lion's Roar had robbed him of every last ounce of his strength. He fell forward on the floor of the battlement. His knees and legs found the stone. The upper half of his body met only dirt and air. Once the bank of dust had parted, Seth screamed when he saw the result of the Lion Spirit's havoc. A twenty-foot section of wall was missing.

"Feel my blade or fall to your death. It makes no difference to me."

The Changeling, its pointed ears straining, turned toward the courtyard below. Its lips fell downward in a frustrated frown. Slamming doors and booted feet rumbled beneath them. The rangers were coming.

"You've awakened the Jalora's playthings. Pity. You've spent your time on the Erthe all the more quickly."

Its curved blade cut through the distance between them. Seth reached for the hilt of his sword, but the Valdeonian steel remained inert beside the lip of the battlement where he'd left it. Rolling toward his weapon, Seth kicked at the creature's legs to throw it off balance. The battlement disappeared abruptly beneath him, and he grabbed desperately at the edge of the chasm as he began to fall.

A hand grabbed his wrist. Cal, wide-eyed and pale, gritted his teeth and started to pull Seth up. Other hands joined Stallion's, lifting Seth back to the parapets. Henry and Bear plopped down on their backsides, breathing hard. None of the apprentices were fully dressed. Cal had only managed to pull on his trousers and boots.

"I'm glad of your timing, my friends." Seth rubbed a shaking hand across his face.

Breathless, Cal asked, "What is that thing? It looks like a nightmare."

The Changeling pointed its sword at Western Beta forming a circle around it. Phoenix stood at their head, burning with the Jalora's power like the fiery bird inhabiting his Heart of the Warrior Ring. Fury filled the night as the rest of the rangers joined their commander. Connecting the Jalora's power, the rangers trapped the Changeling in their center. White Tiger and Dragonfly were among them, faces solemn as they waited for the deacon to speak.

"You've lost, Creature of Evil. Surrender or perish."

A slow grin formed across its lips. "Poor Jalora plaything. You've no idea what's coming for your weakened legion."

"Careful, Phoenix!" Seth shouted. "The Changeling uses evil magic."

"You've spoiled the surprise, Lion Bearer."

In a fluid movement, the Changeling sheathed its weapon with one hand and threw a powder on the stone with the other. Flame and smoke puffed in bright orange between it and Phoenix. Seth covered his eyes against the blinding light. The Changeling was outside the circle of rangers when Seth opened his eyes again. A fanged smirk hung beneath taunting eyes as it stood by the outer wall.

"After it, rangers! I want the creature's head!"

Phoenix flew at the Changeling, his sword swinging downward at incredible speed. Black feathers circled in a whirlwind of magic until a bird fluttered where the creature had once stood. Cawing derisively at their deacon, the blackbird soared over the side of the wall like a shadow fleeing the sun. Phoenix's blade struck empty air. He made to follow the creature, but White Tiger put a hand on his arm. They argued in low, urgent voices. Phoenix finally nodded, but his stubborn glare remained fixed on the open marsh.

The rest of the battalion, taking White Tiger's cue to stand down, wandered over to the edge of the new chasm in the battlement. Mantis cast a quick look at Seth and began murmuring in a low tone to those standing around him. Dragonfly gave the gossiping ranger's shoulder a hard bump as he walked through their numbers. Mantis frowned at his back but made no move at the slight.

Dragonfly leaned over and offered Seth a hand. "Let's get you to safety, Ice Lion."

Unable to stand, Seth rested his back on the stone once more. "The Changelings and their pet Dirge took something from the outpost. They said they were taking it back to someone called Lord Gorman."

"Very well," Dragonfly said with an unsettled nod. "I'll search what's left of the Changeling you…killed."

Dragonfly pushed at the ragged remains of the dead Changeling with his boot. Finding nothing, he turned to the other lump of cloth. The Dirge lay where Seth had killed it. Henry, drawn by curiosity to Dragonfly's side, stared keenly down at the black rags. The rangers staggered away as Dragonfly turned the

Dirge on its back. Disgust. Curiosity. Anxiety. The emotions hung over their bodies as they regarded the Sarcion's gruesome assassin.

"Look at its face," Henry said. "It is one of the undead. What has come among us?"

"Evil." Seth closed his eyes. Pain. It suddenly became all he could focus on now.

Riley was leaning over him when Seth next opened his eyes. A fierce gaze of bright blue sparked in flares of worry and frustration. Riley shook his head when he saw Seth was awake. The Logan temper was up. Seth would have no chance of escaping his squire's wrath this time.

"You ran off to explore on your own again and put a giant hole in the wall. Don't worry. Repairs are already underway. It seems to me you would have learned your lesson in the Obsidian Citadel. What do I have to do? Lock you in the barracks at night?" Riley put the finishing touches on his bandaging and stood away. "Those Changelings aren't anything to play around with, Seth."

"They stole something from the outpost."

"Indeed," Phoenix said in the doorway. "Dragonfly found this in the dead creature's robes."

He came to Seth's bedside and took out a roll of parchment. Unfurling it, Phoenix held the old document up for Seth to see. It was a map of North Marsh, drawings of trails that ran through miles of bog and grass. Mountains, forming a bowl around the swamps, lined the top and bottom of the parchment. A large corner was missing in the northwest section of the map. The rest of the document, however, seemed whole.

Seth swept his eyes to the bottom. A date written over a hundred years before rested along the edge. Someone, well before their time, had taken great pains to make the map accurate.

Running a finger along the trail lines, Seth found their outpost. No. It wasn't their outpost. Another massive manmade structure rose above the marsh a few miles from them. Ruins of an earlier time, perhaps?

"You've discovered something? A reason as to why they wanted this map?" Phoenix was watching him closely. "You are part of Western Beta, Ice Lion. Keeping secrets and putting your comrades in harm's way won't go unpunished."

"My ranger needs his rest, sir." Riley stepped between them. "I think this should wait until he's up and about."

"Very well, Logan." Phoenix rolled up the map again. "Be assured we will talk soon."

Seth let out a relieved sigh when the ranger left. He had an idea of why this Lord Gorman was willing to risk so much to steal the map. Seth and the Jackal were looking for the same relic. He had to get out of this outpost and search the ruins before the Jackal tried again—and succeeded.

Chapter Twenty-One

JULIAN STOOD ON the eastern shore of the Constantina, rolling hills and grassy meadows behind him. The river twisted in slow bends down the center of Valdeon, its snaking body dividing the kingdom in more than just geography. A low-hanging moon's reflection covered the leisurely waters. Perhaps such a moon was an omen of further bloodshed.

Lifting his eyes to the distant shores of the West, Julian could think of no other outcome. Plains grass, thriving in rock and heat, waited on the Western range. Such land bore hard men. San Marimosa, the West's greatest stronghold, had withstood invasion. Its men stubbornly insisted on living on, and were a pestilence that must meet fire to eradicate. Death would find them behind their mighty walls once he wore the Regent Medallion.

A soft flutter of wings touched the air behind him. Leaves rustled on the willow grove's weeping branches as a bird landed below its canopy. Frequently fascinated by his Changeling cousin's shapeshifting, Julian found he couldn't turn away from the Western shores of the Constantina. Fate held him in its grip, whispering promises of power.

"He is here, cousin." His nanny's scored face came to stand between him and the view. "The mortal is a boar."

"Good." Julian grinned. "Then he can be properly motivated."

Boar. The Changeling used this term often to describe those mortals of whom they particularly disapproved. Gorman's barbarian warriors were a favorite subject of their disgust. The Jackal general didn't have quite the firm hand on his allies as he supposed, an opportunity Julian vowed to explore further.

Bouncing light from a crystal lantern peeked through the branches. A brutish man with legs the size of tree trunks and a thick, boulder-like body followed uncomfortably behind one of Julian's Changeling fellows. Ambling awkwardly on a crippled foot, the mortal seemed lost among the group of creatures from children's fairytales. Hair, shaven close to a rough scalp, exposed a jagged scar plunging from the crown of his skull down the side of his face. Indeed, the term "boar" was an overly generous description of the ugly beast.

"My Lord Prince," he said. "I am called Tabor, chief man in these parts."

"Are you? I understand you have information for me about the location of a certain barbarian tribesman."

An ugly sneer cast Tabor's features into a grotesque mask of hatred. "Jorge Pacarro, yes. I know where he is." Tabor smoothed at his weak leg. "I gave him a sound thrashing, but the barbarian was able to get in a final shot before he ran like the coward he is."

The Pacarro tribesman was sometimes known as the invisible death. Able to move unseen through both forest and civilization, he was a man who could keep up with rangers in battle. In no stretch of the imagination had this thug gotten the better of Jorge Pacarro.

Julian's laugh broke the silence hanging over the river. Dullard! The branches above their heads shook under the flapping wings of a dozen blackbirds. Tabor recoiled under their rustling wings and sharp talons. Casting an uneasy glance at Julian, he spat an awkward chortle.

"It would appear I have the right man to aid me in my search." Julian patted the jingling coins in the purse hanging from his belt. "My gratitude would be very generous, naturally."

The creases dug deep into Tabor's rock-like forehead. "I can't pay my men with gratitude."

Julian's Changeling nanny leaned closer to the brute, baring its fangs with an impatient sneer. "He means he has lots of money to spend, and it's yours if we're successful in finding the Pacarro tribesman."

"Of course!" Tabor grinned, the greed glistening in his eyes. "I'll take you to the forests outside of San Lucida. He was last spotted there."

"Very well," Julian said. "Go prepare your men. We'll be with you shortly."

Tabor blanched when his Changeling escort beckoned its long-nailed finger. Following the creature under the branches toward shore, he gave Julian a last dubious look and was gone. The boar needn't worry. Barges rather than death awaited them on the waters.

Julian had heard rumors of secret ports where commerce flourished. Trading weapons, drink, and human flesh, the merchants were frequented by the Jackal and Valdeonian opportunists alike. The journey north would be eye-opening, to say the least.

"Our spies already search the forests surrounding San Lucida. Why do we need him?" the Changeling nanny asked.

"My dear cousin. The Jackal drove them from their homes," Julian told it. "They will resist these invaders. Give them a fellow Valdeonian to trust and a little money to spend. You will see a change." He spread his arms wide. "Besides, I am their prince. Have not your spies reported that these refugees await their deliverer?"

Fluttering black wings pushed through the weeping branches. Exploding out of its feathered body, another Changeling came toward them at a run. His black orbs were a jumble of mischief and anticipation.

"Lord Gorman's favorite Jackal pets have come among us, cousin." Its lips struggled with a grin. "Our barbarian friends are exuberant in their killing. They found your ship. The mortal crew met their end quickly."

"The Jackal general is no fool, cousin." Julian's Changeling nanny didn't share the messenger's glee. "He has come for you."

Gorman was a constant nuisance in Julian's eyes. The general wasn't pleased when Julian was within reach, but he wasn't satisfied with his absence either. Julian was an irritant to Gorman as well. Good. Every ounce of discord he could stir in that metal helmet was a point won.

Finding the Regent Medallion was of utmost importance. Indulging the Jackal general's whims would have to wait. Then again, the Jackal seemed determined to locate him. His killing of Julian's crew was a good indicator of Gorman's temper. Pity Marcellus and Zoya hadn't journeyed with Julian on this trip. The Jackal's impulse to kill first and think second could have relieved Julian of his two burdens. Julian tugged irritably at a twig dangling from the nearest branch.

"I may have to go with the Jackal to keep the peace until we're ready to strike. Stay here, cousin. They mustn't see you. I will go out to meet Gorman's messenger boys," he said. "Marcellus and Zoya have betrayed me. My family is all I have left." He placed a hand on his nanny's shoulder. "You know what to do, Chancellor of Valdeon."

Julian pushed out of the tangled branches and bramble surrounding the banks. He turned back and saw himself standing beside the Constantina. His Changeling nanny had replicated Julian's features with disturbing thoroughness. He laughed and nodded at the creature. Julian, despite Lord Gorman's best efforts, could be in more than one place at a time.

"Handsome devil." Julian chuckled as he made his way through the tall grass.

Then he waved when he saw the Jackal troop marching over the rolling hills of the meadow. Smoke and fire from his burning ship made a grim backdrop for their bloodied armor. Stone-faced and devoid of imagination, they demonstrated in their expressions that the beauty of Valdeon was utterly lost on them.

"How delightful. Will you join me for a peaceful walk in the countryside?" Julian invited.

"You are to come with us, Andarian. Lord Gorman commands your presence." The Jackal troop leader thrust a finger toward their prey. "Bind him."

"I would be honored. You won't hear any objections from me."

"Any trouble and you'll be dead. I know of many places to hide a body in North Marsh."

What was Gorman doing in no man's land? Julian let out an irritated sigh as they pulled him forward. He was well acquainted with North Marsh and its northwest coastline. Julian had trapped his father there and defeated Leo's defenders. Being in such a carcass-infested bog again wouldn't be pleasant.

Chapter Twenty-Two

NIGHT HUNG OVER the forest with oppressive heat. Jorge, unable to sleep, moved through the trees like an avenging phantom. The men he'd placed on guard duty were undisciplined merchants and farmers. Though they'd seen their homes overrun in the night, the guards didn't respect the darkness. He'd caught one sleeping and another smoking a foul weed capable of addling the mind. Jorge's discipline had been swift and painful. He could no longer indulge in exercising patience.

Moving unseen among the gentle beams of moonlight, Jorge entered a lonely stretch of trees rimming a gulley. His feet made no sound as he came within a yard of the slumped figure sitting on a rock. The guard, not yet out of boyhood, snored in soft hums.

Jorge stayed hidden among the tree trunks. His were not the only pair of eyes watching the boy sleep. Erthe Mother! Yellow glowing orbs peered into the darkness as the creature stalked closer, its massive paws moving with silent steps toward the oblivious prey. Mad with starvation, the cougar was at its most dangerous.

Jorge reached for his hatchet, but its comforting weight was missing. He cursed himself for a fool. He'd left his favored weapon beside his bedroll in camp, a mistake capable of costing him his life this night. Pulling his knife, he crept slowly around the gully's rim to circle soundlessly behind the predator. The beast, focused on its prize, was unaware it was also prey.

Then the great cat prepared to pounce. Jorge flew out of the trees. He had his knife in the great cat's neck before its paws could land. Fur and sinew twisted beneath his bloodied grasp. The beast threw its head back and forth, trying to reach the man's face and arms. Screeching growls filled the night as Jorge wrestled the cougar. Heart beating wildly, the animal struggled for a few agonizing moments, then fell still at last. Jorge lowered it to the ground with a grieved sigh. Killing a starving animal wasn't sporting, but he couldn't very well have it feeding on the people in his charge.

He lifted the cougar and threw its body at the guard's feet. Death was seldom a silent visitor. Erthe Mother! Still, the boy snored softly. Straight hair fell in dark panels across his round face. Hairless cheeks and a stick-thin frame gave away his age. He suspected the boy couldn't have been more than thirteen or fourteen years old.

"Will it take claws to wake you?" Jorge gave the boy a good whack on the arm.

The child bolted upright. Wide eyes stared at Jorge and then moved to the dead animal at his feet. His thin frame leaned forward, alert and curious. Undisguised excitement crossed his face in the form of a wide grin.

Jorge folded his arms, struggling to suppress his temper. "Death came for you this night, boy. Worse, it could've had one of the babies."

"You killed the beast with just your knife?" The boy stared open-mouthed at Jorge. "Can you show me how to be a hunter like you?"

He jumped off the rock, bringing his lanky body upright. It was Jorge's turn to be surprised. The boy seemed to have no fear of his death. Jorge regarded the child's wide eyes and open curiosity. The leader of his rag-tag troop sighed. This boy would be a good man to have around if he could develop discipline.

"What is your name, boy?"

"Antonio, My Lord." The boy blinked up at Jorge and threw in a quick salute.

"I will teach you the ways of the hunter. The first lesson you must master is discipline. You must stay at your post, alert and ready even though sleep calls for you. Isn't that right, my son?"

"Yes, Father." Duarto huffed, stepping out of the trees with an impatient growl. "It is also important to be armed for the task and not, for instance, leave your weapon behind at the camp."

Antonio jumped out of his skin with a startled cry. His anxiety immediately gave way to curiosity and awe. Duarto, for his part, was pleased he'd made the boy jump.

"Yes. A foolish mistake on my part. Now, Antonio, I expect you to be alert when I come to you at sunrise," Jorge told him. "I go to clean my kill. Its pelt will be a welcome comfort on hard ground."

Duarto helped his father drag the cat off into the trees well outside the perimeter of their camp. Drawing more predators for the sake of a pelt was foolhardy. Jorge knelt beside his kill and began the careful work of skinning. He found little flesh on the cat's carcass, but it would be enough to feed the small children for a few days.

"We must find more willing young men like Antonio." Jorge looked up at his silent son. "They will need someone to lead them. Someone who has had military training and is a strong leader with the great skills of the Pacarro."

"I'm nothing compared to you, My Father. It is you who must lead them."

Jorge began pulling the soft fur away from the flesh. "I cannot lead the hunters and the people at the same time, my son. We must have a Pacarro tribesman at the head of the hunters."

"Will you help me to be worthy of your trust?"

Jorge stood and rested the skin over his arm. "The skill I can help you improve, but you are already worthy of my trust, captain."

After butchering the carcass, they buried its remaining inedible pieces deep in the dry ground. Jorge bound the meat in dried fern leaves. His son handed him one of the thin ropes from his hunter's kit. Jorge took it with a nod. He tied one end of the line around the bundles and threw the other end over a tree branch. Tugging at the rope, Jorge secured the meat well off the ground. It would be safe from predators until morning.

A night owl hooted among the tree trunks behind them. Birds of the night no longer flew in Valdeon. The call was a signal from the hunters that they had returned. He'd sent them to search the trail they'd journeyed across during the day. Someone had followed Jorge and his refugees. They had to know who, and why.

"Take the lead, captain." Jorge tilted his head in a quick movement toward the trees.

Duarto stood straighter, his face unreadable in the darkness. He jogged forward toward the west. The hunters fell into step behind their new captain, accepting his leadership without question. Good. Their approval would make Duarto's difficult command a bit easier.

The men cleared the gulley and continued to run soundlessly through the trees toward the westernmost point of the huddled refugees. Staying well out of the glow of the many campfires, Jorge and the hunters remained within the trees lining the trail the people had covered during the day.

One of the hunters, a man who'd frequently visited Jorge's land to barter for wine, stepped out of the trees. His name may have escaped Jorge's memory, but the man's skills as a tracker became clear. The hunter held out a small stick with fabric wrapped around the tip. It was white with bits of lace clinging to the edges.

"They're getting closer," Duarto said, running suspicious eyes back toward camp. "We must find a way to trap these cunning spies in our numbers."

Jorge examined a group close to the edge of the camp. Three elderly women gathered around the small fire, their worn faces filled with grief and exhaustion. He didn't remember them from San Lucida. Erthe Mother only knew how long they'd walked from Southern Valdeon to reach a place they'd assumed would be safe. A diminished hope danced in their eyes as they ate their small meal. Perhaps the regent of Valdeon was proving to be a disappointment.

"Come, captain," Jorge said in a low voice, turning away from the women. "It is time for the hunters to hunt."

Disappearing into the trees once more, the hunters continued west along the trail. As they went, Jorge swept his eyes across the dirt stretching into a long, winding path before them. The people had taken his lessons seriously, hiding their tracks and being careful not to break branches unnecessarily. Still, he could see telltale signs of human traffic. They must do better. Amateurs couldn't fool the predators who followed them.

Duarto held up a hand, signaling them to stop. He pointed a finger toward a bend in the trail. Jorge crept closer to the tree line for a better look and saw a solitary figure kneeling on the dirt trail. Dressed in the trappings of a hunter, he blended with the dirt, trees, and rock. His hands worked rapidly at his treacherous task. Jorge recognized the marker he was building as identical to the one they'd found earlier.

Then the traitor stepped away from his handiwork. Neto, Jorge's oldest and most trusted friend, turned toward the east with a satisfied grin. The raw pieces of Jorge's heart fractured. Charging out of the trees, he growled a war cry full of hurt and anger.

"Why have you betrayed us, Neto?" Jorge slammed a furious fist into the other man's jaw. "You were a trusted friend, someone I allowed into my home!"

Neto's usually somber expression fell away as an uncharacteristic smile spread across his face. Two dagger-like fangs protruded over the flesh of his lips. Black orbs replaced the normally tranquil eyes. Dark hair flowed down from this fiend's head to cascade in thin rivulets across its shoulders. Sharp features cast a terrifying visage under the obscured starlight.

"Changeling!" Jorge pulled his knife.

"I know someone who would dearly love to hear about the medallion around your neck, Andarian." It pulled a curved blade from beneath the black cloak wrapping about its body. "Perhaps I will cut off your head and take it for myself."

"You won't get the chance!" So shouting, Duarto plunged his blade into the creature's back, twisting with a manic zeal. He followed the Changeling's shuddering body to the ground. It lay still on the dirt, but Duarto's hunger for revenge wasn't sated. He stabbed again and again until the sweat poured down his face.

"Easy, my son." Jorge pulled him away. "It's dead."

"What of Neto?"

Jorge shook his head. "I don't know. I pray this thing of evil hasn't pretended to be our friend for too long. It might have communicated to our pursuers the direction we take the people next."

"Then we backtrack and see how much they know," Duarto said between gritted teeth.

"I don't think we have a choice." Jorge let out a deep breath. "We must be swift and silent."

Hatred drove their pace toward the unknown. This hunting trip was a risk. The people's protection had been left to untrained men guarding them against the darkness. Jorge hadn't assigned leadership to anyone who knew where their promised sanctuary was located. If he and his men died this night, what remained of

Western Valdeon would perish. Sometimes taking a risk, however, was the only option.

They retraced their steps from the day's march, reaching the previous night's camp. Nothing. They saw no sign of the predators who hunted them, but Jorge found another marker the Changeling had left behind. He carefully pointed it toward the southeast. The misdirection might buy them time, should he and the hunters fail to terminate those who would kill them.

Continuing past the campsite, Jorge searched for signs of passage among the dried ferns of the forest. Night began to give way to sunrise. The last stars twinkled among the branches of the trees. The hunters were running out of time.

Then he smelled meat. Its aroma sent his stomach lurching with a growl. Even the Pacarro couldn't hide from hunger forever. Moving carefully up the rise, Jorge dropped onto all fours. The bright glow of several fires filled the camp. Loud laughter and voices echoed among the trees. Food and drink passed merrily between about thirty men. They were mercenaries all, but no Jackal. The fools seemed confident no one would challenge their march through the countryside. Jorge guessed the Changeling was the brains behind their searching.

"Father," Duarto whispered with a strangled gasp. "I've found Neto."

Jorge eased away from the overlook of the camp. Swallowing his anger, he followed his son to a large lump at the side of the trail. The body was shoved haphazardly into a bundle of dried pine needles and other rotting debris. Neto had been dumped like unwanted trash. Dead eyes stared up in fear at the nothingness. Turning his friend's body gently, Jorge cringed at the dark blood staining the dead man's back. His killer had met its end in the same fashion.

"We must leave him," Jorge murmured. "Sadly, this is no burial for such a good friend." He began to unfasten Neto's belt. "Nothing must be wasted. Take extra care when you cover him. It's best those mercenaries don't suspect we know he's dead."

Slowly stripping Neto's body, Jorge said a prayer to the Erthe Mother for his safe passage into the afterlife. Tears wouldn't come. He wrapped the weapons, hunter's kit, and boots in the bloodied tunic. Its new owner would start his life as a hunter with Neto's legacy as armor.

Duarto cast his eyes toward the mercenary camp. "I would dearly love to see their blood flow this night, but so many men…"

"No. We return to the people." Jorge stood, cradling the bundle. "Thirty men could pass through our camp creating a river of blood. We must double our efforts to evade them. Hurry now. The sun rises soon."

Chapter Twenty-Three

SUN STREAKED THROUGH dried branches, sending patterns of light onto the trail. The hunters shared Jorge's silent sorrow for Neto as they ran. Grief had been a constant companion since Valdeon fell; Jorge had underestimated its ability to intensify. He'd lost so many who were dear to his heart. Curse these Changelings and their human minions. Jorge was tired of loss and defeat. He must find a way to expose the remaining spies in their camp and stop the slaughter of those left in the West.

They ascended a rise and came to the spot where Duarto had killed the Changeling. Young Antonio and the malcontent, Santos, were standing over the body. Poking at it with a stick, Antonio wrinkled his nose. Santos tugged at the boy, head shaking with disgust.

"Why aren't you at your post?" Jorge pushed out of the trees in a sudden rush.

"My watch is over, My Lord." Antonio jabbed the dead Changeling again. The light of morning did nothing to dispel the gruesomeness of the creature's appearance. Gray skin had taken on a blue tint while its dead black orbs stared at the nothing of evil's afterlife.

"Did you kill this creature?" the boy asked.

"It's Duarto's kill. Why are you this far away from camp?"

"You didn't come this morning to lead. People were worried." Antonio shrugged. "I came to look for you."

"I followed the boy. We can't have him wandering off alone." Santos stood up straighter under Jorge's glare. "You think more of them are among us, don't you?"

Out of all the men in the camp, Santos was the last person Jorge wished to have paid keen attention to his comings and goings. His bushy silver mustache swayed from side to side while he waited for an answer. Mistrusting eyes narrowed as they scanned Jorge's face. Here was a mind used to exposing lies. Best to give him the truth.

"This creature has been leaving signs along the trail for the group of mercenaries hunting us. You must keep this to yourselves. I don't want panic in camp."

Antonio nodded quickly. "Can I help? Trap the next one, I mean."

"The impetuousness of youth. Our regent has a loyal worshipper." Santos burst out in a laugh and shook his head. "You may not like me, Jorge Pacarro, but you need me."

Santos waved a hand over his head and continued to make his way toward camp. Jorge scowled at the irritating man's back. He felt tempted to tie Santos to a tree for another roving cougar to find.

"We must bury the Changeling. We don't want the mercenaries to discover we've found their deception." Jorge lifted Neto's legacy and handed it to Antonio. "These belonged to a good man. Wear them with honor and never forget he gave his life protecting us."

The boy reverently caressed the buckskin. His fingertip pushed past the dried blood and lifted the back of the well-worn tunic. Antonio, jaw tightening as he removed his finger, raised his eyes to Jorge. A solemn oath passed between them then—Neto's buckskin bearing witness to it.

"Come along, boy." Duarto kicked at the Changeling corpse. "I'll show you how to remove blood from buckskin later. Pay close attention. If you are to be a hunter, then you must know how to hide signs of our passing. Properly disposing of a carcass is part of the job."

Antonio, setting his gear respectfully on a rock, eagerly joined two of the hunters as they dragged the body off into the trees. The boy grinned with a pride Jorge hadn't seen in some time. Even their grisly task didn't deter his enthusiasm.

Santos's words echoed in Jorge's ears. He didn't need worshippers. Trust and perhaps a little faith would see them to the caves. Maybe he should heed his own advice. Rubbing lightly at the gold medallion around his neck, he wished he knew how to activate its power. Or what the extent of its power was, for that matter.

A twig snapped on the trail leading from camp. Three old women shuffled slowly toward Jorge. Their widow's lace and old bones were out of place against the grisly backdrop. They clung to each other as if frightened of the trees about them. Since they frequently fell behind the end of the procession, other generous souls had aided the old women in their march toward the caves.

Kicking dirt over the pool of Changeling blood, Jorge turned to face them. The gentle rebuke upon his lips faded as they drew near.

Worn lace and calico fell away as dark robes materialized. Grizzled hair, pulled tightly against wrinkled skin, began to shift until smooth, gray flesh stretched across their faces and hands. Black orbs, shimmering with amusement, stared at Jorge. Here was evil exposed at last.

"Sometimes it is those we least suspect who can be the most dangerous," one of the old crones said with a cackle.

"You underestimate us, Changeling." Jorge pulled his dagger. "It will be your undoing."

Drawing their swords as one, the three Changelings came at Jorge in a blinding whirl of black and steel. He readied his body, standing in the dirt road alone against the soldiers of evil. His thoughts turned to the gaunt, hopeless faces waiting in camp. Exposed to the elements and left like sheep among wolves, were they lost? No. Duarto could lead them. Jorge gritted his teeth as the first blade struck his dagger. His son, he knew, would not leave his father. Even now the hunters were running toward them.

Then a brilliant golden light burned beneath his tunic. Its heat seared the skin on Jorge's chest. He hissed at the sudden pain, struggling to remain in the warrior's stance. The golden light raced along his skin and down his arms. Jorge dropped the dagger as its handle grew too hot to hold. His hands pulsed with power. He thrust them outward as an electric energy stiffened his muscles.

"What foolery is this?" One of the Changelings snapped its fangs at Jorge. "Julian said nothing about such magic."

Julian, the bastard prince, wasn't content with the betrayal of his people. He still desired the Regent Medallion. Very well. He and his followers would feel its power. Releasing all his hate and pain, Jorge aimed his hands toward the Changelings. The golden light pounced on the evil creatures like a wild animal. It covered their bodies with burning fire, devouring flesh and bone. Even their metal weapons fell away to dust on the ground.

"Jalora, spare me!" Jorge screamed.

The brilliant burning of the Regent Medallion extinguished with a pop. The heat of its magic blackened the tree trunks, dirt, and rock. The three piles of Changeling ash fluttered in the movement of running boots. Duarto and the hunters stopped at a circle about the ash, staring with awestruck horror.

"By the Erthe Mother!" Duarto cried, taking tentative steps toward his father. "It was like the light of a thousand suns."

Jorge dropped his arms, wincing as the burned skin on his hands touched his trouser legs. Duarto took him by the arm and helped Jorge to a rock. He sat down slowly on the warm surface. Pain. It blurred his vision and sent waves of spasms through his weakened body.

"Your hands," Duarto said, swallowing his shock. "They're burned raw. What of the rest of you?"

"My chest where the medallion rests on the skin."

Duarto carefully opened Jorge's tunic. Flinching, his son pulled free the buckskin as much as he could.

His dismayed eyes told Jorge the burn was terrible. Grabbing at the chain, Jorge ripped away the medallion before it could permanently stick to his body. He pulled his tunic closed and placed the necklace on top of the fabric.

"My Lord!" Antonio pointed past the burn marks in the ground. "In the trees!"

Mercenaries flooded toward them out of the thinning branches. Brown cloaks marked their clan of thieves, but these scavengers had traded the rest of their clothing for the spoils of wealthy Valdeonian households. Brandishing heavy chains, the first line of attackers marched toward them. Swinging the metal links upward, they smashed them hard against the burnt ground.

Duarto helped Jorge stand as the rest of the hunters took up positions behind the father and son. Backs to each other, the hunters readied their weapons to fight the mercenaries pouring in from all directions. Jorge cursed himself for a fool. They'd grown careless and left themselves open to ambush. The trap was complete.

"Can you use the medallion again?" Duarto asked.

"I don't know how it works." Jorge cradled shaking hands against his torso. "We must fight our way out of this for the sake of the people."

Jorge and Duarto pressed against each other's backs, waiting for the final rush of men and blades. Greedy faces met their determination. These men cared nothing for Valdeon or Andara. Money was their only desire, and Jorge had none to offer. Anger rose again in his heart, but this time the power didn't come.

A balding man with brass rings in his ears and a leering smirk stepped out of the mob. He shook his head at the little group of hunters standing with hatchets and daggers before their heavy metal weapons.

"Give us the medallion, barbarian. Perhaps we will spare some of your people then—the pretty ones we can sell. A few of the men and children may fetch a price as passable slaves. The rest we won't waste food and water on." He spat on the ground. "Don't tell me you haven't weighed each body's value, Regent of Valdeon. They told me you were clever."

"We will give you nothing, scavenging dogs!" Jorge stood straighter, ready to fight despite his burns.

Then the day blew apart. Dirt, rock, and tree limbs burst into the air in whirling chunks as another explosion thundered along the road. Bits of mercenaries were among the pieces showering down in a dreadful red rain. Duarto pulled Jorge to the ground. The other hunters joined them, covering their heads against the hurled debris.

After the passage of some time, fire and thunder stopped at last. Jorge lifted his head as snapping twigs, and merry laughter filled the lethal scene. Santos climbed down out of the trees and jabbed a blade absently into one of the dying mercenaries. He waved a stick of explosives playfully in his other hand.

"Twenty years of explosives experience with the UR Army should earn me my place among your men. You need me, Regent of Valdeon. And I'm happy to oblige as long as you plan to get even with the men who took my homeland."

Jorge came to his feet to face the irritating malcontent. He regarded Santos more closely. Here was a clever man who knew how to hide the scent of gun powder and explosives. He knew how to transport it and could make it work to their advantage.

"My thoughts exactly," Jorge said. "Once we see the people to safety, I think it's time we cause some trouble for our unwanted guests."

Chapter Twenty-Four

THE OPPRESSIVE ODOR of healing herbs hung heavy in the infirmary—sour scents mixed with sweet in an overpowering stench. Gagging, Seth covered his nose. Even the dank stink of the marshes would smell better than the aroma of healing.

"Hold still!" Riley slapped at the invisible wrinkles in Seth's tunic. "Arthur has just started to set his medicine to boil. It can't smell bad enough for you to carry on like a toddler."

"What's in it?" Seth regarded the bubbling yellow concoction. "Never mind. I don't want to know. And don't try to put any of the stuff on me."

Agile fingers moved quickly, tugging at fabric until the Lion's squire was satisfied with the tidiness of the uniform. Fussing with the sling holding Seth's right arm, Riley nodded. He was, at last, pleased with his ranger's appearance.

"You're on light duty, so you have no need to take your arm out of the sling."

"The wound wasn't deep enough to warrant all this fuss." Seth sidestepped Riley's grip and headed toward the door.

"Are you sure you won't wait for me, Seth?" Riley called. "I have to finish up the kitchen work, but after we could go up to the battlements for a look at *The Protector.* It'll be different seeing the ship from outside this time."

Firefly had returned with fresh supplies. Rumors of mail circulated the outpost, even finding their way into the infirmary. Though they hadn't sent word to Seth's Aunt Charlotte or Riley's family before leaving Lea, the chance of mail from home still gave them hope. Seth's friend had spoken of little else once Gudal had shared the news.

"All right. Meet me outside the mess after dinner. We'll head to the battlements for a look."

Seth hurried out the door, eager to feel the fresh air on his face again. Sheets of heavy rain pummeled the muddy courtyard. Wet drops struck the awning over his head in fast, rhythmic pings. He sucked in a long breath. Even the reek of North Marsh couldn't snatch away his sense of newfound freedom.

Stepping out into the rain, he began to cross the empty courtyard at a jog. Late afternoon sun remained hidden behind blankets of rain clouds. Wet drops splashed at his hands and face. Gloom may have driven ranger and squire alike inside, but Seth welcomed the sensation. He was glad for the chance to take a solitary walk. His thoughts were best explored out in the open, rather than confined to a sick bed.

Drunken laughter parted the falling droplets. Mantis, Gecko, and a handful of their comrades sat under the awning of the mess. The rangers, passing a jug between them, were engrossed in their conversation. Seth set his steps toward the shadows of the storage shed and as far away from them as possible.

"Ho, hero!" Mantis called. "Where are you going? In search of cheering crowds, I suppose?"

He leaped off the patio on unsteady legs and stomped across the muddy courtyard toward Seth. Gecko, sneering as he thrust the jug into another ranger's hands, followed his friend. The others disappeared through the double doors of the mess hall. Their curious glances and whispered talk continued as they gave Seth a last look.

"I asked you a question, apprentice. Where are you going?" Mantis asked, grabbing at Seth's arm. "Are you too important and busy to chat with your comrades now that you're a hero?"

"No, sir."

"You seem nervous, Valdeonian." Gecko grabbed Seth's tunic and slammed him against the wall of the storage shed. "Very wise."

Seth cringed at the pain in his shoulder and turned his nose away from the strong stench of liquor on Gecko's breath. Fury stirred in the depths of his heart. The Lion Spirit was waking. These drunken fools had seen what he'd done to the walls of the battlement. Didn't they understand the dangers of provoking his anger?

"What do you want?"

"You fight with the skill of a bishop ranger, yet you are still an apprentice. I saw the Jalora's power burning around your body and its remnants on the stone where you destroyed the wall. The Jalora is with you, so the Lion Ring can't be fake. The others mutter behind closed doors, worried about what your half-breed blood means for the Legion. But we…" Mantis wagged a finger at Gecko. "We don't fear you, Ice Lion."

A low growl rumbled in Seth's chest. The Lion Spirit's anger was growing. He squeezed his fists harder, struggling to control its deadly power. Seth pulled away from the Gecko's grip.

"Yet you waited to ambush me when I was injured."

Mantis threw an angry fist to Seth's mouth. Hot blood trickled down Seth's chin from the fresh cut on his lip. He thrust his free arm upward to block the next strike. Mantis's fist grazed the shed wall as Seth threw the ranger's body off balance.

"You dare call me a coward?" Mantis pushed away from the shed wall on unsteady legs. "I'll make you sorry you were born a D'Antoiné."

Suddenly, the drunken ranger flew up into the air as a solid ash shape pounded into his torso. Gecko cried out when Mantis slammed into him, sending them both onto the mud. They skidded several feet across the courtyard. The man-sized barrier of ash stopped in the space between Seth and his attackers. It was Dragonfly. He stood in the First Stance. His sword trembled as the fury of the Jalora burned angrily about his body. The dire warning from Seth's ancestors inside the Realm of Mist and Dreams was coming true. In place of the Right-Hand, the Jalora had indeed sent someone else to protect its Lion's honor.

Donny, Dragonfly's squire and younger brother, rushed out of the muddy courtyard and pulled Seth toward a bench out of the rain. Fear. Shock. Disappointment. The wild emotions swirled about Dragonfly's squire in vibrant colors. Seth, horrified, had no words as Donny pulled his sword. He was ready to kill to protect his new charge.

"I call you both cowards," Dragonfly said, his voice heavy with dangerous promise. "An honorable man would not ambush another while he is wounded. A ranger certainly would never attack one of his own unless the Jalora commanded it."

"This is not your affair, Dragonfly!" Gecko bounded to his feet, pulling his sword as he stood.

Mantis, however, remained in the mud. Staring intensely at Dragonfly, he didn't move or speak. Seth's attention was drawn to the unbridled fury bursting about his ranger protector. Dragonfly was unyielding. Mantis acquiescing wouldn't save his life. He had offended the Jalora, and it wanted its due. If Seth didn't stop Dragonfly, blood would spill.

Pushing off the bench, Seth ran past Donny and hurried to stand between the Jalora's punisher and Seth's attackers. The three rangers didn't move or seem to notice Seth trying to block their view of one another. Gecko in particular was ignoring the visible signs of the Jalora's displeasure. His blade shook violently. He was eager to strike in a drunken rage.

"Stop this! A brawl in the mud is no way to settle things."

Dragonfly's gaze flicked momentarily onto Seth. He eased out of the First Stance with a sigh and sheathed his sword. Wiping the wet droplets of rain from his hair, Dragonfly let his arms drop to his side. His body relaxed as the Jalora's fury left him.

Turning his cold gaze on Mantis once more, he said, "I owe Seth D'Antoiné a life debt. If you attack him, you attack me also. Do you understand me, Charles? Next time, I won't hesitate to execute you, as is my right."

Mantis came to his knees and bowed his head. "My hand will never again lift against the Ice Lion. I so swear, My Sovereign Lord."

"Leave me," Dragonfly commanded.

Seth looked at his friend in awe. He had no idea Dragonfly was lord of anything, yet there he was bringing a skilled ranger like Mantis to his knees. Mud splashed and slurped as the two men stomped away toward the barracks. Gecko, still angry, tried to circle back, but Mantis pushed him forward with persistent shoves.

Turning his attention again to Dragonfly, Seth was astonished to find the stern authority was gone and his unassuming air had returned. All this time Seth had been worried about his own problems, never pausing to consider others had their secrets. Who was Dragonfly? Probing his friend out of curiosity didn't seem right.

"Thank you for…" Seth's words failed him. Dragonfly had been willing to kill for his sake, but he'd also been ready to stop at Seth's pleading. No gratitude on his part was big enough for such an act of friendship.

"You'd better let me have a look at you." Donny guided him back to the bench and pulled off the torn sling. Riley wouldn't be pleased when he noticed the mishap. Donny checked Seth's shoulder for additional damage and then moved to the split lip. All the while, Dragonfly stood guard and silently watched the barracks.

"I don't understand why they wanted to hurt you," Donny murmured as he dabbed ointment on Seth's cut. "Ronny and I have known Charles all our lives."

"They're frightened of me, though Mantis denies it."

Seth then nodded his thanks. He pulled on his hood and stepped out into the rain again. The drops pinged against the fabric in steadying beats. Concentrating on their rhythm, he let the anger and unease leave his body.

"These rangers have lost their faith in the Jalora's wisdom." Dragonfly, following, shook his head. "A D'Antoiné has always worn the Lion Ring. It is the king of rings. In times of great trouble, the Lion Ring is what leads us to victory. No one can be certain what will happen if…"

"If someone with mixed blood bears the ring, you mean," Seth interrupted.

"You're my friend, Seth. Who or what you are doesn't matter. My faith in you will never change."

"Well, isn't this romantic? Enjoying your stroll, ladies?"

White Tiger's stealth was infamous among the apprentices. He'd proven his skill once again this night while Seth and Dragonfly were distracted. Sharp eyes scanned them with quick certainty. Seth had the distinct impression the old ranger didn't need the Jalora's magic to read them or their memories of what had happened in the courtyard.

"Phoenix has you on guard duty at the hole in the wall until midnight. Get to it."

"I'm heading there now, sir." Dragonfly threw White Tiger a quick salute and hurried across the courtyard with Donny following closely behind.

White Tiger turned to Seth, not bothering to watch the two of them retreat to the battlements. "Would it be too much to ask for you to get the mail from *The Protector*, Ice Lion?"

Biting back an honest answer, Seth saluted and headed along the wooden walkway toward the UR courtyard. He wrapped the wind about him and skipped across the muddy field between raindrops. Stopping under the battlements, Seth signaled the guard to open the massive gates. Hunched and hooded soldiers waved back. They huddled over a massive chain wrapped around a series of gears. Their sergeant barked an order, and the men began to pull. Locks already unfastened for their visitors, the gates groaned slowly open.

Seth darted through the opening when it was wide enough for a man to squeeze through. The gates groaned closed behind him, temporarily leaving Seth exposed to the marshes. Darkness had begun to push the fading sun from its perch. Hoots and distant growls lifted from the bogs. North Marsh was waking.

Heart pounding, Seth took a tentative step away from the gates. *The Protector* floated placidly beside the docks, its presence a hope for safety. Willing his body forward, Seth raced along the path without stopping until his boots hit wood. He sprinted up the steep docks toward the waiting ship. Laughter thundered above his head when he slipped and teetered precariously to a stop at the gangplank.

"Get back to work, you worthless dogs, or I'll have your heads!" A ranger appeared in the opening at the top of the gangplank. "Identify yourself and your business, apprentice."

Clean-shaven and flawlessly groomed, *The Protector's* first mate, Thunderbird, had been a silent presence of discipline during their three days aboard ship. Seth moved up the gangplank with a small sigh. The first mate knew very well who had come seeking entry. Ignoring the disapproving look Thunderbird gave Seth's uniform and boots, Seth saluted.

"I am called Ice Lion, sir. White Tiger ordered me to pick up the mail."

"Very well. We have a high priority parchment for Phoenix. Wipe your boots. Firefly doesn't like mud on his ship." Thunderbird walked toward a small closet-like enclosure. "Do hurry, Ice Lion. We have a schedule to keep."

Seth scraped the mud from the bottom of his boots against the side of the gangplank as best he could. A little part of him was pleased he'd missed spots along the toes. Firefly's agitation at the small evidence of disorder would give Seth something to muse over during his next round of guard duty.

Thunderbird stepped inside the small space and stood with hands clasped behind his back. Seth, perplexed at his intentions, warily stepped inside. He stood awkwardly beside the ranger as they waited for what Seth couldn't guess. Then the floor moved, shooting them upward. Yelping in undignified panic, Seth pressed his back against the quaking wall. Thunderbird let a pleased grin flutter on his lips.

He motioned for Seth to turn around. Small slivers of light flashed past them as they rose inside the belly of the ship.

"It's called a lift. No other vessel in our armada has one. *The Protector* is the flagship in all the latest Legion innovations."

"I think I prefer the stairs, sir."

"Times are changing, apprentice. We must change with them."

The lift shuddered to a stop as its entry opened onto a bustling room full of rangers preparing to set sail. Seth, still pressed against the lift wall, soon pushed his body away and hurried after Thunderbird as he stepped onto the bridge.

"A guest from the outpost, sir." Thunderbird saluted. "Ice Lion has come for Western Beta's mail."

Firefly sat like an emperor in his captain's chair, sipping a cup of what looked like strong tea. The deacon ranger gave no acknowledgment of their presence or his first mate's words. He remained silent, staring out over the marsh behind a wall of glass. Its gloomy sunset was rather beautiful when seen at this height.

Gaze dropping to the bogs stretching out to the horizon, Seth noticed several long tracks of stone. He suspected these weren't natural. They must be the remnants of pathways he'd seen on the old map of North Marsh. Nature had overtaken pieces of the path, but it didn't necessarily mean the stone had sunk into the bogs. Blade and boots might be able to traverse them.

"Making new friends, Ice Lion?" Firefly sneered, handing a sealed parchment to Thunderbird. "See Phoenix gets this straight away. I need a response before we set sail."

"Yes, sir." Seth took the parchment from the first mate and tucked it inside his tunic.

Thunderbird pointed to a large canvas bag hanging on a hook beside the lift. Taking it to be the mail, Seth lifted the bag with his free arm. Its bulk made him stagger backward, but he managed to steady his body before falling. Seth refused to embarrass himself in front of Firefly and his bridge crew. Stepping back inside the dreaded lift, he waited for the contraption to move.

"I have an excellent view of the docks, Ice Lion," Firefly told him merrily. "It should be quite amusing to see you fall in the mud."

Thunderbird slapped at the side of the wall with a nod and Seth began to fall. He clutched at the bag with a poorly restrained cry. The slow descent suddenly ended with an unsettling bounce. Seth burst out of the lift and hurried across the corridor then down the gangplank like a man freed from prison. Hurrying to base while ignoring the hungry growls from the bogs about him, he shouted up at the walls until the gates mercifully opened.

Adjusting the cumbersome bag, Seth staggered across the mud toward the Legion buildings. The canvas was already getting wet. If he took too long, the rain would soak through. With a pause to lean against one of the storage sheds, he rested the heavy bag on a barrel well out of the mud. He wouldn't be the one to drop someone's precious letter from home in the muck of North Marsh.

"Young idiot!" White Tiger splashed up beside him. "Give me that. Why didn't you get one of the sailors to help?"

"I have an important parchment for Phoenix," Seth said, handing him the mailbag.

White Tiger gave Seth a look the apprentices had seen many times. "You'd better clean yourself up. Phoenix has a way of discovering the truth. He isn't as understanding as I am."

Bending over to view himself in the distorted reflections of the water barrel, Seth straightened his appearance as best he could. Rumpled uniform aside, his split lip was a telltale sign of brawling. He pulled the hood of his cloak down as far as it would go. If he stayed out of the light, perhaps the deacon wouldn't notice. It was raining after all so that his wearing a hood was perfectly natural.

His residence a private cottage befitting his station, Phoenix enjoyed a certain level of privacy not afforded to those of lesser rank. After climbing the rain-soaked stairs to the commander's quarters, Seth walked along the railings toward the front door. As the cottage's occupant whistled a happy Geltic tune from inside, Seth knew Phoenix must be enjoying some rare leisure time. Seth caught the strong aroma of paint. After a sniff, Seth peeked around the door jam. Phoenix sat perfectly still on a tall stool. His fingers held a small paintbrush dipped in a cheery blue. He was utterly engrossed in the large canvas before him.

Seth cleared his throat. Phoenix scrambled to his feet, and the stool toppled with a loud bang. Splotches of bright colors covered the long white jacket he wore. Phoenix, patently flustered, snatched a rag off the floor and hurriedly wiped his hands.

"Excuse me, sir. Firefly needs your reply before he sets sail." Seth stepped inside and handed Phoenix the parchment. Trying hard to ignore the spots of blue transferred to the page, Seth stayed put as the deacon moved to a small writing desk beside the window.

Seth's eyes strayed to the painting. A woman with long golden hair and intelligent green eyes stared out of the portrait at her surroundings. She was stunning. The enigmatic smile on her face spoke of sharp wit. Expert details within the painting illustrated her beauty and charm in their subtlety. Seth turned an astonished look on his commander. He didn't know anything about culture, but for his money, Gregory Baldemar was a true artist. Seth wondered if the lady knew how much her prince worshipped her.

"What do you think of the painting, Ice Lion?"

Phoenix shuffled the parchment about the desk as his finger fumbled to grasp his wax and stamp. Blue eyes darted quickly from his desktop to the painting. Here was a man who possessed deadly skill with a blade. How was it possible those same hands could create such beauty?

"I think it is remarkable, sir. She seems as if she would step out of the canvas and into the room at any moment."

"I wish it were true." Phoenix swallowed with a small nod. "The lady is Alicia Lambert, my fiancé.

You were kind enough to rescue her aunt and cousin in Lea."

Seth remembered well the experience of charging into the thieves' district to rescue the unlucky ladies. They'd been shopping for wedding items on behalf of the young bride in the painting. Seeing the love Phoenix bore for his Alicia, Seth was sorry he hadn't brought back her possessions as well.

"I hear *The Protector's* engines. Firefly isn't a patient man. Take this back to the ship, apprentice."

Phoenix handed Seth the parchment. He was about to turn when the deacon grabbed his arm. Phoenix threw off Seth's hood and clutched at his face for a closer look.

"Who did this?"

Seth shifted uncomfortably and remained silent. It would be worse for him if the commander found out. Power gripped his mind as Phoenix's probing began. The touch was none too gentle this time. Seth was hard pressed to block.

Phoenix sighed angrily. "Fine. Have it your own way, but I will find out who did this."

"I had better get the reply back to Firefly before the ship sails, sir."

Hurrying down the stairs of the cottage, Seth cast a look back. Phoenix stood in the doorway. Anger. Regret. Violence. They stormed around his body in frantic spirals. Seth turned away with a sigh. If Phoenix took revenge on Mantis and Gecko, then the battalion would undoubtedly come to hate Seth. Trapped behind walls with nowhere to hide, would he face more threats from his comrades?

Chapter Twenty-Five

HUNGRY RANGERS FILLED the mess. Their forks clinked against dinner plates as food vanished before them. They may have been mighty lords of noble birth, but men were men at dinnertime. While they leaned across tables to swap stories, their many languages spoken at once made the glasses on the sideboard jingle. Riley, as he spent more time around them, realized they were indeed men rather than the god-like idols people assumed them to be. Gods, after all, weren't prone to spilling soup on their sleeves.

Riley scratched absently at the back of his hand. He and his fellow apprentice squires had spent the afternoon setting up warmers on the long sideboard. One of the blasted things had left a small burn mark while he wasn't paying attention. Arthur had made the mishap what he called a "teaching opportunity." He'd showed them a mixture of herbs that acted as a burn ointment. Riley hadn't minded. He'd learned something valuable from the incident.

"They're late today," Selby said behind him.

Standing in line, the squires waited for their turn at the vegetable ladle. Eager hands scooped bowls of steaming ham and cabbage onto the fancy plates. Back and forth the squires would go, putting second and third helpings of the dishes before their rangers. Selby was right. If Seth and his friends didn't hurry, the best cuts of meat would be gone.

Gudal suddenly stepped out of line and headed toward the sideboard. Selby and Lucas joined him. Bear's massive body was hard to miss even in a crowded mess hall. Stallion and Badger walked gloomily beside him. The apprentices sank on the bench with slumped shoulders. Riley shook his head. White Tiger must have worked them hard again today. Great gulls. Where was Seth? Before he'd left the infirmary, they'd agreed to meet here. Had Seth forgotten?

Riley leaned a hand on the wall and lifted onto his toes. Searching over the heads of the dining rangers, he scanned the many faces. Seth wasn't in the mess hall. Well, no telling what Seth's curiosity had descended on while he was romping around on his own. Riley rubbed the back of his neck with a frustrated grunt. If he left the line now, he might miss his ranger.

"Perhaps Ice Lion went back to the barracks," Selby said, passing him with a plate full of food. "I'll ask Badger if he's seen your ranger."

"Aye. Good idea."

Seth promised to take it easy. Was he wandering the soggy outpost on his own again? He'd seemed impatient and sullen as they'd parted earlier. Ice Lion needed a friendly ear. They hadn't had a great deal of time to speak with each other since arriving at this water-logged outpost. Something was bothering Seth—Riley was sure of it. Best to get it out of him before Ice Lion ended up in trouble again.

Selby leaned over the apprentices' table, speaking to them in a low tone. Shaking heads told Riley what he needed to know. It was time to go looking for the wayward Ice Lion. He was about to turn around and head back to the kitchens when the mess hall doors boomed open.

Phoenix filled the doorway. Eyes blazing with fury, he marched through the tables. Riley fancied he saw small flickers of light coming from the ranger's golden head. But he wasn't the only one who'd noticed the deacon's power burning about his body. Ranger and squire alike stopped what they were doing and remained entirely still. Every eye in the hall followed their commander as he stormed to the center of the room.

"Someone in this battalion has attacked a wounded man." His cold blue eyes scanned the rangers at each table. "My apprentice will not divulge the names of his assailants, but I will have them all the same."

Seth! Riley pushed out of line at a run. Without hesitation, a hand grabbed him by the back of the collar and lifted him off his feet. It was Dragonfly. He put a finger to his lips. Then the ranger sat down and pulled Riley behind him. A strange heaviness descended upon Riley's body. His breath came in anxious gulps. His heart seemed to struggle inside his chest. Invisible needles pricked his skin.

Sneaking a look around Dragonfly's shoulder, Riley immediately regretted not staying hidden. Phoenix had crossed the distance like a bad thought. The outline of his body rippled with erratic waves of light, making him appear as if he'd grown to several times his real height. The ferocity in his gaze froze Riley in place.

"You know something, acolyte. It must be important for you to abandon your post."

Dragonfly maintained his respectful posture. Riley admired his ability to stay calm in the face of such undisguised fury. In contrast, Riley was itching to run for his life. He'd seen Phoenix angry before, but never like this. He had murder in his eyes.

"The matter has been resolved, deacon."

"Not by me." Phoenix leaned in closer. "You may have been sent here at the Dragon's request, but I still command this battalion."

An invisible hand shoved Riley away from the rangers. He skidded to a stop a few feet to the side. Bodies tense, Phoenix and Dragonfly maintained constant eye contact. The serene faces of the two rangers couldn't hide the struggle of wills between them. Riley looked from one man to the other. They'd tear each other apart.

"What in the green, green fields do you think you'll accomplish by quarreling with one another?" Riley put his fists on his hips. "We'll have the rain barrel in here in a minute to cool your tempers if you don't stop."

He had no idea if anyone possessed the courage to support him, but his threat seemed to have the desired effect. Phoenix took a pace back and let his shoulders relax. Dragonfly, released from the mental struggle, fell into a casual stance. The two rangers continued to regard each other, nonetheless, with a dangerous intensity.

"Why do you protect those who lay violent hands on their comrade?" Phoenix asked. His anger hadn't gone far.

"Ice Lion has no desire to see them harmed. I cannot act against his wishes."

Aye. That sounded like something Seth would say. He was too forgiving to suit Riley. First, his best friend had tolerated Pavel Sandor's foul temper for his mother's sake. And what did Seth get for his trouble? The Tslavic assassin, disguised as their school's headmaster, had poisoned Seth and his mother. Then Phoenix had put a dagger to Seth's throat back in Lea before the deacon realized Seth was the Lion Protector. Riley grumbled at the phantom memory of Esteban the Hawk's weapon at his own throat. The bishop ranger had broken the code by threatening another ranger's squire. It was an insult to the Lion and something Riley wouldn't forgive. He shook his head. If Riley had Seth's powers, he'd have thrown them all in a deep hole by now.

"You see," Phoenix said. "The Lion's squire has more common sense than his ranger."

"Here now!" Riley gave both men the full brunt of his sour frown. "Isn't probing another ranger's squire against the rules?"

"Forgive us, Lion's squire, but we must use every avenue in the protection of your lord." Dragonfly sighed and closed his eyes. "I release the knowledge you seek, Partisan, for our Lion's sake."

In an instant, Phoenix had what he'd been after. Exploding in an angry growl, he twisted his body with a speed Riley hadn't imagined possible. He fell upon

Mantis and Gecko like a fierce storm. Their heads smacked together with what sounded to be a painful whack. Phoenix dropped the two rangers on the floor before him.

"What did you think would happen if you harmed the Lion?" Phoenix took an angry breath. "I am the Master's Partisan. Have you forgotten yourself and who you serve? Be gone! If I look at you any longer, even Ice Lion's magnanimity will not save you. White Tiger." He threw the words over his shoulder at his second-in-command standing quietly by the door. "Give them the worst assignment your fertile imagination can concoct."

Then Phoenix was gone, leaving uncomfortable whispers to circle about the room. Nobody moved. Neither ranger nor squire dared look at Mantis and Gecko, who remained on the floor. Their squires, Riley noticed, had judiciously exited to the kitchens.

"I never want to see our commander's temper again," Cal the Stallion said at Riley's shoulder.

The apprentices and their squires had come to stand with Riley. Fists still lifted in warning, they'd been ready to stop any nonsense from behind. He nodded his thanks. Seth had gained something here in the muck of North Marsh. He'd found loyal friends who'd stick with him no matter what the cost to them.

"Go back to your dinner, apprentices. You'll be standing guard at the base of the hole in the wall with Dragonfly tonight." White Tiger moved past them without a glance. His attention riveted upon Mantis and Gecko. Their punishment, no doubt, would be the worst sort of hell. Riley could have no sympathy for them, not after what they'd done to Seth.

"I'd better find my ranger." Riley gave Dragonfly an awkward smile. "I'm not sure what happened tonight, but thank you for helping Seth, sir."

"It was my greatest pleasure." Dragonfly stopped Riley again. "Keep Ice Lion out of the mess tonight. The rangers are...unsettled. And if you would do me a great favor, Lion's squire." He nodded in the direction of the barracks. "If you discuss the events of this evening, would you omit what happened between Phoenix and me? My brother has had a troubling evening."

"Fair enough." Riley gave Dragonfly a quick nod and hurried out of the mess, leaving the murmuring diners behind him. Finding the kitchens empty, he made his way past dirty pots and messy counters. Arthur might not like his shirking the cleanup, but he suspected the old squire would understand. Riley's first duty was to his ranger.

Grabbing his cloak off its hook in the squire's mudroom, he pushed out the door and into the unrelenting rain of North Marsh. A man could drown in this water if he weren't careful. Riley headed back to the barracks stomping along the slippery wooden path.

The warm glow of the fire in a newly kindled potbelly stove danced about the walls of the barracks' mudroom. Its heat took the chill from Riley's body. No time to dawdle in comfort, however. Seth's cloak was missing. Turning the latch with determined fingers, Riley breached protocol and ran through the halls still wearing his muddy boots. Arthur would have him mopping the entire building in the morning.

"Ice Lion. Hello in the house! Are you in here?"

Crystal lanterns flickered inside the apprentices' chambers. Empty beds and a vacant space greeted Riley. He slapped a hand on the door jamb and kept moving. On the run toward the common area, Riley stopped dead and stepped inside. Seth wasn't in there either. Then again, Riley doubted the apprentices even knew of its existence. White Tiger kept them hopping with little opportunity for leisure time.

Riley popped his head into the squire's barracks for a quick look. Empty. Donny was probably still guarding the wall in his ranger's place. The squires all slept in the same long room with the exception of Roland and Arthur. They had quarters befitting their rangers' stations. One day Seth would be a deacon ranger—Riley knew it in his bones. Then he would have a room to himself. He shook his head. Seth had to survive North Marsh first.

A quick jog in the night's chilly drizzle brought Riley to the infirmary—no Seth. The squire took a deep breath and stepped off the path into the muddy courtyard. Heading back out into the rain and darkness, he ran across the yard. Where would Seth be after a sound beating? Aye. He'd be hiding from his anger, no doubt. Most likely he would be in some place rangers didn't frequent.

Snapping his fingers, Riley exited the Legion courtyard and entered the world of the UR Army. Bright lights burned from the lively mess hall at the far end of the outpost. Music and laughter sent merry tones over the mud and into his ears. Riley tapped a finger on his hip to the beat of the tune. Part of him missed the casual banter among regular folk like himself.

Most of the squires were nobles used to stuffy castles and even stuffier company. The atmosphere was a little too much to stomach sometimes for a woolie farmer from Marianna.

Seth, though he was named crown prince of troubled Valdeon, had been born and raised on the same island as Riley. He'd never cared for pomp and circumstance. He'd choose to hide among regular folk until his temper left him. Riley was sure of it.

A mournful creak rasped from the wall. Riley spun about, grabbing for a sword he'd left in the barracks. The walls cast monstrous shadows over the courtyard. Creeping closer, he let his eyes search the darkness of their base. Then he noticed the gates were open wide enough for one man to pass through. Great griping gulls! Could Seth be out in the marsh?

He eased through the opening in the gates, cringing at the growls and howls from the bogs about him. Why hadn't the UR guards closed the barrier? What a nightmare. *The Protector* had already set sail. No one had any reason to be roaming around the docks. Every soul in the outpost had been warned not to go outside the walls after dark. What was Seth thinking?

Then he felt it—power pulsed from under the docks. Riley recognized the sensation. He'd tried to follow it on Carlotta when Seth had disappeared into the jungle each day. The Jalora was in North Marsh and speaking to its Lion.

Slipping and jerking down the path, he followed the Jalora's unmistakable presence. Here he was going outside the safety of the gates after dark with no sword. The night's madness had overtaken him. Yellow orbs glowed with hunger as they watched him walk. The beasts made no move to approach. They, too, were frightened by the Jalora's vast power.

Stopping at the edge of the wooden docks, Riley was overwhelmed by the raw energy all about him. He stumbled to his knees under the weight of it and crawled along the boards toward a small glow of pulsing light. Riley peered between the cracks in the board. By the green, green fields. Seth sat upon an old barrel. His face was aglow with the pulsing light of the Lion Ring. Its bright fingers touched every inch of the surface below the docks until even the smallest shadow was cast out.

"This quest you have given me is impossible," Seth said. "And now the rangers hate me. Why must I stay with them?"

Riley's ranger sat silently for a moment as if he was listening. Then Seth's head dropped to his chest. He ran trembling fingers through his wet hair. Riley's best friend's shoulders drooped in utter defeat.

"Of course, it will be as you say. But, can't you give me another clue? I don't know where to look." Seth slammed a hand against the barrel. "I need to know if the thing is in the old ruins. Very well. I'll go tonight. It isn't far." He jumped off his seat and sank into the mud. "Wait! Why can't I go? Don't leave! Not yet!"

The glowing light swept along the grass and mud beside the docks. Its power sent waves of dark liquid spraying over the curious beasts waiting for a quick meal. Yelping, the animals ran for open marshland. The Jalora continued its dance along the docks, rattling the boards as it flew over them. It brushed against Riley, stopping for a moment to cling to him and then disappeared into the rainy night. Shaking a bit, Riley eased onto his belly and dangled over the side of the dock.

"What's happening to me?" Seth threw a rock into the marsh and watched it sink into the mud.

"You could be going mad, talking to yourself," Riley told him.

Seth grinned and shook his head with a frustrated laugh. Well, a laugh was better than a shout. Riley hung his legs over the side and dropped down into the mud to stand by his friend.

"A rumor is going around you were roughed up," Riley said.

The squire gripped Seth's arm and put a hand gently on his lord's chin, lifting his face, the better to examine him. Ointment glistened on the split lip. A squire, Donny most likely, had tended to Seth. Riley owed his new friend a favor.

"Mantis and Gecko did this?" Riley asked. "Why?"

"How did you know? Did Dragonfly tell…"

"Don't look so surprised. Nobody had to say a word. Phoenix stormed into the mess yelling about someone roughing you up while you were injured. He said you wouldn't tell him who did it, but he wanted the truth right then and there."

"And did Mantis and Gecko confess?"

"They didn't get the chance." Riley grinned. "Phoenix has a nasty temper."

"Fantastic." Seth sat back down on the barrel. "They attacked me because I frighten them, Riley.

If what they said is true, then the rest of the rangers feel the same way. Why did Hawk send me here?"

Riley rested a hand on Seth's shoulder. "Come on. A hot meal will do wonders. You can tell me then what impossible quest you're on this time."

"You heard?" Seth nodded and sighed. "The Jalora commands I look for a lost relic. It's supposed to be hidden in the marsh someplace."

By the green, green fields. This quest sounded harder than finding the Book of Ancients hidden in the middle of the Obsidian Citadel. Life as the Ice Lion was never going to be easy.

"Do you know what this thing is we're looking for?" Riley bumped Seth's good shoulder. "Yes, *we*. And don't think you're going to be running around the marsh on your own."

"I have no idea what it is." Seth hesitated a moment. "I was told I would know when I'm near it."

"Sounds mysterious, and mysteries are best solved on a full stomach. Come on, let's go back to the barracks, and I'll grab us a plate of delicious boiled meat and vegetables." They both grimaced. "Well, at least it's hot."

Seth's spirits seemed to have lifted for now, but Riley well knew his lord's impatience. He would have to keep a careful eye on his ranger from now on. Charging out into the marsh alone could be a death sentence, even for the Ice Lion.

Chapter Twenty-Six

COLD ASHES PUFFED into the air, escaping the soles of Wolf's boots. Any embers had died days before when fire and sword had finished their work. Trickles of hesitant snowflakes struggled to reach the ground. Wolf wiped the tiny bits of white off his face. Their icy touch would be the only burial for the unlucky victims who'd met their end.

This pile of rubble was the third Buellander village they'd discovered on their journey for the truth. Jaguar, an expert tracker, was able to read telltale signs on the ground. All of the communities had shared the same systematic end. The Jackal rounded up their victims in the village meeting house, locked them inside, and set fire to the building. These barbarous villains had grown slack this time. Wolf let his arms fall limply at his side. They'd allowed a victim to slip out of their death box.

Desperate to escape the flame, a woman had broken away from her captors. Strawberry hair peeked out from the scarf she'd worn about her head. Green eyes, filled with wild fear, stared into Wolf's soul. Her pale face had faded into a bloodless mask. Protective arms remained wrapped about the tiny baby stretched limply upon her breast. Wolf choked on his horror.

A Jackal sword had pierced them both in a single strike and nailed them to the ground.

Though Wolf turned away, the mother's frightened eyes still burned into his memory. He'd carry the image with him for eternity as another innocent he couldn't save. Then, in his mind, her skin began to change its pigment. The horrific imaginings of his dead wife and children came to him in the ashes of the Buells.

"Dulcina," he whispered.

"Wolf." Jaguar grabbed his shoulder, snatching him away from his recollections. "We have company."

Revulsion. Anxiety. Suspicion. The emotions hung about the branches of evergreen. Wolf, engrossed in his contemplation, hadn't sensed the Jalora's power approaching at their backs. He lifted his arms slowly, signaling his guardsmen to do the same.

"Why do you hide?" he asked at last. "Do we not serve the same master?"

Five rangers, their swords at the ready, stepped out of the trees. Their leader, a deacon level two, pulled off his hood. Straight black hair fell in thick strands about his stern face while ice-blue eyes glared at Wolf and the Lords of Valdeon with severe concentration. Known as Eagle, he'd become a legend during the border wars as he'd fought beside Edmund the Leo.

Wolf pulled off his hood and gave the ranger a nod of greeting. They'd never been more than idle acquaintances. The bad blood between the De Vincente and the D'Antoiné families had soured a few relationships for Wolf with Leo's more ardent supporters. Eagle ranked near the top of Leo's greatest admirers.

"A murder scene in the wilds of Western Buell is the last place I'd expected to find you, Wolf," Eagle said. "Word reached us of trouble in Lea. It seems Esteban the Hawk claims you've gone mad. He says you believe yourself to be the Right-Hand."

"He dares try to discredit Wolf when it is he who aids the Jackal against Andara!" Ferret sent hot spittle into the trampled snow. "I've seen it with my own eyes, sir."

"Let Hawk screech in the night like a wounded bird. The truth will out eventually." Wolf silenced Ferret with a glare.

His young guardsman hadn't noticed the continued ribbons of suspicion around the group of rangers. They were troubled and confused by Hawk's accusations. Ferret, their occasional comrade, now disputed the bishop's claims. Wolf had undeniable proof of being named as Right-Hand. Hawk, however, must rely on fear to feed his lies. Unfortunately, fear was a powerful weapon when used by a cunning manipulator.

"And what do you believe, Eagle?" Wolf asked. "You still have your swords drawn. I wonder if you'll use them against the Sacred Guard."

"Two powerful servants of the Jalora make the same claim." Eagle lifted an eyebrow and shrugged. "Why not return to Lea and provide proof you are the Right-Hand. You'd settle the matter and put the Bishops Council at ease. Dragon's word is the only thing keeping them from each other's throats."

"I have more pressing matters here. We've no time to play politics." Wolf gestured around him at the burned village. "You'll find more villages in this state.

The Jackal has built a fortress nearby. They plan to use the Buells as a pathway for a large invasion force."

"You have a plan to stop them. Very well." Eagle sheathed his sword with a definitive thud. "Young Ferret is an excellent linguist, but you'll need a guide who knows this land."

"What about the warning from Lea?" one of Eagle's companions asked.

Wolf had earned a chance from Eagle to prove their claims about the Jackal invasion. His men wouldn't give their trust so easily. The rangers were in an awkward position. Each of them had sworn to serve the Sacred Guard, whether or not a Jalora Master walked the Erthe. Now they were being asked to choose between two of the guard's highest-ranking members. That presented an impossible choice.

"Soldiers in the field don't have the luxury of political banter," Eagle said. "Our blood and sweat keep evil away from the innocent. Not the politicians' useless words. Never forget it. Now, return to the battalion. Put North point Outpost on high alert."

"Yes, sir."

The rangers, relieved to have someone of a higher rank make their decision for them, immediately ran to obey. Eagle stepped through the snow bank and joined Wolf in the desolate ruins of the village.

"You trust me then?" Wolf asked.

"I trust my eyes." Eagle rested his gaze for a brief moment on the woman and her babe. "Come. I know of a wandering camp of nomads who plague the foothills of the Bloodtooth Mountains. It's a favorite den for smugglers. They've managed to elude us for many months. I believe they're able to detect our presence as we approach somehow."

A few awkward hours dragged by as they journeyed northwest along the foothills. The young Lords of Valdeon remained subdued, eager to avoid Eagle. His account of Hawk's manipulations in Lea had both surprised and angered them. Wolf, for his part, was troubled by the news. The Bishops Council would have easily detected such lies before Valdeon fell. The Jalora's power was waning quickly. Andara needed its Lion at full strength. His body tied together the Jalora and the land. Should the Lion fail, every soul on the continent was in peril.

Eagle's silent form suddenly shifted. He leaned on the bridge of the *Wind Chaser*, looking down at the vast sea of evergreen trees whooshing by beneath them. A triumphant laugh erupted from his mouth in a hearty baritone.

"We've got them!" Eagle pointed at a spot on the tree-lined horizon where clouds of smoke steadily rose into the skies. "You'll want to ease up on your speed, My Lord the Fox. We don't want them to know we're coming."

"Why would such evasive nomads allow the smoke from their campfires to be so visible? It's rather convenient," Fox answered, bringing the engines to a slow stop. "I don't like it."

"I always suspect a trap," Eagle said. "It keeps me alive. Let's go, Wolf, before we're spotted."

He gave a last nod to Fox and then hurried down the stairs to the deck in a rush of excited anticipation. Wolf well understood his desire for the hunt. These thieves and smugglers had eluded Eagle and his men for many months. To put such desires aside for the time being was best, however. More than thievery was at play here.

"I don't like this, Wolf." Fox's eyes remained on the staircase. "The *Wind Chaser* is an easy target against a blue sky."

"If you see any signs of trouble, I want you to do what you must." Wolf stopped at the top of the stairs. "Collect Ice Lion at North Marsh Outpost should I not return. Take him to safety."

Wolf descended the steps and walked onto the deck as Eagle was speaking with the young rangers and their squires. Engrossed in his tale of the hunt for these smugglers, the young men had momentarily forgotten their anxiety Eagle's presence had inspired.

"We can enter the village from the trees to the north. They may be overconfident about their cleverness," Eagle told them. "If we're lucky that is."

"Creatures out of childhood nightmares serve the Jackal cause. We must show caution." Wolf turned to his men. "Jaguar. Ferret. You're with me. The rest of you stay alert aboard ship. We may have to make a quick exit."

Anger. Frustration. Disappointment. These emotions fumed from Tulio the Rabbit. Grief, once casting a heavy shadow over this young guardsman, had turned into unappeasable hatred. Wolf had seen what such loss could do to a man. He'd been in this state once until the Jalora had taken him in hand. The Jalora had reminded Wolf of his sacred duty. Grief and anger had no place among the Sacred Guard until Ice Lion was safely seated upon his throne.

"May I speak with you, sir." Tulio's face was a mask of red determination. "Please."

"You have your orders." Wolf moved to the launch the squires had prepared for them.

"But I would be of more use to you on the ground!"

Wolf grabbed Tulio by the collar and shoved him against the bridge wall. "Your anger almost compromised our last scouting mission into the Jackal fortress. Why do you imagine I can trust you now?" Wolf released him as the burning shame came to Tulio's face. "Go below and spend the time contemplating your unsettled heart. Ask the Jalora for its perfect wisdom."

Stepping onto the launch, Wolf gave one last look at those remaining onboard. The reproof he'd given Tulio was a reminder for the rest of them as well. They were the Lords of Valdeon, bound by their very souls to the Lion as his Sacred Guard. Loss of control was inexcusable. They must master their inner demons before the Joining or suffer a worse fate than mere physical death.

Eagle took the rudder and lifted their launch off *Wind Chaser's* deck. He brought them down at a steady speed to skim over the treetops. Scanning the vast sea of green forest, he seemed to find what he'd been searching for and sailed half a mile to the south. Pointing with a nod to Wolf, Eagle hovered over a small break in the trees. Burnt limbs from an old fire budded with fuzzy green life. The tree's withered arms, however, hadn't parted far apart enough to embrace a launch.

"Use the ropes to tie the launch to the thickest branches you can find. Keep it solid and in place." Eagle took one of the ropes and leaped onto the nearest tree. "I hope you don't mind a climb down."

Wolf grabbed another rope. Following Eagle's example, he jumped into the waiting embrace of the boughs. These northern pine trees were massive. Their trunks were thicker than three men huddled together, and their height reached taller than most buildings in Valdeon. Sticky pine tar gripped at his hands and uniform. Wolf wiped at the clear sap. Curse it. The sap wasn't coming off without help. Basilio wouldn't have an easy time getting the determined substance off the cloth.

Using the Jalora's gifts of speed and agility, the rangers raced down the tree trunks and landed soundlessly on the forest floor. Winter had brought thick snow to this part of Andara. Wolf sank to his knees in the white powder. None of the Valdeonian rangers were accustomed to the sudden chill. Eagle, on the other hand, seemed not to notice. He trudged forward, gradually accelerating until his boots skipped across the top of the snow.

"That's a neat trick," Jaguar said.

"Yes, it's practical too. Come on."

Wolf picked up speed until the snow fell away from his boots as well. Ferret had spent a great deal of time under Eagle's command. He had no problem keeping up, but their comrade from the grasslands of western Valdeon wasn't having an easy time. Jaguar grumbled colorful curses as he stumbled. Chilly white flakes sprayed onto his face and down his tunic.

"Keep up, ranger. We don't want to lose you in the snow." Eagle threw an amused look at Jaguar.

Running at top speed across the snow, they traversed the forest with the ferocity of a chilly winter wind. Wolf's nose caught the scent of burning wood and roasted meat. Eagle, too, apparently had noticed the signs of civilization. He gave the signal to stop. Crouching down at the base of a massive tree trunk, he put a finger to his lips. Wolf knelt beside him to peer past the tree. Here, at last, was the nomadic camp. It wasn't what Wolf had expected.

A series of one-room buildings tucked away under the massive evergreen branches formed a makeshift village. Several small homes gathered close together, while an active market shaped the village hub. Wolf was astonished by the working smithy's shack and the busy trading post where women entered and exited at a brisk rate. Impossible to see from overhead, the village had been carefully designed to match the dirt and green of the trees. No small wonder this place had escaped the Legion's notice.

Men dressed in leather and furs walked between the buildings, bartering with their neighbors for goods or merely chatting to pass the time. A significant number of them were flocking to a larger shack framing the opening to a small cave. Kept well away from the village proper, the building seemed the social center for Buellander males. Women of apparently questionable moral compasses laughed and greeted them at the door. Coins exchanged hands as the women escorted them inside. Wolf shook his head. He was glad the younger of their numbers had stayed aboard ship.

"Drink makes a man's tongue and his wallet free." Eagle stood and pointed to the rough-looking pub attached to the brothel. "Shall we move closer?"

Wolf would have preferred caution over Eagle's need to take risks, but Eagle did have a point. They'd not learn anything useful squatting here in the snow. He nodded, allowing Eagle to take the lead. They were in his world of snow and trees now. Following someone who knew how to navigate such terrain was best.

Staying close to the trees, they moved behind the rickety pub. The structure was roughly put together and had the appearance of a contraption easily taken down and erected again. On closer inspection, Wolf noticed all the buildings were of the same design. Eagle had been correct. This entire village was portable.

"Welcome, rangers!" a coarse voice said behind them. "We're honored."

Armed men swarmed out of the trees to surround them. Most were Buellander thieves. The others who flowed out of the buildings like metallic harbingers of death, Wolf recognized well. Jackal. These villains had hunted him in the forests of Varianne as he tried to escape Valdeon. They'd come in the darkness and burned an entire country in one night. Now the Jackal was preparing to do the same to Andara. How could four rangers stop them?

Chapter Twenty-Seven

BANG. BANG. BANG. Steel hilts slammed relentlessly on metal chest plates. The sound pounded against Wolf's ears, bringing the blood rushing from his troubled heart. Had this been what the innocents of Valdeon heard when the Jackal had invaded their shores? These killers had been met with fear then. Here in the wilds of the North, they'd meet fury and death.

He counted thirty warriors circling about them in the slush and mud. Disciplined and seasoned soldiers, they stayed in a perfect formation. The Buellanders—notorious cowards all—stayed back, preferring their barbarous friends to fight for them. Hooting and laughing, they threw taunts at Wolf and the other rangers.

"The Jalora's curse upon every last one of you," Wolf told them. "You may escape me this day, but you can't outrun your fate."

Every Andarian, good man or blaggard, feared a curse from a member of the Sacred Guard. Such a damning was more than mere words. Magic was behind their sentiment, and it beckoned to be unleashed by the Jalora's will. A curse from a Lord of Valdeon was a death mark upon a man's very soul. Its magic struck the transgressor, his family, and every possession he owned.

The Buellanders stopped laughing. Silent fear crept among their numbers as they made useless protective hand motions before their bodies.

The Jackal, unimpressed by such displays of superstition, used the distraction to attack. Bloodstained braids banged against metal chest plates as the Jackal came at them. The foul odor of dried blood and unwashed bodies struck first. Wolf brought his death mask to his face. Its power blocked the putrid stench. His sword met the first blade. He knocked it away and drove his weapon through metal and flesh until it burst out of the vermin's back. Giving the hilt a vicious yank, Wolf pulled his sword out of the body. Grim satisfaction swelled in his heart as he regarded the dead man. Vengeance. It could consume a man, and yet the Jalora didn't scold him. Their Master, too, felt pleasure at this taste of blood.

Then they swarmed him. Blood and braids. Metal and swords. Wolf pulled more of the Jalora's power about him. He brought his blade up in a deadly arc, sending severed hands flying. Four rangers against thirty seasoned soldiers? In his current temper, he felt as if he could kill them all on his own a thousand times over.

"For Valdeon!"

Rabbit burst out of the trees, spraying snow and pine needles in his wake. He zipped between the Jackal in a whirlwind of ash and steel. Their youngest came about in a full circle to send a wave of snowflakes at the Buellander traitors trying unsuccessfully to see the mad wind among them.

Then Tulio's wild dash stopped a few feet from Wolf. Sword hand extended, his blade pierced one of the Jackal soldiers coming at Wolf's back. Tulio gave Wolf a quick nod and zoomed away again, striking at knees and necks. His body was a blur of deadly revenge. Tulio the Rabbit was believed to be the fastest man on Andara. He'd been challenged to many a foot race to prove the claim. Tulio had yet to lose. Wolf just hoped his speed would keep him alive now.

More ash uniforms flew out of the forest moments later. Fox, Raven, and Yuli echoed Tulio's war cry. Fury. Bloodlust. Revenge. The dark emotions pushed the young rangers into the fray. In moments, their swords dripped with the blood of the villains who'd taken their homeland, until one remained. Though gravely injured, he went on the attack. Jaguar, cutting the air with his blade, relieved the villain of his head.

"He would rather have died than be taken," Jaguar said, shaking the blood from his blade. "I think it's some honor for them."

"Another reason these barbarians are dangerous," Wolf said. "An enemy who does not fear death will be difficult to chase from our shores. They will force us to kill them to the last man."

"Fine by me. I've heard rumors of these barbarians among some of the traders," Eagle said, kicking at one of the dead bodies. "They call them the metal beetles because they swarm through the trees and are hard to kill." He nodded at the young rangers. "I'm grateful you decided to join us after all."

"So are we," a rasping voice filled with shards of broken glass and septic toxins said. "All of the Sacred Guard in one place. Fortune smiles on us."

A sudden lurch in his heart forced Wolf's attention toward the brothel. Evil had crawled its way into the village, spreading dread in its wake. Twisted thoughts of terror and panic crept into Wolf's mind. Fighting the fear, he planted his feet in the slushy snow with a stubborn will.

Three shrouds floated through the Buellanders like a nightmare. Swirling waves of madness surrounded their new attackers' bodies as famished cries roared under the tree boughs. Then the beasts sang their terrible song. Gray skin peeled in short strips from their boney fingers. Jagged teeth dripped thick saliva as they snarled hungrily. The Dirge had come to join the battle.

Screams echoed against the shacks. The Buellanders scattered, punching and pushing at each other. They'd do anything to escape the personification of death among them now.

"Of all the evil ever to crawl out of hellfire," Eagle said, clutching at the hilt of his sword like a talisman. "What are those?"

"They are the Dirge. These wraiths are the Sarcion's favorite weapons against mortal men." Wolf sheathed his sword. "Get behind me. All of you!"

The three shrouds floated closer, drawn by their uncontrollable appetite. Boney fingers flexed with desire as they reached for their mortal prey. These monsters were themselves surprisingly fleshy. Wolf had met such creatures in battle before, when they'd tried to attack the Lion on Marianna. The Dirge had been walking corpses then. These creatures still possessed the appearance of men.

Then a burst of winter air caught the shroud of one of the nightmares. Its chilly fingers tore the cowl away from the Dirge's rotting skull. Large patches of flesh not yet overtaken by gray betrayed his lineage. The thing before Wolf had been Valdeonian once. It opened its mouth with another ravenous snarl. Two rows of jagged teeth dripped with its poisoned blood. Any humanity the creature once held was gone.

"The Right-Hand has come among us," it said, straining with the words. "I long to taste his flesh."

"You speak? How is this possible?" asked Wolf.

"Do you imagine the Jackal lack volunteers to join the Sarcion's elite soldiers?" another said, snapping its jaws at the rangers. "Its rewards are many, Right-Hand. The weak of our people starve, but we—the strong—eat our fill!"

These lost souls may have been desperate innocents once, but they'd chosen evil over their people. Wolf would show no mercy. He gathered all the hate and anger he possessed into the center of his heart. Next, he pulled the energy about his body until it threatened to suffocate him. Then he let loose the power of the Right-Hand. The Voice pounced upon the Dirge, cracking bones and exploding what remained of their innards with relentless fury.

This righteous cleansing didn't stop until the three filthy shrouds lay flat on the wet snow. Wolf, sickened by the greed and foolishness of the dead creatures before him, put an arm against his stomach. He wanted to retch. He wanted to scream. A larger part of him wanted to mourn for the innocent still held hostage in Valdeon.

Jaguar tentatively touched Wolf's arm. "Is it…is it over?"

"Find me someone who is smart enough to answer questions."

Jaguar gestured to his guardsman and led them toward the shacks. "Break down the doors if you must. We will have answers."

Wolf leaned against the building of the makeshift pub with a tired sigh. He hoped the drain on his energy would lessen as the days passed. The progression of events would turn to the better once the Lion and his guard joined. Jalora willing, both he and Seth survived until then.

"Are you well, My Lord Right-Hand?" Eagle came to him and handed Wolf a canteen.

"You believe me then?" Wolf snorted and took a long drink.

"How can I have any doubts after what I've witnessed today?" Eagle pointed at the crushed shrouds. "We have a weapon against evil, at least."

"Yes, we do, and it is my sacred duty to protect him."

"The Ice Lion," Eagle said with a nod. "Many, rangers and UR leaders alike, have strong opinions on his future." He looked at the crushed Dirge again. "Foolishness. They must obey the Jalora's will."

"Yes. Let's hope the rest of the Legion remembers who they serve before it is too late."

Lies. Avarice. Betrayal. They exuded from the cowering Buellander Jaguar held by the collar. Dragging his victim through the slush, he threw the fat little man at Wolf's feet. Wide eyes stared up at Wolf from ruddy cheeks. This man loved his drink. The gold bracelets about his wrists and ankles spoke of his craving for riches as well.

"Mercy, Mighty Lord!" he cried and clutched at Wolf's cloak. "I'm just a victim here. These brutes invited themselves into our village."

Deceit. Gluttony. Cowardice. The foul emotions hung about the man like a filthy blanket. Wolf grabbed him by the tunic and lifted him until his feet dangled awkwardly above the ground. Valdeonians, by nature, stood much taller than the average Andarian. They were practically giants compared to the much smaller Buellanders. Pleased by his advantage, Wolf shook the little man.

"Do you think you can lie to me?" he boomed. "I will take the knowledge from you, coward."

Images of conspiracy and money changing hands appeared in Wolf's mind. Disgust and fear came to him as this Buellander welcomed the Dirge, offering them free access to the women in his brothel. Disgusted, Wolf moved onto the next set of images. Many more of the shrouded monstrosities existed, but unclear was where the Jackal had taken them.

Wolf dropped the man back in the snow. "The Jackal prepare to march on Northern Andara. They've already landed on the nearly uninhabited northeast coastline of North Point. These thieves don't know specific details, but they do know the Jackal are preparing for a north and south push toward the UR Commonwealth."

"We must destroy the fortress," Fox said. "I'm out of ideas as to how."

"I've been to Stone Fang Fortress," the little man said, greed shimmering in his eyes. "I can tell you where they keep their explosives. They have plenty. Why not destroy them with their own goods?" He grinned and spread his arms. "I know exactly where they keep them. I'll tell you. For a price."

"I dare say it won't be what you're expecting." Wolf grabbed him again.

"Mercy! I beg you!"

"Oh no, traitor," Wolf said, bringing forth his death mask. "You will receive no mercy."

The Legion's most disturbing weapon—the death mask. Its cold, silver surface showed a mortal the exact time of his death. Of those lucky souls who'd survived with their minds intact, many said they experienced the pain of death as well. The Buellander shared their luck this day. Wolf released the mask and let the sobbing little man fall to rock and moan in anguish, beating raw fists upon his chest. Try though he might, the little man couldn't escape the terrible fate he'd seen in the cold silver.

"We must be swift," Wolf told his men. "Many of these Buellanders have escaped into the trees. Our presence and our knowledge of the enemy's plans will be good secrets for them to sell. We must strike the fortress before they have a chance to warn the Jackal."

"I saw a launch moored in the trees," Eagle told them. "It will get me back to my battalion. I must report what I've seen. All that I have seen." He shook Wolf's hand. "Be swift, Right-Hand. Safe travels."

"You as well, ranger."

Ferret frowned as Eagle disappeared into the trees. "It's a shame we can't lock up these Buellanders though. The cave looks to be big enough."

"Hell can have them. We're out of time," Wolf said. "Back to the ship. May the Jalora grant us speed."

Chapter Twenty-Eight

A CHORUS OF hungry howls roused Seth from sleep. They sounded uncomfortably close. Impossible. The beasts of North Marsh couldn't breach the walls of the outpost. Seth scanned the dark space above him in a daze. His eyes finally adjusted to the filtered light of nighttime. He was no longer in the barracks. Somehow, he'd left the safety of the outpost to sprawl on the moss-covered road leading to the docks.

Hurrying to his feet, he looked down at his bedclothes and bare toes. No mud. It was impossible to travel from the legion barracks to the outpost gates without attracting the slimy stuff. Unless, of course, someone had carried him. Was this another prank at his expense? Low growls prodded him closer to the outpost. The stunt would turn deadly if he didn't get back inside.

"Open the gates!" he called up to the battlements. "This isn't funny. Mantis! Gecko!"

He twisted the hem of his nightshirt, waiting for the reassuring sounds of metal on metal signaling the locking mechanism. Silence, however, met his order. A long howl just beyond the docks called more beasts to their dinner. Stomach twisting with fear, Seth saw yellow orbs watching him from the grass.

"You can't leave me out here," he shouted up at the battlements. "I've no weapon."

Perhaps that was the point. The story would be simple. Ice Lion had another episode and went into the marsh after dark. The beasts tore him apart. No one would suspect foul play. Who was behind this plot? Mantis and Gecko may have hated him, but they were rangers, not killers. Could this be another Changeling ploy?

Seth threw his body against the massive wooden surface with a growl. Then he fell forward as the great gates gave way under his weight. Righting his body before he could land in the mud, Seth tumbled through the opening and into the courtyard. It was empty. No guards. No firelight from the battlements. Darkness and the ever-present sound of rain on rooftops greeted him.

"Guards! We have a breach at the gates," Seth called. "Is anyone there?"

Cold mud oozed between his toes as he moved toward the UR barracks. He had to find help. The outpost was exposed and would quickly fall by the weapons of men or the jaws of the marsh.

Seth's foot kicked against a cloth bundle. The lump sent him sprawling on his hands and knees into the mud. A rare glimmer of moonlight illuminated the lifeless face. The body was that of Dragonfly. His dead eyes stared at the gates as a lifeless hand clutched at the gaping hole in his stomach.

Other heaps filled the courtyard. Rangers and UR soldiers had fallen together, their lives lost protecting the outpost against strange invaders from distant shores. Many of Seth's comrades had ignored the wet and cold to fight in their bedclothes. The strike had caught them completely off guard.

Seth forced himself to his feet and ran wildly through the dead men. He had to get to Legion HQ. Maybe some of the rangers had barricaded themselves inside. Overturned crates and tables from the mess fortified the Legion courtyard. Hope prodded his legs forward.

"It's Ice Lion," he called to the wall of debris. "Is anyone there?"

Then he saw them. Phoenix and White Tiger had made a last stand before the barricade. Golden hair caked with blood, Phoenix had been pierced dozens of times by vicious strikes. White Tiger had fallen beside him, his body partially covering their wounded commander.

"No!" Seth screamed as he saw the other man who'd dared to stand with them. Riley Logan hung upon the barricade, his body pinned spread eagle to its wooden exterior. He'd been made to suffer for his service to the Ice Lion.

Seth sank to his knees, sobbing. Why had he allowed Riley to journey with him to such a forsaken place? Riley should be home on Marianna with his family and his Beatrice. They'd have been married by now, despite Riley's insistence he didn't want home and family.

Blowing out a ragged breath, Seth stood once more. He was on his own. It was up to him to find a way to warn the Legion about the fall of North Marsh Outpost. He climbed over the barricade and raced to the steps of the battlement. Scaling the stairs slick with blood, he stopped at the top. Bodies covered the stone platform. So many brave men had died. Surviving this night would take a miracle.

He had to reach the alarm bell on the other side of the battlement. If anyone was within hearing range, they would come. No one tried to stop him this time. Seth ran across the temporary bridge they'd installed over the hole he'd put in the wall a few weeks before. The thickest concentration of bodies lay in a pile at the base of the opening beneath him. All of these deaths were his fault. If he hadn't lost control, the wall would still be intact, and his friends would be safe.

Gritting his teeth against the guilt, Seth pushed on until he was just feet away from the alarm bell. He stood beside the unused bell cord, inches from grabbing it. Why hadn't anyone thought to sound the alarm?

"We come for you, Ice Kitten."

A Changeling stood right beyond the bell. Its features drew sharp angles as the vicious grin opened to reveal dagger-like teeth. The Changeling lifted its blade into the air, signaling in a wide arc over its head. Hundreds of mercenaries crawled across the battlements toward them. They came closer, banging chains against their swords. The clamor was deafening.

"You won't win, Creature of Evil. The Legion will stop you."

The Changeling laughed and shook its head. "Your Legion will fall without their Jalora to protect them. Andara is a ripe fruit, ready to be plucked. And you, Ice Lion, will be just another sad tale told at our campfires."

Seth dove at the cold hand of a nearby dead soldier and pulled the man's sword free. Taking the First Stance, he brought the death mask to his face. Surprise had aided him last time when he'd killed the Changeling. This time, the creature and its allies were ready for him. Hoping he wasn't alone, Seth grasped the bell cord like a lifeline. He began tugging it with all his might.

Dull buzzing filled his ears. Focused on the Changeling before him and its oncoming allies, Seth ignored the obnoxious noise. Suddenly, tight bands grabbed his sword arm, forcing his body out of the First Stance and pulling him off balance. The buzzing grew louder. Its pitch resonated in his brain with painful stabs as he struggled. Another band pulled against his neck in an unbreakable grip. The Lion's Roar began to rumble angrily in Seth's chest. He wouldn't try to stop it this time.

Then something hot and flat slapped against his face. The buzzing in his ears reached a shrill pitch and suddenly stopped. Phoenix stood before him alive and well. The angry hue of Phoenix's burning blue eyes was in sharp contrast to his white nightshirt. Mud covered his feet and the bottom hem of his garment.

"You're alive! How?"

Three other men had accompanied their commander. Mantis held Seth's sword arm, while Gecko hugged his torso. White Tiger, much to Seth's embarrassment, had a strong arm wrapped around his neck.

"What the devil is going on here?" Phoenix folded his arms as if to prevent himself from striking Seth again. "Answer me, Ice Lion, and stop ringing the alarm! You've woken the entire Marsh."

Frozen fingers clutched at the cord. Seth, with great effort, opened his hand and let it fall from his grip. He relaxed his body in submission. The Lion's

Roar pressed against his control for a few more disgruntled moments and then subsided back into sleep.

"Ice Lion came onto the battlements screaming like a madman about assassins," Mantis said, pulling the sword from Seth's hand and handing it back to a pale-faced soldier. "Frightened the wits out of the corporal here. Luckily, he gave up his sword without a fight."

"We have a sleepwalker," Gecko grumbled, gesturing toward the hole in the wall. "It's a miracle Ice Lion didn't take a stroll over the side."

"It wasn't a dream." Seth's anger flared again, prompting the Lion's Roar to rumble low in his throat. "Invaders are coming. Don't you see? They've followed me here."

Phoenix turned to glare at the crowded battlements. "Get back to your posts or to your beds. The show is over for tonight."

He pulled Seth by the front of his bedclothes down the battlement steps. Their bare feet sank into the cold mud. Seth shivered as it oozed between his toes. Strange. He'd experienced the cold and wetness during his vision. Seth stumbled onto the wooden pathway as other sensations brought him sharply back into reality. Phoenix's fist tightened as he pulled Seth toward HQ. Anger pulsed about his commander as Phoenix threw open the door to his office. White Tiger's calm presence followed while he observed them both.

"I'm not dreaming. You must believe me, sir! The Changeling warned they were coming for me."

"You were not given permission to speak, Ice Lion. I've been far too lenient with you, it seems. What if someone had been seriously injured tonight?" Phoenix sat heavily in his chair. “It is natural to have nightmares about these creatures after what you’ve gone through, but waking the entire outpost…”

Seth slammed his fists on the desk. “I wasn’t dreaming, Phoenix. You must let Riley and me leave before it’s too late! You can’t stand against them.”

“We shouldn’t discount visions or dreams given to a Lord of Valdeon,” White Tiger said, pushing away from the wall. “I think we should discuss this when the sun is up.”

“Morning may not be soon enough.”

Seth wiped irritably at the wet hair clinging to his face. What would he do if they didn’t believe him in the light of day? He couldn’t allow an entire outpost of men to die just because they happened to be in the same place as he. The Ice Lion must disappear again.

“I formally request permission to transfer, sir.”

“The Obsidian Citadel, I suppose?” Phoenix grunted.

“They found me there as well. Do you honestly think those Valdeonian cutthroats were stalking around Lea to cause trouble? They were looking for me!” Seth leaned across the desk. “I must join Wolf.”

Phoenix bolted upright and clutched agitated fingers on the edge of his desk. “That’s enough, apprentice. Return to barracks and report for regular duty in the morning. Understood?”

Seth saluted. “Yes, sir.”

Closing the door behind him, he stormed across the patio toward the steps leading to the courtyard. Riley waited outside the entrance to Phoenix’s office. He had Seth’s clothes and boots in his hands. His squire shrugged when Seth failed to stop and fell into step beside him.

"He doesn't believe you, does he?" Riley asked, cursing when Seth shook his head. "He's seen enough to know better. What do we do now?"

Seth rested a hand on his squire's shoulder, grateful at least one person believed him. "We stay alert."

Chapter Twenty-Nine

SETH FOLLOWED A respectful distance behind White Tiger. Morning's weak fingers touched the top of the battlement walls as they marched through the constant rain. White Tiger's pace didn't slow as he stepped off the planked pathway into the mud. Where was he taking them? The Legion buildings ended after a short distance, leaving only paddocks and bare walls. Sighing with acceptance, Seth stepped from the planks into a field of mud. He hadn't dared ask what hellish duty the old ranger's furtive imagination had concocted.

Movement caught his attention at the base of the wall. Two men crawled out of its stone belly and stomped in the mud toward a hand wagon. One of them waved two fingers in the air. Steaming cups of tea for him and his friend appeared. Seth, chasing the lingering effects of sleep from his mind, finally understood. They were part of the repair team for the gaping hole Seth had inadvertently blasted in the wall with his power.

White Tiger returned their salute as he stomped past them. He waved a finger at Seth and nodded toward the sizable opening. Scaffolding crawled up the rough sides of the barrier wall. Rope hung in thick strands off pulleys anchored within the stone.

Though several rows of rock lined the gap, Seth could still see the unending marsh beyond. Several armed soldiers, muskets ready, stood guard at the top.

"I've heard you're good at building things, Ice Lion." White Tiger folded his arms with a frown. "It's high time you help repair what you destroyed. Here comes your crew."

A squad of UR soldiers marched toward them through the mud. Each man carried wood or tools on his shoulder. Apprehension. Fear. Respect. Seth sensed their emotions from across the distance. Sergeant Duncan was at their head. He seemed to be the only one pleased to welcome Seth.

"You have a new squad member, Sergeant. I think you know the Ice Lion." White Tiger lifted his eyes to the top of the battlements. "Gecko's in charge of the day's repairs. I trust you'll be on your best behavior, apprentice. Now, get to work."

Gecko. Seth let out a disgruntled sigh. Of course, it had to be his remaining tormentor. Mantis had kept his promise to Dragonfly. Seth was glad of it, not just for his own sake, but for Dragonfly's as well. He didn't like this fighting among rangers. It would tear the Legion apart.

"How can I help, Sergeant?"

"We're ready to set a further row of stone, sir." Sergeant Duncan gave him an encouraging smile. "They could use another strong man on the ropes."

Seth followed the team of soldiers to the remains of the innermost layer of the wall. Gecko must have decided to first seal up the hole to the bog. The approach made sense. They'd have a much easier time of repairs without worrying about the inhabitants of the marshes.

Resting a hand on the short wall, Seth immediately yanked it away again. The Lion Spirit's fury still radiated off its surface in angry spikes of energy. Such raw power. How would he ever control it? His father's warning echoed in his mind. Leo had told him many would try to use his gifts. Now he understood. The Lion's Roar was a terrible weapon. If someone could manipulate it, or rather him, then they would control all of Andara.

The uncomfortable heaviness of guarded stares was upon him. His team circled a rope dangling inside the hole. The line ran through a series of pulleys mounted over their heads. Its end was wrapped tightly about a massive square stone. Seth leaped over the short wall to join them.

"Where did you get these stones?" he asked. "I hadn't noticed spares tucked away in the outpost."

"No one knows where they came from, My Lord," one of the soldiers murmured, casting a glance up at Gecko. "They appear each morning. We stop for the day when we're out of blocks."

Seth placed a hand on the hard surface. The Jalora's magic rippled in the stone at his touch. He smiled at the sensation. Others were as bemused as he by the whirls of white within the gray. The UR soldiers took a step back and made protective signs toward the heavens.

"You'll find no evil in this magic," Seth told them. "The Jalora protects us."

“Blessings upon you, Lion.” A weatherworn hand tentatively touched the surface. Grizzled hair thinned on the man’s balding head. Harsh lines carved in old features spoke of many years in service to the army.

“The name’s Bill, My Lord.” He gave Seth a grin. “I don’t suppose you’d ask if the stones could be stacked back on the wall?”

Seth laughed and shook his head. “I’ve learned the Jalora has a purpose for everything it does. Today, it wants me to lift stones.”

“It was worth a try,” Bill said with a shrug. “Come on, you lot. Rope at the ready. Lift!”

Seth hauled in unison with the others. The rope pulled taut. Chirps from the chorus of pulleys echoed against stone as their block began to sway a few inches from the ground. It ascended in rhythmic starts and stops until the block reached men waiting on the newest level of completed rows. Holding the rope steady, Seth and the team jogged forward as their mates swung the stone over its place in the wall. Then they released the fasteners and the block dropped the last couple of inches with a clunk.

The next stone was already secured to the rope when they’d finished. Seth and the team’s steady pulling began again. Bill whistled a pub tune, breaking the monotony of their repetitive motions. Seth joined in with a laugh. He’d missed working alongside ordinary men to accomplish a good day’s work. He was almost disappointed when they stopped for a break. The top workers needed to catch up on the mortar work.

"Glad you're on our squad, Lion." Bill handed him a canteen of water. "We're three stones ahead of the others."

Seth took a long drink from the container and handed it back with a nod. He leaned against the completed section of the wall and wiped at the sweat on his brow. These UR soldiers were a team, working together toward a common goal. The Legion must embrace this spirit of camaraderie or fail in its mission to protect Andara.

Sudden prickles of warning raced up his spine. The Jalora was unsettled. Standing upright away from the wall, Seth waited. He sent his power through the opening into the marsh. Padded paws scampered along the few solid strips of ground, but none of them approached the outpost. He brought his power back inside and set it hunting among the buildings.

"What is it, sir? Trouble?" Sergeant Duncan asked, pulling his sword. "On your feet." He kicked at the nearest soldier's boot. "Something's wrong."

Bill and the rest of their team sprang into action without complaint or question. They'd left their weapons behind when they'd reported at the wall. Grabbing pieces of board and pipe, they gathered closer to their sergeant. Seth too had been ordered to leave his sword in the barracks. The Ice Lion, however, had other more dangerous weapons.

Protect the innocent!

Seth's power firmly gripped his attention and pulled it toward the other team of men hoisting stones. Their bundle swung precariously over the wall. The soldiers at the top of the scaffolding cried out as the rope snapped. The massive block plunged through the scaffolding like a meteor. It fell toward the ground taking two men with it. Frozen in place between the repaired barrier and the short wall, their teammates could only watch as the rock and men plummeted toward them.

Climbing on the droplets of moisture in the air, Seth grabbed the two falling men by their collars. He skidded across slick air currents drifting sluggishly over the short wall taking his two passengers with him. Their wide eyes filled with terror and shock as the blurred body of their rescuer brought them down to the ground. They slid safely in the mud away from the wall.

Screams drew him back toward the scene. Bang. Scaffolding snapped apart as the massive stone plunged faster through the repair riggings until it was almost on top of the remaining crew. Seth didn't have time to pull them all away before the granite struck. Then he noticed the section of rope hanging free from the rigging. Seth flew at it, fingers clutching tightly about its rough surface. He circled round and round the men until the line gripped them securely. Then Seth pulled as hard as he could. Their bodies sprayed mud as the momentum brought them to a crashing halt against the legs of Seth's teammates. The massive block slammed into the ground with such force, it sank in the mud, buried down about 10 inches.

"What the devil goes on here?" Gecko stomped through the mire with angry strides. "Clumsy idiots! We'll miss an entire afternoon's work."

"Did you not hear the Jalora's call?" Seth asked, the power still pulsing about him. "It is for us to make certain these men are safe."

"You care about their safety now, do you?" Gecko stormed closer to Seth. "This hole is your doing. Any harm that finds them rests solely on your shoulders, Ice Lion."

"Here now, ranger. Ice Lion saved their lives today." Sergeant Duncan came to stand at Seth's side. "You've no right to say such things to him."

"How dare you question me, peasant!" Gecko brought his power to full force. "I am a ranger in the Jalora Legion."

"You are a hot-headed fool!" Seth stepped between them and let the Lion's Roar rumble. "I'm warning you. This man is under my protection."

Gecko spat at Seth's boots. "Does he know his protector is being driven mad by the mixed-blood polluting his body? You won't last long as Bearer, Ice Lion."

I will tolerate no disrespect or insult. If this fool attacks my Lion, then he openly attacks me. Punish the Guilty!

An ash cloud suddenly covered Gecko. Its form moved too quickly for Seth to see any features. He did, however, make out the steel bar striking Gecko with incredible speed and accuracy. Then the attack stopped abruptly. A ranger stood between Seth and the rest of the Legion battalion who had gathered along the wall. His curly hair dripped with sweat and the light rain, impatient to fall. The ranger's faithful squire was next to him, panting hard. At that moment, Seth realized the Jalora had not been speaking to him.

"I am called Coyote, the Lion's First Marked," Jason boomed at the curious members of Western Beta who'd come to see what trouble Ice Lion had caused this time. "Make a move, and I'll kill you where you stand!"

Radiating with the Jalora's power, Coyote stayed in a ready position until the rangers began to back away. He gave them one last contemptuous glare and dropped the pipe at Gecko's feet. Turning his back to Western Beta, Jason gave Seth a relieved smile. He rubbed a hand against his unshaven face. Tired eyes lifted to examine something just past Seth's shoulder.

"Are you well?" Boyd asked.

"Yes, we're unharmed." Seth turned to the Coyote's squire, taking in his rumpled clothes and baggy eyes. "You both look as if you've been traveling hard. How is it you've come to be here in North Marsh?"

"An excellent question," Phoenix said, standing a few feet behind Seth on the other side of the short wall. The distaste on his face as he stared at Coyote was unsettling. Jason returned the gaze with equal disdain. White Tiger, clearly noting the tension between the two rangers, stomped purposefully between them.

"Here's another question," White Tiger snapped. "Why have you breached the security of this outpost and protocol by flying over the wall?"

He pointed to a launch hovering lazily a few feet above the mud. Shades of brown and white made patterns in the paint. The surface reminded Seth of mountains or a rocky seashore. It wasn't painted or designed like any vessel he'd ever seen before. Others found the craft of interest as well. The apprentices had somehow escaped their duties and came to explore the little launch. Cal the Stallion's eyes, however, were transfixed on Jason. Here was the legend of a Lion's First Marked come to life.

"I commandeered that vessel from the Jackal fortress in the Bloodtooth Mountains just north of here. I trust, apprentices, you can find a place to moor it in safety. It needs to get me to the Obsidian Citadel in one piece."

"Yes, sir!"

A few of the most alert climbed in the vessel and began playing around with the controls. The engines sputtered and whirred. But then a sudden lurch threw its occupants unceremoniously onto their backsides. Cal crawled to the rudder and gripped it tightly. He gave Coyote a sheepish grin and turned the launch slowly toward the Legion courtyard.

Coyote, completely unfazed, reached out a hand to Sergeant Duncan. "Well met, Lion Friend."

The sergeant smoothed at the three, deep, claw marks Seth's power had ripped into his skin. The squad hurried to circle about their sergeant, giving him nods of admiration and slaps on the back. Seth, for his part, hadn't realized he'd marked the man.

"Our Lion holds the courage of his UR comrades in high regard," Coyote said. "You join a small, but auspicious group."

"If you're done strutting about, I'm waiting for your explanation." Phoenix's glare hadn't softened.

Coyote winked at Seth with a grin. He hopped over the short wall and made his leisurely way toward Phoenix and White Tiger. Jason had taken a dislike to Phoenix. He seemed to derive great enjoyment from purposely goading the deacon.

"What's going on? Someone claims we had a breach," Riley said, climbing over the short rim of the wall. "Is that Jason Coyote?"

"Yes, and he's about to cause a small war with Phoenix," answered Seth.

"Aye, I'm sure and rightly so." Riley whistled. "Phoenix knocked Coyote out when he was trying to help you in Lea. Rumor has it the deacon put Jason and Boyd in a cell. I dare say we're about to witness one devil of a fight."

Seth rolled his eyes to heaven and let out an irritated sigh. Too many were fighting among themselves for his sake. Why couldn't they understand? The Jalora guided Seth's steps. He followed its word alone.

"Perhaps you should go, Riley."

"Oh no," Riley responded with a grin. "I wouldn't miss this for the world."

Phoenix seemed to fill the space as his power pressed dangerously against the walls of the battlement. His fierce blue glare burned into Jason as Seth's First Marked came closer. White Tiger pressed a hand against Coyote's chest, keeping him at a discreet distance from their commander. Jason, body tense, stopped. Seth held his breath.

"Have you grown deaf to the Jalora's voice?" Jason let his hand fall casually on the hilt of his sword. "Why would you leave our Lion under the charge of a treasonous blaggard? If I had not been here to obey its will, Seth…"

"You forget yourself." Phoenix let his hand drop to his belt. "I protect the Lion, though it has become a full-time occupation."

"We can see how well you do your duty, Partisan," Coyote retorted, pointing to Seth. "You and your men offend the Jalora with your rudeness to its Lion." He stood up straighter. "I'm sure the Right-Hand will say as much when he arrives at the outpost."

"Wolf is here?" Seth bounded over the short wall and spun Coyote about. "He's in North Marsh? Is he well? Why didn't he come to me in Lea?"

"Easy," Jason said, gripping Seth's shoulder. "Esteban the Hawk tried to murder him in the forests outside of Lea."

The Lion's Roar grumbled in Seth's throat. He gulped in angry breaths. Images from Coyote's mind ran across his consciousness as he probed his Lion Friend. Thick woods. Many mercenaries and then his uncle, Esteban the Hawk Prince. The bloodlust in Esteban's eyes was unmistakable.

"You saved him." Seth gripped at Jason's arm.

"Wolf is the reason I came. He was worried about your safety, and it turns out he was right." Coyote ignored Phoenix's disgruntled protest. "Dragon tricked him the night he was supposed to meet you, but Wolf is a wise man. He knew where you were going and follows. We were on our way to this outpost, but fortune had other plans."

Coyote lifted his voice for the crowd of men to hear. "We spotted enemy ships sailing toward the Buells.

Wolf suspected mischief and was right again. The Jackal built a base in the Bloodtooth Mountains to our north. They plan an invasion."

"Impossible," White Tiger said. "Dragon would have sensed something."

"The Jalora's power has diminished. Wolf believes it conserves its energy for other things." Jason cast an uncomfortable look at Seth. "The Lords of Valdeon are trying to find a way to slow down the invasion until I can warn the Legion. I sail to Lea just as soon as I make sure Seth is safe."

"I must go to Wolf." Seth slammed a fist into his palm. A handful of rangers wasn't enough. The Lords of Valdeon would need him to sabotage the invasion. Perhaps they could take the entire battalion and head north to join them.

"Wolf wanted me to tell you he comes for you soon," Jason said. "I can't take you to him and warn the Legion in time. You must stay put until he comes for you. Wandering around North Marsh is a sure way to get yourself killed."

Wolf has his task. You have yours.

Seth nodded reluctantly. The Jalora was right, but its reasoning didn't make his impatience any easier to bear. Wolf and the Lords of Valdeon were saving Andara. And what was Seth doing? Hauling cargo and repairing walls. He was the Lion Protector after all. What use was it for him to hide behind walls?

"We'll leave you now, Deacon," Coyote told Phoenix, who at the mention of Wolf, grew quiet. "Thank you for the offer of your hospitality. Come along, Lion's squire. I quote one of your favorite

Marianna sayings—my stomach has a hole in it!" Jason glared at the rangers of Western Beta. "I think I prefer the company of courageous men today. Come, we'll seek out a meal at the UR mess."

Coyote put a hand on Seth's shoulder, guiding him away from Phoenix and toward the base of the wall. The entrance to the UR courtyard wasn't far. He began whistling a Geltic tune loudly enough for the deacon to hear. Seth kept his eyes forward. The slight and insubordination were enough to land any ranger on White Tiger's blacklist. Mention of the Right-Hand, however, seemed to give Coyote special consideration not awarded to anyone else, including the Lion Protector.

Chapter Thirty

THE UR COURTYARD echoed with the typical hustle bustle of army life. Seth found the activity reassuring. Soldiers moved crates from one storehouse to another at the insistence of their attentive sergeant. Others pulled flat carts loaded with vegetables and flour toward the mess. Seth's attention landed on a fortunate group of young men playing field ball. Apparently even the UR soldiers had more free time to spare than the unlucky Legion apprentices.

"Phoenix has a nasty temper," Riley warned Jason as they stomped their muddied boots on the wooden pathway. "Making him angry isn't a good idea."

"You don't like him either and don't seem to have a problem letting him know it." Coyote chuckled when Seth gave him a sour frown.

"I'm protected by the code, sir. He's fond of telling me the rules are the only reason I still have my head," Riley explained.

Coyote burst into laughter and slapped a hand on Riley's back. The gesture propelled his much smaller frame toward the mud. Boyd grabbed Riley before he could tumble off the edge.

"Neither of you should provoke him." Seth stopped and leaned against the storage shed. "Hawk ordered him to bring me here. I don't think he liked the idea. Who could blame him? His entire battalion is uneasy because of me. A half-breed bears the Lion Ring." He kicked a small clump of mud from his boot. "What will become of Andara when red blood mixes with red blood?"

"Sarcasm from you?" Jason tilted his head. "I'm not sure how I feel about what I'm hearing. Come on, Seth. What else happened?"

"They think I'm an oddity, Jason. I hear the whispers as I pass them in the corridors. Ice Lion performs the moves of a bishop. Have you seen the hole in the wall? When will he lose control again?" Seth turned his head to look at his three friends. "Now the rangers think I have marsh madness after my vision."

"Vision?" Jason let his arms drop and stood with his full attention on Seth. "Tell me everything."

"I was standing outside the open gates. The Changelings and their Jackal allies had overrun the outpost. I alone was left alive. The Changelings in my vision said they were coming for me."

"And what did the Phoenix say?" Jason asked, bending closer.

"He doesn't believe me. No one but Riley does."

"I believe you," Jason said. "Wolf must hear of your vision. But we've no time to warn him." He shrugged with a sigh. "I see no help for it. I must take you to Lea with me. Wolf will understand I had no choice."

Jason suddenly pulled Seth behind him. Mantis stood in the entrance to the Legion courtyard. Fury. Resentment. Confusion. The emotions pulsed about him as he stared down their group. Mantis had heard about the fate of his friend, Gecko.

A swirl of movement came to a stop beside Coyote. Here was Dragonfly, his typically pleasant face twisted with lines of contempt. Other streaks of ash flew past Mantis in the opening and came to stand with their group. A hand rested on Seth's shoulder. Bear had arrived, and he'd brought friends: Stallion, Badger, and the apprentice squires stood on the pathway with fists raised.

The hammering and chatter stopped abruptly as several UR soldiers dropped their tools. Grim scowls greeted Mantis with silent rebuke. Each had a hand on their sword hilts as they watched the ranger turn around. Mantis left the UR courtyard with as much slow dignity as he could muster.

"Quite the day you've had, Lion." Sergeant Ralston gave him a nod. "Call us if you need anything. Back to work, the rest of you."

"Thank you, Sergeant."

Seth returned the wave offered him by the group of UR soldiers as they resumed their play. The men of the UR had made their allegiance clear. They'd follow the Lion Protector even if the Legion did not. The responsibility of their loyalty added a burden on Seth. He would move the heavens to be worthy of their faith in him.

"You play field ball?" Jason asked.

"Does he play!" Riley folded his arms with a crooked grin. "Seth was Marianna team captain."

"Why don't we join them?"

"Phoenix may not allow it, Jason. The day hasn't been a peaceful one."

Jason snorted, his mischievous grin focused on Phoenix as their commander kept a steady pace behind them. The deacon returned Jason's smirk with restrained dislike. White Tiger—in comparison—wore his disapproval of Coyote as he would a prized overcoat.

"Well, Deacon. I'm glad you were able to step away from your office for a brief while. Bolstering the troops with words of wisdom, eh?"

"Yes, acolyte," Phoenix said, evenly. "They're also learning discipline. I feel I must instill this in them quickly before certain ill influences taint their minds."

Coyote nodded slowly. "And you think playing with stones will teach them?"

"I suppose you have another view."

"Field ball requires teamwork and discipline." Jason leaned casually against the shed. "Care for a game? The apprentices, Dragonfly, and I against you and the team of your choice."

Seth's friends exchanged excited looks. A game of field ball would relieve some of the monotony of North Marsh. Seth groaned. The bad blood between Jason and Phoenix ran deep. Their confrontation at the wall was far from over. He knew it in the twisting of his gut.

"Young devil!" White Tiger growled. "This is a military outpost, not a schoolyard."

"You would make an excellent scorekeeper, White Tiger." Jason's grin grew wider when the old ranger sputtered. "What about it, Phoenix? Care to put those disciplined rangers of yours to the test against the apprentices?"

"I've no time for games," Phoenix told him, moving past Coyote to head toward the Legion courtyard.

"Just as well, I suppose," Coyote called. "Wouldn't want to interrupt their drinking and we certainly wouldn't want you to get your nice uniform dirty in all this nasty mud."

Riley and the apprentices stepped back as Phoenix turned toward Coyote with blazing eyes. Seth's gut twisted again. Bloodshed seemed more and more inevitable the longer the two rangers spent in one another's presence.

"I look forward to wiping that impertinent grin off your face, acolyte."

"Many have tried, Deacon." Jason slapped his hands together. "Come, apprentices, Dragonfly! We have a game now!"

Boyd helped Jason off with his sword, cloak, and tunic. Hands yanked at Seth's garments as well. Riley wasn't about to miss such excitement. The other apprentice squires and Donny weren't long in joining him to help their rangers prepare for the game. Not for the first time, Seth wished his and Riley's roles were reversed. Worrying was pointless. Jason and Phoenix would have their fight, no matter what Seth said.

"I've heard tales of the brashness of Lion Friends." Cal unfastened his belt and handed it to his squire. "Remember this, Jason Coyote. The code protects you from harm. We are not protected."

Jason laughed, slapping Cal on the back. He jumped off the wooden platform and into the mud. Marching across the courtyard, he spoke to the soldiers with animated gestures. They eagerly handed over their ball. Then the soldiers hurried in all directions, passing the word along. Seth groaned. This game was happening whether he wanted it to or not.

Phoenix, for his part, had been quick to assemble his team, acolytes all. Seth recognized them as receivers of Coyote's admonishment. To Seth's relief, Mantis wasn't among them.

"I like field ball as much as the next man, Ice Lion." Bear leaned his sword against the storage shed. "I don't think this will be a friendly game."

Seth nodded his agreement and walked with the others toward the muddied courtyard. He took an irritated breath when he saw Riley Logan already placing bets, his carrot curls bouncing between squires and UR soldiers. The love of gaming, it would seem, was common among men in all walks of life.

"Give me the ball." White Tiger snatched it from Coyote's hands. "Who are the team captains?"

"I'm captain for our team," Phoenix said, eyeing Coyote.

"And the apprentice team?" White Tiger asked, casting a disapproving look at Jason.

"I should think that would be obvious. Ice Lion is the captain of this team."

"What?" Seth was taken aback.

"You were Marianna team captain." Jason winked at him. "We're bound to win."

The apprentice team gathered in a huddle, every eye looking toward Seth. This game was for higher stakes now. Seth reached back into his memories of simpler days on Marianna. He'd known the boys he'd led then for many years. He could anticipate their moves and motives. His new friends had completely different histories.

Use what you've learned from the Islander boys of your youth. Seek to learn from each of your new team now. Many lives depend on you to lead, My Lion.

"I play best in the offensive position," Seth told them. "Each of you, take a spot."

Jason slapped his hands together as if pleased at the new tone of authority in Seth's voice. His additional teammates weren't as confident as they positioned themselves in the mud. Dragonfly joined Seth at the center of the courtyard. He gave Seth an encouraging smile and moved into a relaxed stance as they waited for the other team.

Phoenix and his players took up their positions opposite Seth. Facial features completely blank, Phoenix wasn't giving any moves away. The rangers opposite held the attention of the jittery apprentices. They were perfectly aware of how intimidated Seth's team was by their presence. Weeks of hazing and orders had conditioned them. Seth would have to change their minds.

"Ready. Steady. Go!"

White Tiger threw the ball straight up in the air. Phoenix's height was an advantage as he slapped it away from Seth's hands. The ball was headed toward the apprentice goal post before Seth landed back down in the mud.

Badger zipped across the line to try and block the ball, but Phoenix was too fast for him. The crowd along the courtyard gave a cheer as the ranger team scored its first goal. Phoenix jogged past the apprentices as Bear took the ball.

"First point to me, Coyote. Don't look so surprised," Phoenix sniped. "I'm no stranger to this game."

"This is one team that won't let you win." Jason gave him an unfriendly smile. "You'll have to earn the next point, Prince of Heidelbrecht."

"Are you through chatting, ladies, or can I throw the ball back in play?" White Tiger spun the ball in his hands, glaring at them with anticipation. Despite his original objections, he seemed to be enjoying his role as referee. Seth signaled his team to be at the ready and waited for the sphere to hit the mud.

Bear was on it first. He kicked it toward the ranger team's goal at the end of the courtyard. Taking the move without help from his teammates, Bear soon found himself boxed in by the ranger team. One of them kicked the ball out of his reach and zoomed like a muddy lightning bolt to strike the apprentice team goal.

"The second point goes to the ranger team," White Tiger called over the cheers of the crowd. "Throw me the ball, Coyote."

Ignoring the order, Jason kept his muddy boot on the sphere. A sudden expectant glint sparkled in his eye. Then he kicked, propelling the ball with pinpoint accuracy at the unsuspecting Phoenix. The ball smashed their commander full in the face. He staggered back a few steps, eyes watering.

"I believe that makes us even." Coyote spat onto the mud.

"Young devil!" White Tiger snatched the ball, staring at Phoenix's dripping nose. "I ought to do more than throw you out of the game."

"No, Tiger. We'll call it a poorly executed move." Phoenix wiped at his nose. "I suppose I had it coming. Know this, Jason Coyote. Strike me again, and I won't hold back, Lion Friend or no."

"Come on, Jason." Seth pulled at his friend's arm. "No more fighting today, all right? We must come together as a Legion, not split apart as enemies."

"Not even you can change human nature, Seth."

Phoenix's team moved back to their positions. They each stayed within their zones, waiting for their captain to give them signals. Each played well in his role. Seth regarded Phoenix again and noticed the deacon watching him. He seemed to be waiting for something. Then Seth looked to the apprentice team. Each of them played in random positions, trying their best to make it through the game. They were intimidated by the other team. Phoenix, Seth realized, was using it to his advantage.

Well done, My Lion. I have promoted Phoenix because of his strong leadership skills. Learn from him.

"Apprentice team!" Seth called, gathering the ice walls about him once more.

They joined him at their goal and huddled together. Frustrated, his teammates had all but given up. Coyote was the only one who met his eye. He'd gotten the revenge he'd intended.

"We must change our strategy if we're to win this game. Bear, you protect the goal. There isn't one ranger—not even the Phoenix—who can get past you.

Dragonfly and Coyote will stay in the defensive line, while Badger and I act in the offensive."

"I've never played in that position before, Seth."

"You're quick, Badger. They won't know what hit them."

"And what about me?" Cal asked.

"Stallion, you're our secret weapon. I want you to play center. You're good at both defense and offense. Come up the very center of the field, when I give you the signal."

Stallion grinned and nodded. The team then broke out of the huddle and moved to the newly designated positions. Seth stood before Phoenix, carefully blocking so as not to give their strategy away.

White Tiger threw the ball up again, and this time Seth reached it first. He zipped past Phoenix and headed into the middle of the other rangers. Just when they moved to surround him, Seth passed the ball to Badger. The young apprentice ran toward the unprotected goal and slammed it against the post with a yelp of victory. The apprentices lifted their young friend and cheered with the crowd.

"One goal to you, Ice Lion," Phoenix said beside him. "Well done."

Seth nodded his thanks. They moved back into position and worked closely together. The apprentices were nearly tied with the ranger team when the sky opened up to a downfall of rain. Seth ignored the hard drops slapping at his face. Now Phoenix wasn't letting them get any more goals through. He had beefed up his defensive line and was waiting for Seth as he came closer with the ball.

A flash of lightning shot across the sky. The play outside was growing dangerous, but neither team wanted to quit. Seth wiped a hand across his rain-soaked face, looking for an opening. He slipped a little in the mud and quickly righted himself. An idea began to form. Seth let a little grin come and bolted forward toward the tall deacon. He kicked the ball as hard as he could over the Phoenix's head and slid on his back in the mud through his opponent's legs.

Seth righted himself and raced toward the goal. He slammed the ball against the post with a cry of victory. UR soldiers, rangers, and squires alike cheered. The apprentice team circled about Seth, whooping in excited chants of triumph. Even rangers on the opposing team slapped him on the back. Hungry for the chance of victory, he reached down to grab the ball, but White Tiger was too quick.

"This ball and I are going in for a drink out of the thunderstorm!" White Tiger yelled across the field. "I say we have a tie and need to finish up the game when the weather permits."

The players reluctantly agreed and followed him into the mess where rum and slices of meat and cheese were waiting for them. Some of the rangers, once wary of him, patted Seth on the back as he came inside.

"I am proud of you, Ice Lion," Phoenix told him as they sat down at one of the tables. "You led your men well. Remarkably, even Coyote listened to your orders. He wants to take you with him to Lea."

"Yes, sir. He does."

I have given you a task, Lion. You must complete it before Andara can be saved. It is not time for you to leave yet. Phoenix must continue to protect you."

"You don't agree with him." Phoenix watched Seth's face intently.

"The Jalora commands I stay in North Marsh." Seth took a sip of the rum. "I will speak with Jason."

Phoenix gave him a nod. His eyes lifted, and the distaste came back to his face once more. He moved away as Jason parted the crowd to reach Seth carrying three glasses of victory rum. Boyd followed, looking a bit disgruntled. He brought two plates overloaded with food and set one down before his ranger. Boyd dug into the other plate with hungry zest.

"I'm glad to see you have so many new friends," Jason said, lifting his rum. "Come, let's share a drink. I fear my time in North Marsh grows short."

The apprentice team joined them, singing a merry tune. Drinks and food soon covered their table as the other rangers offered their congratulations on a game well played. Jason, Seth noticed, was careful about his drink. He'd grown quiet and contemplative as they waited for the storm to diminish.

"The thunder has rolled to the west," Jason said, touching Boyd's arm. "Will you see us off, Seth?"

They hurried through the mud to the storage shed where the apprentices had secured the Jackal launch. Boyd gave Seth a quick nod of parting and began to unfasten the vessel from its tethers. He pulled it outside, leaving Seth alone with Jason.

"I must go now, Seth. Time grows short, and I worry for Wolf." Coyote rested both his hands upon

Seth's shoulders. "The Jalora told me it commands you stay here in North Marsh. I don't like leaving you, but we must trust its wisdom. Swear to me now if you ever find yourself alone and in trouble, you'll send for me. I will come to you without fail."

"I promise."

"Swear it upon the Jalora, Ice Lion, or I won't have the strength to get aboard my launch."

"Very well. I swear upon the Jalora I'll call for you if I'm alone and in trouble."

Coyote let his hands fall away with an exhale. Troubled eyes scanned Seth's face. Then he jogged out of the shed and into the rain-soaked night. Jason crawled into the launch and balanced on the rows of seats. He dropped to a bench as Boyd fired up the engines.

"May our paths cross again soon, Lion," Jason called and gave him one last wave. "Beware Esteban the Hawk. He's a traitor to Andara. Wolf is the one you must trust now."

Rain, light and gentle, tapped at Seth's face as he kept his eyes to the skies. The Jackal launch's engines lifted into the air and flew over the outpost wall with a small boom. Sending all his hope with the little vessel, Seth prayed Jason would reach Lea in time to warn the Legion.

"Your friend has a lot of brass." White Tiger came to stand behind him. "It will get him in trouble one day with the wrong person."

"I hope not, sir."

Chapter Thirty-One

WOLF CROUCHED AGAINST the damp stone wall of the cave. Scarred and wet from the brutal excavation of its body by the voracious digging tools of Andara's invaders, the mountain seemed to be bleeding. According to the Buellander thief, the Jackal had named their defacement of the Andarian mountainside, "Stone Fang Fortress." Judging from the jagged remains hanging above him, Wolf believed the name was well deserved.

Boots struck stone, announcing an approaching squad of Jackal soldiers. Their foul stench hung in the damp cave even after they marched past. Oblivious to Wolf's presence, their attention remained focused on the back of their squad leader's head. Barbarous they might be, but the Jackal soldiers were extremely disciplined. This same, unflappable loyalty to their leader was what gave them the upper hand during Valdeon's fall. Andara would suffer the same fate if its leaders continued to bicker.

"Are you sure you know what you're doing?" Berto asked.

"No, as I've mentioned half a dozen times, I've only seen this done once," Raven answered with an irritated sigh. "It should work if Basilio wired the barrels correctly."

Basilio was a man of surprising talents. He'd aided a tunneling crew in the rocky wilds of Portsmouth as a young man. Though many years had passed, Basilio had retained fundamental knowledge of rigging explosives. Wolf's squire, however, was no expert either.

Raven, to his credit, continued splicing together cord connecting several tubes of Jackal explosives. Not only had their hosts been amiable enough to store all the gunpowder and ammunition in one pile, but they'd also been careless in the storage of their mining equipment. If Andara's luck held, the Lords of Valdeon would blow every scrap of Jackal weapons and equipment to oblivion. The Legion needed time to prepare. Thank the Jalora, the Legion had already started recruiting men and making weapons when Valdeon had fallen.

A hateful presence touched the tendrils of Wolf's senses. Recoiling, he withdrew his power. Esteban the Hawk emerged from the entrance to one of the caverns. A Changeling followed respectfully behind him. What bangtail mischief was this? Wolf had known Esteban lusted for his brother's throne, but this unholy alliance with creatures formed by the Sarcion's dark hand was unforgivable.

Hawk held up a hand to draw the attention of a Jackal commander. They greeted each other warmly. Curse the betrayer prince! Wolf pushed a fist against the surface of the stone. Quite obviously the two villains knew each other and had been meeting for Hell only knew how long. They were old allies plotting to overthrow an entire continent. Hawk's smile of friendship was more than Wolf could stand. Esteban's death was long overdue.

"I don't like his choice of friends," Raven whispered, his voice hollow with betrayal.

"Get back to your tasks. Time grows short," Wolf told them. "Hurry and light this cave up. I have a new mission now. The Hawk Prince dies today by my hand."

Jaguar grabbed his arm. "You can't go now. We've almost finished. What if you don't make it out of the cave in time?"

"I'll worry about my escape." Wolf pulled away with an impatient grunt. "Blow the cave and then get to the ship. Don't forget to collect the others. I've sent them to guard our escape route. Meet me at Corpse Point. We'll fetch the Lion together."

"This is madness."

"Perhaps, but I won't allow the true villain behind this treason to escape."

Wolf moved away from the protective concealment of the barrels and along the wet cave walls. Hawk and his Changeling companion bid their parting pleasantries to the Jackal and began walking toward another far cavern. Wolf followed the wall in a parallel course until he came within feet of their destination. Intensifying his mental block, he squeezed anxious fingers around the hilt of his sword when Hawk stopped at the opening.

"Why the delay? I've given you the location of the map. It outlines all the old Legion routes across North Marsh."

"Your Lion killed one of my cousins and recovered the map. I'm most eager to confront him about his insult to our family."

"Did he?" Hawk laughed. "Curb your bloodlust. I've taken years to develop this plan. We attack North Marsh Outpost on two fronts. The Jackal from this base in the North and our mercenary friends from the West." Fierce mania filled the energy around his body. "They will be surrounded and outnumbered. Then Heidelbrecht and the other lazy countries will be easy to pluck like ripe fruit."

"And what of this Lion?" the Changeling asked. "We can't guarantee he will survive the battle."

Hawk flew at the creature and slammed it against the wall. It bared its teeth for a brief moment before bowing its head in submission. Hawk, it would seem, was also the Changeling leader. All the more reason to kill him.

"I've told you I need the boy to fulfill our plans. He'll be my puppet." Hawk released the Changeling and stepped away. "If he should happen to fall, I have a contingency plan, but it will be less appealing for everyone."

Protect the Lion!

Wolf, a slave to his sudden concern for Seth, spun away from them. He hurried through the mouth of Stone Fang Fortress. The power of the Right-Hand urged him forward without regard for stealth or safety. Racing to the launches Coyote had found a few days before, Wolf ripped the mooring lines from Stone Fang's cliff face. Rock pulled away with the rope as several of the vessels floated haplessly toward open air.

Wolf jumped aboard the nearest launch and set sail at a reckless speed.

Heavy rain and wind slapped at the tiny vessel as soon as he descended over the waters. Dank marsh zipped by below him in blobs of green and brown. Flying without map or navigation, he followed the urgent pull of the Lion's heartbeat. Perhaps this single-minded concern for Seth's safety was the cause of his lapse in judgment.

Two hands hung on the side of the launch, which rocked as Esteban the Hawk pulled his body aboard. A murderous fire burned within the depths of the Hawk's eyes. Releasing the rudder, Wolf drew his sword. He must reach Seth quickly. No more time for games. Esteban D'Antoiné would soon draw his last breath.

"Let's have done with this, Hawk Prince. I've no time to spare."

"Xavier De Vincente, you've always been the burr in my boot. No more." Hawk pointed the tip of his sword at Wolf's heart. "I have a continent to conquer, and you're in the way again."

Hawk came at Wolf in a rush, his sword sweeping down in a deadly arc. Slapping away the weapon, Wolf threw his fist into Hawk's jaw. Esteban staggered backward then wiped the blood away with a furious growl. He flew forward again. Wolf, dancing upon the wind, whirled out of the way and landed in the midsection of the hull. Hawk's blade struck the engine with a boom. It sparked and fizzed, finally dying in an erratic display of light.

"Give up, Wolf. You aren't going to warn the Lion. Don't you understand? You'll never be the Right-Hand."

The launch, engine sputtering smoke, plummeted toward the marsh. Wolf braced his feet against the sides of the hull. Their vessel rocked wildly like a leaf in a windstorm. It wouldn't stay upright much longer.

"You're mad!" Wolf fell to his side in the shallow hull. "Neither of us will survive this fall."

"You might be surprised. Goodbye, Lord of Valdeon." Then Hawk's face twisted in an outraged growl. "No!"

An engine roared above them. It was Basilio. He'd followed Wolf in his reckless attempt to go to the Lion. Wolf brought his leg up and kicked Hawk hard between the legs. Scrambling to his feet, he jumped at and into the launch as Basilio drew closer. Esteban's hateful gaze locked on them as he plummeted in his burning vessel toward the marsh.

"May he rot in that boggy prison with the other carcasses." Wolf turned to his squire. "Hurry! The Lion is in danger. We must reach North Marsh Outpost before the mercenaries can attack. What of the sabotage?"

Just then, the mountain exploded behind them. Rock, metal, and wood rose into the air on a spout of fire. Stone Fang Fortress closed its mouth with a piercing scream. The Lords of Valdeon had done their duty well this day. They'd blocked the Jackal's march to the North, but what of the Southern infestation? Wolf must reach Seth and North Marsh Outpost before the mercenaries pounded at their gates.

Chapter Thirty-Two

SETH LEANED AGAINST the railing of their training paddock. An uncommon full sun had come out to grace them this day. Celebrating the rarity, Seth had cut their training short and let his friends relax in the warming rays. The other apprentices didn't mind the short class. Any change in their dull routine was welcome.

"What does he want?" Cal asked, nodding his head toward the courtyard.

Mantis approached them at an irritatingly casual pace. An expectant grin struggled to stay off his lips. He'd resumed his torment of the apprentices after Jason had pummeled Gecko. Carefully adhering to Dragonfly's orders, he'd kept his harassments to verbal slights. Judging by the skip in his step, Mantis must have particularly unpleasant news to make him happy this day.

"Enjoying the sunshine, are we?" Mantis stopped at the railing, his eyes remaining on Seth. "Such a fine day too. Pity the apprentice testing has been canceled. The weather's perfect for it."

"What do you mean?" Bear pushed away from the railing.

"Phoenix is afraid to send you boys out into the marsh alone. I suppose he fears Ice Lion will have another nightmare and fall off Mount Crumble." Mantis sneered as he waved a gloating goodbye. "Enjoy the rest of your class. I'm sure you'll test. Eventually."

Bear slammed a fist onto the railing. His burning glare followed Mantis as the acolyte walked back to the courtyard. Disappointment. Anger. Frustration. They circled about the young man's body in agitated waves.

"What does he mean by apprentice testing?" Cal asked.

"The Jalora decides when a ranger advances to the next level of service," Bear said. "Sometimes it can happen during battle or after some heroic feat. Often, during peaceful times, apprentices are given the opportunity to advance by a test. Their commander determines when and where the challenge takes place." Bear leaned his weight against the railing again. "I thought I would advance this year for certain. My swordsmanship has improved, and I'm a senior apprentice. I don't understand."

"Phoenix will come around, Bear." Badger gave him a reassuring smile. "You'll see. He can't hold off on testing for long."

"I'm glad he's waiting until we get out of this carcass-filled bog." Cal waved a hand at the wall. "Mount Crumble, indeed. It sounds horrible."

"You're wise to fear it," Bear said. "Mount Crumble is what the Legion jokingly calls the old ruins a few miles west of here. It is a dangerous place. Only the lightest foot can step on its face."

Seth noticed his solemn friends looking down at their feet or anywhere else to avoid his eye. They must resent him for their missed opportunity, but was it true? Or was Mantis telling a vindictive half-truth?

"I'm going to speak with White Tiger," Seth told them. "Wait here."

"Don't do anything rash!" Cal called.

While his heart pounded to the beat of his angry strides, Seth stomped up the stairs of the mess and pushed inside. The testing might be his only chance to search those ruins for the lost relic. He found White Tiger sipping on a cup of hot tea at one of the tables. Sharp eyes watched as he crossed the distance. White Tiger set his cup down when Seth came to a stop next to the table. The old ranger pressed his palms on the linen surface as if to summon more patience.

"And why so angry today, Ice Lion? The sun is out. You should be in a better mood."

"Is it true you've canceled the apprentice testing?"

"Put a 'sir' on the end of that, Ice Lion." White Tiger shook his head and picked the cup back up. "Phoenix decides when he will test his apprentices, not you."

Fury instantly surged to form a low growl at the base of Seth's throat. The Lion Spirit didn't like to be questioned, not even by a ranger. Seth took tight control on its anger, calming both their tempers with a series of deep breaths. He saluted White Tiger and marched back out of the mess.

White Tiger didn't understand. They were all servants of the Jalora, and when it commanded they perform a task, then it must be done. Besides, holding back his friends over concern of Seth's lack of control wasn't fair.

Standing at the commander's door before he realized where his feet had taken him, Seth struggled to calm his emotions. His storming in like an angry thundercloud hadn't moved White Tiger. Most likely such an approach wouldn't work on the Phoenix, either. He must convince the commander to allow the apprentices to test. The desired outcome — Seth's recovery of the relic — might very well be the key to Andara safety. He'd have to come up with a more compelling argument.

Honesty is the best approach, My Lion.

Seth took a deep breath and knocked on the door. The Jalora's permission to share its secret with Phoenix was a welcome relief. Seth was getting nowhere on his own. An arm reached over his shoulder and pushed the door open. Phoenix gave Seth a nod and stepped around him to enter his office. How long had the commander been standing there watching Seth dither?

"You want a word with me," he said, moving to the desk.

"The apprentice testing, sir. It's important the challenge proceeds."

"Indeed?" Phoenix clasped his hands behind his back. "And when will you tell me why you are so eager to explore Mount Crumble? Why do you search this outpost night after night, I wonder." Phoenix sat down on the edge of his desk when Seth didn't answer. "Take a seat, Ice Lion."

Seth swallowed his impatience and plopped down on the chair before the desk. Stiff and unyielding, it was an uncomfortable object of torture. He shifted in the seat as the deacon settled in for what Seth hoped wasn't a lecture about Legion codes or military protocol.

"Many centuries ago, in the days of Paulo D'Antoiné, Andara's second Jalora Master, war spread across the land. Many died from violence and the famine it wrought. Paulo the Azure Lion and the Lords of Valdeon were the lone justice on Andara. No one would stand with them against the hordes who ran across the continent. No one but my ancestor Delwyn Baldemar. He and his men joined the forces of Valdeon to stop the hordes and restore peace."

Phoenix smiled down at his ring with pride. "In honor of his loyalty, the Jalora gifted the Phoenix Ring to my ancestor. It was the first Heart of the Warrior Ring created after the original nine gifted to the Sacred Guard."

The proud smile slowly faded. "The Bearer of the Phoenix Ring has another duty when a Jalora Master walks the Erthe. He is Partisan to the Master. I am honor bound to protect the Sacred Guard as they care for the Lion during his fits of rage or power. This duty rests on the very soul of the man who bears the Phoenix Ring. Heidelbrecht is Valdeon's oldest ally. As Partisan to the Master, I cannot refuse a request from the Bearer of the Lion Ring. I beg you to reconsider your plan. North Marsh is full of danger."

"I'm afraid I cannot be swayed in this, Phoenix." A little pang of guilt crept into his conscience when Phoenix shook his head unhappily. "The Jalora has given me a quest, sir. I must complete it soon."

Phoenix leaned a bit further, concentration hard upon his face. "You look for something? Can you tell me what?"

"I'm supposed to look for what was lost, but I have no idea what it is."

Phoenix jumped up with a sharp intake of breath. "The Creed of the Guardian! It reveals itself at last." He reached across the gap between them and rested his hands on Seth's shoulder. "You must have heard about 'The Sign of the Coming?'"

Phoenix recited:

"The skies thunder the moment he is made, and the stars fall from the heavens at his birth.

"His strength of heart shall be a fortress to those without comfort.

"His kindness shall know no bounds.

"He shall be known as 'Lord' by his allies he draws to him with ease.

"Many will know him when what was lost is found, as the Creed of the Guardian shines

"The Lion Child Vessel declares his naming as the Sacred Guard draws near.

"Crimson circles the Ring of the Lion until his mighty roar, at last, is heard.

"This marks the coming of the Red Heart."

"Don't you see?" asked Phoenix urgently. "The Creed gives you authority over the Legion. We are one step closer to restoring the Jalora's power and defeating the Jackal."

Seth nodded. "Once I find it."

"Yes, once you find it." Phoenix marched about the room in excitement. "We'll take a troop of rangers to

Mount Crumble. Did the Jalora give you any clues as to its hiding place?"

"Supposedly, I will know when I'm close," Seth said, then rubbed anxious fingers through his hair. "The Creed of the Guardian. What is it? What does it look like?"

Phoenix shook his head. "I'm afraid I don't know. The legends only speak of it after the Creed attaches itself to the Lion's sword."

"Then it could be anything like a jewel or a scabbard." Seth reluctantly smiled at the keen interest on his commander's face. "The apprentices, sir, they've earned the opportunity to test."

"And it would be awkward for a battalion of rangers marching about." Phoenix tapped the silver band of his ring in an energized tempo against the desk. "Very well. If the Creed is waiting to make itself known to you, it may not want a loud affair. I'll allow you and the apprentices to go on this test, Ice Lion, on one condition. Promise on the treaty between our people if trouble finds you, then you'll signal immediately. I'll have rangers on the battlements watching for any signs. We'll be prepared to join you at the greatest urgency."

"I swear it will be so." Seth got to his feet with a new surge of hope. "Thank you for your trust in me."

"One last thing, Ice Lion." Phoenix folded his arms with a grin. "If the Creed isn't at Mount Crumble, then you must promise to allow me to help you look."

"That's a promise I'm happy to keep."

Chapter Thirty-Three

LIGHT RAIN FILTERED an early morning pink sky over the walls of North Marsh Outpost. Seth and the other apprentices followed Bear through the Legion courtyard. The battalion had kept silent about their impending challenge, but Seth suspected Bear knew what was about to happen. He'd tested before—though unsuccessfully.

Passing through the entrance to the UR area, Seth was astonished to see every ranger in Western Beta assembled in the large courtyard. They lined the path leading to the outpost's main gate. Cal whistled low at the unexpected sign of support from their battalion.

Several of the acolytes had encouraging words for Bear. He'd earned this chance for advancement. Seth hoped the Jalora agreed and would finally promote Bear to a full ranger in the Legion.

"I've got a bad feeling about this." Cal gave his friends a shrug. "Not that I'm afraid. Let's say I'm concerned."

"You should be afraid," Bear told him. "The last time I tested, White Tiger had to pull me out of a burning ship. I nearly died." He tugged hard on the hem of his tunic. "This time will be different. I'm ready for anything."

"I wish you hadn't said that, Bear."

Cal pointed at the gates of the outpost. Phoenix, blue eyes set firmly on them, stood before the entrance. His body shifted in impatient gestures uncharacteristic of the typically composed and commanding presence he adopted before his men. Their deacon, they could deduce, was as eager for the test to begin as his apprentices.

White Tiger stood solemnly beside him. Arms folded and a sour frown under his mustache, the old ranger didn't share the deacon's enthusiasm. He returned Seth's gaze with a disgruntled sigh.

"Apprentices!" Phoenix raised his arms, quieting the rangers. "You've been trained by the best. Now it's time to see how much you've learned. White Tiger and I have placed a flag somewhere on Mount Crumble. You will retrieve it and bring it back to me by noonday tomorrow."

"That doesn't sound too bad," Badger said.

"Have a care. Dangerous bogs and predators await your steps between here and the ruins." Phoenix stopped for what Seth suspected was dramatic effect. "Use what you have learned. Trust in the Jalora."

White Tiger beckoned to the ranks. Riley and his fellow apprentice squires hurried through the line of rangers. Each of them carried heavy packs. Pride. Anxiety. Anticipation. The emotions clung to the young men as they came to join their rangers. These squires, in a way, were also testing.

The Squire Corps' most vocal apprentice splashed in the mud toward his Lion. Riley awkwardly balanced Seth's sword and belt atop the bundle in his arms.

Seth grasped the weapon and strapped it around his waist while his squire lifted the cloak from his shoulders. Slipping his arms through the straps of his pack, Seth staggered a bit as Riley let its full weight fall on Seth shoulders.

As he adjusted the straps, Riley tugged hard, then murmured, “This has your handiwork all over it, Seth.”

“I’ll be back soon.”

“You’d better be, or I’m coming after you.” Riley slapped the pack and returned to stand with the other squires.

The gate rumbled open, letting the noises of the marsh seep through. A little of Seth’s excitement waned as the reality of danger came to the forefront of his mind. This test wasn’t going to be as easy as he’d supposed. Death waited for the unlucky out in those bogs. They’d have to focus on staying alive first before Seth could go searching for any relic.

“Signals have been placed in each of your packs. Use them if you run into trouble.” White Tiger pointed at the open gate. “Stop puttering about like mud hens. Get moving. Good luck and have fun, boys.” He held Seth’s gaze with an intense urgency. “Hurry back, Ice Lion. I don’t relish explaining to Xavier the Wolf why you’ve left the outpost.”

Laughter pushed at their backs until they were well down the path toward the docks. Then—as with the sudden flip of a switch—the laughter was silenced by the slamming of the outpost gate. They were on their own.

“Which way?” Badger asked.

"Mount Crumble lies to the west," Bear said. "Legion rumors speak of hidden trails through the bogs of North Marsh. We'll need hours to find them."

"Unless we have a map."

Seth pulled out the rough drawing he'd made from memory. Having this guide wasn't cheating since he'd seen the many paths around North Marsh prior to their commander planning the challenge. Unrolling the parchment carefully, he held the page out before him. Bear and the others circled, staring at the map over his shoulder.

"I caught a glimpse of the original map the night those Changelings tried to steal it. The solid lines appear to be the hidden paths. The diagram had other markings, but I'm not certain what they were supposed to represent."

"I say we follow the ones we know," Cal suggested.

"Agreed. Bear, can you lead us west?"

"I believe so," Bear said, running a finger along the parchment. "Here is our route."

After a few missteps, their feet found firm ground. Filtered sunbeams touched the murky waters of the bog. The light danced on the surface, unable to penetrate the thick presence of death beneath the pools. Bear took point, while Seth brought up the rear. The chance to escape White Tiger's unending list of chores might have been a reason for celebration, but the overwhelming eeriness of the bogs snatched away their good humor.

"How could the stench be worse out here than inside?" Cal hopped over the rotting remains of a small rodent-like creature.

"Perhaps the stone walls filter some of the odor," Badger said. "I think we will all have a better appreciation for the outpost by the time this test is through."

Morning passed quickly. Toward afternoon, Seth couldn't resist casting a few looks back. The walls of North Marsh Outpost grew smaller until they finally disappeared in the distance. Hours had flown by with no sign of Mount Crumble. Doubt in the hand-drawn map began to crack Seth's confidence.

"Don't worry, Seth. We found hard ground," Badger said. "I consider it progress."

"Yes, but I don't know if we march toward Mount Crumble or deeper into the center of the bogs." Seth held a hand to block the waning light of a rare sun. "Do you see the small rock formation over there? We can climb to the top for a better look."

They made their way on a winding route toward the rocks. Seth let out his frustration upon the unruly marsh grass arcing over their trail. He'd expected the Creed would call to him and perhaps help him on his way. But the relic still gave no sign or glimmer of magic in any direction.

"The sun is beginning to set." Bear brought them to a halt. "We must find shelter soon. It's suicide to be in the bogs of North Marsh after dark. The creatures of the night will certainly find us."

Distant howls, as if in agreement with his warning, trumpeted behind them. Their notes hung in the heavy air several seconds before being taken up by another voice. The strange series of sounds, lonely one moment and violent the next, were more intense than any they'd heard from the top of the battlement walls.

"What horror has found us?" Badger cried.

"Marsh wolves. They gather for the hunt, and we're the prey. Run!"

Bear hurried down the mossy path at a breakneck pace. Seth and the others followed, forgetting their careful search of hard versus soggy ground. Pounding paws thundered on the stone behind them as sharp claws scraped against the path. A pack of yellow eyes pierced the distance, hungry to make the men's acquaintance. The wolves yowled! Massive heads of dark gray fur lifted in frenzied howls as they ran.

"The rock formation," Seth shouted. "Climb as fast as you dare."

Heart racing, he gulped in frightened breaths of dank air. Teeth snapped at his heels. The hungry pack was almost upon them. Then his boots hit the slippery rock. He stumbled to his hands and knees. A sharp pain ran up his arm as a piece of jagged rock sliced his palm. Ignoring the blood, Seth continued upward and followed the sounds of rock sliding violently toward the ground. The wolves stopped at the base of the stones, pacing with snapping jaws.

"Why aren't they following?" Badger asked.

"Who cares!" Cal kicked a piece of rock into the group of wolves. "May they go find an easier dinner tonight!"

Bear bent over and carefully picked up a rock. Its body contained a strange mix of black, rust, and clear crystal. Bear pushed at the end of the shale with his thumb, and the piece broke off with a snap. He sniffed the remaining stone and wrinkled his nose.

"It smells of old wagon wheels and sulfur. Such a harsh smell. No wonder they don't follow us. The rocks must hurt their paws."

"No, not rock." Seth knelt to examine a larger clump of material. "It looks like metal and glass fused into one. I don't know what this pile of rocks used to be, but whatever destroyed it must have been as hot as the sun."

"I see something." Cal pointed toward the top of the formation. "It almost looks like an opening."

Climbing higher on the slippery pile of rubble, they came to a narrow ridge. Seth pressed his boot carefully on the rusted surface. In its past life, the rim had been a metal girder. Satisfied it was stable, he put his full weight on the beam. Shale slipped down into the marsh as he walked across it. The rim might have been solid, but its foundations rested on muddy ground.

"Careful," he told his friends. "Take light steps."

A hole opened in the rubble close to the ridge's end. Seth, carefully avoiding the sharp edges of the entrance, stepped into the darkness. A sharp cry from Cal told him the others hadn't learned the value of caution around the surface of the formation. Seth stretched out his powers using the Sight to survey the space. He was in a small cave made of fused metal and glass. Someone had stored blankets and crates of food and water inside. Wood had been carefully placed across the floor to protect inhabitants from the spiky ground.

"Do you think the Legion uses this as a lookout?" Badger asked, fidgeting with the knob on a crystal lantern atop a makeshift workbench.

Light from the lantern burst into the darkness, illuminating every square inch of the cave. A small band of silver flashed between two crates at the rear. Seth reached for the dagger abandoned on the floor. The image of a Jackal growled in its handle. Handing it to Bear, he lifted the crate lids. Bags of flour and dried meats had once filled the now-empty containers. The cave's occupants had been here for several weeks.

"This is a spy's cave then?" Bear asked. "It's too far from the outpost to do much good."

"We need to report this to Phoenix," Cal said.

"Listen, we don't know how long ago any spies were last at the cave. Perhaps they were chased off the night Ice Lion killed those Changelings." Bear drove the Jackal dagger into a crate lid. "Come now. I've trained so hard for this testing. We all have. Why jump to conclusions and forfeit based on a guess?"

"It isn't a guess," Badger said, opening up a parchment at the center of the cave. "Some Jackal spy has been trying to draw paths from the west coast to the outpost and beyond. Look, some of the trails go to the borderlands like Framburg and Heidelbrecht."

"I recognize these dashes they've used for paths. Our solid lines represent men walking single file. These other lines could hold large groups of men…like an army." Seth shivered as the memory of his vision came again. "I've seen them come. They will overrun the outpost."

"In this vision of yours," Cal began. "Was everyone dead?"

"Yes, except for us. We weren't at the outpost." The cold fingers of fate twisted viciously at his gut. "I think we were here in the marsh on this testing."

"We must take these maps back with us." Badger began digging through other parchments in the spies' pile. "The invaders can't use them if they're safe with us. Maybe we can stop the events of your vision?"

"Let's get a few hours of rest, and then we must go back to the outpost." Seth put a hand on Bear's shoulder. "I'm sorry."

Lying on the ground fretfully, Seth covered his eyes with his forearm. The others had fallen into a light slumber, but sleep wouldn't come for him. If Phoenix was correct about its nature, then the Creed of the Guardian must give the Bearer of the Lion Ring additional powers. It could help him stop the invasion. Why in the green, green fields wasn't the relic reaching out to him?

"Have you considered the reason the Creed's magic isn't calling is that it isn't here?" asked a voice.

Seth took his arm away. Elk and Cougar stood at the opening of the cave. Their uniforms were perfectly clean as if they'd found a way to circumvent the muddy bogs.

"I believe it's hidden somewhere on Mount Crumble," Seth rebutted. He sat up and rubbed at his eyes.

"You may be adept at drawing maps, but you're not very good at reading them." Cougar chuckled and held his arms wide. "Welcome to Mount Crumble."

"Of course, it is," Seth murmured with a disgruntled sigh. "If the Creed isn't here, then where is it? Andara's time grows short."

"What you seek is in a sunken place. Beware, young Ice Lion." Elk stepped away from the door and turned. "Evil is two steps ahead of the Legion. And it has many agents."

A silent figure crawled through the opening of the cave. Careful feet moved noiselessly over the wooden floor until the intruder stopped beside Cal. Violence. Greed. Amusement. This agent of evil, as Elk had named him, had no trepidation for what he was about to do. Pulling a dagger from his garments, the spy lifted his dagger high.

Seth rolled out of his blankets and dove at the interloper. He slammed into the man's torso, sending them both to the edge of the protection of the wooden floor pad. A sharp breath burst from the villain's mouth in a great whoop. Flipping him to face downward, Seth pressed the spy's cheek against the pointed edges poking out of the floor. He left his own face open and got an elbow in the nose. Eyes watering, Seth fell away from the villain.

"You aren't going anywhere!"

Bear grabbed the spy as he was running for the exit. Holding a massive arm around the man's neck, he squeezed hard until the spy stopped struggling. Henry, ever the practical one, turned on their crystal lantern. The spy blinked his watering eyes and stared at them. Thin brown hair jutted out at awkward angles from his balding scalp. He laughed. A tooth, chipped and blackened, hung in the center of a murderous sneer.

Then he apparently noticed Henry's yellow ring and began to laugh. "Apprentices! Just my luck. Did the real rangers let you out to play then?" He slapped at Bear's arm. "Let me go. I've no time for you."

"I recognize your accent, Buellander." Seth wiped the blood from his nose. "Why would you help these villains who seek to invade your homeland and enslave your people?"

"Money, of course," the spy spat out with a grunt. "What's it to you?"

His high-pitched laughter hit the pointed walls of the cave, echoing in irritating beats against Seth's ears. The beast inhabiting his shared body began to wake. Its ravenous appetite for blood flared as if someone had rung a dinner bell.

"Tell us of the invasion. You were drawing a map of the safe paths across North Marsh for them. When do they attack the outpost?"

"If you were real rangers, I'd be afraid. All their reading of minds and such." The spy rubbed at his neck when Bear released him. "Being apprentices, you won't know how to do any of those things then. And your Jalora doesn't condone torture."

"It would depend upon what type of torture you mean," the joined voices of Seth and the Jalora said, bringing the death mask to full strength. "Do you recognize me now, villain? I am the Lion Protector."

Seth grabbed the intruder's face and forced him to look into death's gaze. Terrified eyes opened impossibly wide as the ancient magic claimed the last of his courage. Seeing his own death with brutal clarity, the spy screamed. Seth pushed aside the man's terror and probed his thoughts. The Lion's Roar grumbled at what he found within the man's memories.

Andarian mercenaries had hired this cowering cur and furnished the cave with supplies and mapping tools. Money had been exchanged with other human hands. The Buellander had met his Changeling allies only once on the pathways just out of sight of the outpost.

Seth dropped the death mask with an angry growl. "This man is a mapmaker only. He doesn't know their invasion plans or anything about the attack on the outpost."

The spy pushed away from Bear and threw his body to the side. Heaving violently, he vomited into an empty crate. His audience waited unmoved and unrepentant. The spy sat up at last and turned vindictive eyes on Seth. He wiped his mouth with shaking hands.

"I know this," he said, staring at the Lion Ring. "You've been marked for death by the Changelings. You'll die soon."

"What a coincidence. So will you." Seth grabbed a few pieces of rope tying the crates shut. He tossed them to Cal. "Tie him up. Don't bother being gentle."

Chapter Thirty-Four

"COME NOW," Bear pleaded. "Give me an hour! We have the spy in hand."

Bear, stepping back onto the steel beam at the lip of the spy cave, slipped precariously off the side. Seth grabbed his arm and pulled him upright. The constant drizzle of rain had returned home to North Marsh. It would make the surface of Mount Crumble all the more hazardous.

"We must warn the outpost," Seth said.

"I don't understand, Ice Lion. You were the one who was so keen to find Mount Crumble. You talked the Phoenix into the testing. Don't try to deny it." Bear lifted his arms into the marsh morning. "What could an hour's delay hurt?"

Indeed, Seth had been keen. His single-minded push to find the Creed had been for nothing. He sighed. But perhaps their journey hadn't been a waste after all. This spy and his map would help them prepare for an attack on the outpost. He might have misjudged the timing in his vision as well. Come to think of it, Bear, Henry, and Cal hadn't been with him at the gates.

"Very well, Bear. We've come all this way. What do the rest of you think?"

"As much as I hate wandering around in this boggy mess, I'd like to finish what we've started," Cal said.

"Would it be cheating to get a bit of help from our spy?" Henry asked, grinning at the Buellander.

The spy spat a stream of obscenities in Lydec, stabbing two fingers rudely at Seth. A pink tongue pressed against his chipped black tooth as he delivered a particularly brutal curse. Red burned along Seth's face and ears. The Buellander was creative in his insults.

"He declines to help us," Seth told them. "And wishes us all a painful end."

Cal gave the spy a good whack on the back of the head. "Fine. You'd probably lead us in the wrong direction anyway. And I hope Badger accidentally drops you in a bog."

"Our best direction is up," Bear said. "We should be able to see something from the top of Mount Crumble."

The climb to the top was an exercise in patient tenacity. Rivulets of rainwater raced from the top of the ruins toward the hungry bogs below. Their wiggling bodies made finding solid footing almost impossible. Each step they took sent a landslide of shale plummeting downward. They'd had the good sense to wrap their hands in cloth to protect against slips on the rough surface. Even so, Seth's palms were taking a beating.

Their prisoner wasn't much help. He seized every opportunity to resist Henry until Cal gave the spy a hard right in the jaw. Deciding straining their patience wasn't a good idea, he begrudgingly stopped resisting. His hatred for the apprentices, however, remained a wild thing, looking for an escape. Henry sensed his ill will too. He stayed alert, his hands continually checking the ropes binding their prisoner.

"I don't believe it!" Cal yowled with a laugh. "Our path took us to the wrong side of the ruins."

A bright red flag flopped lazily in the morning rain. Someone had planted its pole in the center of a small island at the base of Mount Crumble. Strange black sand surrounded the flag. Its soot-colored grains blanketed the landmass until the waters of the bog stopped them.

"Andara has benefited from our mistake," Seth said. "We might have missed our spy and his secret cave altogether if we'd gone the right way."

Henry shouted in triumph. He pulled his unhappy prisoner along with him down the side of the mountain of rubble. Seth followed, using his arms to maintain his balance. Falling on the fused metal and glass was an experience he'd already endured and didn't enjoy.

"Hurry!" Henry called to them. "We're almost there!"

Bear rushed to stop him before he stepped away from the base. "They've put the flag in the center of a bog. Step in there and the mix of sand and water will pull you to your death."

"Phoenix would have left a solid path. Shall we try this way then?" Henry asked stepping toward the left.

The spy screamed out in warning, but he was too late. Henry sank into the oozing black muck taking their prisoner with him. Their bodies disappeared below the surface in seconds. Seth rushed into the bog at the last place he'd seen his cousin. Throwing himself onto the mush of black sand and murky water, he drove his arms into its sopping body, reaching for the two men to rescue them before they drowned.

"Help us!" Cal grabbed Seth's ankles as his head sank closer to the water's surface.

"I've got you," Bear called from his position as an anchor on the shifting rock.

Stretching. Reaching. Grasping. The muck slipped through Seth's panicked fingers. Finally, he touched a solid object. He'd found Henry's collar. Grabbing on tightly, he told Cal and Bear to pull. As he slid backward through the marsh, he struggled to keep his mouth and nose above the mucky surface.

"Henry!" Seth kept a tight hold on his cousin's collar. "Keep pulling! We're almost to the rock."

After dragging Henry and his prisoner to the shore, they all collapsed on the thin rim of solid black sand. Sputtering for breath, Henry gagged violently. Wet muck trickled out of his ears and every opening in his uniform. Seth waited beside him until Henry's coughing subsided.

"I'm glad you're well," Cal said, slapping Henry on the back. "But you, spy, are lucky we didn't leave you in the bog."

While coughing up all he'd inhaled, their prisoner cast murderous eyes on him. Cal stood and pushed the man over as he passed. His boots stomped on the shale surface of Mount Crumble. As he twisted about, Cal scanned the base of the ruins with an unhappy scowl.

"You don't suppose Phoenix and White Tiger used their powers? That's hardly fair." He slapped at the muck on his sleeves. "We can't hope to compete with a deacon."

"Young idiot. They used their brains." The spy pointed to their right. A thin branch of moss and rock stretched across the waters. The land bridge ended a good five feet from the flag, but it was traversable by those with the skills of an apprentice. A common man bound with rope, however, wouldn't make it across the gap. All the apprentices must finish the challenge according to the Legion rules. Seth looked at the empty marsh surrounding them.

"You won't be able to go with us," Seth told the spy. "I suggest you wait here. Don't make us come looking for you."

"Where would I go bound as I am?" He muttered several more curses as they left him.

Bear was already scouting a path to the small land bridge when Seth left the spy sitting on the shale. Walking carefully on the strip of black sand along the shore, Seth joined the other apprentices on the land bridge. Blocks of stone formed a small pathway leading to nowhere. Perhaps it had been used for some purpose long ago. Seth shrugged. Regardless, he welcomed solid ground beneath his boots. Signs of careful cleaning were evident on the surface of the stone as they walked. Phoenix and White Tiger had given them clear signals for a safe path after all.

"I think you should be first, Bear."

Seth gave him an encouraging smile as they stood on the edge of the land bridge. Ringlets left by raindrops made circles in the dark water; blades of marsh grass poked their vibrant bodies through its surface. The veil of green had been cut down by a metal blade to make their jump easier. This apprentice test had been designed to be a more straightforward challenge. Fate, it would seem, had provided other ideas.

Seth's friend returned his smile with a battle cry. Then Bear jumped. The others cheered as he came to a landing upon sandy, but solid ground. Cal and Henry went next. Then Seth joined them as they circled about the flag. It waved to them in greeting. Transfixed, he and his friends watched the bright red fabric dance on the weak breeze.

"We pull it down together," Bear suggested.

They each put a hand on the pole and pulled. After unfastening the flag from its pole, Cal folded it neatly. He brushed away bits of dried sand shifting from his sleeve to the red fabric. Cal pointed to the base of Mount Crumble and let out a curse.

"Where do you suppose he thinks he's going?"

The Buellander spy had cut his bonds on the sharp rocks and was scurrying away toward the east. Shale and sand slipped beneath his boots as he wobbled on his feet. They'd lose sight of him in a moment when the base of Mount Crumble curved toward the northeast.

"Wherever he's going, he won't get there quickly." Henry chuckled at the spy's departing back.

"You saved our lives, Seth." Cal shrugged and looked down at his boots. "That wet rat might have... Well, here. You carry the flag."

"Agreed," Bear and Henry echoed.

"We'll all see it safely into Phoenix' hand." Seth tucked it in his tunic for safekeeping. "Morning is leaving us. We'd better take our spy back to the outpost."

Seth looked across the water toward the shore. "Where did he go?"

"Back to the spy cave, I hope." Bear took the lead as they hurried away across the land bridge.

Sudden prickles of anxiety raced along Seth's spine as they fought their way again up Mount Crumble. Something was wrong. The Jalora was unsettled. He pushed his feet harder, but the aggressive movements sent the shale sliding. Test done, he was free to use his full power. With the wind wrapped about him, Seth danced on the raindrops as they fell.

Finally reaching the top of Mount Crumble, Seth let his boots touch down lightly on the slippery rock. He could see mercenary troops crawling slowly through the bogs toward the outpost. The Buellander spy must have signaled them when he'd found the apprentices asleep in his cave. Jalora save them. Seth's vision was coming to life on the pathways of North Marsh.

"What is it?" Henry asked, coming to a panting halt beside him. "By my blood. How is this possible?"

"I've been such a fool!" Seth slammed a fist against his leg. "I should have sent the signal as soon as we tied up the spy last night."

He'd promised Phoenix. Now his lapse in judgment had jeopardized the outpost and Andara. Four apprentices couldn't stop the hundreds of trained warriors bound for murder. The outpost was doomed to its fate.

"What should we do?" Henry cried.

"The rangers will see them." Cal ran a nervous hand across his face. "They have to see them."

"In my vision, the outpost was caught unaware," Seth said, staring out at the open marshes. "These villains attacked at night. We still may have time to warn the battalion."

Bear shook his head. "Look at the land between us and the outpost. It's all marsh. We'll never make it unseen."

"The signal flares." Seth took off his pack and emptied the thin cylinders onto the rock. "Phoenix said he'd have rangers stationed on the walls to watch the skies."

The others scrambled to fetch their flares. Henry lifted his pack with a groan and dumped out the water trapped inside. The wet cylinders broke apart when they struck Mount Crumble's surface. Seth touched the rest of the flares. They were all damp from their plunge in the bog.

"These are too wet to ignite," Bear said. "What now?"

Seth ran nervous fingers through his wet hair. He knew of one force that could ignite anything it touched, but once he released it, would he be able to control it? Seth was the Lion Protector. It was time he embraced the role.

Standing up again, he found a sturdy foothold against the shale. "Put the flares in my pack. Throw them into the air as hard as you can on my signal, Bear."

He turned to stare out at the treacherous Andarians crawling toward the east. A hollow ache filled his heart. Releasing his power would draw evil to the small group of apprentices like a deadly tidal wave. No matter his actions, Legion blood would spill this day.

"Please, Jalora, help me! Summon the Lion Spirit."

Seth nodded at Bear. Using all his strength, he sent the flares high into the air. The pack sailed up into the heavy clouds. Then like a harbinger of doom, it fell back toward the Erthe again. Seth pressed his boots into the ground and braced himself. Nothing happened. Sick at heart, he began to panic.

You call me now, boy? Why? Do you suppose I am content to frighten these paltry mortals? No. I long for the taste of their flesh.

"You shall swim in blood this day, Spirit," Seth told it within his mind. *"I won't try to stop you this time."*

Very well, Bearer. Marvel at my power!

Then the Lion Spirit burst to life. Its roar thundered from Seth's throat, shaking the foundations of Mount Crumble. Its force struck the pack with a mighty boom. Explosive color filled the cloudy sky of late morning while rolling waves of energy pushed past the thick banks of rain and drew down thunder from the heavens.

"By my father's beard!" Bear cried, falling to his knees.

"On your feet, apprentice," Seth and the Jalora told him. "They come."

Chapter Thirty-Five

THE MERCENARY ARMY swarmed toward them like locusts in a wheat field. Seth could see the ancient pathways now as the aggressors' charging feet crushed the moss and grass covering the stones beneath them. Seth and his friends had mere moments before the first of hundreds reached Mount Crumble. Hatred. Greed. Revenge. The destructive emotion hung over the enemy numbers, prodding them forward.

"We've nowhere to run," Cal cried.

Fear. Desperation. Then finally acceptance. The apprentices came to stand in a half-circle behind Seth. Hopelessly outnumbered, they remained in position. Each knew his duty and would see it done, no matter the cost.

"We ruined their plans," Henry said. "Didn't we?"

"I choose to believe so, yes." Bear pounded a boot on the shale. "Our battalion will have seen the Lion's warning. No one could have missed it."

They fell silent as the war cries of the mercenaries rose up to strike them. Death was coming on swift feet. A strange sense of regret hit Seth. He hadn't said a proper goodbye to Riley or written a final letter to Aunt Charlotte. Bear and his other friends would leave this life with unfulfilled potential. It wasn't right.

You have no room for self-doubt. I call upon you as Lion Protector, my champion and savior of the innocent. Take your men and win this day for me!

The Jalora came to Seth in full power, filling his body with a hunger for battle. Bloodlust entered their shared mouth as they looked on the mortals charging toward them. The Lion's Spirit would feed well this day. Seth and the Lion's Spirit turned suddenly to the apprentices and pulled their sword.

"We will show them Andarian courage! Who can stand against the Legion?"

The apprentices pulled their swords as one. "All shall fall!"

"Protect the innocent! Punish the guilty!"

Running in attack formation, they dove down Mount Crumble. A shower of shale dislodged by their boots flew at the mercenaries. The mob covered their faces and slowed to a staggering crawl. Seth stopped on solid ground a few feet from the enemy's line. His men landed beside him to take ready positions in the First Stance. As good and evil faced each other, the marsh fell silent.

Then the Lion's Roar thundered across the bogs. Thousands of rangers from the past and present mixed with its fury. The Horde's Cry, it followed the Lion's Roar through the line of their attackers. Men and weapons blasted into ash clouds before Seth's eyes. The screams of the dying faded as wild laughter filled Seth's ears. He was thirsty for more blood, and so many of these mercenaries were willing to oblige his gruesome appetite.

Hungry! I want more!

The Lion Spirit's euphoria engulfed him. Faces and body parts of his foe streaked by as he fought. They'd lost their humanity. Mortals. So weak. He would crush every last one of them under his boots!

Another part of his mind—the Jalora and its eternal calm—stretched out to his servants. *"Bear, patience. Let them come to you. Stallion, steady your arm. It will strengthen your thrusts. Courage, Badger, and take one strike at a time. Focus on your opponent's move."*

The infestation of mortals approached with increasing speed. Their rangers would be overwhelmed. Seth and the Jalora wrapped the wind about them. Their joined body moved on the droplets of moisture hovering over the marsh. Seth, finding the army's center, halted in a sea of mercenaries. He adopted the First Stance and threw his head back as the Jalora's rapture washed over him again. The Lion's Roar shook the ground. Seth pounced like a wild beast in a blood frenzy. Cutting through bone and flesh, he spun faster in the bloodied midst of the enemy. He gulped in great breaths of air, the Jalora's power nearly consuming him.

A ranger pressed against Seth's back. His movements were elegant and precise. What strength he had! Breathing in power, Seth allowed the sense of calm and reason to subdue the Lion Spirit's frenzy a bit. He turned his mind outward.

"Hold the line, rangers!" Seth and the Jalora commanded across the distance. "Evil shall not escape our justice this day!"

The air crackled around him with power as he pushed forward through the men. As he moved, he lost the connection of energy he'd had with the ranger who'd fought at his back. No time to find him again. The treacherous mortals, abandoning their scheme to invade Andara, were running for the open marshes. Seth raced after them. Not a single one would escape punishment.

"Partisan!" the Jalora commanded. *"Protect the Lion!"*

"Stay close, Seth!" someone behind him screamed. "Don't go on your own."

Those words faded in the brutal sounds of battle. Bloodlust pulsed through Seth, fueling his body. He wouldn't stop hunting. Not until they were all crushed at his feet. Terror's foul stench hung in the wake of fleeing bodies. Mortal fools. Even now, many of them ran off the ancient pathways and into the bogs where death was waiting.

Then a figure stepped out of the shadows, blocking Seth's path. The euphoria seeped away, leaving him feeling drained. Seth, on his own now, blinked at the creature. He recognized the sharp features, long black hair, and cruel orbs. Changeling! They'd found him again.

"I've been looking for you, Ice Kitten. We must settle a little matter of revenge."

Its appearance began to change in rapid shifts of birds, animals, and humans. Confusion flooded Seth's mind, blocking the Jalora's presence. The sword dropped from his hand with a muffled clank. What was happening? Sinking to his knees, Seth grabbed at his pounding head.

"You have grown very powerful, Ice Kitten. Has your Jalora warned you of the dangers to that power? No?" The Changeling settled back into its original form with a laugh. "Of course, it wouldn't. The Jalora likes pliable slaves."

The thing circled about Seth slowly, just out of reach. Sharp teeth descended over the creature's thin lips. Though it hadn't pulled a weapon yet, Seth well knew the Changeling was prepared to kill. Seth had been lucky the night on the battlements when he'd killed its cousin. In his current state, without the Lion Spirit's strength, Seth was no match for the Changeling.

"You remind me of a newly turned Dirge," the Changeling said, kicking absently at a clump of marsh grass. "The Jackal start with ten mortal men. Half don't survive the serum they so eagerly desire. Three or four mortals manage to endure its poison. Unfortunately, they discover a rather unpleasant side effect. They become willing servants of the Sarcion or anyone else who will feed their need for flesh."

The thing approached closer to a weakened Seth, staring at him appraisingly. "You, Lion, remind me of the remaining half-man half-Dirge among their group. A strand of human sanity remains until the scent of blood is in the air. It discovers true power in the flesh of others. The Dirge feeds gladly on the power, becoming obsessed and addicted. Soon it goes mad. The power consumes the Dirge until nothing is left, but a dying lump of flesh."

Standing only feet away from Seth, the Changeling pulled its sword. "Don't worry, puppet. I will spare you from such a fate. Your death will be quick, though not painless."

Chapter Thirty-Six

EXPLOSIONS OF CRIMSON and yellow burned within the clouds over the marsh. The raw power erupting in their depths could only mean one thing. Wolf closed his eyes and focused on the Lion's heartbeat. He wasn't at the outpost. Bangtail mischief. Seth had gone to Mount Crumble for some reason. What was Phoenix thinking?

Then a jarring thrust came across their connection. The Spirit of the Lion Ring had been released unrestrained into the marsh. What fevered nonsense was this? The boy had been allowed to roam around the bogs without protection. Something had angered the spirit of the ring, and now Seth was in real peril. If he didn't pull back the power soon, its strength would devour his soul.

"Faster, Basilio! The Lion is in danger."

Wolf stood as the launch's speed increased. The boggy landscape zipped by beneath them. Traces of trampled grass and exposed stone covered its surface. An army had passed this way. Wolf moved to the front of the launch and reached out with his power. Nothing. Growing agitated, he glared at the distant pile of rock.

Then a flash of metal lit up the sky. Battle. A great many traitor blades struck against the swords of the good. Seth was right in the middle. Glowing with the brilliant light of the Jalora, he was a beacon for every attacker in North Marsh. A golden head bobbed up and down among the fighting men. Phoenix was trying desperately to reach Seth. Their Lion, however, had been cut off from his men. Gripped in the bloodlust of the Lion Spirit, he hadn't noticed.

A flock of blackbirds waited on the branches of long-dead trees. Seth, still lost in the Spirit's power, walked right into their midst. He fell to his knees as a Changeling materialized from the trunks of the dead grove. Though Wolf couldn't hear the Changeling's taunts, Seth's elevated heartbeats were enough to signal the gist of their conversation.

Wolf leaped off the launch and danced on the droplets in the skies above the marsh. Racing with all the speed his new power afforded, he was a lightning bolt of sheer fury. Time itself stood still as his body pushed aside the frozen rain. His sense of wonder or any prickles of fear redirected into one single purpose. Protect the Lion.

A Changeling held its blade over a helpless and confused Seth. Wolf grabbed his dagger and threw it. The knife split the air like a lightning bolt, striking with such force, it penetrated the back of the creature's skull. His weapon soared onward until it collided with a crumbling column. The blade penetrated rock to its hilt and remained suspended within the stone.

"For the Lion!" The Voice of the Right-Hand boomed across the distance, striking a grove of dead trees. Blackbirds erupted into an agitated cloud of feathers and beaks. Brittle bones snapped. Feathers and flesh ripped until each of the Changeling flock littered the ground. Most maintained their tiny bird forms; a few, however, had almost completed their shapeshifting. Small black feathers lingered in their hair and skin.

Wolf, sword drawn, came to stand protectively over Seth. Nothing must come near the Lion. Using the Right-Hand's power, he scanned the marsh for any movement. His intensified Sight revealed the retreating backs of the would-be invaders. Mercenary scum. Justice would find them, no matter where they tried to hide.

Several figures ambled from the battlefield. Forms were blurred by the colors swirling in the depths of their emotions, and Wolf couldn't see their faces. Their intent, however, was all that mattered now. He spun toward them and held out his sword in warning. Ready to strike, he waited for them to step inside the circle of dead feathers.

None shall approach while the Lion is helpless!

A tall blond figure grabbed one of the others by the arm. "Have a care, Badger. Can you not see the Jalora surrounds the Right-Hand? He will kill you if you approach Seth right now. Stay here."

Then the blond figure moved a little closer. The man kneeled slowly and held up his left hand. A Heart of the Warrior Ring shimmered brightly under the heavy clouds. Wolf touched it with his power. The cry of a Phoenix filled his ears. Gregory Baldemar. He was a friend and Partisan to the Lion. The fury of the Right-Hand began to dissipate. Wolf's vision slowly cleared as details sharpened into recognizable Legion uniforms. The Jalora's servants had arrived.

"Guard us," Wolf ordered.

Sheathing his sword, he knelt beside Seth. The Lion's amber-flecked eyes rolled wildly as the power began to overtake him. Wolf rested a hand on the Lion's head. Immediately, Seth grabbed that hand and pulled it to his chest. He cradled Wolf's hand as he rocked.

Sitting down among the feathers and gore, Wolf pulled Seth close. "It's over. You have no more reason to be angry, yes?"

"Have to kill them all! I must protect the outpost and Andara."

Seth's body shivered violently as he fought for control. Wolf placed his other hand on the boy's forehead. The Lion's eyes opened with a start. They stopped rolling, trying to focus.

Summoning the Voice again, Wolf whispered low to him. "The outpost is safe, Seth. You've stopped the invasion. Close your eyes and rest. I'm here to watch over you."

"Wolf? You're here." Seth reached into his tunic and pulled out a red flag. "Will you give this to Phoenix? It's important."

"Of course. I will hand it to him myself, yes? Now sleep."

Seth leaned against Wolf with an exhausted sigh and let his head roll onto the proffered chest. Sleep had found him at last. The danger was over for the time being. Andara had come dangerously close to losing its Lion. Even so, he was safer at North Marsh Outpost than in Lea with traitors hunting him.

Hushed whispers reached Wolf's ears. He reluctantly lifted his gaze from the precious soul in his care to find

Western Beta standing in a protective circle around them. Phoenix remained at the edge of the bloodied feathers, waiting fretfully for Wolf's word.

"You may approach, Gregory Baldemar. It is safe." Wolf handed the flag to Phoenix. "I'm waiting for an explanation."

"I decided to test the apprentices."

"Don't you mean, Seth convinced you to conduct the testing on Mount Crumble." Wolf smiled with an understanding of the man in his care.

Then Wolf turned to the older ranger who'd huffed his agreement. "You are called, White Tiger. Our Lion may not like the tasks you give him, but he appreciates the fact you don't treat him differently than the other apprentices. I thank you for your common sense. You've helped to keep his temper in check. And your training prevented the death of Seth and his friends this day."

"I did my best for Ice Lion, My Lord Right-Hand." The old ranger bowed, causing a stir of surprise from the younger men about them.

"Wolf, about Mount Crumble," Phoenix began.

"Later. We must get the Lion to safety."

Basilio pushed through the staring rangers. Holding the mooring line tightly, he dragged the borrowed launch behind. Wolf's squire stopped at the edge of the circle of feathers and waited patiently for his lord's command.

"We take the Lion in the launch. Phoenix, you will make certain every last one of these mercenaries has met his end. Western Beta has broken their back while the Lords of Valdeon have snapped their necks by damaging the Jackal fortress. But these actions will delay their invasion a few weeks only."

Three young rangers, Seth's friends, came tentatively toward him. Awe. Concern. Loyalty. They'd shown trust and courage in supporting Seth on their adventure. The Lion could use more allies like them. Wolf gave the young men a beckoning nod. They stalked closer on tentative boots.

"Will he be all right, my Lord?" one of them, a Tslavian, asked. "You need not be wary of me. By our joined blood, I will protect my cousin."

"Very well, Henry the Badger. You, Bear, and Stallion will carry the Lion to our launch. We head to the outpost."

Wolf tried to rise, but the Voice had weakened him. Basilio knocked ranger hands away and helped Wolf up. He swayed and then righted himself. For the Right-Hand to show weakness wouldn't do. But Wolf needn't have bothered. Western Beta Battalion stared at Seth's unconscious form as he was carried past them. They would never forget the thrill of fighting alongside the Lion Protector.

"My Lord Right-Hand!" called out a voice.

Loyalty. Protectiveness. Strength. The acolyte approaching them exuded the qualities, though his manner was modest. Covered in blood from the fray, he pushed past Phoenix without a word and came to kneel before Wolf.

"I am called Dragonfly," he said. "Please allow me to accompany you in the launch. Evil's will may still be roaming the marsh."

Wolf touched the ranger's mind with his power. Dragonfly did not resist. Instead, he completely opened himself to the contact. Here was a man whose loyalty to the young Lion was absolute. Cardinal Dragon had thought so too and had sent him to protect their Seth.

"You honor the Lion. I thank you, Dragonfly. Such good sense is needed here in the search for traitors. Others must guard us. Acolytes, you will accompany us to the outpost," Wolf said as the young rangers placed Seth tenderly inside the launch.

"Acolytes?" The one called Stallion grinned as he stared down at his ring.

"You stood with the Lion against great odds. I would say you've passed the hardest test any apprentice has ever taken." Wolf crawled into the launch and sat on the bottom next to Seth.

White Tiger gathered together the new acolytes and growled quick orders. The young rangers nodded, giving him an earnest salute. They climbed inside the launch when Basilio started the engines. Sitting with their sword arms unobstructed, the new acolytes earned an approving nod from White Tiger.

"Search the spy cave your men found," Wolf told Phoenix. "It may contain other clues as to what the Jackal has planned for us next. The Legion has grown slack in its watchfulness. We must remain vigilant if we are to defeat our enemy."

The launch lifted into the air at a gentle incline. Then Basilio leveled its flight and opened wide the throttle. Mount Crumble's inhospitable shale surface retreated over a rain-soaked horizon. Wolf, keeping a protective hand on Seth's arm, closed his eyes.

Something had drawn Seth to those ruins. Wolf hoped what the Lion had sought had been resolved.

Chapter Thirty-Seven

RILEY LEANED AGAINST the stone lip of the battlement, hard raindrops peppering his hood. Ignoring the irritating splatters, he stared uneasily across the marsh in the direction the rangers had gone. The Lion's Roar had sent the outpost into a state of frenzy. Every last soul immediately came to high alert. The big explosion following afterward had mustered them out into the courtyards double quick.

Riley and the other squires had grabbed their packs and raced to the gates, but the rangers had already gone. Riley and the rest of the Squire's Corps were left to linger on the battlements. He hated waiting for any news. The Lion's squire should be out in the bog with his ranger. Others shared his impatience, too. Gudal, Selby, and Lucas took their turns pacing beside him. If trouble had coaxed out the Lion's Roar, then what misfortune had the other apprentice rangers found in the deadly bogs of North Marsh?

"See anything?" Arthur asked, coming to stand beside him.

Riley shook his head. "I don't like Seth being out there on his own. Keeping us back here at the outpost isn't right."

"Phoenix will look after him," Arthur said. "Squires can't fly across water and muck. We'd slow them down."

"Is that a launch?" Lucas pointed to the horizon.

The little vessel came straight for the battlement walls at a breakneck speed. Painted in the same rocky camouflage as Coyote's stolen launch, it must have come from the Jackal fortress. The vessel zipped over their heads, close enough for Riley to feel the whoosh of air as it passed. Bear, Badger, and Stallion waved as they flew overhead.

"Where's Seth? Why isn't he with them?"

"Hold your fire!" Arthur yelled at the UR soldiers manning the battlements.

Racing down the steps toward the Legion courtyard, Riley and the rest of the corps charged toward the apprentices. Roland was the first to reach them. He nodded a greeting to Seth's friends. The young men spoke to him with frantic gestures. Riley, still too far away, couldn't make out what they were saying. Then his heart froze as they lifted two unconscious men out of the launch. The first was a Valdeonian of middle years. The other was Seth.

"I knew sending them out on their own was a mistake," Riley grumbled as they jogged across the courtyard. "Who is the other man? He looks familiar."

"That, Riley Logan, is Xavier the Wolf. He is the Lion's Right-Hand." Arthur held Riley back as the apprentices carried Seth and Wolf toward the officers' quarters. "Have a care. For some reason, Basilio isn't following his lord." Arthur spat in the mud. "He's the meanest thing on two legs, so be on your best behavior."

"Aye. The Wolf's squire and I have met."

Basilio had treated Riley's wound back on Marianna the night they'd escaped the Jackal. Wolf's squire was a good healer, but he was a little too free with his opinion to suit Riley. The man had fallen on hard times since then. The patch covering his eye spoke of a battle he'd almost lost. His face was gaunt, either from hunger or disease. The strength of his disapproval, however, hadn't faded one hair.

"Where is the Lion's squire?" Basilio's voice boomed across the courtyard, echoing against the stone walls. "There you are, woolie farmer! Where were you while your lord lay helpless in the mud? No doubt, you were drinking with your friends."

"Wait just a moment," Riley growled, his temper rising. "We were ordered by the Phoenix to stay behind."

Wolf's squire stormed through the muck like a charging bull. He didn't stop his angry march until he was nose to nose with Riley. The rest of the squires—including Arthur—backed away. Riley planted his feet in the mud. The Logan temper was up and ready to slap back Basilio's insults. This Valdeonian hothead had no business questioning him about Seth.

"You are squire to a Lord of Valdeon. The only orders you recognize come from your lord." Basilio's fist struck Riley like a horse's hoof, sending him to his back in the mud. "Useless fool! Would that the Right-Hand had allowed me to kill you when I had the opportunity on Marianna."

"Stay down, Logan!" Arthur warned when Riley began to rise.

"I'll not lie in the mud for any man."

Basilio's next strike snapped Riley's head back with a jerk. He had time enough to feel the mud in his hair before darkness took him. Dull, gray nothingness parted. Then a patch of emerald green appeared on the horizon of a vast angry ocean. Marianna. He was almost home. Riley stretched his hand out, grasping at the lush hills. Empty air met his fingers as he began to fall toward the waters.

Splash.

Riley broke the wet surface, sputtering out a mouthful of water and curses. Basilio stood over him with soap and a scrub brush. The one-eyed Valdeonian demon had stripped him. Indecent. Riley, covering his tender bits, sniffed at the water with a disgruntled huff. It reeked of flowers.

"By the green, green fields. I just bathed at the Obsidian Citadel less than a month ago. Now I smell like a woman!"

"A shepherdess covered in sheep muck perhaps." Basilio shoved the soap and brush into Riley's hands. "Clean those nails as well. Do a good job of it, woolie farmer." Basilio pulled out his dagger. "You don't want me cleaning them."

Arthur was right. The man was meaner than a wounded ram. Riley put soap to brush and started scrubbing. He did his best to ignore the Wolf's squire as the man fiddled with Riley's uniform and boots. 'Shameful' and 'disgraceful' were bandied about in Valic. Riley was glad the rest of Basilio's tirade involved words he didn't understand.

"Get dressed, woolie farmer." Wolf's squire pointed to the clean and neatly folded uniform on the bench.

"Our lords have awakened. I would serve them their dinner before it grows cold."

Dinner, under the command of the Wolf's squire, was a precise military exercise executed with all the seriousness of a medical procedure. He'd insisted each ranger must have the opportunity to enter into conversation with the Lion and his Right-Hand. Riley and the other squires rearranged the mess hall until Basilio was satisfied. The fusspot was scandalized the rangers could see their food before plated and had them hide all the side tables in the kitchen.

"He certainly seems to know what he's doing," Donny whispered as Western Beta took their seats before the Right-Hand.

Xavier the Wolf appeared a little leaner and more haggard since the night they'd first met on Marianna. The Right-Hand, however, hadn't lost an ounce of dignity. He was a man who commanded respect just by walking into a room. That regard showed in the eyes of the emotionless rangers who hung on Wolf's every word. Seth had thought him to be king before he'd learned the Bearer of the Lion Ring was Valdeon's crown prince. Riley could see it in Wolf now. He was the type of man to lead a nation.

"I suppose the new arrangement makes sense while we have a guest." Riley gave Wolf a sour frown. "We'll move things back when he leaves and takes his demon squire with him. Accusing me of putting my thumb in Seth's potatoes. Basilio's gone off his head. Now he won't let me serve my ranger. Look at him fuss. I think he's trying to prove he could be squire to both of them."

Seth, for his part, didn't seem to notice. He was entranced by the famous Right-Hand as were the other men in the mess hall. Riley's ranger hadn't even commented on making A-2, one level beneath White Tiger. Riley couldn't fault the Lion's good humor though. Seth finally fit in with the other rangers.

Riley had tried to share in their celebration, but Basilio gave him a good knock. None of the other squires dared to step a toe out of place either. Respect rather than fear seemed to keep them in awe of the foul-tempered Wolf's squire.

"Walk with me, Seth." Wolf suddenly stood and headed toward the mess door. Seth, without so much as a question, hopped up to follow him. Phoenix nodded to his rangers. Western Beta warriors all hurried to their feet, respectfully falling in line behind the Wolf and the Lion.

"Don't stand there like a pile of sheep dung." Basilio slapped Riley on the arm.

Taking a swift pace toward the rangers crowding the mess hall entrance, Basilio barked something in Valic behind the crowd. Western Beta, much to Riley's surprise, immediately parted. Riley hurried after Basilio, more than a little impressed.

Wolf's squire gave him a sideways glance. "I am squire to a Lord of Valdeon. It gives me a certain authority over the Legion."

"What kind of authority?"

"Don't concern yourself, woolie farmer. I dare say you won't be in the Squire's Corps much longer."

Basilio put a finger to his lips, silencing Riley's angry retort. Wolf and Seth waited under the awning.

The Right-Hand had a light grip on Seth's shoulder. He held the other hand out to the side as if waiting for something. Basilio was there in a flash. He helped his ranger into his cloak. Riley, wanting not to be shown up, started for the rack behind them. Wolf's squire, however, was already helping Seth into his cloak. Brazen bully. The Valdeonian demon was trying to take the Lion away from him.

Then their rangers were off, disappearing soundlessly into the rain-soaked sunset. Even Phoenix and his men seemed astounded at the speed of their departure. Western Beta was after them with an excited spray of mud, leaving Riley alone with Basilio.

Wordlessly, Wolf's squire stepped onto the planks and adopted a steady pace toward the western edge of the Legion courtyard. They walked side by side in an uncomfortable silence. Riley had many questions about what was happening to Seth. Basilio, however, wasn't someone he'd willingly ask for information.

Reaching the edge of the courtyard, they found Western Beta forming a half-circle in the mud before the steps of the battlement. Their swords were drawn. White Tiger and several of the rangers were missing. Riley guessed they guarded the staircase located in the UR courtyard. Western Beta was treating this Right-Hand like a king or dignitary. Basilio, clearly pleased by the respect they were showing his lord, walked directly through the rangers without stopping. Riley once again followed him.

The two squires found their rangers staring over the marsh in the direction of Mount Crumble. Seth, pointing a finger along the horizon, seemed to be giving

Wolf an account of how he and his friends had come upon the site. Wolf burst into a pleasant baritone laugh when Seth growled like a marsh wolf. Neither of them seemed to notice their squires taking up positions behind them.

"I have got to practice my Valic," Riley whispered.

"A pointless exercise." Basilio stood up a little straighter. "Now be still. The Right-Hand speaks."

"You were looking for something on Mount Crumble, yes?"

"The Jalora commands I find The Creed of the Guardian. It is somewhere in North Marsh. I'd hoped it find it at Mount Crumble, but it wasn't there," Seth told Wolf with a frustrated sigh. "I don't know where to look now."

The Creed of the Guardian? What in the green, green fields? Riley frowned at Seth's back. Somehow, he'd figured out what this relic was that the Jalora wanted him to find. Why hadn't Seth taken the time to tell his squire rather than wandering through the marsh, almost getting himself killed? And why had he shared his secret so quickly with this stranger?

"News of the Creed gives me great hope, Seth. It's one more step in the journey to achieving your destiny." Wolf turned his eyes away from the horizon. "Perhaps the Jalora will reveal its location when the Lords of Valdeon come together again."

The two men turned away from the battlement wall as one. Wolf led them back down the stairs toward the waiting rangers. Basilio swelled with pride when Western Beta bowed as Wolf came among them.

"I am honored to celebrate this night with all of you," the Right-Hand said. "It has given me hope to carry along."

"You're not leaving?" Seth asked.

Riley was startled by the sudden unhappiness infecting his ranger's voice. This Wolf had quickly become a hero in Seth's eyes. The Right-Hand had saved their lives, yes, but the blatant worship was too much. Riley, for his part, wasn't sure he completely trusted Xavier the Wolf. He didn't like the hold this Right-Hand had over Seth.

"I go to join the other Lords of Valdeon. They wait for me." Wolf placed a hand on Seth's shoulder again. "We will be back soon to fetch you."

The Right-Hand walked back toward the mess, shaking hands and greeting the other eager rangers. Seth moped unhappily behind him. Wolf, almost as if he sensed the Lion's mood, turned and put an arm around the younger man's shoulder. He whispered steadily in Valic.

Basilio slapped Riley's arm and motioned for him to follow. They moved toward the same shed where Seth's friends had hidden Coyote's launch a few days earlier. Basilio pulled open the doors. The little vessel that had brought Wolf here hovered between the crates and barrels.

"Assist me with the launch," Basilio ordered. "I must see the Right-Hand to Corpse Point before the young Lords of Valdeon do something rash."

Riley was happy to help the other squire. Anything to see Basilio's back. He pulled aside the tarp covering the inside of the launch. A few small crates of food lined the bottom. Blankets and bandages were stuffed between the benches as well. Basilio had been busy when he wasn't tormenting Riley.

Slapping the tarp back down with a huff, the Wolf's squire untied the launch's mooring line and began to lead it back out into the rain. Riley followed behind with a sense of relief and joy he guessed was shared by the other squires.

Then Seth suddenly pushed away from Wolf. "No! You aren't telling me everything."

For the first time since Seth had put on the Lion Ring, Riley could see his face contract. Seth's countenance dropped into the unhappy pouting of a small child. What was happening? This behavior wasn't like Seth at all. He'd never thrown a tantrum to Riley's memory. Not even as a toddler.

"You must remain here with the battalion. We will come to you as soon as I find a place of safety."

"No, Wolf! You're in danger. I know it. You must take me with you. I can fight!"

Western Beta backed away while the mud about the courtyard began to bubble. Wood and metal groaned as the Lion's power filled the space. He'd bring the whole outpost down upon their heads in a minute.

Wolf picked Seth up as effortlessly as if he were that small, pouting child. Then the Right-Hand and his bundle disappeared. Riley spun around, trying to pinpoint where Wolf had taken Seth. The rangers, he noticed, were staying absolutely still.

Riley jumped out of his boots when the Phoenix's door slammed. "Here now!" cried Riley. "What's he going to do to Seth?"

Sweeping Riley's legs, the Wolf's squire dropped him into the mud. This time, Basilio's blade was at Riley's throat. Riley froze as the tip pressed into his skin. Hard resolve formed on the Wolf's squire's face.

"Come between the Lion and his Right-Hand again, woolie farmer, and I will kill you myself!"

Another blade slammed against Basilio's weapon, knocking it away from Riley's neck. Roland, tongue still silent, glared into Basilio's eyes with an unspoken warning. Neither man moved. All the while, the rangers stayed still.

"Very well, Roland." Basilio took a step back and sheathed his weapon. "You saved the life of my lord and Tulio the Rabbit. I owe you a life debt." He kicked a clump of mud at Riley. "This mutton-headed boy is still under your care for the time being."

"Basilio," Wolf called from a few feet away.

Whipping winds! Xavier the Wolf was fast. None of them, rangers or squires, had heard him approach. Basilio hurried to his lord and held up Wolf's sagging body. He didn't seem hurt precisely. It was as if he'd run a thousand miles with no sleep.

Wolf turned to Phoenix. "I owe this Marianna boy's father a life debt. You will assure he stays alive until I return. Then it is up to the Lords of Valdeon to see him safely back home to his family."

Riley opened his mouth to object, but Phoenix lifted him by the collar. The blond giant's massive hand covered Riley's mouth and nose in a sweaty grip. Wolf didn't comment on their struggles. He remained focused on crawling into the launch without falling.

Basilio helped his lord until he was safely aboard, and then jumped in after him and grabbed the rudder.

"Keep that mouth shut for a change," Phoenix hissed. "The Right-Hand has spoken. He could have easily ordered your death, and I would have had to obey."

Riley pulled away Phoenix's hand. "No need to smother me."

Basilio gave Riley one last glare before he piloted the launch upward. The little vessel zipped away in the darkness, up and over the wall. Then it was gone. Good riddance to both of them. Riley pulled out of Phoenix's grip and splashed his boots down in the mud then marched across the courtyard to join Seth with as much dignity as he could muster.

This Right-Hand fellow might be a person of importance to the rangers, but he'd not tell Riley what and where. Nobody was going to send him home. He'd sworn an oath to Leo. More importantly, Seth was his best friend. He wouldn't leave him no matter who objected.

Chapter Thirty-Eight

WOLF LEANED BACK against one of the crates at the bottom of the launch. Exhausted from taming the Lion's anger, he let his eyes close. The sweet smells of carrots and ham emanated from beneath the tarp. A smile crossed his face. The Sacred Guard would eat well this night in celebration. Wolf had found their lord and could report the Lion Protector was worthy of his title. Seth had shown courage, and his cleverness was evident. He'd certainly earned a great deal of respect from Western Beta after Mount Crumble. The UR soldiers, Wolf noted with satisfaction, already admired him before the testing.

Most importantly, Seth was wholly devoted to the Jalora. He'd been sincere and respectful as they'd spoken together of his quest to find the Creed. A quick probe of Seth's mind had allowed Wolf to explore his memories and his emotions. Seth had two confidants. The first was his childhood friend, the little woolie farmer—who was loyal enough, but entirely unsuitable to be the Lion's squire.

Seth's second confidant was the Partisan. Gregory Baldemar had taken great pains to earn his trust. Perhaps this was the reason he'd been so accommodating to Seth, letting the boy run around stirring up bangtail mischief. Phoenix had been correct about one thing. Seth needed a team of rangers to help him look for the Creed. That team, though, wouldn't be Western Beta. The Lords of Valdeon would accompany their Lion this time around. They'd missed Seth's naming, but they wouldn't neglect this opportunity to see history made.

Then the skies lurched violently around him. Thunder rumbled in his unprotected ears. No. He detected nothing natural about this attack. Black splashed and stained the gray skies as another boom echoed over North Marsh. Something struck their hull with a hard thud. Then an explosion ripped a hole at the bottom. Its force sent the launch spinning out of control.

"I can't hold it!" Basilio shouted, fighting with the rudder.

His efforts were futile. Already, spray from the waters below slapped at Wolf's face. Nothing would possibly save the launch. They were plummeting into the bogs. A swim was inevitable, provided they even survived the impact. Wolf struggled to wrap the Jalora's power about his body with the sudden adrenaline rush. Too late. Their launch smashed into the waters bow first. Splinters of wood and chunks of food flew everywhere. Wolf covered his face against the stabbing fragments.

Blackness. Silence. Cold. Then the sudden shock of wet and weeds brought him back to consciousness. Wolf thrashed against the watery arms of North Marsh. He was underwater, imprisoned by dead roots and bits of their tarp. Ripping himself away from death's grip,

Wolf kicked the tarp from his body. Once he broke the surface, he took in a great gulp of air. Basilio floated nearby. Wolf grabbed his squire and dragged him from the wreckage. Basilio's head was bleeding, and he was still unconscious. The squire was in grave danger of breathing his last in the bog. Wolf must get his squire to solid ground.

Fighting the grasping fingers of dead branches and wet strands of moss, Wolf swam toward a small formation of rock. His outstretched hand slapped against solid ground. Pulling Basilio up by the tunic, he lay his squire down on the marshy grass of the small solid island. Wolf then crawled onto its surface and collapsed on his back. Rain struck his face in light drops. He closed his eyes, letting the air rush in and out of his lungs.

Then the presence of mad ambition crept toward them across the small mass of land. Wolf rolled swiftly to his feet. Esteban the Hawk stood in the center of the island. His naked sword waited unflinchingly to taste blood. Uniform clean and no visible signs of injury, he appeared unharmed after their last encounter. How had the villain survived the inescapable crash of their launch?

"I should have let Jason Coyote kill you when he had the chance," Wolf said, pulling his sword. "Then again, punishing traitors is the Right-Hand's job."

"Indeed, it is. That's why I'm here, pretender."

"I've been called as the Lion's Right-Hand, Esteban. You must accept this and serve." Wolf tensed at the spark of malicious fury in Hawk's eyes. "The Jalora won't have its word questioned."

"Any witnesses to your naming as Right-Hand are no longer in the world of the living." Esteban let the cold grin come. "I am the Hawk, after all. Which of us do you think the Jalora Legion will believe? The Bearer of the Hawk Ring who has served the Jalora Master as Right-Hand from the time of Mikel D'Antoiné? Or the mad ravings of a lowly guardsman who lost his mind at the murder of his family?"

"Dragon knows."

"The Jalora's power has dwindled. Dragon's abilities aren't what they used to be. Many in the Legion and Andara question his leadership. It is my word against yours, Xavier the Wolf."

"The Voice of the Right-Hand will be difficult for you to explain away. Western Beta has witnessed my power on the skirts of Mount Crumble. What will you do when an entire battalion of rangers bear witness to my naming?" Wolf gripped the hilt of his sword tighter in anticipation. "I will convince the Legion, while you, Hawk Prince, will be punished as the traitor you are."

"You won't get the chance."

Hawk sprang at Wolf. Swinging his blade downward in a deadly blow, Esteban pressed all his weight into the attack. Weakened after calming the Lion's temper, Wolf staggered as their swords hit. His boot slid in the mud and brought him closer to the water's edge. He spun out from under Hawk's sword. Slicing upward, he scored a hit along Esteban's torso. With a kick at the Prince of Valdeon's backside, Wolf sent Hawk sprawling on his hands and knees in the mud.

Esteban spat out an angry growl and abandoned the Legion's Dance of Death, charging at Wolf again.

Hawk adjusted his stance, calling to him power foreign to Valdeon and Andara. Swift circles of sickly light formed about his body as Hawk spun his blade. A glimmer of recognition teased Wolf's brain. He'd seen these movements before, but where? Hawk, taking advantage of Wolf's surprise, pushed him back to the center of the island. In a vicious strike, he thrust the tip of his sword toward Wolf's eye. Stopping it inches away from his face, Wolf brought his full power to him and twisted with all the speed his supremacy would afford. He came to Hawk's side and smashed a fist against his temple. Hawk crumpled on the ground.

"More proof I am the Right-Hand," Wolf said. "What other explanation is there for your defeat at the hands of a deacon ranger?"

Esteban, on his hands and knees in the muck, spat a pink spray of blood. Breathing hard, he gingerly shook his head. Braying laughter, soft at first, settled over the little island. Wolf took a step back as the Hawk Prince's unnerving chortles escaped from his mouth.

"Very well, Wolf. I concede you were named Right-Hand by the Jalora. You have strength, speed, and power, but none of it will matter when you're dead. The Jalora won't have any choice but to name me as your replacement."

"I don't plan on dying anytime soon, Hawk Prince."

"Oh, don't worry, Wolf. I've made the arrangements for you." Hawk waved a fist into the air. "He is here."

Two troops of Jackal appeared out of the bogs to surround them. How had they hidden their presence from the Jalora? Wolf had his answer when a band of

Changelings walked through their circle. He'd been beaten again by trickery and betrayal. Wolf regarded Hawk. Their exchange and the battle had been nothing more than a diversion. Esteban was no better than Julian. They'd both betrayed Andara for their own ambitions.

"You're playing both ends against the middle, Esteban. What can you possibly hope to gain from this enemy who will surely betray you?"

"You'll never know, Wolf." Hawk turned to one of the Changelings. "Here is my side of the bargain. Do a proper job when you kill the Wolf's squire. He doesn't like to stay dead."

One of the Jackal soldiers shrugged. "The Wolf's squire is gone. We didn't find a body."

"Hunt him down!" Hawk growled. "He mustn't be allowed to warn the others."

Faithful Basilio. Hope was still alive this dark day. Wolf's squire was a cunning warrior, accustomed to traversing landscapes undetected. He was almost as gifted as a Pacarro tribesman. Wolf prayed Basilio's skills would be enough. Andara's fate rested on Basilio's shoulders.

Chapter Thirty-Nine

JULIAN FLICKED IRRITABLY at a smudge of moss on his sleeve. North Marsh hadn't gained any charm since his last visit when he'd tracked his father, Edmund the Leo, to Sea Point Outpost on the shores of northwest Andara. Leo's precious Jalora had almost dragged Julian into the bogs to his death. Almost. Naturally, he wasn't keen to revisit this land of wet muck.

The pile of rubble acting as Leo's last stronghold could at least boast of a coastal breeze. This tiny lump in the middle of the marsh, in contrast, was stifling. An eternity of bog stretched out to the horizon from every vantage point. They were, quite literarily, in the middle of nowhere.

"Try to be a polite guest," Lord Gorman said. "I'd hate to lock you in the ship's brig."

"I'm sure."

The Jackal general's metal mask turned to glare at Julian. He couldn't see beneath its hard surface, but Gorman's annoyance came through in the tone of his voice and the impatience sparkling in his imperious blue eyes. Gorman, son to a Luminawni mother and crown prince of Akutar, held a power that was impressive. Julian wondered for the thousandth time what he hid under his metal skull.

"I can understand your restlessness," Gorman said. "The battle between Andara's best warriors is rather disappointing."

Xavier De Vincente and Esteban D'Antoiné had chosen to act out their families' long-held feud in the middle of this miserable marsh. While he'd had a good seat for the performance, Julian held mixed feelings about the winner. He hated his uncle, Esteban the Hawk. His sudden appearance after decades in hiding was an unpleasant and unsettling surprise. Curse him! Esteban's lust for the throne of Valdeon was legendary. He was another rival Julian didn't need. Then again, rivals could be killed—even powerful bishops in the Jalora Legion.

The winner of their impromptu battle, however, was the one who brought out the worst sort of venom in Julian's heart. Xavier the Wolf was the Altar of Providence's champion. He'd thwarted Julian's plan to claim the throne in San Leonora and had declared himself the young Lion's protector. The Valdeonian court, swooning like school girls, had believed him without question. Though Valdeon fell, Wolf's very memory still evoked hope and the spirit of rebellion in the hearts of the people. Julian despised Wolf with every ounce of emotion he possessed.

His Changeling cousins stepped aside with a respectful nod to Gorman as he entered the circle surrounding Wolf. Julian followed, swallowing his unexpected sense of dread. He'd spent his youth fearing the ranger and plotting revenge for every slight the man had thrown his way. Why was he hesitating now?

Suddenly, like a suppressed nightmare, he was standing face to face with Xavier the Wolf. Despite the mask of emotionless justice covering Wolf's face, his burning hatred was evident. The ranger had never trusted Julian. Though Leo had accepted Julian as his son, somehow Wolf had known of his questionable parentage. The ranger had warned Leo to guard against Julian's intentions. He'd been right. Too bad for Leo he hadn't listened.

"Julian D'Antoiné, I name you a traitor and mark you for death!"

Wolf flew toward him, ready to deliver a death blow. Sounds faded into the moment as Julian's eyes followed the blade's descent toward him. The Jalora's power held him fast, ready for Wolf to deliver its unyielding justice.

Then Lord Gorman stepped between them. His metal hand caught Wolf's sword with a clang and pulled it away as if it were a toy he coveted. Bringing his other fist downward, he slammed his knuckles against Wolf's head. The Lord of Valdeon crumbled to the ground.

"Another of your many admirers, Julian?" he asked.

Wolf was one of the Legion's most powerful rangers. If Gorman could disarm and then trounce him so easily, how would Julian stand against this Jackal general when the time came to rid Valdeon of him and his kind? Was this the reason Gorman considered Julian an annoyance rather than a threat? Perhaps the general's overconfidence could be used against him somehow.

"Restrain him," Lord Gorman ordered. "I want the Jalora's plaything to stay in one piece for the time being."

Gorman held his outstretched hand over Wolf's sword. "This Right-Hand is a surprise. No one touches the weapon. It will mean your death. The Jalora's power waits to strike."

Right-Hand? A new sense of revulsion sent a swelling of disgust through Julian's body. If they were proclaiming Xavier the Wolf to be Right-Hand, then it meant the fools believed his half-breed brother was the next Jalora Master. The timing of his visit from Whisper and the offer of an alliance made complete sense now. If Lord Gorman defeated Andara's Jalora Master in battle, then it would be an unchallengeable win for the Sarcion. Perhaps an opportunity remained for a true prince of Valdeon to seize the throne.

Seth was a weak fool. He'd have to become much stronger for the fledgling plan forming within Julian's mind to work. The opportunity for Julian to win his half-brother's trust was long gone. But perhaps Julian could manipulate him in other ways. After all, the Lion was created to protect the throne of Valdeon. He didn't have to survive the ordeal.

"Let me have the pleasure of ridding us of the source." Hawk raised his sword to strike down Wolf.

Gorman grabbed Hawk's wrist and tossed him as though he were a wounded bird. Esteban landed unharmed several feet away. He rolled to his feet with a predator's growl. Standing between Hawk and the unconscious ranger, Gorman held up a warning finger.

"Why not kill Wolf now and be done with it?" Hawk asked, wiping the droplets of blood from his chin.

"Those were not my orders." Gorman motioned with his fingers. "Our Master Interrogator is to spend some time with him first. Who better to know how to breach the Jalora's magic surrounding the Altar of Providence than a Lord of Valdeon?"

A Changeling stepped inside their circle. Flowing robes of midnight blue swept across the ground as it walked. Strange symbols stitched in silver lined the hem. Thin strands of white spilled over its shoulders. Julian, though he'd never met such an ancient creature, sensed this member of the tribe's power matched its advanced age. The Master Interrogator's sharp teeth made a wide smile under dark orbs when it saw Wolf. Crossing the distance at tremendous speed, the old Changeling came to stand over its prize.

"A Jalora plaything! It will be a welcome challenge, my lords." The Changeling bent down, examining Wolf's hard face. "How much time am I allotted?"

"Have your fun," Gorman said. "Just don't forget to bring the Wolf Ring to me when you've finished."

It stood back as Jackal soldiers picked up Wolf's unconscious form. They carried their prize toward the other side of the island. Cackling like a mad old woman, the Master Interrogator followed. The circle of younger Changeling heads turned away as he passed. A strange reaction, considering it was such a powerful creature. Such traits were highly prized among the Changeling family. Perhaps the nature of its interest in Wolf was what offended them so.

Gorman turned to Hawk. "Are you coming, Master Spy?"

The title fit Esteban the Hawk Prince well. He'd managed to hide from the Legion all these years, gathering information and making plans to destroy them. Julian reluctantly set aside his loathing of the man and allowed a bit of respect.

"May I have a moment with Julian, my lord?" Hawk gave Gorman a strained bow. "A father so rarely gets a chance to speak with his long-lost son."

Father? What was he saying? Gorman continued his trek back to the ship. His laugh echoed with earsplitting screeches within the mask. Julian, stunned motionless, stared wordlessly at Hawk. He'd heard the scandalous whispers of Hawk's infidelity with Julian's mother. But it wasn't possible. Hawk was a ranger. His Jalora's punishment for such behavior would have been immediate and fierce. Of course, the ranger before him was waist deep in treason against his Legion.

"You are such a disappointment, child."

Then Esteban the Hawk's appearance began to change. The scar on his face faded, and wrinkles appeared in its place. Neatly trimmed hair stretched downward to spill over Hawk's shoulders in a long white waterfall. His black orbs stared intensely into Julian's eyes, banishing any last hopes of frail humanity.

"Tell me what's happening? How can you be a Changeling?"

"My magic is strong. As long as I have this." His demonic father lifted the Hawk Ring before Julian's face. "I can fool anyone, including that pompous windbag, Dragon. You see now, child. I took Esteban's arm and his brother's wife." Its laugh was a hideous cackle of spittle and stench. "I even bore a son to take the throne. Ha! A wasted effort. I handed you Leo and his heir. You should have killed both of them on Marianna. Then I warn you to kill Chancellor Benito, but you fail me there too!"

"You are the Dark Stranger who opened the secret gates of the city wall." Julian spat at the Changeling's feet.

"Obviously, dullard. Your failure left me no choice. It's our good fortune that I'm a cautious fellow and thought to develop a backup plan."

"And the real Esteban?" Julian looked into the creature's face. "What have you done with him?"

"He's spent his years in a place far from Andara. The unlucky dupe may be dead by now." He dropped his hand bearing the Jalora' talisman, allowing the Hawk mask to return. "Esteban, however, is not the prince of Valdeon we need to worry about, now is he? From now on, you will fall in line. Do as you are told. Don't cross me, Julian. Papa will have to punish you."

It turned, striding across the moss and muck. Julian wrapped his arms around his body. What wickedness had entered their world? This creature—his father—would never be satisfied without a throne. Julian had killed one father already. A second wouldn't be too emotionally trying.

Chapter Forty

JORGE PRESSED AT the dry ground with light fingertips. Pink and raw from the Regent Medallion's power, the burns he'd incurred were slowly fading from his body. Even so, he planned to avoid misadventure until his recovery was complete. Careful eyes scanned the ground again. He saw no sign of anyone's passing. Then again, rangers left no prints. He lifted his eyes to the small rock formation setting in front of the entrance to a short ravine. It was a marker, most certainly, but who had left it?

"Stay in the trees," Jorge told his son.

Duarto held up a restraining hand to his hunters. They pulled their hatchets, ready to strike if need be. Jorge gave his son a nod. The hunters, under Duarto's leadership, were a disciplined team. Such expertise would be needed even more in the days to come.

Passing through the dried branches lining the foothills, Jorge stopped at the base of the cliff for a better look. He ran his hands along the rock. Carved smooth by ancient waters, the cliff face contained no handholds. Not even a mountain goat could scale its surface. Dangerous to traverse, the Border Mountain Range had very few walking trails. Jorge wasn't aware of any in this part of the terrain. Hawk had chosen well.

Jorge kept low, making his body a smaller target as he moved toward the entrance. The rock formation hadn't been there for more than three weeks, based on the signs in the dirt. He carefully lifted the top stone, then rolled away the others placed beneath it. A hawk in flight was painted in white chalk. Jorge quickly erased the symbol and stood.

"We've arrived at long last," he said, calling for Duarto. "Come, we must find the opening."

Patterns in the rock shifted as they entered the ravine. A few short steps brought them not to rock walls, but rather through an opening. The cave's entrance waited for them like the promise of paradise. Jorge stepped inside. He placed a hand on the inner wall as it took a sharp left. Something or someone had created complex patterns in the stone to camouflage the cave. Human eyes would merely assume the ravine was empty. Clever. Perhaps the Jalora had aided Hawk? Such questions must be put on hold until the ranger paid them another visit.

"Duarto, give me the torch." Jorge waited as his son set the material aflame and then held the light up inside the opening. "By the Erthe Mother!"

A massive cavern lined with shimmering crystals stretched out before them. It was large enough to hold twice the number of people they'd brought with. Small shafts of light struck the cavern floor in even patterns, almost as if human hands had constructed them as chimneys for cooking or comfort.

"Father," Duarto gripped Jorge's arm when he took another step. "Who is our benefactor? I mean, do you trust this person?"

Duarto had a practical point. Their enigmatic benefactor's location for the past decade or more was a complete mystery. Who could be sure of Esteban the Hawk's intent? Jorge sighed. He didn't know what to believe anymore. He only knew his people needed refuge.

"I trust the Regent Medallion to warn me. It will go into the darkness before us."

Jorge lifted the medallion out of his tunic and pointed it toward the inside of the cave. A shaft of sunlight caught its golden surface, illuminating the darkest corners of the cavern. Jorge walked inside with the hunters following cautiously.

"Food!" Antonio cried, pointing to their right.

A large alcove rested toward the back of the cavern. Barrels of food, water, and medicines were neatly stacked inside. Were those blankets and jugs of rum? How had Hawk managed all this?

"That must be enough for a year!" Duarto burst into happy laughter, a sound Jorge thought he would never hear again. "Jalora bless our benefactor!"

Yes. Esteban had kept his word, but how had he created this cave? Jorge had a sinking feeling their mysterious friend wanted the Regent of Valdeon in a location where he could swiftly get his hands on him again. But now he forced his worries away. It was time for celebration.

Duarto and the people had been through enough hardship to last a lifetime. Let them be at ease today. Soon, they would be on the offensive. A war still brewed in Valdeon. He and his men were tired of hiding. The refugees of the West would take every opportunity to rebel against the Jackal. Then they would make a stronghold for the Lion to return and muster his forces.

"Bring the people, Duarto! Let them share in our abundance."

Good humor followed Jorge as he walked through the cozy camps set up within the cave. Smiles, happy talk, and laughter filled the space, muffled from outside travelers by the cave's unique design. Jorge smiled. His people had reached safety at long last. They were eating hot meals of meat and fruit for the first time in many months. To see them contented was satisfying. Here in the midst of their happy banter, his feeling of unease seemed out of place.

He exchanged greetings with several well-wishers and headed toward the cave entrance. Stars hung over the ravine, twinkling peacefully in their heavens. Taking a deep breath, he enjoyed the earthy scents of Valdeon's mountain range. Sage, pine, soil—their aromas took him back to the green fields of his orchards. Then grief swelled unexpectedly in his heart. Perhaps sorrow's specter never really left a man until he crossed the horizon to join those gone before.

Then the Regent Medallion blazed with vibrant golden life. His consciousness left his body and flew out of the ravine. It soared like a predator bird over the trees and glided south. Across the plains grass on the western side of the Constantina River, a large force of thieves and cutthroats—Valdeonians all—marched northward toward the forests. Tabor was at their head.

"Father?"

Duarto shook him hard. He and the other hunters surrounded Jorge, watching in awe as the golden light retreated into its metal home. Santos stood with them, wearing his perpetual frown. Jorge rubbed at his eyes. Still dizzy from the sudden flight, he leaned against his son.

"Tabor and a hundred men march toward our forest." He took the canteen Antonio offered him and gulped down the water. "We don't have much time. They'll be at our door in a few days."

"Why don't we welcome them properly, my lord regent?" Santos grinned and patted the pack at his side. "I can make things very…explosive for them."

"By all means. I'm especially happy to meet Tabor again. We have unfinished business."

Indeed, they did. Tabor was an opportunist of the worst kind. He'd taken advantage of Jorge's absence from San Lucida to rob and molest the refugees. The hunters had made short work of the other criminals while Jorge had maimed Tabor for life. But he'd do more than injure the bully's foot when next they met.

Chapter Forty-One

SETH SHIFTED AWKWARDLY in the tense silence hanging over the office. His first meeting with the senior ranking officers of the battalion was turning out to be an exercise in patience. He took his cue from White Tiger. The old ranger stayed silent and still, waiting on the will of his commander.

Mantis stood at attention beside Gecko. Their attitude toward Seth had shifted from antagonistic to awkwardly polite. He supposed the sentiment was an improvement, but even so, he envied the new open friendliness they shared with Bear, Badger, and Stallion.

Gecko shifted on his feet with a small wince of discomfort. Though still recovering from the trouncing he'd received from Coyote, he'd rushed with the other rangers to the battlefield at Mount Crumble. Gecko had fought with his comrades to protect their apprentices, the outpost, and Andara. Seth prayed the Jalora would take Gecko's actions into account and judge Gecko and Mantis worthy of forgiveness. White Tiger certainly thought they were and had kept them hidden away during the Right-Hand's brief visit.

"Roland!" Phoenix paced about the office, shuffling papers in every nook. "Where are the parchments I drew up last night?"

Seth shifted his eyes from Phoenix to examine the rest of the room. Their deacon had been at work for a long space of time before summoning his officers. Old parchments covered his desk while crumpled bits of torn paper spilled onto the floor. Empty breakfast dishes lay abandoned upon one of the shelves.

"Here we are." Phoenix swept up four rolled parchments in his arms and turned to face them. "An armed force has managed to ambush us in a land we are supposed to be guarding. I agree with the Right-Hand. The Legion has allowed itself to grow lax in its stewardship of North Marsh. We can see now what happens when a careful eye is not kept to our coasts."

Phoenix paused for a moment, letting the silence hang heavy about his men. "The Jalora spoke to me last night. It commands we correct this lapse. I'm sending each of you into a region of North Marsh to patrol and report back what you find."

They gathered around his desk as Phoenix pushed the four new parchments to one side and unrolled another. Dust from many decades clung to the old skin. Faded ink, carefully cleaned, exposed many lines on its inner surface. It was a map of North Marsh similar to the one the Changeling had tried to steal. This map, however, was complete.

Phoenix ran a finger along the trails, outlining the four regions of North Marsh. The first—located to the southwest—was marked as "Free Wilderness." He pointed to the southeast along the borders of Framburg and Heidelbrecht. Then he tapped on the Bloodtooth Mountain Range toward the northeast where Wolf and the other Lords of Valdeon had found and destroyed a Jackal fortress.

Seth's gaze followed the Bloodtooth Mountains along the northernmost shoreline to the piece of the map which had been missing on the Changeling's stolen parchment. Sea Point Outpost rested on the northwest corner of Andara's coast. Someone had long ago drawn a line through it and had written the words "taken by nature."

"A sunken place," Seth murmured.

Then a strong pull of power gripped at the center of his chest. Fate called to him at that moment. He knew he must journey to Sea Point Outpost. Going there would take several days of dangerous travel through rough terrain. The Jalora's quests were never easy.

"You will break up into four groups and spend the next few days scouting North Marsh. Each team will be assigned four A1s." Phoenix turned to them with a furrowed brow. "Under no circumstances will you engage the enemy you find—unless you have no other choice. I want you all back in one piece to report."

"I volunteer to search the northwest region, Sir."

"Not the northeast, Ice Lion?"

Seth leaned across the table. "I must search the northeast region, sir."

He opened his mind to Phoenix then, allowing the deacon to probe his impressions of Sea Point Outpost. Bright blue eyes sparkled with excitement as the possibility of the Creed's location became clear. Seth returned the grin struggling on Phoenix's lips. Here was a kindred spirit.

"Mantis takes the southwest, Gecko takes the southeast, White Tiger takes the northeast, and Ice Lion takes the northwest. I've copied each section of the map. Take your assigned sections and get some sleep. You leave at first light. White Tiger will have your team assignments soon."

Gecko and Mantis accepted their parchments and exited the office. Talking of dinner and drink, they seemed indifferent to their future exploration of North Marsh. Seth, in contrast, was keen to begin. The possibility of finishing his quest flooded his mind with inexhaustible excitement. A sleepless night was ahead of him for sure.

White Tiger stopped at the door. "Have you considered what Xavier the Wolf will have to say about his Lion romping around North Marsh?"

"It's only a few days, sir. I'll be back before Wolf returns to the outpost," Seth said.

"Is that so? And what if you aren't?" White Tiger grunted unhappily. "I like my head right where it is."

"There'll be no trouble. I'll speak to Wolf."

"Oh, that makes everything all right does it?" White Tiger waved a finger at Phoenix. "I'd at least send him with an experienced team."

"Bear, Badger, Stallion and I know how each other fight, sir. I want to take them with me."

"Wouldn't you prefer to select some of the more experienced rangers, Ice Lion?" Phoenix asked, doing his best to ignore the huff of disapproval from White Tiger.

"I trust in my comrades," Seth said. "We will see each other through this assignment."

Phoenix let out a slow breath and gave Seth a strained smile. "The rangers you have chosen are all good men, but not very experienced. Why don't you take someone who has been in the Legion as an acolyte for a few years? The region I've assigned you is full of danger. You will need skill to make it back safely."

"You must trust me, Ancient Ally. I will bring these men back alive. You have my word."

"Very well. Just don't forget to bring yourself back alive too." Phoenix nodded at White Tiger. "Make the assignments. I'll leave the fourth man on Ice Lion's team to your discretion."

White Tiger slammed the door behind him. His frustrated muttering followed as he stomped down the steps. Seth held a great deal of respect for White Tiger. He hadn't intended to offend the old ranger or belittle his opinions. Perhaps to travel so far in the marshes was a bit rash, but Wolf would understand. He knew the importance of Seth's quest to find the Creed.

"My old friend is a man who keeps his feet on the ground. He isn't fond of mysteries or surprises." Phoenix leaned against the desk. "I must confess I'm none too pleased to let you go without me. Alas, someone has to stay and guard the outpost."

"I wish you could come with us too," Seth said. "Thank you for your trust in me, sir. I know I'm asking a great deal."

"Let's say I'm returning a favor." Phoenix sat down on the corner of his desk. "Remember the story I told aboard our transport ship as we traveled from Lea."

"The ephemeral who became a deacon?"

"Yes. I was that ephemeral, Seth. Your father befriended me when no one else would. He trained me in every way you could imagine. His mentorship encouraged me to be the best ranger and the best man I could be. I loved Edmund like a father. Not a better man has ever walked in this world. He was family to me." Phoenix paused with an awkward smile. "I've grown rather fond of you too, Seth. And after what I've seen in our time together, the throne of Heidelbrecht has adopted you."

Seth shook the Phoenix's outstretched hand. "I'm grateful for your gift of friendship. It is very welcome."

"Call me Greg," the deacon said with a wink. "Little brother."

As he left, Seth closed the door behind him. He stopped at the bottom of the stairs and stared into the mud puddle before him. Even now, the power beckoned him toward Sea Point Outpost. Its pull was almost painful, as though a chain attached to his chest was tugging at him. But he must exercise patience. Charging blindly to the north could mean he'd lose some of the men who followed him. Finding the Creed was important, but so were the lives he held in his hands.

Seth stomped a boot into the mud puddle with a splash and watched the tiny waves ripple along its surface. Many counted on his success. He saw their pleading faces in his dreams each night. If the tales of the Creed's power were true, every soul in Andara had new hope.

Chapter Forty-Two

"WHY SO HAPPY, squire?" Seth laced up his boot with a grin. "We're going into danger."

"Aye. I'll gladly stare the devil in the eye rather than stay behind these walls one more moment."

Whistling happily, Riley continued to pack Seth's kit. Expert hands positioned each item in its proper place with impressive speed. In mere moments, the squire had both of them organized and ready to march. Riley Logan had found his true calling.

"You may get your wish, Lion's squire," Bear said, handing his crossbow to Gudal.

Seth slapped Riley on the back and joined his friends in the corridor. Exiting the barracks with their squires in tow, they met their fourth team member in the courtyard. White Tiger had selected Dragonfly to join their squad, and Seth was glad for the addition. He nodded at Dragonfly and his squire, Donny, and then looked to the men under his command. The rangers knew what they would meet out in the marshlands. Their squires, on the other hand, hadn't encountered the beasts waiting in the bogs.

"We journey through terrain with many dangers," Seth told his team, pulling on his pack. "Stay close to the group. Nobody wanders off the trail, and above all else, keep your eyes open."

Marching along the wooden pathways, they entered the UR courtyard. Seth let out an undignified groan. The other three squads had already taken up position before the outpost gates. None of them had brought their squires along. Riley hadn't given Seth much choice. He'd threatened to follow if Seth wouldn't take him too.

White Tiger, Mantis, and Gecko stood at the head of their men, waiting for him. Perfect. He was late for his first mission as a squad leader. Hurrying to take up position beside Gecko, Seth stood at attention before the gates.

"Now we're all here," White Tiger said pointedly in Seth's direction. "Open the gates!"

Chains, cogs, and pulleys grumbled in a chorus of protest. Despite its reluctance, wood parted slowly before them. Seth fidgeted restlessly, unable to keep his eager feet still. Soon he'd reach the end of his quest. He and his men, however, must pass through deadly obstacles first.

Framed in the entrance, North Marsh waited with its hungry jaws. Howls greeted them. Though the night was reluctantly giving way to morning, the four-legged inhabitants still gathered around the gate in hope of an easy meal.

"Move out!" White Tiger marched forward, leading the rangers of Western Beta into the mouth of the marsh.

The gates groaned shut as the last of their numbers stepped out onto the path to the docks. White Tiger barked an order. Then he and his men were gone in a swirl of ash. The other squads darted away from the gates and headed toward their assigned destinations. Seth and his men stood alone before the foundations of the outpost.

"Bear, take point," Seth ordered. "Dragonfly covers the rear. Stallion, Badger, and I will be on guard."

Their steps were more confident this time as they marched toward Mount Crumble. The journey was undoubtedly quicker than previously, even though their pace remained at a steady walk for the sake of the squires. Unlike on the full day spent rambling about during testing, his squad cut its time down to little more than an hour over the stone pathways across the marsh. Seth suspected Western Beta's charge from the outpost to Mount Crumble had taken less than half the time as they crossed the distance at a ranger's speed.

"Great flying gulls. What a stink!" Riley put a hand to his nose. "I'll never get it out of our clothes." Based on the groans and gags, the other young squires weren't keen on the smell either.

Squire Gudal stopped suddenly and swung the crossbow off his shoulder. The string twanged as he let an arrow fly into the grass clump lining the bog to their left. Dark fur crushed the blades of grass as a marsh wolf fell onto its side. Instantly, black muzzles began to rip and tear at the fallen beast's body. Riley gave a disgusted cry as the other wolves stopped following their human prey and fed upon an easy meal instead.

"I'll not be fetching that arrow, eh?" Gudal slapped Riley on the back with a laugh.

"I've seen you do worse." Bear shook his head with a chuckle. "My squire has a good idea there. Better if we all keep our eyes open and our weapons at the ready. We journey into the tall grass soon."

"Aren't we stopping at the spy cave then, sir?" Henry asked.

Seth looked up at the midmorning sky and shook his head. "We can make several more hours at this pace. Though we must find shelter before sunset."

"What happens at sunset?" Riley asked, jumping across a gap in the stone path.

"The deadlier creatures of the night come out to hunt," Bear called over his shoulder.

Fear. It blossomed like a poisoned flower over the squires, but to their credit, they didn't say a word. Each of them remained steadfast and disciplined until Donny pointed excitedly at an area not far off their path. The squires, overwhelmed with curiosity, jogged toward the site. Seth and his squad of rangers followed. Something angry and powerful had completely flattened any grass, dead trees, or ruins in a wide strip of destruction.

"The Right-Hand's temper is fierce," Cal said, awe circling his body. "North Marsh will show signs of the Lion and the Wolf for many years."

Then Seth noticed the granite column, the lone object still standing erect within the scene. A dagger, buried to its hilt in stone, protruded from the surface. The image of a silver wolf ran along the black leather hilt. Reaching out, he wiggled his fingers within the remaining tendrils of the Right-Hand's power.

"Great day in the morning. Xavier the Wolf did this?" Riley whistled. "So, the pile of metal over there must be Mount Crumble. By the green, green fields. What a battle!"

"It was, Logan," Cal said, scanning the landscape. "I can guess where all the bodies have gone."

"Let's keep moving. We have a good distance to go before sunset."

Seth grabbed the hilt of Wolf's dagger and yanked it out of the stone. He tucked the weapon in his pack for safe keeping. Wolf would be glad to get back the blade, a weapon of fine Valdeonian steel obtained in a happier time and place.

Most of the battle had occurred at the foot of Mount Crumble. A few signs of clashes, however, were present along the trail. Western Beta had been tenacious in the hunt for stragglers. Seth and his companions covered several miles along the northwest trail before their squad found evidence of Phoenix and his rangers ending their pursuit.

Hours passed as Bear led them toward open marshland. Bear had been right. Miles of tall grass waited for them ahead. It was hard to believe water rather than soil was the foundation for the solid wall of green. Then the stone trail ended abruptly at a tiny island of wet moss and mud. Recent boot prints curved toward the southwest and disappeared again on a stone walkway leading to the free wilderness. Mantis and his men had passed this way.

"Our paths split here," Seth said, running a finger along his squad's section of the map. "But, I don't see our trail."

"Wait a moment." Bear stopped beside a tall boulder and knelt in the mud.

"What is it?" Seth asked.

Bear gave him a pleased grin. "Footprints are still on this ground though a few days have gone by since the mercenaries passed this way. We can backtrack their journey."

"Good work, ranger! Let's move."

"Ice Lion, do you think we may encounter Jackal stragglers on the trail ahead?" Dragonfly asked quickly.

Seth regarded him for a moment. Concern. Trust. Friendship. The emotions made gentle waves about Dragonfly's body. He wanted to tell Seth to show caution while trying to respect the Lion's command at the same time. Here was a true ally and someone Seth trusted completely.

"Excellent point, Dragonfly. We should proceed with caution. Let's keep our eyes open."

They stepped through the wall of marsh grass to find a well-traveled stone path a few feet from the boulder. Towering a good ten feet toward the heavens, the canyon of green narrowed to a man's width across. Their bodies pressed together in a long chain. One wrong step in either direction and the unlucky man would drown in a sea of grass. The march was suffocating. Seth, feeling boxed in, forced his gaze on the surrounding wetlands as he walked. It was no use. Mortal eyes couldn't look past the natural walls. He'd have to wait for the Jalora's warning if danger came for them.

Minutes spent in the overpowering green tunnel seemed to span a lifetime as they shuffled along the narrow stone path. Then Bear stopped suddenly. Seth looked around his shoulder. Bear had stopped because they had nowhere to proceed. Another wall of marsh grass closed over the trail. Reaching his arm through the blades, Bear slowly parted them.

"Ice Lion. Up ahead." Bear held a finger to his lips for silence. "I think it's a hunter's blind."

He knelt on the stone, allowing Seth to see over his shoulder. Gently opening the veil of tall grass blocking their path, Seth scanned the area before them. Someone had cleared a circle of dirt in the middle of the marsh field. Four tall pillars of stone stood at the southwest corner of the loop. Massive vertical logs bricked into the rock, towered over the bogs.

Bear stood and quietly pushed his body through the grass. Seth followed, holding the curtain of green open to one side until they were all through. Resisting his body's desire to take great gulps of air, he joined Bear behind a large clump of boulders.

"I can make out a platform on top of the pillars, but the structure's too tall to see its surface clearly."

"Aye. Looks like a blind to hunt rangers," Riley told them, pointing up at movement against the darkening sky.

"What now?" Cal asked. "We can't go around without being seen."

Phoenix had ordered them not to engage the enemy unless it was unavoidable. Seth ran a hand through his hair. Getting past the blind was key to completing their mission. Confronting any guards above them seemed inevitable. His eyes scanned the pillars again and rested on the platform, which was about twenty feet high. A rope ladder was attached to its side and had been pulled up to rest on the very edge of the platform. He could use his power to climb on the raindrops and reach the top, but any agents of evil in the area would be alerted to his presence.

"What's on your mind, Ice Lion?" Dragonfly asked.

"Flying, ranger."

Seth spotted Cal, Bear, and Gudal at the edge of the grass just beyond the foundation of the platform. Cal picked up a rock and threw it as far as he could. It landed in the bog with a splash. Seth gave them a wave when the shadow patrolling the platform moved toward the noise. Bear and Gudal dashed to the base of the tall platform. They gripped their arms together and crouched.

"I don't know about this, Ice Lion." Henry took deep breaths as he waited for them to position in place.

"I think it's insane," Riley grumbled with a glare at Cal. "And I don't appreciate being called short."

"Just lower the ladder while Badger takes care of whoever's up there." Seth nodded at his cousin. "Go."

Henry flew toward Bear and Gudal at a run. He jumped onto the joined arms of the two men. They catapulted him up toward the platform. Henry, staying in a perfectly aerodynamic form, landed upon the platform without a noise.

Riley was immediately behind him. Bear and Gudal threw his smaller frame up toward the heavens. Whipping his limbs about like a wounded goose, he teetered on the lip of the platform and then fell unceremoniously forward.

Seth, at Riley's cry of surprise, abandoned the plan and ran at top speed toward Bear and his partner. They quickly compensated for his extra weight and sent Seth sailing up to the platform. He flipped over once and landed on his feet with a thud.

Henry sat cross-legged beside a pile of harvested plants. An animal with the features of a giant rat stood before him. Henry held out one of the bulbous roots and laughed as the creature's whiskers wiggled. Small paws gripped at the plant with a sniff. The little being, taking a tentative nibble, allowed Henry to hold its dinner as it ate.

Riley grumbled Islic curses in the giant rat's direction. He'd landed face first in a pile of the creature's mushy roots and dead frogs. Seth burst into laughter. Mopping bits of mush from his face, Riley glowered at both rangers.

"Ice Lion!" Dragonfly called from the base of the platform.

Still suffering from fits of laughter, Seth kicked down the rope ladder. Dragonfly and Cal were the first to the top. The remaining squires followed. Bear, the last to climb, pulled the rope ladder up after him. Eight men and the rat-like creature easily fit on the platform. The structure could be used to hold supplies for several days of future scouting missions.

"Well, what critter is that?" Cal asked. "Logan seems keen to share its food."

"It's a muskrat," Gudal told them. "They usually stay near the water and are cautious of humans. You must have a way with animals, Badger."

"Great flying gulls. I think we can do without its pile of dead things," Riley said, running another linen across his face. "Come along, ranger. Say goodbye to your new friend. We must set up the camp."

"Your practicality is unarguable, Lion's squire." Badger gave a grin Riley couldn't see.

Seth sidestepped the muskrat as it ran past him to the edge of the platform. He turned his attention to the view surrounding them as the squires began their work cleaning the campsite. The landscape looked the same in every direction—grassy and wet. If more blinds were positioned about the marsh, they weren't visible from this location.

Notably missing in the surrounding bogs was the next section of the path leading to the north. Seth had seen it drawn on the map. What if the stone walkway had sunk into the bogs? Perhaps the rangers could journey to the coast and then make their way north. Somehow, they must find a way to reach the northwest coast or risk failing Andara.

"Well, we can report at least one place for UR personnel to keep watch in this vast sea of wetlands." Seth sighed and ate the cold meal Riley had handed him. "Badger and Stallion, you take the first watch. Dragonfly, Bear, and I'll relieve you in a few hours."

The acolytes allowed the squires to sleep. Brave they might be, but the Jalora didn't grant them the stamina it gave its rangers. They were exhausted. Seth, on the other hand, couldn't stay still for sleep. The hidden path north filled his thoughts. Giving up on his attempts to rest, he sat on the edge of the platform and stared out at the darkness.

"You're doing well with your assignment, Ice Lion." Dragonfly sat down beside him. "These men have grown to trust you."

Seth turned to regard his friend's silhouette in the darkness. "Did White Tiger ask you to keep an eye on me?"

"He didn't like sending you out here on your own, Seth. I think he sometimes underestimates you. You've already learned to trust your instincts." Dragonfly put a hand on Seth's shoulder and gave it a reassuring pat. "I have faith in you, Ice Lion. Your heart is true." He backed away from the edge. "I'm for bed before my time on the watch."

"Sleep well, my friend."

Faith. Seth needed to have a little now. The Jalora had sent its Lion here and given him a clue to follow. It was time he trusted in his fate. The way north would become clear to him. It must. Everything depended on his traveling to Sea Point.

Then he saw his next clue waving against the tall marsh grass about twenty yards to the west. It was Cougar! The old ranger put a finger to his lips in warning and disappeared into the grass once more. Apparently, Elk and Cougar weren't ready to make an appearance yet. No matter. Seth was grateful for their guidance. The Creed waited for him. Soon his quest would be over, and he could join the Lords of Valdeon as they fought to stop the invasion of Andara.

Chapter Forty-Three

RILEY SHOOK THE droplets of North Marsh dew from his cloak. Miserable place. He had needed several minutes of fighting damp cloth to finish arranging their things. He tied Seth's bedroll beneath his pack and secured it with a yank. His ranger hadn't slept well. The drizzle of rain falling on their bodies had been bad enough, but those hellhounds, hungry for man flesh, had howled beneath the platform all night long. Their plaintive baying would give Riley nightmares for months.

"I hadn't expected to miss boiled vegetables," Lucas said, stuffing a roll of dried meat into Stallion's pack. "I can't decide if our rangers aren't hungry or they just hate the taste of old barrel meat."

Selby shook his head with a grin. "They feel the Lion's excitement, I think. Youth has no time for practicalities."

"Aye. Though why Seth is so thrilled is beyond me." Riley stood and cast a wary eye across the sea of green. "The marshlands have already lost their charm."

The moment Seth's boots touched the ground at sunup, he'd gone off to the west. Riley's vantage point atop the platform gave him a good view of the Lion as he prowled the terrain. He hadn't liked Seth running off on his own. Dragonfly, ever the sensible one, agreed. Not wanting to undermine Seth's leadership, however, he'd ordered the squad to stay atop the platform. Now, Dragonfly stood on the edge, scanning the wetlands to their west. Bear, Stallion, and Badger took up positions on the platform as well. They kept keen eyes on the land about them.

Then the tall grass rustled wildly as if a great beast were charging through its blades. Seth burst out of the wall of green. Face streaked with mud and bits of grass clinging to his curls, the Lion let out a cry of triumph. He made for the base of the ladder, waving at them. Out of breath from exertion or excitement, Seth clutched at the rope with a laugh.

"The Lion has found something," Gudal said.

"Aye. Seth won't be happy until we've all followed him. Better hurry and finish packing."

Riley picked up their packs and climbed down the ladder. Spinning Seth around, he helped him put eager arms through the straps. His ranger was about to burst with news, but kept his impatience in check as the rest of the squad descended the ladder.

"I've found our path to the north."

Of course, he had. Riley held in his sigh. Seth wouldn't be satisfied until he'd gotten them to the northwest coast. He had been tight-lipped about the reason, but Riley guessed it had little to do with their official mission. Seth must've discovered a clue as to the location of this Creed he'd spoken to Wolf about.

"It doesn't look well traveled. How do we know it goes all the way to the coast?" Stallion asked. "What if we get stuck in the middle of the marsh with no way out?"

Riley shared the cautious young man's concerns, but he'd never admit it to Seth. His ranger stood facing all of them, head nodding slowly. As squad leader, he could ignore their concerns and order them to follow, but this was Seth. Lion Protector or no, he'd never pretend to be better than anyone else.

"We'll make it to the northern coast. I know it." Seth paused, his amber-flecked eyes scanning each of them. "I was ordered to go on this path."

"What do you mean, Seth?" Dragonfly asked. "Phoenix and White Tiger didn't mention anything specific about this trail. Are you saying someone else is here in the marsh with us?"

And there it was. The secret Seth had been hiding was coming out at last exposed in the long silence. Even his tight shoulders and lifted chin betrayed the hidden truth. Riley's best friend had been keeping secrets from him again.

Seth shifted his eyes away, unable to meet Riley's gaze. "Two rangers have been helping me search for…for something. They showed me our path. This stone trail takes us to the coast."

"Two rangers?" Dragonfly exchanged worried looks with the rest of the squad. "Will they be joining us then?"

"You don't believc me?"

"Of course, we do, Seth." Badger began carefully. "Have you considered they might not be on our side? What if they're Changelings trying to lure you out in the open?"

"A sensible question." Seth ran a hand through his wet hair. "Changelings are the creations of evil. I don't believe they could wear a Heart of the Warrior Ring. Besides, these two men were friends of my father, Edmund the Leo. They swore an oath to help me."

Riley didn't need ranger powers to see the skepticism surrounding their squad. If two rangers had been hiding in or around the outpost, thinking Western Beta would have sensed them was reasonable. He regarded Seth standing alone under the platform.

Riley swallowed his doubts and joined Seth close by. "If the Lion says two rangers are helping him, then that's the way it is. I should think you'd all learn to believe him after what you've seen."

"My apologies, Ice Lion. Your squire is quite correct." Dragonfly gave the young man a respectful bow. "We will follow you."

Aye. Riley hoped that he was right. Seth was too trusting sometimes. What if these men *were* Changelings? And just how long had they been visiting Seth? Riley didn't like the whole idea one bit.

"Come along, Lion's squire," Seth said, bumping his shoulder fondly. "I would have you at my side."

Seth stepped through the grass wall and was gone. Riley jumped across the green barrier to follow his ranger. Right or wrong, he'd watch Seth's back. That's what friends did.

Chapter Forty-Four

JULIAN FOLLOWED BEHIND his sire—now wearing Esteban the Hawk's form. He'd been hushed like a child as Esteban and Gorman spoke in low tones. Strained politeness on Gorman's part spoke of a long hatred between the two. They barely tolerated each other's presence. The conquest of Andara appeared to be the aspiration bringing them together. Julian, for his part, hated them both equally.

"I'll just stay out here like a good dog, shall I?" Julian called once both predators had boarded the launch.

"To leave you on this island forever would give me great pleasure, but alas it seems your father still desires your life to be spared."

"Sentimentality isn't an emotion I possess, Julian. Stay here until someone comes to fetch you." His father's Hawk mask fell into a cold scowl. "It's a pity my only progeny hasn't grown into more of a man."

"Perhaps my Changeling blood is stronger."

Julian, tucking his resentment away for the time being, turned from their departing launch. He wandered toward the makeshift torture chamber created by the blue-robed Changeling. Biting teeth of unspent magic snapped at him as he passed the Lord of

Valdeon's abandoned blade. Resting in the center of a circle of scorched ground, it waited for the next unlucky fool. Julian kicked a clump of marsh grass onto the black leather of the hilt. Popping and burning with a quick zap, the grass withered to burnt crisps in moments.

"May you rust under the clouds of a thousand storms." Julian spat on the steel blade. "You still won't suffer as much as your defeated lord."

Xavier the Wolf's unconscious body was chained spread eagle between four steel posts. Julian leaned in closer, examining the mess of purple flesh covering his enemy's face. Stripped of his ranger uniform, the powerful Lord of Valdeon looked like any other helpless mortal. Nasty cuts and bruises crisscrossed his torso while burn marks from some earlier battle covered his forearms.

Torture. These arrogant foreigners may have done their research on the landscape of Andara, but they knew nothing of its people. Julian could've told them Wolf would never yield. He was a stubborn one. Unconditionally devoted to his Jalora, this Lord of Valdeon would not betray its secrets.

Julian poked Wolf's leg with the toe of his boot. Wolf moaned then fell silent again. Not dead yet? Curious. Hawk certainly wanted him dead, which meant Julian's keeping him alive would be advantageous.

"Here you are, abomination. I've heard the Master Spy was able to mate with a human, but I must admit I had my doubts."

The Changeling they called "Master Interrogator" stood only feet away from Julian, its blue robes sprinkled with Wolf's blood. Moving with surprising speed for its advanced years, the Changeling came within reach. Picking at Julian's skin and clothes, it began examining Julian as if he were a particularly disgusting form of rare fungus.

"Yes, the news was a surprise to me as well." Julian ignored the creature's derisive glare. "And how is it my sire was able to accomplish such a rare feat?"

"Our cousin is ancient and very powerful." It grabbed at Julian's tunic, lifting the fabric to expose his scales. "Spawning an offspring with a human is unnatural and unwise. I warned him against contaminating our race. Nature will always restore the balance."

Julian didn't appreciate the inference but maintained his well-practiced attitude of respect. Many of what he guessed were the older Changelings, didn't like his sire. The younger in their family who'd been with Julian in Valdeon didn't have the sense to hate such dangerous magic. Or they recognized an opportunity.

"I wonder why he took such risks," Julian said.

"You don't know then?" The old Changeling chortled, rubbing together its wizened hands. "Your sire has lofty aspirations. He was once king to the Changeling family until Uther conquered our lands. The Master Spy wants his power again. Uther has promised to make him…what would you say?" Then it looked down at Wolf. "Yes, Uther wants a Right-Hand like the Wolf is to the Lion."

"Wouldn't his son, Gorman, be Uther's Right-Hand?"

The Changeling wheezed another laugh, drool dripping out of the sides of its mouth. "Uther despises his son. He has pitted Gorman and the Master Spy against each other in a contest for the role. The winner will have riches and limitless power."

An idea began to form in Julian's mind. Now he knew what Gorman and his sire prized above all else. Their quest would be their undoing—he'd make sure of it. But first, he had to settle the little matter of Xavier the Wolf.

"My human caretakers never cherished me as a child. Not until my cousins surrounded me with their acceptance did I feel as if I had a true home. I may have come into our family dishonorably, but I am loyal." Julian let angst and self-deprecating emotion enter his voice. "Seeing such recklessness in a leader pains me. My sire was thinking of himself rather than our family when he made me." Julian bowed. "Forgive me. I have spoken out of turn."

"You speak with wisdom, young one." It tilted its head to regard him more closely. "I see it in your eyes. You have an idea?"

"If neither Lord Gorman or the Master Spy were to become Uther's champion that might be in the best interest of the Changeling family." Julian motioned down at Wolf. "We have the Lion's Right-Hand. What if he could be turned? What if his loyalty shifted from the Jalora to Uther? Perhaps the emperor would be grateful enough to give Valdeon to the Changeling family as a reward." Julian shrugged and dropped his arms. "Then again, to turn the Wolf would take a skilled artist. He has a strong will."

"It is possible, clever boy." The Master Interrogator smiled slowly. "Remind me not to turn my back on you."

"I will leave you to your craft," Julian said with a bow. "My king."

He walked at a slow pace toward a crumbled bit of ruin at the center of the island. Behind him, chains rattled as the Changeling prepared to board his ship with Wolf dragging along behind. A predatory grin spread across the Changeling's lips as laughter rumbled low in his chest. Human or Changeling, the desire for power was irresistible. He gave an irreverent salute as their ship lifted into the air. The vessel took flight, carrying Julian's scheme with it.

Chapter Forty-Five

WOLF STRUGGLED TO open his eyes. One of them, the left, refused to respond. His right eye, swollen and weeping fluid, opened a crack. He was, blessedly, out of the drizzling weather. The posts, his chains, and the putrid little island were gone. Steel bars and a single porthole replaced them. The foul creatures had taken him aboard their ship.

In an effort of stern will, he eased his bruised and bloodied body against the exterior wall of the cell. It shuddered steadily beneath his back. Closing his eyes, Wolf listened with an experienced ear accustomed to traveling aboard airships. The vessel's engines hummed low. They'd moored somewhere. Were they still in North Marsh?

Seth. He was in danger. Hawk had gone completely mad. Groaning, Wolf tried to get to his feet. It was no use. His body was too damaged from the abuse he'd taken at the Changeling's clawed hands. The one they called "Master Interrogator" was an expert at cutting and beating. Wolf smoothed at the slashes on his thighs. Curious the creature hadn't broken a bone or cut off an appendage. He held up his Heart of the Warrior ring. The Wolf Spirit paced restlessly within its crystal. It too was impatient to be rid of these Changelings.

They'd wanted to know how to get at the Altar of Providence. Wolf rocked his head back and forth against the wall. No torture evil could conceive would make him disclose such sacred things. Besides, he could tell them nothing. The Jalora's magic alone controlled access to its altar.

Burning tendrils of energy warned he wasn't alone. Lifting his weeping gaze from the cuts on his legs, Wolf glared across the cell. His tormentor had returned. Long white strands fell across its blue-robed shoulders. Emotionless black orbs waited, as they had those many hours of torture, for Wolf to speak. Eyeing the creature defiantly, he was determined to resist with all his will.

The Changeling, however, didn't make a move to enter the cell. It stood, silently staring at him. Something in its manner had changed. The creature no longer possessed the arrogant mischief its kind wore like a mantle. Gone was the frantic glee it had sported as they relentlessly tortured him.

"You are strong, Right-Hand." It lifted the sharp chin, examining him curiously. "Emperor Uther could use a man of such strength to support him. He longs for a champion such as you."

"And what of your pet Hawk or Julian the bastard prince?"

"Esteban's ambitions are dangerous to his allies." Venomous dislike burned in the Changeling's eyes. "Julian is a buffoon and an abomination. No, Right-Hand. Uther must have you."

Wrapping its fingers around the bars, the Changeling grinned slowly. Wolf pressed his back harder against the wall as evil's magic crept toward him. A sense of wrongness filled his heart. He gagged upon its horrible flavor. Somewhere past the spell, he heard the Changeling's wheezing laughter.

"Uther offers you a gift, Right-Hand."

Then the cell disappeared. Wolf was suddenly back in San Leonora standing in the atrium of the Palace of Kings. Brilliant sunlight streamed through the glass. He turned his face to soak in its warmth. The scent of roses and fresh-cut grass came through an open door on the gentle breeze. The sensations seemed so real, but how was this possible?

"You have fond memories of this place."

The Changeling stood next to him. Its presence was an insult to the Palace of Kings. Evil, it would seem, had resorted to seduction and beguilement. Its trickery was pointless. He would not be swayed no matter what bangtail mischief the creature threw at him.

Wolf's gaze followed the Changeling's wizened finger to his left. Figures stood silhouetted in the doorway. Jaguar, Fox, Raven, Otter, and Rabbit entered the atrium. The young Lords of Valdeon hurried forward to join him. They looked happy and excited as if celebrating the restoration of Valdeon.

Then the atrium darkened. Broken glass lay strewn across chipped marble. Tapestries torn haphazardly rested over shattered fragments of Valdeonian artwork. The mood of Wolf's guardsmen began to change as well. Pain. Fear. Death. These emotions visited the young Lords of Valdeon as he watched. Their images writhed across the ruined marble before him. He cried out as the flesh finally rotted from their bones.

"You can save them," the Changeling said, waving its hand.

The Lords of Valdeon, now restored, stood before Wolf, smiling and waving. This time, they weren't in the atrium. Now they stood before the Altar of Providence. Wolf saw his own image seated on the throne. The Crown of Sorrows burned brightly about his head. Had the creature gone mad? Or perhaps it didn't understand. Only the Lion might sit upon or touch the golden surface of the Lion Throne. All others would be struck down by the Jalora's magic.

"You waste both our time, creature of evil."

"The throne of Valdeon isn't enough to entice you? Very well." It waved its hand again. "Perhaps something dearer to your fragile mortal heart then?"

Golden hues dazzled under the brilliant crystal chandeliers of the Great Hall. Deep-red velvet curtains hung beside tall glass doors leading out into the fragrant gardens of the Palace of Kings. Music and laughter filled the room. Leo was throwing another party. Which of the king's many festivities was the Changeling showing him?

Another clue in the form of his old friend and mentor, Fox, approached. He was Rafael's uncle who'd died several years before. Wolf remembered the delicate lace originating from San Angelica he'd worn on his elaborate tunic. This occasion was his old friend's last party before he'd died in battle.

No. Wolf stepped away. He well remembered what had happened that fateful night. How could he forget the most important moment of his life? Curse the Changeling devil! He'd found the core of Wolf's heart.

A soft tap sent thrilling shivers up his arm. Wolf turned unable to help himself. Anything to view her beloved face again. Dulcina, heaven's own songbird, graced him with her beautiful smile. His heart became hers just as it had the first time he'd seen her.

The ladies of San Leonora played a courtship game with their potential lovers during Leo's parties. They bribed servants and squires to find out the favorite color of the man they fancied. Decorating strips of fabric with the colors, they wore them over the shoulder and across their bodies. The game gave their potential suitors a bit of encouragement. Dulcina stood before him dressed entirely in a gown of rich burgundy—his favorite color. She'd certainly captured his attention. They'd danced the entire evening together and were married soon after.

"I have come to thank you for saving my nephew's life," she said.

He began to weep. How had he forgotten the sweet tones of Dulcina's voice? Unable to reply, Wolf took her in his arms and started their first dance. Soft skin. The aroma of delicate roses. Memories of his beloved wife came back in a rush. He'd tried to hold his grief in check, but he'd failed. Releasing the caged emotions now became agonizing.

The warmth of her hand in his faded and was gone. He cried out, living the incredible loss once more. The Great Hall disappeared. Smoke from his burning orchards filled Wolf's nostrils just as it had the night Valdeon fell. Dulcina stood before him. Her long hair wafted about bruised shoulders. Their two little sons, Danel and Gaspar, held her hands. Their mute stares broke the remaining pieces of his heart. Stinging wet fell down his cheeks.

"No," Wolf turned away from his murdered family. "They aren't real. None of this is real."

"It could be, Right-Hand." The creature stood beside him once again. "I can't bring back your dead wife or your children, but I can replace them."

Beautiful women hailing from every country in Andara filled the throne room. Some Wolf recognized as wives or daughters of fellow rangers. His stomach lurched. Hundreds of children clung to their mothers' skirts, each little face having Wolf's features. They cowered in fear and respect as he passed them.

"Uther will give you many wives. They, in turn, will give you children enough to fill your Great Hall. Think of it, Right-Hand. Any woman you want. A wife for each day of an Andarian month."

Wolf brought forth his power and wrapped it about his body. The images of women and their frightened children popped out of existence. He was back in the cell aboard the Changeling's vessel. Cackles of appreciative laughter filled the small space. The Master Interrogator's black orbs regarded him with irritating mirth.

"You have made two mistakes, creature of evil. I do not want the throne of Valdeon or any other throne."

"And the second?"

"I serve the Jalora," Wolf told it. "Never will you make me betray its trust."

"A most unfortunate answer, Right-Hand," the creature told him, taking its hands from the bars of the cell. "I offer you your freedom and the throne of Valdeon. Women will see to your every desire and children will fill your halls. The young Lords of Valdeon too will be given their lands back to live in peace. What more can I offer you?"

"Get away from me! You have nothing I want."

"We shall see. Think on these things, Right-Hand. My patience runs thin."

Chapter Forty-Six

SETH RUSHED ALONG the thin stone path like a man pursued by ravenous beasts. They'd marched half a day through tall grass before the landscape had opened up. While he appreciated being out of the suffocating walls of green, the new scenery was a troubling reminder of the dangers of North Marsh. Miles of decay and fetid water surrounded them on either side. The surrounding landscape was unsettling, considering the stone path was a man's width wide. One slip off the narrow trail and an unlucky soul could drown in the murky drink.

Silent and glum, his squad kept their concerns to themselves with one notable exception. Riley Logan stomped along the stones several feet behind Seth. His temper spiked erratically each time Badger accidentally bumped into him from behind.

"Honestly, Seth." Riley shifted his pack irritably. "I'm not a horse. Can't you slow down a bit?"

"You don't want to be stuck out here in the middle of the great bogs at night, do you?" Seth chuckled silently. "Pick up the pace, Lion's squire."

In truth, Seth had no choice. The Creed of the Guardian called to him with relentless insistence, its magic pulling him with unrelenting force. He wasn't sure he could stop his own body from moving toward it.

Seth smoothed at the handle of Wolf's dagger nestled inside his tunic. The Lords of Valdeon were doing their part to stop the Jackal invasion. Seth must complete his quest. Andara's fate rested in the Lion Protector's ability to find the Creed.

His squire's much shorter legs finally kept pace with his own. Irritation. Worry. Doubt. They circled about his body despite his best friend's endeavors to hide them. Try as he might, Riley Logan was an open book even to those who didn't possess the Jalora's gifts. But one of many virtues shined brighter than the rest—Riley's unshakable loyalty. Seth felt lucky to have him as a friend.

"Bear thinks we'll need a few days to reach the coast." Riley's intense gaze burned as Seth looked over his shoulder. "Didn't you tell me Phoenix gave us only that long to patrol and return to the outpost?"

"Dante, the Leo's squire, showed great wisdom when he chose you to serve, Lion's squire." The joined voices of the Jalora and Seth fell over their group. "You are quite right."

Thick mist rolled off the bogs from every direction. In seconds it devoured the squad. Cries of shock and fear rang in tinny echoes from its gray body. Seth's squad stumbled about as if blinded. Curious. Seth would seem to be the only one whose sight could pierce the mists.

"Stay still! You'll step right into the bogs," Dragonfly warned from the ground where he'd stumbled. "Don't trust your eyes. Something about this fog is unnatural."

"Donny? Where's Donny?"

"I'm here!"

"Selby? Lucas? Are you both still with us? What about Gudal?"

"It's me, Riley. Follow my voice. I have a rope. We can tie ourselves together."

"Aye. Good idea. Sound off."

Five names echoed in the depths of the mist. The squires stumbled over each other as they tried desperately to stay on their feet. The rangers, Seth noted, weren't doing much better. They clung to each other like frightened children in the darkness. He must lead them back toward the light.

Then a welcome face appeared in the distance. Elk waved to him. Seth returned the friendly gesture. He took a step forward, but someone grabbed at his trouser leg. Dragonfly. He remained where he'd fallen. Fear swirled about him, but the concern wasn't for his own sake. He was trying to protect Seth.

"Fear not, my faithful," Seth and the Jalora said. "We are in the Realm of Dreams and Mist. Nothing will harm you here unless I allow it. Many miracles will you see in your service to your lord. It is best to accept this now."

"Rangers," Dragonfly shouted. "Form a chain!"

Pulling out of his grip, Seth picked up one end of the rope circling about the waists of their squires and put it into Bear's empty hand. Seth's other hand grasped tightly to Cal's arm and placed the rope into Henry's grasping fingers. Returning to Dragonfly with his human chain in tow, he took his friend's hand and pulled him to his feet.

"Hold tight now." Seth tugged at the chain and began pulling them forward through the outskirts of the Realm.

Elk appeared out of the mists again to walk beside him. "It calls, Lion. We're close."

"Yes, I feel its magic."

"Who is that?" Dragonfly asked.

Seth, ignoring his question, pulled them through the borders of the Realm and back to North Marsh. Brisk ocean breezes greeted them as they stepped onto the rocky coast. He breathed in the fresh briny air. How he'd missed its sweet aroma.

"What in the green, green fields happened?" Riley asked. "We're there! How?"

Seth looked out across the violent waves as they crashed against the rocks. The loneliness of this northern land stirred something in his soul, a strange mix of peace and uneasiness. Memories of his childhood on Marianna deepened his feelings of isolation. He pushed this sense of the past aside and conjured happy images of Carlotta instead.

"It's funny how the same ocean can look so different on more than one shore," Seth said.

"Aye," Riley answered beside him. "So are you going to tell us how we got here?"

A small stone plopped in the water a few feet before him. Seth turned to the west. Cougar waved an impatient hand, beckoning him to follow. He was right. Andara didn't have time to waste while Seth mulled over old memories.

"No time," Seth said, hurrying forward along the shore. "Our guide waits."

"Give us a moment, for pity's sake." Cal sat down on a rock, retching. "Let us collect ourselves. You may be used to that realm of nightmares, but my stomach is not."

"Cougar calls us forward. We must go."

"On your feet, Stallion. That goes for the rest of you as well," Dragonfly ordered. "The Lion is on the move."

Seth hopped lightly along the stone shore. The others weren't as graceful, their boots sliding on the slick pebbles. Cal, as usual, had spoken his mind. The Realm of Dreams and Mist had indeed taken a toll on his friends. Pale and wobbly, they hadn't left the realm without experiencing a few unpleasant side effects.

"Where are these rangers?" Riley asked, chewing on one of his healing roots.

"They've gone ahead to mark the path. Don't worry. We're close. Hurry now."

A short walk brought them to a small inlet lined by a rocky beach. Seth knelt and rested a hand against the pebbles. Evil had landed here. Its foul touch was still palpable though several months had passed.

"By my father's beard, this must be the trail to Sea Point Outpost." Bear pushed away from the bramble covering a trailhead just off the shoreline. He touched the path with a tentative boot as Seth hurried to his side. A sharp tug at Seth's chest was confirmation enough they'd found their way. Seth ripped away the bramble and stepped onto the path. They soon came upon evil's crime.

"What horror happened here?" Riley murmured.

Skeletons lay strewn before the crumbling remnants of a once great outpost. Many bodies had been ripped apart, and their bones chewed on. A shiver of disgust ran along Seth's spine. The Dirge had feasted well during the assault. These bones were the final vestiges of Edmund D'Antoiné's defenders.

"My father and his men made their last stand against Julian and his unholy allies here," Seth told them. "They came to this lonely place knowing they would never leave."

"Greetings, Ice Lion, to you and your loyal men."

Elk and Cougar stood a few feet before them. Seth gave them a salute. His squad, still unsettled by the day's events, numbly followed his example.

"Where did they come from?" Cal whispered.

"It waits for you, Lion," Elk said. "Come. We will take you to it."

"Have a care, Seth." Dragonfly put a hand upon his arm. "Something's not right. Or at least not natural."

"You will all wait for the Lion here," Elk commanded. "It isn't safe."

Then he held out his hand to Seth. Power tingled along Seth's fingers when he touched Elk's skin. Reality fell away. Seth saw only the light of Elk's power. The warning words of his friends faded as his boots left the ground.

Chapter Forty-Seven

BOOTS TOUCHING LIGHTLY upon the crumbling bastion of stone, Seth followed in the wake of Elk's power. The ranger's white hair and sharp features radiated with light as if he were standing under a noonday sun. Lifting a hand to protect his eyes, Seth didn't resist as his body propelled forward.

"You've come at long last," Cougar said once they arrived at the top of the wall. "Welcome to Sea Point Outpost."

Elk released Seth's hand and joined Cougar at a lone section of the barricade. It seemed to be the last remaining structure of the outpost still intact. Seth scanned the ruin anxiously. His gaze found only miles of bogs and an angry ocean surrounding the dead ruins. The Creed was here. Its power tugged at the invisible chain connected to his heart. And yet, the elusive relic remained hidden. What was he supposed to do now?

Then a dazzling beacon pierced through his uncertainty. Its source—a glowing block of stone at the center of the wall—volleyed a beam of light on him. Seth stood motionless, mesmerized by its power. The block pulsed in a steady rhythm as if in time with Seth's own heartbeat. The Creed of the Guardian was making itself known to him at last.

"We have spent these many months protecting the Creed. Long have we waited for you to come." Cougar pointed to the glowing wall. "Touch the stone, Lion. Take your birthright!"

Seth approached the wall with uncertain steps. Such power. He could use it to protect Andara, but would its strength consume him? The Jalora hadn't explained what would happen to its Lion if he touched the Creed. Then again, the result didn't matter. He must stop the Jackal before they spread across the mainland like an infestation. Seth pressed his left hand on the stone's hot surface. His crystal burst into life as the Lion Spirit of the ring pounced at the wall with a desperate hunger. Then the world disappeared.

Diamond skies sparkled over a midnight beach. Their reflection made glittering dots across the rolling ocean waves. Edmund the Leo, several years younger than when Seth had first met him on Marianna, sat on the sand. Foamy waves brushed over his bare feet. His father, eyes locked on the stars, seemed not to notice.

Suddenly, Leo let out a shout of warning and rolled to the side. A fiery comet plummeted to the ground where he'd been sitting only moments before. Seth leaned over his father's shoulder as the glowing square grew cool. The square was the size of one fire brick at the back of an oven, but its power was as immense as the cosmos. Strange letters written with starlight flashed in a last, burning throb and then faded into the white tile.

"What does it mean?" a younger Cougar asked Leo.

"It means the next Jalora Master has been born."

"Your heir has been chosen then?" Elk queried.

"Yes. I was not worthy to father such a precious soul. Some other man has the honor. Let us hope he does his duty to his son well."

Seth had seen firsthand the heartbreak his father had endured. His wife—frightened of both their families—had taken her baby into hiding. Leo hadn't known about Seth for the first seventeen years of his life. Old regrets. Seth reached a hand down to touch his father's shoulder with a sigh. The hand passed through the memory of Leo like a ghost of what might have been.

"Come, Edmund," Cougar said. "The Jalora has entrusted you with the protection of the Creed."

Leo carefully lifted the precious relic. "Will you help me, my dear friends?"

"Upon our souls, we swear."

The beach suddenly fell away. Seth was back in the ruins of Sea Point again. Steel struck steel. Men shouted as they stood between the invaders and their failing outpost. All the while, a mournful tune echoed against the ruins. It spoke of terror, hunger, and death. The Dirge had taken the field.

"This is madness," said Dante, his father's faithful squire. "We must call the Lords of Valdeon for help."

"The door is closed to us. Wolf would insist on taking my son from me. I won't lose him again."

Leo turned to Elk and Cougar. Haggard from life on the run, their grave faces spoke of what they'd endured in Julian's persistent hunt. Cougar, despite his seeping belly wound, stood up straighter. Elk put an arm under his shoulder to hold his friend upright.

"You know what you must do, rangers." Leo gripped their shoulders as if borrowing some of the strength he found in their friendship.

Elk and Cougar nodded gravely. The three friends embraced, and then they pushed apart with an anguished cry. Its sound filled Seth with dread. His father fell to his knees beside a flat stone and stretched out his left middle finger. The Heart of the Warrior Ring pulsated as if it were offering Leo encouragement for what he must do. Then his father slammed down the blade of a dagger on his finger. The outpost shook as the mighty Lion's Roar thundered in a last show of defiance.

Leo, his time as Bearer of the Lion Ring complete, sunk to the stone with a moan of heart-shattering grief. Dante wrapped a cloth around his bloodied hand. Leo picked up his severed finger as his squire worked. The crystal within the Lion Ring was black with death. He cradled it against his chest with a sob.

"You must protect the Creed now," Leo told his companions.

Struggling to his feet, he leaned heavily upon Dante. They stumbled toward another hole in the ruins. Seth had heard from Dante's lips how they'd planned their escape. Soon Leo would find his son and heir. Seth's adventure as Bearer began a short time later.

Turning back to the men Leo was forced to leave behind, he waited to see the last moments of their lives. Elk pulled the white square from his tunic and placed it on the center stone of the wall. Cougar pressed his hand against the surface to help hold it in position. Once a firm tile, the Creed's matter began to change. Liquid replaced its hard form. Soft edges wrapped around the corners of the block in shimmering velvet.

"Jalora, hear us!" Elk shouted. "We pledge our souls to our duty. We will stand the watch until the Lion returns."

Then their screams banged against Seth's ears. Horrified at the ruthlessness by which the Jalora had extracted their souls, he pressed his hands to his head. The two brave men, bodies writhing in unimaginable pain, collapsed on the ground. Cheeks wet with their shared grief, Seth let his arms fall as the images faded.

"We have done our duty," Cougar said. "We have kept it safe for you."

"Look how it pulses with your strength!" Elk leaned close to him. "Pull your blade and call to it, Lion."

Seth gripped the hilt of his sword as a low growl rumbled in his throat. He pulled his weapon and held the blade toward the heavens. Throwing back his head, he let loose the full might of the Lion's Roar. The Creed's white surface burst from the wall and struck his blade. Pressing his boots into the stone, he struggled to stay upright.

Then holy fire burned in swirls within the steel of his blade. Arcing. Falling. Connecting. The fire began to form words as if by an invisible scribe. Slowly at first, the magical hand wrote faster and faster until the last letter glowed brightly within the steel. Then the fire abruptly vanished.

Elk and Cougar, offering cries of joy to the empty marshland, stepped away. Two skeletons sat side by side. Their bones bleached with searing magic, the remains had stayed safe from evil's touch. Tattered uniforms were proof the harsh climate of North Marsh spared no one.

"We attached our very souls to this place, waiting for your coming," Elk said. "Our watch is done. We can return home to the arms of creation."

"How can I ever thank you?" Seth swallowed hard.

"Return our legacy to the Legion," Cougar said. "That will be thanks enough."

Then they closed their eyes as their ghostly bodies began to flicker. Elk and Cougar ascended toward the brilliant sunlight. Their happiness spilled down on Seth, giving him hope for the future.

Boots thundered toward him. Riley and the others burst onto the top of the ruins. They'd grown impatient waiting for his return. Seth turned to greet them. Then they caught sight of his glowing blade and the writing on it. Awe. Confusion. Hope. The mixture of emotions swirling about his squad started Seth laughing.

"You've come. Good," Seth told them. "You must bear witness to this moment."

"I've never seen writing like this before," Riley said in a whisper. "What does it say?"

"It's the old language," Dragonfly said, gaze irresistibly held by the Creed. "Can you read the words?"

"I can, ranger." Seth set the tip of his sword lightly on the stone before him. "It says 'Held within the Lion's hand, this blade shall never fall. All who hear his mighty roar will answer the Master's call."

"The Creed of the Guardian!" Bear shouted triumphantly. "Everything becomes clear."

The rangers fell to their bellies. Stretching their arms toward him, they lay still and waited for his word.

Their squires, stunned to silence, hurried to follow the examples of their lords. Riley Logan, his carrot curls whipping about as he looked across the floor of men, stayed on his feet. Seth laughed. Here was one soul who would never treat him like a holy relic, and he was glad of it, too.

"Rise, Lion Friends." Seth pointed to the remains of Elk and Cougar. "We must honor these brave rangers who dedicated their very souls in my service."

"Ghosts!" Riley staggered away, falling on his backside.

His squad lifted off their bellies to stare at the bones. Miracles and the supernatural would not be taken lightly by such practical men. Seth smiled. Their faith and loyalty deserved extraordinary honor.

"Wait. Did you say Lion Friends?" Henry lifted his left sleeve and grinned at the markings.

"I am glad you are all with me on this momentous day, my friends." Seth bent over and took the Elk and the Cougar rings. "Come, we must see these loyal men respected. Then we return to our outpost. We must report to the Legion."

"Indeed, we must," Dragonfly agreed, still staring at the Creed from his knees. "Hope has come to us at last."

Chapter Forty-Eight

WOLF RAN THROUGH the fields of slaughtered horses toward his smoldering villa. His pasture of rolling hills, slick and bloodied with the carnage, bucked violently beneath his boots. The ground shifted, distorting into a horrific imitation of reality. Wolf, unable to maintain his balance, dropped to his hands and knees.

"Dulcina! Children!"

Suddenly, he was in the courtyard of his estate. He rose to his feet and moved toward an inescapable destiny. A burgundy scarf lay abandoned at the trailhead to his orchards. Perhaps this time he would save her. Running faster, he pushed through the burning branches. Endless twigs scratched at his face and hands.

"Where are you? Papa is here!"

Then he found them. Dulcina and the children stood at the center of a circle of fire. Nooses still hung about their necks. They pointed at him as one. Their eyes, once filled with love, held unrelenting judgment. Wolf screamed and fell to his knees. He'd failed them again.

"Such guilt, Right-Hand." The Changeling stepped out of the flames, eager fingers gripping at its blue robes. "Why cling to this old life? Peace awaits you under Uther's house."

Rough wood and cold steel surrounded them once more. They were back in his cell within the Changeling ship. Wolf sat with his back against the exterior wall, while his tormentor stood a few feet away. The thing was growing careless with all this bangtail mischief. Another illusion designed to use Wolf's grief against him. Why did the creature persist? Did it not understand after these long hours of physical and emotional torture? Wolf would never betray the Jalora.

"Your Uther is a fool," he said. "If you both were wise, you'd kill me while you have the chance."

"You will not turn then? Pity. Uther won't like my failing to break you." The Changeling's grin fell. "Then again, another exists from which he'll take more amusement."

A small boy, no more than four or five years of age, appeared in the space between them. Frightened amber-flecked eyes pleaded with Wolf. No. Not even this cruel Changeling would risk such sacrilege against the Jalora. The precious soul standing before them was the personification of innocence. Used to house the Jalora as it walked upon the Erthe, the boy wasn't meant to experience cruelty. The Lion Child Vessel held his arms out to Wolf, whimpering and begging for comfort. Then a collar and chain appeared around his neck. A metal-clad fist yanked at the restraint, pulling the little Lion backward.

Rage burst from Wolf's very core. "You will never touch him, creature of evil!"

"So, I have found your weakness, Right-Hand."

"You have found your death!"

Wolf, seized by the Jalora's fury, brought forth the power of the Right-Hand. Its Voice struck the Changeling in the torso, throwing it backward against solid bars. A new entity, ancient and unimaginably strong, joined with Wolf as together they twisted the steel cage. Metal groaned under the invisible fists of vengeance.

Then the Right-Hand's power faltered as Wolf's weakened body collapsed. But the ancient magic raged on. It filled the cell, the ship and the very air about him. Mightier than even the Lion's Roar, this new power was consuming Wolf. He released the last of his will and let it flow from his body into the floor of the vessel and back toward the ground. The wood beneath them split into pieces as the ship began to break apart. Water and mossy ground flashed before his eyes. They were falling fast.

Wolf rolled toward the twisted steel and braced his body. Would he escape the decaying arms of North Marsh for a second time? His fate rested with the will of this new power released upon Andara.

Chapter Forty-Nine

SETH TURNED AWAY from the dying flames of the funeral pyre. He tucked the two Heart of the Warrior rings inside his tunic with a sigh. They'd given Elk and Cougar a proper burial. Time was short. The rest of the defenders must await nature's hand. He moved to the trailhead Leo and Dante had taken in their escape. Remnants of broken stone indicated the path was a sentry's at the rear of the outpost. Yes. Seth had walked this path before.

Clean-cut stone held his quiet feet as Seth walked down toward the beach. Torches—newly delivered from Lea—flickered to life as he passed. Though he had no need of such aids to see his way, those following him insisted upon safety.

He passed over a bridge arcing over one of the small inlets. Two timelines crossed his memory. Was he Enrico the Granite Lion, Fifth Jalora Master? Or was he merely seeing Edmund the Leo and Dante escaping their Jackal hunters? Seth wasn't viewing the outpost with his own eyes or in his own time now. The Creed of the Guardian had boosted his power an incredible degree, but he hadn't expected it to give him memories.

Waves struck rock close by in all the timelines. He was near the shore. Stopping a toe's breadth away from the waves, he turned back for a last look at Sea Point Outpost. It hadn't been this decaying graveyard on his previous visit. No. Enrico's last visit. Green things had grown here once under a bright sky. Massive stone stood in impervious blocks to safeguard northwest Andara. What had happened?

"The Granite Lion died," Seth murmured.

"I asked if you were hungry." Riley tapped him on the arm with a piece of dried meat. "You'll need your strength if we're to return from the edge of the world."

"Come now, Lion's squire. We grew up on the edge of the world." Seth tore off a piece of meat and popped it in his mouth. "You've got a short memory."

They'd spent the night among the ruins not far from the funeral pyre. Riley hadn't liked it. His islander superstition warned against staying in places where ghosts roamed. Seth's reassurances did little to ease his angst.

"Dragonfly," Seth called to his Lion Friend. "Are we all here on the beach?"

"Yes, My Lord." Dragonfly made a quick count to be certain. "The squires have finished the breakfast and have packed our things. We're ready to head back to North Marsh Outpost."

Seth nodded slowly, hiding a grin at Dragonfly's subtle hint about returning to the Legion. Here was a man of honor, ever conscious of his duty. He was also one of the most practical men Seth had ever met. A worthy choice for his Lion Friend. Dragonfly was correct. The time had come to leave this place, but Seth had one more task to perform.

"Behold!" Seth and the Jalora thundered over the shoreline.

The ground rumbled and groaned as the Erthe opened up to swallow the remains of Sea Point. Gigantic jaws chewed at the stone and bones. Then a geyser of dirt and muck burst into the air. Riley hid behind Seth as its spray pummeled the shore a few feet from them.

"By the green, green fields!" Riley cried. "What's happening?"

An enormous mound of sculptured stone pushed out of the ground where the outpost ruins had been. Blazing eyes glared over the open ocean to their west. Massive jaws growled as they fought their way to emerge from the land. Shoulders, a torso, and legs followed quickly. The mountainous Lion shook its mane with a final roar and sat down just beyond the shoreline. The beast, towering over one-hundred feet high, could easily rest its stony jaw on the battlements of North Marsh.

"It's a warning to those who would dare invade the northwest corner of my land." Seth and the Jalora regarded the faces of their awed servants. "This sentinel will alert the Altar of Providence if danger comes from across the waters."

Dragonfly smoothed a hand along his left arm where Seth and the Jalora had marked him. "We must see you back to the safety of the outpost, My Lord Lion."

"I don't think it will be the straightforward trip we had coming here." Cal pointed to the south. "What about the shoreline? It seems clear."

The consensus around their evening campfire was to absolutely avoid any further travels within the Realm of Dreams and Mist. Seth had reluctantly given his promise not to take them through its borders again. A man's nerves, Riley had told him, could only take so many unsettling sights in such a short time.

"Walking along the coastline might get us far enough south," Bear said. "Many fishing ships sail along the southernmost part of North Marsh. Sometimes they will journey up to the central coast, but they don't land."

"Why is that?" Dragonfly asked.

"The Great Bogs lie directly to our east," Bear said, adjusting his pack. "It's riddled with deadly traps. Think of it as a no-man's land."

"Sounds lovely," Riley muttered. "And when we reach far enough south? Will we find a way through the bogs to the outpost, Bear?"

"No doubt we will. How else could the Jackal make it to Mount Crumble?"

Seth's eyes followed the rocky shoreline as it journeyed toward the South. Miles and miles of open landscape remained unprotected. The Lion Sentry would defend Andara from foreign invaders, but what about common thieves and mercenaries? Phoenix was right. The Legion must guard this coast with sharp eyes.

Their journey down the coast was much simpler than the hike north. His squad took advantage of the fresh sea air. Its clean, brisk breeze did wonders to improve their moods. Henry and Cal waved their arms and cawed in high pitched chirps as they chased the seabirds along the shore. Their laughter danced merrily upon the breeze. The antics earned a reluctant smile from the serious Dragonfly.

The morning passed under an ocean sky. Seth's childhood had been spent in a similar environment. Its familiar sights, and sounds drew his mind into long ago memories—his own this time. He hadn't noticed the shore's sudden change until Bear called a halt. Seth joined him at the edge of a broken beach. Sand and pebbles abruptly ended. Grass walls replaced them around the inlet. The natural barrier skirted the shore, blocking their view of the other side.

"I didn't miss this tall grass, I can tell you." Riley's groan of disappointment reflected the group's sentiment.

"What now?" Henry asked. "I don't see any signs of a trail through the grass."

"We have another way open to us if you allow me…" Seth began.

"Oh no, Ice Lion." Cal tugged a blade of grass from its roots. "I'd rather swim than go through those mists again."

Then distant notes from human voices drifted toward them as the ocean breeze paused to catch its breath. Straining to penetrate the grass barrier with his senses, Seth sent his power over the tops of the blades. Anger. Frustration. Greed. More wanderers in the marshlands. Whoever they were, their loyalties didn't lean in favor of the Legion.

"We aren't alone," Seth said. "Bear, and I will have a look. The rest of you wait here. Keep your eyes open. We don't want to be boxed in from behind."

Parting the thick wall of grass and reeds, Seth moved carefully toward the inlet. Bear came behind him, crossbow held firmly in his hands. Seth could hear the voices now. Silent and invisible to human eyes, Seth and Bear remained undetected by the wanderers. A short hike brought them to the muddy banks of the inlet. Two men, oblivious to their audience, shouted angrily at one another in Lydec. Shoving and kicking in impotent rage, they seemed not to notice water flowing over the side and onto the deck of their flatboat.

"Buellanders," Seth whispered to Bear. "What are they doing this far south?"

"Smugglers." Bear spat with distaste. "The fools will lose their plunder if they don't stop fighting."

The flatboat continued to rock precariously on the still waters several feet away from shore. Finally, one of them, a portly man with a stubbled chin, stepped in the wet. He slapped the other man away and barked urgent orders. They pushed their flatboat to shore right in front of Seth and Bear's hiding place.

Jumping out, the smugglers landed in ankle-deep mud. Both wore weatherproof leathers dyed to camouflage their bodies in the bogs. Broad-brimmed hats extended well past their collars. Such contraptions were sure to guide the raindrops away from exposed skin. They'd come prepared for long bouts of exposure in the foul weather.

Both strangers ran hands over a large fissure in the rim of their boat. Their circumstance could vastly improve if they'd unload a small portion of their cargo. Piled to a height much taller than the average man, the tarp covering their spoils bulged to the point of tearing.

Seth could make out the distinct shape and color of rum barrels.

"I told you not to get too close to the metal hull!" The portly man wagged a finger at his companion. "I just painted this boat not two weeks ago."

"Don't blame me," his friend whined. "Those Jackal don't like to work. They don't want to hoist the supplies aboard their ship any farther than they have to, do they?"

Seth nodded to Bear. The time had arrived for a little justice from the other side of the coin. Stepping out of the grass, Seth regarded the smugglers who prized money over loyalty to their people. They were about to experience worse fortune than wet cargo.

"Problems with the boat?" Seth asked.

"Move yourself! It's the Phants."

The thinner of the two jumped back on the boat. Tripping over muddied boots, the smuggler grabbed his musket. He raised it and fired. Seth, spinning to the right, watched the slow bullet float by. It cut through the blades of grass sending bits of green popping into the air.

Taking a step forward, Seth leaped at the flatboat and landed on the smuggler's side. His sword cut through the musket with one slice. The smuggler's wide eyes stared down at the two halves of the musket barrel lying on the deck where Seth's sword had cut them.

Lifting his blade, Seth examined the surface. No scratches or burn marks. Curious. The magic of the Creed held many extraordinary powers. He would need a lifetime to delve into them all. He sheathed his sword with a frown.

"Phants?"

"It's what the criminal element calls members of the Legion," Bear said, throwing the portly smuggler back on deck. "I'm told we look like death's phantom horde as we hunt down our villainous prey."

Bear kicked at the cargo and then threw off the canvas cover. Cases of rum and tobacco were carefully secured to the deck with more rope and metal fasteners. These smugglers valued their goods above all else, for they left very little room for weaponry.

"What's all this?" Riley's orange strands broke through the reeds.

He wasn't alone. The rest of the squad pushed across the natural barrier and came to stand on the bank of the inlet. Fear. Disappointment. Remorse at being caught. They circled in depressed waves about the Buellanders. Groaning with unrestrained despair, the portly smuggler threw his arms about the closest barrel of rum.

"Smugglers," Bear told the approaching party. "They were selling contraband to their Jackal allies."

"First ghosts and now smugglers," Cal said, sheathing his sword. "Missions with you will never be dull, Ice Lion."

Seth stood over the blubbering Buellander. The man's tears were real. It was grief for his lost profit, however, rather than the idea of punishment by the Legion's hand. Fear of the Jalora's justice was waning among the criminal element of Andara. Disturbed by the smuggler's lack of respect, Seth shoved him away from the cargo with his boot. The Legion must focus their fight on the Jackal. They didn't have the time or means to combat Andarian traitors as well. A war fought on two fronts would exact a bloody price.

"You've broken Andarian law. Have you no concern for the safety of your people?"

The smuggler gave Seth a churlish glare. "We must make a living, ranger. Our families starve..."

"Do you think you can lie to me?" Seth sent a sliver of his power to wrap about the smuggler's throat. "Tell me of the Jackal."

"Mercy, mighty lord." The man put his hands before him with a cry. "They have a port hidden within the Great Bogs, not two miles from here. We found it abandoned. No harm in taking advantage of an opportunity. Isn't it enough we've lost money?"

"So, you stole the goods inside and then hoped to sell your cargo to the Jackal at Stone Fang Fortress in the Bloodtooth Mountains." Seth leaned closer, allowing his fiery glare to stoke their fear. "Your customers won't be there either. The Lords of Valdeon have destroyed the fortress." He stood back again, folding his arms. "I offer you redemption. We need guides to show us the way back to North Marsh Outpost."

"And how much are you willing to pay?" The portly smuggler's greed helped him find his courage again.

"Have a care," his friend said. "Our boat won't hold them all."

"Then we shall have to rid the boat of its cargo," Cal said, gingerly jumping aboard.

"No, ranger! That is valuable property."

Cal tossed the first crate overboard. "Not anymore."

The Right-Hand is in danger. Go inland, Lion. Save your comrade!

"Everybody on the boat!"

Shoving the remaining cargo across the deck and into the inlet with a burst of strength, Seth hurried to one pole as the rest of the squad quickly boarded. Bear grabbed the other. They pushed away from the banks and out into the middle of the still water.

"What's going on, Seth?" Riley asked.

"Where are you taking us, ranger? There's no outlet here!" the smugglers shouted, trying to pull away from their captors. "Madman! Your route takes us directly into the Great Bogs."

"Shut up, you!" Riley shot a warning glare at them. "Ice Lion knows what he's doing."

Seth wished Riley's faith in his plan was justified. He had no idea where he was going. His only guide was the constant sense of panic pulling him toward the east.

Chapter Fifty

RILEY BRACED HIS feet against the hull as the flatboat skipped along the murky water of the bogs. Seth and Bear pushed the poles like men on fire, using their powers to propel the little boat at astonishing speeds. Suddenly, they stopped rowing. Riley leaned around Lucas's shoulder as they coasted forward. Dead end. The smugglers had been right.

"We told you, Lion. This journey is a madman's folly. The Great Bogs will kill us all."

Cal the Stallion reached down and slapped the smuggler's head before he could lean away from the ranger's strike. Putting a finger to his lips, Stallion pointed to Seth. Riley turned with the rest to watch their Lion standing completely still on the front of the bow. The shore was approaching quickly. Riley held his breath as Seth prepared for some physical movement. Then the Lion jumped.

"Great flying gilley monsters, Seth!" Riley shouted as his ranger landed on the shore. "That wasn't funny."

"Bring the prisoners," Seth called. "I don't trust them to stay put."

Dragonfly took up Seth's abandoned pole and helped Bear push them closer to the muddy shore. Stallion and Badger disembarked first, dragging their struggling prisoners with them. Riley and the squires followed. Great flying gilley monsters, indeed. This whole section of Andara was one soggy mess. Riley tried to keep his feet out of the death traps of sucking mud as they moved east. Seth, he noticed with a grumble, had already disappeared into the grass.

The uncertain minutes crept by as Riley tried to spot Seth in the massive bog. Bear, though, thanks to his tracking skills, knew precisely where the wayward Ice Lion had gone. His massive body remained tense as he followed seemingly invisible signs. Riley stayed close, marveling as the ranger's steps never faltered.

Then Bear pointed. Seth stood in the grass ahead of them, sword before him. He held up his hand in silent warning. Bear, Dragonfly, Stallion, and Badger pulled their weapons as one and stood in the First Stance. Riley and the other squires took up positions behind the rangers.

Grass and reeds rustled among the clumps a few yards in front of Seth. Someone was coming—six someones in fact. Rangers bounded through the grass and stopped before Ice Lion. They weren't from Western Beta. By their great height and dark hair, Riley could guess from which country they hailed. What in the green, green fields was a squad of Valdeonian rangers doing in the middle of the Great Bog?

"The Lords of Valdeon," Badger breathed. "They've come for the Lion."

"Here now," Riley said, storming around the squad to join Seth. "Nobody is taking my ranger anywhere."

Standing among men over a foot taller than he, Riley felt his temper fading quickly. The Lords of

Valdeon, all staring unabashedly at Seth, gave no indication they'd noticed Riley's presence. Tingles of power ran along his arms and spine. Gasping at the touch, he smoothed at the hairs on his arms standing on end. Riley sensed these men were different than the other rangers. Perhaps the indicator was their solemn manner or the raw power radiating off their bodies as they drew near Seth. They commanded respect from the rest of the Western Beta squad. None of Seth's friends, especially Dragonfly, dared move.

"Young idiot," Basilio the Wolf's squire said, grabbing Riley by the nap of the neck. "Stand away. You're embarrassing your lord. And me."

"Where did you come from?" Riley pulled away.

Basilio looked like a shipwreck. His uniform was torn and muddied. Bruises covered his face and hands. A wet bandage, hastily wrapped around his head, darkened with blood. Whoever had treated his wounds hadn't done a thorough job. Riley reached for the bandage and had his hand slapped away for the trouble. Fine. The man could develop an infection for all he cared.

"Tulio?" Seth sheathed his sword. "Where is Wolf?"

The solemn-faced young man shook his head and turned away. He appeared to be Riley's age, maybe a bit younger. Whoever he was, this Tulio had met and befriended Seth somehow. Then Riley remembered Seth mentioning friends he'd planned to find in Lea who'd help them get to safety. Those friends must have been Wolf and Tulio.

"He's been taken, Lion." Another ranger with a square face ventured a step forward. "I am called Berto the Jaguar. We've come searching for Wolf. He was supposed to meet us at Corpse Point. We decided to go looking when he didn't come, and ran into his squire. Basilio said Hawk and the Jackal ambushed Wolf."

"We saw wreckage as I flew The *Wind Chaser* over the Great Bogs," another of the Valdeonian lords said. "Forgive me, Lion. I am called Rafael the Fox, a member of the Sacred Guard. May I present Ernesto the Raven, Lucio the Ferret, and Yuli the Otter. Tulio the Rabbit you know."

Dressed in a naval commander's uniform, Rafael the Fox was the picture of elegance. Handsome features shifted quickly from Seth to young Badger who'd just joined them. Riley had seen the hatred Seth had endured from the Tslavic people due to his mixed blood. Here it was from the Valdeonian side.

"I thought it best we hide our ship and go on foot," Fox said as if his attention had not been elsewhere a moment before. "If Wolf is a captive onboard, we don't want to provoke them."

Seth twisted around and pounced on their prisoners. Lifting the smugglers like rag dolls, he held them as their toes swung wildly above the wet ground. A rumbling growl rolled across the grassland. Everyone except the Lords of Valdeon backed away while the Lion Spirit struggled for release. The Valdeonian rangers stood straighter with their chins raised proudly. They seemed hopeful, frightened, and happy all at the same time.

"What do you know of this? Tell me! I have no patience for your lies." Seth demanded of the men in his grasp.

"We heard a ship crash while we were leaving the abandoned Jackal docks. I guessed it to be in a hidden bay to the south. Hoping to find some cargo to scavenge, we journeyed to the wreckage," the portly smuggler sputtered. "Unnatural things guard it. We were trying to hide when you found us."

"What do you mean unnatural?" Badger asked.

"Changelings. We left as soon as we saw them in the wreckage."

"Evil creatures," Riley said. "One of those things captured Seth in Lea. If it hadn't been for Wolf…"

"If it hadn't been for Wolf, many would be dead right now." Seth tossed the smugglers several feet across the wet grass. "Squires. Stay here and guard the prisoners. They must answer for what they've done."

"We mustn't be hasty, Lion," Jaguar told him. "Trying to board the Changeling ship before nightfall is foolhardy."

"Stay here and cower in the reeds then," Seth snapped. "I go to rescue the Right-Hand."

"This isn't like you, Seth," Riley said. "Jaguar has a good point. You must listen. We need a plan."

"Stay here with the Lords of Valdeon, Lion's squire. I have no use for cowards." The Lion's Roar grumbled deep in Seth's throat.

Then Ice Lion raced toward the south with his Lion Friends following close behind. They cast uneasy looks at the Lords of Valdeon as they passed. Jaguar hissed an order to his men in Valic, and the guardsmen followed the Western Beta rangers. Riley, still unsettled from the stinging rebuke, watched them go.

"So, what do we do?" Donny asked.

"Stay here and watch the prisoners." Riley took a deep breath to shake off the hurt. "I'm going to make sure my ranger doesn't get himself killed."

He followed the slight mud tracks the rangers had made. Doing so wasn't easy. A broken blade of grass here, a bent reed there. Riley cursed. Trying to find Seth was impossible. He'd end up lost in a bog hole quick enough. Then another pair of boots stomped up behind him. Basilio gripped the back of Riley's cloak and hurried him to the left.

"Rangers may be invisible if they choose, Lion's squire. Not so for us. This way."

Chapter Fifty-One

THE WRECKAGE JUTTED out in several pieces from the Great Bog. Its design was oddly elaborate and fanciful for evil's helpers. Carved circles and geometric shapes shined in gold sparkles from the wood. Even its massive rudder sported embellishments of gold. Riley guessed the vessel had been beautiful once, before the entire hull had cracked into pieces.

Streaks of ash flew up the side of the biggest piece of wreckage. The rangers were attacking without so much as a plan. Seth, he was sure, led them in their zealous push to rescue the Wolf.

Riley shifted his legs through the muck as fast as he could, but the slimy fingers of the Great Bog continued to slow his pace. Seth was acting like an impetuous lunatic. Aye. The man hadn't changed when he'd put the Lion Ring on his finger—no, to Riley, Seth had stayed the sane person Riley had known since childhood. This Creed of the Guardian was different, though. It'd done something to Seth's mind, and Riley wasn't convinced the change was a good thing.

"Hurry along, woolie farmer." Basilio yanked him upward by the collar. "How do you expect to keep up with the Lion when you have no endurance?"

Reluctantly, Riley had to admit Basilio was almost as sure-footed as a ranger. The Valdeonian's long legs found clumps of grass and stone to rest on as they ran. All the while, he kept a tight grip on Riley until they reached the large piece of wreckage. Basilio found small handholds Seth's followers must have used to scale the ship. Releasing his grip on Riley, Wolf's squire started his climb. Not willing to be left at the bottom like an old shoe, Riley grabbed a handhold and began to follow.

Basilio's legs flipped over the railing above Riley's head. Valdeonian height was an advantage in this case. Riley gritted his teeth and pushed his body to move faster. Another jibe from the Wolf's squire was the last thing he wanted to hear. Reaching the top, at last, he lifted his chin onto the railing and froze.

Taking the First Stance in a perfect half-moon line, the rangers had found the Right-Hand. Seth had been right. Wolf was in terrible shape. A white-haired Changeling clenched at Wolf's hair, yanking it viciously when Seth stepped forward. A few loose hairs were the least of Wolf's injuries. His swollen face bulged in deep purples and reds. Riley guessed the villains had beaten him in long sessions aboard ship. He didn't want to think about what else the unconscious ranger had endured.

"My emperor will be pleased," the Changeling snarled at them. "I have the Right-Hand and the little boy with his magic ring."

Strands of long white hair spilled over Wolf's face as the creature hissed at Seth. Its blue robes were torn and soiled by blood Riley hoped was its own. Long, black fingernails tightened, digging tiny streamers of blood into Wolf's scalp.

"Let the Right-Hand go, creature of evil! I warn you. My temper is fierce."

Riley had been around Seth long enough to know when the Lion's Spirit was pushing to break free. The Changeling, arrogant and greedy, refused to heed the signs. It drew a nasty-looking blade and held it to Wolf's throat with a cackle. Foul, idiotic creature.

The Ice Lion's roar of fury shook the wreckage. Riley, afraid of falling to the Great Bog below, swung over the side of the railing and onto the deck. He held on as wood and metal groaned beneath him.

"I will tear you apart with my bare hands!"

Then time stood still as a flurry of ash crashed into the Changeling. It attached to the creature, striking with unimaginable speed. The shock had infected their group. No one moved to interfere in the Ice Lion's battle with evil.

Seth suddenly stopped. The Changeling's battered body, dangling like a dead trout, swung lifelessly in his grip. Tossing it over his shoulder and into the Great Bog, he looked at the line of rangers as if he'd never before seen them. Riley imagined a pleased grin on Seth's face for a moment. Impossible. The Jalora's magic prevented Seth from showing any emotions. Then Riley remembered the Lion's tantrum as Wolf left North Marsh Outpost. What was happening to his ranger?

Basilio ran to Wolf's side. His face was a mix of fury and horror as he gently touched the wounds covering his ranger. The injuries must be bad for the

Valdeonian to show so much emotion. Suddenly, the flurry of ash was on the move again. It pulled Basilio away from Wolf and sent him flying across the deck. The Wolf's squire slammed against the wood beside Riley.

"Mine!" Seth growled low in warning as he stood between Wolf and the friends he no longer recognized.

"Nobody move," Jaguar ordered.

The Valdeonian showed good sense. Riley and the others heeded his warning and stood still as well. They waited breathlessly to see where the Lion would focus his temper next. The Right-Hand groaned behind him. Wolf was hurting and needed medical attention. In his rage, Seth wasn't thinking clearly. Aye. More likely, the Lion Spirit wasn't thinking at all.

"Seth, it's me. It's Riley. Listen to me. I know you're in there." He stood slowly and held his hands out before him. "Wolf is hurt. Won't you let me help?"

"You ignored my command, woolie farmer." The grating voice didn't belong to Seth. "Perhaps you are not a coward after all. Mayhap you are mad?"

"Leave the Marianna squire be." Seth tilted his head to one side with a visible grin as another voice commandeered his mouth. "He amuses me."

Then a firm hand forced Riley to his knees. The young Valdeonian ranger called Tulio stood beside him. He bowed respectfully to the Lion, though his eyes never left Seth's face. The hand on Riley's shoulder trembled a bit. Still, the young man didn't relax his grip.

"Greetings," he said. "You know me, yes?"

Seth sniffed in their direction and then nodded. "You are Tulio the Rabbit. Of course, I know you. Wasn't it I who chose you to serve me as a member of my Sacred Guard the day you were conceived?"

"You honor me and my house, Holiness." Tulio took his hand away from Riley's shoulder. "Will you allow the Marianna squire to treat Wolf's wounds?"

"Riley?" The cloud of rage lifted from Seth's eyes. "Wolf is hurt. Please help us."

Basilio rolled away from the railing and moved closer. Seth growled, pointing his weapon at the squire. Despite what Basilio had tried to do at the outpost, Wolf's squire was the Right-Hand's best hope. Riley owed Wolf his life. He couldn't watch the ranger die.

"This is Wolf's squire, Seth. He can help."

"Yes. You're a doctor." Seth let his arms drop. "Please help him."

Basilio ran past Seth and fell to his knees beside Wolf. "I'll need your assistance, Lion's squire."

Riley eased around the Lion, who had taken up a guard position between the injured Wolf and the rest of their group. Trusting in his friendship with Seth, Riley knelt beside the Right-Hand with his back to his own unpredictable ranger.

"Help me clean his wounds," Basilio said, taking out his canteen.

Using spare bits of cloth and the clean water they'd carried on them, Riley and Basilio exposed the damage done at the hands of the Changeling torturers. Wolf's body was as purple and raw as his face. Deep cuts with a vicious blade had carved circles at varying degrees of depth into his skin.

"Two broken ribs," Riley murmured, pulling more healing ointment from his pack.

"I see them. Careful with your words." Basilio took a cautious glance at Seth's back. "We mustn't upset them."

Aye. The Lions had seemed to settle a bit. Riley twisted around with the pretense of fiddling with his healing pack. Seth and whoever else remained inside him at the moment seemed content to stand watch. Nodding his head as the Lords of Valdeon came closer, he didn't make a move to attack them.

"May we stand the watch with you, Lion?" Jaguar asked, leading his guardsmen forward.

"Yes. The Wolf must be protected," Seth said. His words were losing some of their power.

Riley shivered as a sudden sense of wrongness came over him. Standing on the railing like a banshee, the white-haired Changeling cackled madly. It dove at the helpless Wolf with claws bared. Basilio threw himself over his ranger, protecting Wolf from the attack. Riley brought his fist up from the deck and smashed it into the foul creature's nose. Bone cracked. The Changeling staggered back with a cry of surprise.

"I won't die so easily," it said as bone and cartilage snapped back into position on its face. "You'll have to do better than fisticuffs."

It pointed a gray finger at Riley. An invisible hand shoved him on top of Basilio, and both squires rolled helplessly away from Wolf. Magic. It must be. How else could such a creature keep the powerful Right-Hand in its clutches?

Then Seth stood in the gap between the Changeling and its helpless prey. "I will give you no mercy for what you've done to my Right-Hand!"

He held his sword to the gray skies and growled in a promise of death meant for his enemies. Riley covered his ears. Light struck the letters of the Creed upon Ice Lion's blade, and the words blazed in dazzling fire within the steel. He brought the sword down, severing the Changeling's outstretched arm. The foul thing fell to its knees on the deck, burning where the blade had touched skin. Seth sliced along the Changeling's side and whisked the blade's tip to its throat.

"You claimed to know of my family, creature of evil. Tell me of the Hawk."

"I will tell you nothing, Jalora plaything."

Seth slapped the flat of his blade against its skin pressing hard until smoke rose from the creature as the Creed's magic burned. Seth pressed harder. Riley didn't like the wrathful burning in his friend's eyes. This vengeful torturer wasn't Seth. The Lion Spirit was hungry for blood again.

"Tell me, and I'll give you a quick death."

The Changeling gurgled a laugh. "Ask your brother. I hope the answer brings you heartbreak."

Then the creature swept sharp claws on its remaining hand toward Seth's legs. Scratching impotently against the Lion's boots, the Changeling fell short of its mark. Seth's shock lasted only a moment. Cold anger then flashed in his eyes. He swung his blade across the evil thing's neck, severing bone, flesh, and hair. Kicking the head with a growl, he sent it flying out over the bogs where it landed with a sickening splash.

Seth threw back his head and let free the Lion's Roar. The sound thundered against the stormy skies with an Erthe-shattering boom. His rage fell onto the deck, slamming them all to their backs against the wood. Riley couldn't move. The pressure was threatening to smash the air right out of him. Great gulls. Ice Lion was going to kill them all.

"Seth, stop." A voice crossed the deck, holding them all in its power. "Come to me."

The Lion's Roar halted abruptly, but its weight still trapped Riley's body. He struggled to breathe as the pressure remained steady. After their adventures together, was this how he met his end?

"You mustn't hurt your friends, Seth."

The voice was Wolf's. Pinned against the deck, Riley searched with his eyes for the wounded ranger. The Lords of Valdeon stood to his left. Their arms joined to form a line between Seth and Western Beta. Basilio was on his hands and knees behind them. His worried eyes fixed on Riley. Somehow the others were able to move behind the protective barrier of the Sacred Guard.

Basilio's eyes broke contact, lifting to a point beyond Riley's pinned body. Riley looked to his right. A weak hand lifted and reached out toward Seth. Somehow the Right-Hand had found the strength to move. Crying out in anguish, Seth hurried to him. He fell to his knees at Wolf's side and gently took his hand. Sobbing, he held it against his chest.

"Please calm down," Wolf said soothingly. "You don't want to bring harm to your friends."

"They've hurt you." Seth gulped in angry breaths like a sobbing child. "They must all be punished."

"You've already punished the Changelings. Look. See your friends? They want to help you, Seth." Wolf lowered their joined hands to his chest. "Please calm down. We must let them help us, yes?"

Seth nodded with a pained sigh. "I'm tired. Why am I so tired?"

He lay down beside Wolf, keeping hold of the calming grip. The blazing flecks of amber in Seth's eyes diminished. Sighing again, he closed his lids. The excruciating weight on Riley's body lifted. He sat up, gulping great breaths of stale marsh air. By the green, green fields. He'd never complain about the stench again.

Releasing a strained breath, Jaguar nodded to his men and stepped out of their line. Basilio immediately returned to Wolf's side. Western Beta hurried to Riley. Bear grabbed him up in his arms and rushed back behind the Lords of Valdeon.

"Are you well, Riley?" Dragonfly asked when Bear sat him down.

"You turned a pretty shade of blue for a moment there." Stallion handed him his canteen. "I thought you were a goner for sure."

"Aye. Me too." Riley gulped at the water.

Jaguar wiped the sweat from his brow. Leaning against the railing as if he'd run a long while against a strong wind, he shook his head at Riley. They'd been holding Seth's power back somehow and keeping it away from the others. Now he knew why the Lords of Valdeon held honor above other rangers in the Legion.

"Now you understand why the Lion and his Right-Hand should not be separated." Jaguar gripped the railing to steady his shaking body. "It is best if none of you mention what happened after the Lion lost control of his power. He won't remember, and the confusion might upset him. We must make sure he stays calm."

Riley promised along with the rest of the squad. He wasn't too sure at what point the ranger considered Seth to have lost control. Ice Lion had been wild since they found the Buellanders. Perhaps waiting to see what Seth recollected and what he didn't was best.

"We have company!" Badger shouted, pointing to the north.

Fox was beside him at the railing in a flash. "It's a Jackal ship. The Lion's power must have attracted their attention."

"Then it is for me to lead them away." Seth stood behind them. Gone was the fire and fury. He was calm now and in control. The human Ice Lion commanded his body again. Riley frowned. Aye. And he was ready to find trouble.

"Take Wolf to safety," Seth told the Lords of Valdeon. "We'll distract them until you can get your ship out of here."

"Wolf won't like it," Tulio said. "He wants you close."

"You're wasting time, rangers."

"Back to the *Wind Chaser*," Jaguar ordered, lifting Wolf over his shoulder. "We journey to Muellerton Outpost in Heidelbrecht, Lion."

"My squire and I will join you there as soon as we can." Seth looked at Wolf's unconscious body swaying over the ranger's shoulder. "Keep my Right-Hand safe. Wolf is of utmost importance."

Basilio pulled Riley to the side as the Lords of Valdeon carefully lowered Wolf down into the Great Bogs. "You understand now, don't you? The Lion won't know you when the power is on him. If not for Wolf, we'd all be dead now."

"Seth would never hurt me. We've been best friends since we were babies."

"Young fool! I'm trying to save your life." Basilio shook his head. "Your friend isn't the only being living in that body. The others—immortals—don't have the same sense of affection as we humans. They are easily offended and have a single-minded manner of thinking."

"Basilio! We must go." Fox called from below.

Wolf's squire let out an impatient breath and hurried to climb down the side of the wreckage to join his ranger. Riley kept eyes on him as he ran behind the Valdeonian lords. Basilio's warnings, he was shocked to find, were meant with the best intentions. It didn't matter who said what. The Right-Hand didn't want Riley as Lion's squire. Would Seth stand up for him? Or would he do as Wolf asked?

Riley supposed he'd learn his fate when they joined the Lords of Valdeon in Muellerton. Then where would these rangers take their Lion? Would they hide him in some out-of-the-way place? Or would they go against all reason and head back to Valdeon? Riley ran a hand through his wet hair. Both their fates seemed to be in the hands of the Wolf.

Chapter Fifty-Two

JORGE, BLENDING UNSEEN among the trees and rocks, watched the predator's camp with an unobstructed view. Tents, erected haphazardly, swayed under the sunset sky. Any stray breeze would knock them over. Campfires burned on open prairie without any thoughts to spreading flames and igniting the grass about their site. Foolish. The entire prairie land was a tinderbox.

"Are they having a joke? They've posted no guard. I don't see hardened soldiers." Duarto shook his head in disgust. "Someone has emptied a town of its drunks. Not one of these sots will see death coming for them."

"It would appear our friend has elected to hunt us with thieves and cutthroats rather than fighting men," Jorge said, chuckling. "I think I'm a bit offended."

Santos patted the satchel he carried over one shoulder. "Those drunken fools are about to be very sorry they left whatever hellhole they haunted."

"Everything's ready then?" Duarto asked.

"Yes. Now we need to get the louts to run toward the forest." Santos chewed at a piece of fuse he'd snipped from one of his combustible contraptions. "They don't seem overly keen to come looking for us."

Twilight painted orange, purple, and pink streamers in the skies over the grasslands. Darkness, their best ally, would join them soon, thank the Erthe Mother. Jorge scanned the endless horizon toward the south. Its emptiness haunted his soul. So many lives had already been lost in this war with invaders from across the seas.

"What's on your mind, My Lord Regent?" Santos asked.

"Phantoms." Jorge faced his hunters as fate's fingers pressed against his chest. "Many souls haunt these lands. It is time we joined them—in spirit anyway. Go into the grass just beyond their camp. Be ready to make enough noise to wake the dead. Santos and I will be waiting for them at the tree line."

"Here, take these." Santos tossed a bag to Duarto. "A few poppers to get the party started."

The hunters each took a handful of the small noisemakers and disappeared into the prairie grass. Jorge swelled with pride as not one blade moved at their passing. They were true warriors now. Soon the enemy would come to fear rumors of their skill. The Hunters of the West would be spoken of in awed whispers just as the Pacarro tribe had once been.

Excruciatingly long minutes crept by as Jorge waited for complete darkness. His hunters were skilled and courageous. Even so, they were outnumbered. One wrong move or stray noise and the game was up.

A lumbering figure exited one of the tents and sat down on a rock at the center campfire. It was Tabor. He lifted his leg and moved it closer to the fire. Jorge's fingers lingered over the handle of his hatchet. Here was a wounded beast he'd be happy to kill.

Then a series of yowls filled the prairie night. Booms shattered the calm as dirt and clumps of grass sprayed over the flimsy tents. Bumbling, drunk, and frightened out of their wits, Tabor's men ran from the safety of their illuminated camp. They charged wildly toward the forest, zigzagging to avoid the thundering booms following them.

Santos grabbed his sides as he laughed. Tears rolled down his cheeks in streams of merriment. Jorge, unable to escape the other man's mirth, joined him. His laughter stopped abruptly when the first man stepped into the field of traps. The ground exploded in a massive wave of fire and dirt. Tabor yelled for his men to stop running, but he was too late. They veered away from one explosion only to trigger another.

"I may have been a little enthusiastic with the amounts of explosives I put in the ground." Santos shrugged. "It's best to be thorough."

The resulting effect was like another sunrise, flashing with fire and lights. Then when the glowing death traps finally extinguished, darkness settled back over the grasslands. Tabor stood alone inside his empty camp. Those spared from the trap crawled back into the comfort of the firelight.

"Stay here," Jorge told Santos.

He stepped out of the trees and carefully made his way through the gruesome field. Bits and parts of men littered the ruined ground. He gave the mess no notice, focusing all his will on his prey. Tabor stood close to the fire, too frightened of the darkness to check on his men. He showed wisdom there. Jorge and the hunters were the darkness now for any of Valdeon's foe.

"Greed will be your end, Tabor."

"Who are you?" The villain twisted around frantically. "Step into the light!"

Jorge came closer on silent feet. Firelight touched his hands and tunic in an eerie glow. He waited. Hoots and yowls circled about the camp and then fell silent in a horrible kind of stillness. Random screams from the dark plains shattered the quiet. Duarto and his hunters weren't allowing any to escape.

Tabor, eyes wild with fear, caught sight of Jorge at last. Recollection slowly came to the brute's face. Harsh laughter forced its way out of his ugly mouth. Stragglers, encouraged by his show of false bravado, began to gather around Tabor as if taking comfort from his still frame. They would be disappointed. None of them would leave this prairie again.

"We've found the barbarian regent at last." Tabor forced a laugh. "Julian will have to pay us thrice his original offer for the medallion around your neck."

Julian, the bastard prince, still hoped to take the throne then. The evil whelp had murdered his father and brothers in pursuit of his prize. Naturally, he'd send such blaggards to slaughter innocent refugees.

"Do you imagine you can sell the Altar of Providence?"

Then the Erthe beneath their boots began to shake. Trunks groaned and snapped along the tree line. Tents, too flimsy to withstand such violence, collapsed in heaps of cloth. As if in response to the mere mention of its name, the Altar of Providence's power had come to the grasslands. Striking the bottom of Jorge's feet, its light raced up his leg. He screamed as the magic illuminated his entire body in its golden fire.

"Mercy!" Jorge begged while its holy fire consumed him.

The Altar's justice, however, would not be swayed. Flames burst out of Jorge's body in a solid beam and struck Tabor. The brute, thrown several feet into the air, smashed back onto the ground with a sickening crack. His screams of agony were cut short as skin, bones, and flesh melted into an oozing puddle of fat and blood.

"Jalora, preserve us!" Tabor's allies called to the very being they'd betrayed.

The flame, as if in response to their pleas, jumped off its forgotten kill and pounced upon new prey. Screams shattered the night anew. Jorge tried to turn away from the horrifying sight, but the Altar refused to relinquish his imprisoned body. The remaining traitors fell to the ground, desperately trying to crawl away from the Altar's terrible justice. All effort was useless. Their bodies joined Tabor's in gruesome puddles within the camp.

Suddenly, the deadly fire blinked out as the Altar withdrew from Tabor's body and returned into the land. By the Erthe Mother. How had he survived its immortal justice? Jorge had felt no compassion or emotion of any kind from the entity consuming him. The Altar's power simply *was* the land. He had no other words to describe the entity's presence as it possessed him.

Duarto caught him as Jorge fell to his knees. Body smoking from the power, he screamed in agony at the touch of the helping hands. His son opened Jorge's tunic. A cry of despair accompanied his troubled expression.

"It's bad, Father," he said. "I don't know what to do."

"The Regent Medallion is too powerful for my body. Such magic was meant only for the Lion."

"Then you mustn't use it again." Duarto took Jorge's hand and held it gently. "I can't lose you too."

Jorge closed his eyes against the pain, knowing their enemies would come again. Next time, Julian would send skilled fighting men, armed and ready. A handful of hunters wouldn't be enough. They needed help.

"We must find a way to hold the West until our true king comes," Jorge said. "Erthe Mother bless the Lion and hasten his return."

Chapter Fifty-Three

RED SAILS, BILLOWING at full capacity, blemished the gray skies over North Marsh. A white jackal ran within its blood hue. The fabric creature, aided by the vessel's powerful engines, charged toward them at a rapid pace. Seth slammed a fist against the railing of the ruined Changeling ship. Wolf and the others needed time to escape. He must find a way to distract the Jackal until Fox could get his vessel well out of range.

"By my father's beard!" Bear leaned over the side of the railing to stare down at the Great Bogs. "What's happening?"

A thick fog—sickly and wrong—was forming in huge banks over the water. Tints of green and black mixed with white as it grew. Ascending in a gigantic wall of thick vapor, the fog stretched out its arms to form hard lines in front of them. Massive appendages of green and black rolled along the bogs in the direction the Lords of Valdeon had taken Wolf.

I rule this land again, Lion. You won it for me. Have no fear. My servants will be well hidden as they escape with the Right-Hand.

"Seth, you promised not to take us into that realm of nightmares again," Cal cried.

"It isn't me. Time to go," Seth called over his shoulder. "We must return to the outpost."

"I think I've found us a ride, Ice Lion."

Dragonfly pointed toward the southwest where another piece of the Changeling ship had landed vertically in the Great Bogs. Hovering beside it was an air launch. Seth grinned and nodded appreciatively at Dragonfly's keen eye.

"Aye. It'll make the return trip faster, but how are we going to reach it?" Riley asked. "We've got a bog hole between us and the ship."

"Have faith, Lion's squire."

Seth wrapped his power about him and leaped into the air. Dancing on the droplets of drizzle, he raced toward the launch. The bogs zipped by beneath him, but Seth no longer feared their deadly traps. Nothing would harm him in the Jalora's realm. He landed gently on the vessel and untied its bindings. Turning the launch, he sailed with a cheery whistle on his lips to retrieve the Lion Friends.

"Will we learn to do such things?" Cal asked as Seth threw him the mooring line. "Run across the water, I mean."

"The Jalora has many things to teach you, ranger." Seth held the rudder steady as they boarded. "Come. Let's collect the squires and our prisoners. I'm sure the Buellanders know a quick route to the outpost."

The launch grew still as his passengers settled in for the long journey home. Seth shared their yearning for hot food and a warm bed out of the weather. He was eager to tell Greg of their adventures at Sea Point.

Not for the first time, he wished his new friend had been along to share in the excitement.

Having the Buellander smugglers as their guides was an eye-opening revelation. They knew a series of water channels that made traveling from the north to the south a half-day's journey rather than the trudging march known to the Legion. Seth had made clear he would leave them in the middle of the bogs if they tried to lie or mislead their route. The Buellanders, accepting their fate, were willing enough to help the Legion map the water channels for future use.

A sudden sense of uncertainty and hurt touched at his mind. Probing his friends was something Seth tried to avoid out of respect for their privacy. This sensation he couldn't ignore. Riley, who settled toward the bow as far away from Seth as he could get on the small vessel. Seth's best friend sat with arms folded and chin down in an undisguised frown. He was unhappy about something.

"Badger?" Seth motioned to his cousin. "Would you take the rudder?"

"Of course!" Henry hurried to grip the handle before a concerned Bear could grab it.

Seth managed to keep his feet as the launch lurched forward at a much faster pace. Bear, grabbing at the bench with a tighter grip, grumbled his opinion of Henry's overexuberant piloting. Seth ignored them and continued to tiptoe between the boots settled within the hull. He made his way to the front and sat down in the empty seat beside Riley. Shoving Riley with his shoulder, Seth stared at the side of his friend's head until Riley couldn't ignore him anymore.

"What is it?" Seth asked. "Out with it, Riley Logan, or I'll dunk you in the bog."

"You and who else?" Riley huffed. "I'm sure Wolf would thank you for it. He doesn't approve of my being your squire."

Seth rubbed a hand across his chin. Wolf hadn't spoken a word to Riley. How could he possibly object? Basilio, Wolf's squire, must have scolded Riley one too many times. Seth would have to sort it out when they reached Muellerton. He needed his allies to be of one mind in the days to come.

"I'll speak with Wolf."

"Aye. Is that so? It seems to me that you and everyone else does what Wolf says, Seth." Riley slapped his hands on his thighs. "The Right-Hand has it in his head he owes Da a debt. He means to take me back to the farm. I won't go."

"An easy thing to solve. Sorry. I didn't mean to eavesdrop, but it's a small ship, and your voice carries," Cal interrupted with a snort. "You just saved Wolf's life, didn't you? Well, now he owes you a life debt. He can't take you home after that, can he? Besides. Show me another squire who's broken a Changeling's nose."

"You did?" Gudal laughed and slapped Riley on the shoulder, sending his friend falling against Seth. "First Harold the Mantis's squire and now a creature out of hell. Riley is the toughest squire in Western Beta!"

Seth wasn't sure what went on in Riley's world, but it sounded as if he'd had his own adventures. One thing was certain. No one would be sending Riley home. Seth needed him now more than ever.

"Look up ahead," Badger called. "It's the blind where we spent the night."

"No wonder the mercenaries had such an easy time getting to Mount Crumble." Cal gave the closest smuggler a good whack. "You'd do anything for money, wouldn't you? They could have made it all the way to Heidelbrecht and Framburg."

Cal lifted a hand to strike the nearest smuggler again, but he stopped suddenly with a yowl of joy. The walls of the outpost rose up out of the marsh to greet them. Seth cheered with the rest of the squad, eager to be within the protective stone arms.

Badger eased the launch down on the dock a short time later. They tied it off and disembarked. Relief. Joy. They circled about the squad as the massive gates opened. Yet only moments later, their happy feelings quickly dissolved when Phoenix and White Tiger marched out to greet them.

Another ranger walked beside the Phoenix. Seth recognized well those sharp green eyes and the hatred swimming in them. Peter Von Wolkhurst, crown prince of Tslavia, had come among them. Seth doubted his visit was out of common curiosity. He hoped it wasn't to exercise his chance for violence against the hated child of Tslavia and Valdeon—namely Seth.

"Gargoyle." Henry groaned and let his shoulders slump.

"Easy, Badger."

The last time Seth had encountered Peter the Gargoyle, he was lying in a cot in the infirmary after Seth had forced sleep on him. This was yet another reason for the ranger to press his advantage, and

Phoenix couldn't do much about it. Gargoyle, as a deacon level three in the Legion, outranked Phoenix.

Seth snapped a salute as Phoenix came before him. "Ice Lion and squad reporting, sir."

Curious blue eyes took Seth in. Phoenix was looking for signs of the relic they'd been so keen to find. Straining to keep his excitement in check, Seth allowed slight hues of success and amazement to appear in the emotions circling about his body. Phoenix, reading them clearly, let a grin escape his carefully controlled mask of discipline.

"You've come home to us at last." Phoenix returned the salute with a quick scan of Seth's team. "All of you seem well, including your prisoners."

"Yes, sir. We have much to report."

"Then you had better do so, Ice Lion," Gargoyle snapped in a heavy Tslavic accent, his words laced with dislike.

Seth clutched at the hilt of his sword. Sensing his uneasiness, the new Lion Friends formed a protective line between Seth and the Gargoyle. Rangers and squires alike pulled their swords. They would kill for him, he knew, no matter if his attacker happened to be a ranger.

"You dare show your sword to me, Henry Von Wolkhurst!" Gargoyle barked.

"I serve the Lion," Badger told him, lifting his left sleeve to reveal the mark of a Lion Friend.

Gargoyle's face blanched to a sickly white as he stared at the marks. "What have you done, blood of my blood?"

Phoenix, finally able to snatch his gaze away from the Lion Friends, hurried to stand in the gap. He turned his back on Gargoyle and regarded Seth with pleading eyes. The young acolytes he'd sent out into the bogs had returned as sacred protectors. Seth and Phoenix had both seen the unflinching loyalty those marks demanded from their bearers.

"Come to my office, Ice Lion," Phoenix ordered, clearing his throat. "The others of you go to your rest and a meal. You too, Logan." He motioned for Seth to step forward. "Welcome, home, rangers."

"Phoenix!" Dragonfly put a hand out to block Seth's path. "I must speak with you."

"Later, Dragonfly." Phoenix reached past him and took Seth's arm.

"It's important."

"I'm sure the Lion can take care of himself," Gargoyle said with a sneer. "He has in the past, though I disagree with his methods."

Seth gripped Dragonfly's shoulder as his friend took a step forward. "It's fine. Go and refresh yourselves. You've all earned it and more."

Mumbles of thanks and reluctance circled the group as his squad threw anxious looks at the deacons. Bear and Gudal each put a hand on Riley's shoulder, prodding him toward the barracks. Dragonfly and Cal took hold of the prisoners and headed toward the brig.

"Take the Buellander traitors to my ship. We will see what else they're willing to share once we reach the Citadel," Gargoyle ordered. "Badger. You and your squire will await me at HQ."

"Yes, Deacon."

Dread. Anxiety. Determination. The emotions surrounded Seth's young cousin. Clearly, this was not the first time he'd been bullied by Peter the Gargoyle. Seth rested a reassuring hand on his cousin's shoulder as they followed the deacons. Henry managed a weak smile and stared back down at his feet.

"Gargoyle will come to see you differently, Henry. You are a full ranger and my Lion Friend now. I will tolerate no disrespect for my loyal few."

Henry gave him a proud smile. "It will be as my Lord Lion says."

Chapter Fifty-Four

WARMTH TOUCHED SETH'S face as he entered HQ, a welcome sensation after so many days in damp and chill. Aromas of hot tea and bread sent his stomach growling. North Marsh Outpost seemed a beloved oasis now rather than the prison it had once been.

Seth waited for Phoenix and Gargoyle to be seated, while White Tiger took up a standing position against the wall to their right. Seth brought the ice walls about him as he endured their heavy stares.

"Report, Ice Lion." Gargoyle leaned back with a poorly suppressed sneer.

Seth pulled out his map of the Northwest. He spread it across the desk and tapped a finger on the trail running past Mount Crumble. Gargoyle's eyes reluctantly followed his fingertip.

"We marched along here and found the Jackal's path through the bogs to the north. My squad discovered a lookout platform located at the edge of an inlet. It is in good condition and is large enough to hold at least eight men. I believe the mercenary forces positioned the platform at the halfway point between Mount Crumble and the northernmost coast. We found no evidence of any current enemy activity on this side of the Great Bogs."

White Tiger, ever the sensible one, grabbed pen and ink from Phoenix's side table. He had Seth go over his route to the platform and carefully documented the exact location. Producing another piece of parchment, he had Seth describe the surroundings with his thoughts on securing the platform.

"We were guided along an old path to the north-west coast." Seth hesitated, looking at the two deacons. "The Elk and the Cougar ordered me to lead my men west along the coast."

"Elk and Cougar?" Gargoyle grumbled, leaning forward with a raised eyebrow. "They were reported missing in action the same time Edmund the Leo disappeared." The deacon fixed his intense eyes on Seth. "What did they have to say for themselves?"

"They made a great sacrifice for my sake. Elk and Cougar's mission was to guide me to Sea Point Outpost. You mustn't condemn them for doing their duty."

"Sea Point?" White Tiger frowned.

"Quiet, Tiger," Phoenix told him with a raised hand. "Continue, Ice Lion."

"I found the stone path to the outpost's ruins. The two rangers greeted us when we got inside. A great battle had taken place several months before we had entered its walls. The abandoned dead were everywhere."

Seth took a deep breath and reached inside his tunic. He held the Elk and Cougar rings before Gargoyle. The black crystals were dull against the silver as if they, like their bearers, had extinguished the last flickers of life. White Tiger cried out in anguish. He'd counted the two rangers as friends, Seth realized.

All these years and he hadn't known whether to grieve for them.

"They'd given their very souls protecting something of great worth," Seth told White Tiger. "Elk and Cougar along with the defenders have been honored by the Jalora."

Phoenix tapped an excited finger on the ink image of Sea Point. "You said they protected something of great worth?"

Seth pulled his blade and rested the tip on the desk. Its fiery letters shimmered under the lantern's glow. Phoenix reached out his hand and then pulled it back with a start. Power sparked from the blade. Strange. It didn't seem pleased to be touched by anyone other than Seth.

"We were right, Greg." Seth tilted the blade again, catching more of the glow. "I wish you could have been with me when we found it."

Read the words carved into the blade, Lion. Gargoyle must carry this news back with him.

"Held within the Lion's hand, this blade shall never fall," he recited for them. "All who hear his mighty roar will answer the Master's call."

"The Creed of the Guardian," White Tiger said, awe swirling about his body.

Glass crashed behind him. Roland stood in the doorway. A tray full of cups and hot tea lay smashed at his feet. Crossing the distance as if pulled by an unseen force, the silent squire joined them beside the desk. These words certainly had a disturbing effect upon any who saw them.

Exhaustion suddenly came with full force in Seth's body. He sheathed the sword again, drawing their attention back to his words. Reluctant to discuss the plans of Wolf and the other Lords of Valdeon, he kept his report short.

"We continued to head south and found those smugglers from the Buells," Seth told them. "They and others like them have been helping the Jackal forces. The smugglers showed us a water channel spanning from north to south. Mapping it would be of great value to the Legion." Turning his gaze on Gargoyle, he said, "Badger and the other members of my team have proven their courage on this mission, sir. If you agree, we would like to help map the channel."

"Indeed?" Gargoyle leaned back in his chair again. "You are free with your praise and your loyalty, ranger. Such devotion is rare between a Valdeonian and a Tslavian."

"He is my comrade," Seth said in Tslavic. "He is also my cousin."

Gargoyle bolted from his chair and circled the desk. "How dare you, Valdeonian dog!"

"My mother didn't share your narrow-minded hatred," Seth told him, the Lion's Roar grumbling deep in his throat. "Tell me. How are you sleeping lately?"

The Lion Spirit's amusement filled Seth's heart as Gargoyle, and the rest of the rangers stepped back a pace. Then an invasive prick of power touched his mind. Gargoyle pressed his probe harder. Seth knocked it aside with an irritated grunt. Returning the probe, he expected to meet a wall of obstinate will. Crying out under the strain of Seth's power, Gargoyle pushed his touch away at last.

"Why have you come, Peter Von Wolkhurst?" Seth asked. "Curiosity can't be your only reason."

"Your First Marked, Jason the Coyote, came to the Obsidian Citadel. He told Dragon of the Jackal fortress in the North." Gargoyle let an unfriendly smile cross his face. "He was also quick to accuse Esteban D'Antoiné of treason. The Hawk Prince was furious and had him thrown in a cell."

"Hawk was in Lea? That isn't possible. Wolf saw him here in North Marsh."

"Xavier the Wolf? I've heard interesting things about him from Esteban the Hawk. He claims Wolf has gone rogue, calling himself the Right-Hand." Gargoyle shook his head with a booming laugh. "You have a problem, Lion. Dissent in the ranks leads to trouble."

"Make no mistake, ranger. Xavier the Wolf is my Right-Hand."

"Perhaps you should explain things to Hawk over tea and biscuits. I'm certain he'll take the rejection well." Gargoyle stepped away from Seth. "The antics of the Valdeonian court are none of my affair. I have more important concerns. The Legion has received reports of Jackal troops in the Northeast and the foothills of the Bloodtooth Mountains. War is upon us. Phoenix, you and your battalion report to North Point within the week."

He produced a small parchment from his tunic and handed it to Phoenix. They exchanged salutes. Gargoyle, without another word, headed out the door and into the courtyard where Badger and his squire waited. Seth felt a wave of pity for Henry.

"He certainly doesn't care for you, Ice Lion." White Tiger shook his head. "Why did you purposely make him angry?"

"The Legion needs Gargoyle's sword in the days to come. I didn't want him yelling at Badger. Those who harm or curse my Lion Friends will be punished. Better if he directs his anger at other things."

"Gargoyle is the crown prince of Tslavia and Badger's older cousin," White Tiger told him. "It is best to stay out of family business, especially if you are Valdeonian."

Seth began to laugh. "It is my business, Tiger. You see, Gargoyle is my cousin Peter, too. He has already discovered he cannot bully me as he does Henry."

"Gargoyle is the least of our worries," Phoenix said. "Have a hot meal and then go to your rest, Ice Lion. White Tiger will have assignments in the morning. Roland, where are you going? We have work to do, and you have a mess to clean up."

The silent squire continued to stare at Seth. He seemed to struggle with the decision of staying in the office or following them out into the courtyard. Seth imagined he saw Roland's lips move as if to speak. Then Phoenix's squire clamped his mouth shut and turned back to the fallen tray of dishes.

White Tiger and Seth walked down the stairs and into the courtyard. The ordinarily gruff and level-headed ranger seemed to be struggling with whirling emotions as they walked. He wore a sad frown filled with regret.

"I have something I would ask you, Ice Lion. What happened to Leo at Sea Point? There is more to the story."

Seth nodded and looked at his father's friend. "Leo asked you to go with him, and you said no."

"I regret it. Perhaps if I'd been there, another ranger might have strengthened the defenses."

"You would be dead too, Tiger. The enemy surrounded the outpost. Leo was forced to cut off his finger to escape with the Lion Ring. Elk and Cougar allowed the Jalora to attach their very souls to the Creed of the Guardian. So many died for my sake."

He'd never forget the sight of their bleached bones or the dark dried blood on the stone. Somehow, he must live up to their sacrifice.

"I may not have been there to fight beside the Leo, but I will not fail his son. Go, get yourself some supper. You'll need your strength over the next few days."

War. Seth had known it was a possibility when he signed up as a cadet in the UR Army. He'd never expected to go to war as part of the Jalora Legion. They were the first to the front lines, acting as a human shield against danger.

His thoughts turned to Wolf. He couldn't join the Right-Hand now, but at least Wolf would be safe to heal in peace. Seth gripped at the handle of his sword. He was the Lion Protector. No longer could he hide behind walls. Enemies of Andara were trying to destroy his world. He must stand against them, but would his new power be enough? Time alone would tell.

Chapter Fifty-Five

JULIAN PEERED INTO the sickly fog. Careful to cover his mouth and nose against the potentially dangerous vapors, he pressed at the thin linen fluttering with his every breath. The Jalora's magic was at play again. He'd seen this particular strategy before over the coast of Marianna as the Jalora had hidden its Lion. Julian was undecided about the implications the fog's presence held now.

On the one hand, he hated his half-brother with burning contempt. On the other, he'd hoped the Jalora had sent its champion to rescue Xavier the Wolf. Wolf's survival was vital to Julian's plans.

A bell rang hollow in the thick air of North Marsh. Sights and sounds faded like phantoms within the bowels of the sickly mists. Red sails, reduced to pale pink, rustled as they were deflated into empty husks. The ship shuddered while it came to a full stop, floating in the eerie gray. Julian's skin began to crawl when the fingers of green and black crept slowly toward them.

Lord Gorman stood at the very tip of the bow, hands clasped behind him. His metal skull turned to face the Jackal officer racing to a respectful stop. Julian drew closer while the barbarian gave his general a respectful salute.

"Portside, My Lord."

Julian leaned over the railing to view what his eyes had missed. A piece of the Changeling ship stood out from the Great Bogs. Its engines and rudder jutted toward the heavens like a dead shark thrown ashore by savage waves.

Then a metal hand grabbed him by the back of the collar, lifting Julian off his feet. Gorman slammed Julian's body through the wooden cover of the cargo hold. Splintering wood rained down on him as he fell deeper into the ship's bowels. Lord Gorman's imposing frame jumped in after him. Gorman's massive shadow extended, kicking Julian's torso down into the floor.

Broken bones and torn flesh struggled to mend under a mesh of new scales. Another strike ripped them apart again as Gorman exercised his anger on Julian's body. A hard fist slammed against his temple and cast Julian into momentary darkness.

Cold. Hard. Smooth. Julian stretched his arms out on the metal floor. Forcing his eyes open, he directed a dazed glare along the lines of his new cage until they reached the open door. Hands covered in cold metal grabbed him. Gorman, his anger not yet spent, punched Julian. The skin on his cheek ripped and sent hot blood down onto his tunic. Even as the gray scales clattered together over Julian's cheek, Gorman struck the other side.

"Do you think me a fool?" Lord Gorman lifted Julian by his collar and threw him against the bars of his cell. "I know you were behind Master Interrogator's treachery."

Julian's sire, sporting the Hawk disguise, leaned against the bars, staring in at his son. Julian shrank from those emotionless eyes with an impotent cry of betrayal. No caring or concern was evident in them. He saw only contempt.

"Now you understand. Daddy won't intervene on your behalf. He doesn't dare," Gorman said. "Changelings value self-preservation above all else. Know your enemies better than your own backyard."

Hawk tipped his head to Gorman. "You count me as a worthy enemy. I'm flattered."

"Don't be. One more misstep and you'll end up in a cage with your useless spawn." Gorman slammed the cell door shut and turned away from them to storm above decks.

"Joined cells. Gorman is sentimental after all. How can we make that happen, Daddy?" Julian, hiding his temporary weakness, laughed defiantly. "You both have been playing me from the start. I'd love to return the favor, Father Mine."

"You think you can stand against me, whelp?" His sire cackled. "I've no time to show you just how wrong you are."

Julian let the hate burn deep inside his heart as he watched the creature follow Gorman above decks. They believed Julian thwarted and cornered. How wrong they were. Let them plot and scheme. He would show Gorman and Esteban just how dangerous he could be. A deadly game was already in play. He simply needed a way to escape and return to Valdeon. Then human blood would flow deeper than the mighty Constantina River.

The End

People, Places, Things

People

Grey Cliff Isles

Cutter - Mercenary leader hired to kill Seth

D'Antoiné, Seth - Bearer of the Lion Ring

De Vincente, Dante - Leo's Squire

Emma - The McCloud's Housekeeper

Gunn, Sergeant - Head of the Marianna Militia

Leo - Valdeonian Warrior and Seth's Mentor (see D'Antoiné, Edmund)

Logan, Andrew - Woolie Farmer, Riley's Brother

Logan, George - Woolie Farmer, Riley's Brother

Logan, Laura - Farmer's Wife

Logan, Michael - Woolie Farmer, Riley's Brother

Logan, Patrick - Woolie Farmer, Riley's Brother

Logan, Riley - Seth's Best Friend and Squire

Logan, Stephen - Woolie Farmer, Riley's Brother

Logan, Thomas - Woolie Farmer

Logan, Tom - Woolie Farmer, Riley's Brother

McBride, Stan - Haven Bay Youth

McCloud, Anne - Seth's Mother

McCloud, Fergus - Headmaster and Seth's Uncle

McDermott, Charlie - Haven Bay Youth

McFadden, Beatrice - Haven Bay Youth, Doctor's Daughter

McFadden, Doctor - The Isle of Marianna's Only Doctor

McKenzie, Alice - Haven Bay Youth

McKenzie, Danny - Woolie Farmer

McKenzie, Mike - Woolie Farmer

McKinney, Teb - Barkeep at Paddy's

McTavish, Angus - Owner of Haven Bay's Mercantile

McTavish, Constable - Haven Bay's Police Chief

Newcastle, Elder - Haven Bay's Elder

Newcastle, Jamie - Haven Bay Youth and Elder's Son

Paddy - Owner and Innkeeper of Paddy's Inn

Sandor, Pavel - Andara's Deadliest Assassin

Valdeon

Basilio - Squire to the Wolf

Benito - Chancellor of Valdeon

Bram - Framburg Healer and friend of Jorge

Cristiano, Felix - Usurper of San Angelica

Cristiano, Rafael the Fox - Member of the Sacred Guard, A Lord of Valdeon

Cristobal, Tulio the Rabbit - Member of the Sacred Guard, A Lord of Valdeon

D'Antoiné, Edmund the Leo - King and a Lord of Valdeon

D'Antoiné, Esteban the Hawk - Former Member of the Sacred Guard, A Lord of Valdeon

D'Antoiné, Julian - Prince of Valdeon

De Costa, Marcellus - Minion of Julian D'Antoiné

De Vincente, Danel - Son of Xavier

De Vincente, Dulcina - Wife of Xavier

De Vincente, Gaspar - Son of Xavier

De Vincente, Xavier the Wolf - Leader of the Sacred Guard, A Lord of Valdeon

De Quintaro, Arturo - Brother of Ernesto

De Quintaro, Ernesto the Raven - Member of the Sacred Guard, A Lord of Valdeon

De Quintaro, Fausto - Steward of Varianne, Former Lord of Valdeon

Hernandez, Inez - Jorge's daughter

Jalora - Embodiment of Good Upon the Erthe

Mendoza, Alberto - Steward of San Marimosa and Father to the Jaguar

Mendoza, Berto the Jaguar - Member of the Sacred Guard, A Lord of Valdeon

Mendoza, Stephano - Captain of the San Marimosa Guard, Cousin of Berto the Jaguar

Mendoza, Yuli the Otter - Member of the Sacred Guard, A Lord of Valdeon

Neto - Jorge Pacarro's lead farm hand

No Name, Zoya - Sister of Julian D'Antoiné

Orryo - Minion of Julian D'Antoiné

Pacarro, Donna - Jorge's wife

Pacarro, Duarto - Jorge's son

Pacarro, Jorge - Former Squire to Cesar Santiago and leader of the western refugees

Santiago, Cesar - Steward of San Lucida, Former Lord of Valdeon

Santiago, Lucio the Ferret - Member of the Sacred Guard, A Lord of Valdeon

Santos - Follower of Jorge Pacarro. Explosives expert.

Sarcion - Embodiment of Evil Upon the Erthe

Isle of Carlotta

Rodrigo - Mayor of Carlotta

Tymon - Aunt Charlotte's companion and protector

Von Bohdan, Charlotte - Seth's aunt and the Iron Queen of Carlotta

The Jalora Legion and Squire's Corps

Arthur - Squire to White Tiger

Baldemar, Gregory the Phoenix - Partisan of the Lion and Wolf's trusted ally

Bear, Anders (Apprentice) - Member of Western Beta

Boyd - The Coyote's squire

Cougar - Friend to Edmund the Leo and Seth's guide

Donny - The Dragonfly's squire

Dragon, Francis (Cardinal) - Leader of the Jalora Legion

Dragonfly, Ronald (Acolyte) - Ranger and friend to Seth

Elder, Jason the Coyote - Ranger and Seth's "First Marked" Lion Friend

Elk - Friend to Edmund the Leo and Seth's guide

Falcon, Tad Lambert (Bishop) - Member of the Bishops Council

Firefly - Captain of the *Protector*. Enemy of Edmund the Leo.

Gecko (Acolyte 2) - Member of Western Beta

Gudal - Squire to the Bear

Lucas - Squire to the Stallion

Manitou, Burgess (Bishop) - Member of the Bishops Council

Mantis, Charles (Acolyte 2) - Member of Western Beta

Phants - A derogatory term for Rangers

Roland - The Phoenix' squire

Shelby - Squire to the Badger

Stallion, Cal (Apprentice) - Member of Western Beta.

Swan, Percival (Bishop) - Member of the Bishops Council

Thunderbird - First Mate on the *Protector*

Von Wolkhurst, Henry the Badger (Apprentice) - Member of Western Beta. Seth's cousin.

Von Wolkhurst, Peter the Gargoyle - Ranger ang Crown Prince of Tslavia

White Tiger - Ranger and Phoenix's second-in-command

Lea and the United Realms

Dawson, Tory - Member of Cadet Beta Three. From Lea. Lion Friend

Claybank, Amery (Twin) - Member of Cadet Beta Three. From the Outpost Territories. Lion Friend

Claybank, Aubrey (Twin) - Member of Cadet Beta Three. From the Outpost Territories. Lion Friend

Dancer, Sergeant - Master Sergeant over Cadet Beta Three. Lion Friend

Duncan, Sergeant - Lion Friend

Finley, Lieutenant - Commandant Sharp's aid

Lambert, Lady Philippa - Sister-in-law of Bishop Tad (Falcon) Lambert, Lord of Ghent

Lambert, Fanny - Daughter to Lady Phillipa

Ralston, Sergeant - Friend to Seth

Sharp, Commandant - Leader of the United Realm Army

Akutar

Changeling - Lord Gorman's Spy

The Dirge - Sarcion's Undead Assassins

Gorman - A Lord of Akutar, General of the Jackal Army

Uther - Emperor of Akutar

Whisper - Emissary of the Akutarian Emperor

The Realm of Dreams and Mist

D'Antoiné, Ignacio - Seth's ancestor and teacher

D'Antoiné, Hugo - Seth's ancestor and teacher

Places

The United Realms of Andara

Amity - Island in the Grey Cliff isles

Bloodtooth Mountains - Massive mountain range running from the Northwest coast of Andara down to Framburg. Acts as a natural barrier around North Marsh

Border Mountains (Also known as the Forbidden Mountains) - Natural border between Valdeon and Tslavia. Origin of Heart Crystals and location of the Temple Cave

Commonwealth - The Small Circular Space of Land Surrounding Lea, The UR Capitol

Corpse Point - Ancient ruin serving as a landmark in North Marsh

Eastland Isle - Located Off the West Coast of Andara

Estabelle - Located in Valdeon, Home of the Hawk

Fort L'Azure - Located in Valdeon, Home of the Rabbit

Fort La Val - Located in Valdeon, Home of the Otter

Ghent - Located in the Central Mainland Region

Grey Cliff Isles - Located Two Days from Andara's Mainland

Haven Bay - Town located on Marianna

Heidelbrecht - Located in northcentral Andara. Ancient ally of Valdeon

Horner - Island in the Grey Cliff Isles

Larkspur - Island in the Grey Cliff Isles

Lea - Located in the Center of the Commonwealth, Capitol of the UR

Marianna - Smallest Island in the Grey Cliff Isles

Mount Crumble - Dangerous ruins located in the center of North Marsh

Muellerton, Heidelbrecht - Outpost and safe haven for the Lords of Valdeon

North Marsh - Located in the Northwestern corner of Andara. Dangerous lands of bogs and wilderness

North Marsh Outpost - Jalora Legion outpost located in the southeast corner of North Marsh

Obsidian Citadel - Located in Lea, Headquarters of the Jalora Legion

Palace of Kings - Located in San Leonora, Home of the Lion

Port City - Located on Eastland Isle, Major Airship Port

San Angelica - Located in Valdeon, Home of the Fox

San Leonora - Located in Valdeon, Home of the Lion

San Lucida - Located in Valdeon, Home of the Ferret

San Marimosa - Located in Valdeon, Home of the Jaguar

San Rudalfo - Located in Valdeon, Home of the Wolf

Sea Point Outpost - Ruins located on the Northwest Coastline of North Marsh

Southbay - Located on Valdeon's eastern border. A contentious neighbor.

Stone Fang Fortress - Jackal stronghold built in the face of the Bloodtooth Mountains

Temple Cave - Located in the Mountains on the Border of Valdeon and Tslavia, Place of Power

Tslavia - Located in the Central Mainland Region, Ancient Enemy of Valdeon

Valdeon - Located in the Southern Mainland Region, Realm of the Lion

Varianne - Located in Valdeon, Home of the Raven

Other Island Nations

Azure Isles - Located South of Andara's Mainland, Ruled by Raiders

Isle of Carlotta - Located Off the Coast of Valdeon

Cottage on the Cliff - Aunt Charlotte's mansion on Carlotta

Foreign Nations

Akutar - Located Far to the East of Andara's Mainland, Home of the Jackal

The Pearl Isles - Located Far to the West of Marianna, Home of the Luminawni

The Realm of Dreams and Mist

Created by the Jalora to model Otherworld, the Realm of Dreams and Mist is a place where time and reality are suspended. This is where the Jalora lives while it waits for the next Jalora Master.

Things

Altar of Providence - Stronghold of the Jalora on Andara. Consists of three parts: The Crown of Sorrows, The Lion's Seat and the Orb of Valdeon

Book of Ancients - Contains the history of Andara. Once opened by the Lion, its magic begins the transformation of the ring bearer into the Jalora Master

Creed of the Guardian - A mystical relic capable of dramatically increasing the Lion's power

Crown of Sorrows - Crown of the King of Valdeon

First Marked - See Lion Friend. This individual is the first person marked by a new Lion. They are honored and respected with almost as much reverence as the Lords of Valdeon

Heart's Blood Talisman - A thumb length silver cylinder worn on a chain. Contains liquid Heart Crystal from the Temple Cave. Obtained by murder several centuries ago

Horde's Cry - Vocal weapon utilized by the Jalora Rangers to instill fear into their enemies. It makes one ranger sound like many

Lion Child Vessel - Captured at the very moment a bearer loses his innocence, this ethereal child is the vessel the Jalora uses to inhabit the Master's body as it walks among the world of men

Lion Friend - An individual who has either saved the Lion's life or has done a great service for him. They are marked by the Lion's power with three claw lines down the left forearm. It is considered treason to harm or threaten a Lion Friend

Lion Ring - Symbol of the Contract Between the D'Antoiné Family and the Jalora

Lion's Roar - Mighty vocal weapon granted only to the bearer of the Lion Ring. Has the power to bring down mountains and devastate armies

Lion's Seat - Golden Throne of Valdeon

Lords of Valdeon - Bearers of the nine original Heart of the Warrior Rings gifted to Valdeon by the Jalora. Lion (Lord of San Leonora and King of Valdeon), Hawk (Lord of Estabelle), Wolf (Lord of San Rudalfo), Jaguar (Lord of San Marimosa), Fox (Lord of San Angelica), Raven (Lord of Varianne), Ferret (Lord of San Lucida), Otter (Lord of Fort La Val) and Rabbit (Lord of Fort L'Azure)

Orb of Valdeon - Conduit of the Jalora's Power to Andara's Ranger

Partisan to the Jalora Master - Traditional role of honor held by the bearer of the Phoenix Ring. The partisan holds a place of power in the Master's court and is considered a valued councilor to the throne

Regent Medallion - Made from the purest gold, the medallion contains the symbol of the Altar of Providence. Its magic grants the bearer power and ruling authority over Valdeon should there be no Lion upon the throne

Right-Hand - This special ranger is second only to the Jalora Master. He is bound by his very soul to protect the Lion and calm his temper when the power threatens to escape

Sacred Guard - In the time of a Jalora Master, the Lords of Valdeon (Sacred Guard) are transformed into a special guard. Their only purpose is to protect the master. They are bound to him forever

Sign of the Coming - Prophecy which provide omens and signs a Jalora Master has been born

Voice of the Right-Hand - This vocal weapon is a rare and destructive gift used in service to the Jalora Master.

About the Author

C. R. Richards is the award-winning author of *The Mutant Casebook Series.* Her literary career began as a part-time columnist for a small entertainment newspaper. She wore several hats: food critic, entertainment reviewer and cranky editor. A lover of horror and dark fantasy stories, she enjoys telling tales of intrigue and adventure. Her most recent literary projects include the epic dark fantasy series, *Heart of The Warrior* and the novel length dark fantasy thriller, *Pariah.* She is an affiliate member of the Horror Writers Association.

For more information on the author's books and upcoming events, please visit her website: www.crrichards.com

Other Books by C.R. Richards

THE LORDS OF VALDEON
(Heart of the Warrior Series - Book One)

THE OBSIDIAN GATES
(Heart of the Warrior Series - Book Two)

CREED OF THE GUARDIAN
(Heart of the Warrior Series - Book Three)

PARIAH

LOST MAN'S PARISH
(Short Fiction)

PHANTOM HARVEST
(The Mutant Casebook Series)

Did you enjoy the book?
Please leave a review and let me know.
I'd love to hear from you!

www.ingramcontent.com/pod-product-compliance
Lightning Source LLC
Chambersburg PA
CBHW030645120726
47905CB00001B/63

* 9 7 8 0 9 9 0 6 6 9 4 7 0 *